WHEN THAT TIME COMES

WHEN THAT TIME COMES

Book Two of the Taylor Morgan Trilogy

Time flys!

Sabra Brown Steinsiek

Sabra Brown Steinsiek

Writers Club Press
San Jose New York Lincoln Shanghai

When That Time Comes

All Rights Reserved © 2002 by Sabra Brown Steinsiek

No part of this book may be reproduced or transmitted in any form or by any means, graphic, electronic, or mechanical, including photocopying, recording, taping, or by any information storage retrieval system, without the permission in writing from the publisher.

Writers Club Press
an imprint of iUniverse, Inc.

For information address:
iUniverse, Inc.
5220 S. 16th St., Suite 200
Lincoln, NE 68512
www.iuniverse.com

Any resemblance to actual people and events is purely coincidental.
This is a work of fiction.

ISBN: 0-595-22223-4

Printed in the United States of America

*FOR
JOSEPH GORVETZIAN and BARRY RUMBLES
WITH GRATITUDE*

FOR
JOSEPH GORVETZIAN and BARRY RUMBLES
WITH GRATITUDE

For everything there is a season and a time to every purpose under heaven: a time to be born…a time to embrace…a time to seek…a time to heal…a time to keep silence and a time to speak…

—Ecclesiastes 3

Acknowledgements

Each book carries with it a responsibility to the readers. Even a work of fiction requires research, help, and encouragement. All the mistakes in this are mine…all of the glory goes to the following:

—To Teri Hanson and the members of the real Taylor Morgan Fan Club who never let up on me for a minute in producing this sequel.

—To Kathy Mondragon for medical research, Bill Jacoby for legal research, and Karen Talley for word processing advice. Their help was invaluable and *accurate*. What I did with it is not their responsibility.

—To my Editors, Jan Jannsen, Renee Bernard, and Jude McMurry because I will *never* get the hang of commas.

—For my advance readers who once again had faith in me: Marsha Baum, Renee Bernard, Cyndi Dean, Teri Hanson, Carolyn Huesemann, Heidi Nesbitt, Beverly Rumbles, Will Steinsiek, and Beth Wetherington.

—To my family for their support, expecially my sister Eileen who takes her role as big sister very seriously.

—To my husband, Will, and my son, Jared, for giving me the space and time I needed to write.

—And especially to all those fans who care about Taylor and Laura as deeply as I do. I hope this was worth the wait.

CHAPTER 1

❀

It was so hot! New York in the summer was not Laura's idea of fun. Albuquerque had been hot, but the air was never this humid and heavy, trapped in the canyons of the city streets with only the breeze of passing traffic to stir it. Even after all this time she wasn't used to it.

Glancing at her watch, she realized that she still had time to get to the theatre to meet Taylor. Flagging down a cab, she acknowledged she'd really rather take a nap but Taylor's schedule left them so little time to be together. And if it wasn't Taylor, it was Meg's recital or Betta's play or her own publishing deadlines that kept them apart.

Sinking gratefully into the relative coolness of the cab, she told the cab driver to take her to the Majestic Theatre, where Taylor's show was playing—had been playing for almost three years now. But he'd given notice that he would be leaving at the end of his contract, only six months away. Betta and Meg would be graduating and heading off to school. Finally, they would have some time for themselves.

Not that she begrudged the time their daughters required. Taylor had adopted Megan when they had realized her mother, Annie, was dying. He had been her godfather and couldn't have loved her more if she were his own. After Taylor and Laura's marriage, Laura had officially adopted her as well.

Elizabetta (Betta to the family) was the niece of their housekeeper and chauffeur. She had lost her parents in an accident two years before Taylor and Meg had lost Annie to cancer. The two girls had become inseparable when Taylor moved to Italy after Annie's death. When Taylor needed to move back to New York to take this role on Broadway, it had caused major havoc in their lives. Megan had refused to go with him and both girls were in tears most of the time. The solution was that Betta, with her Aunt Rosina and Uncle Matteo, would move to New York with them. They'd found a building with two apartments available and renovated them so that a hidden staircase connected the two. Rosina and Matteo lived in the apartment below. Betta lived with the Morgans in the apartment above—Meg's sister and their daughter in all the ways that mattered.

Laura picked up the new batch of brochures she had brought from the travel agency in her publisher's building. Looking at the bright colors and enticing pictures, she smiled in anticipation of showing them to Taylor. There were so many possibilities.

The cab careened into the loading area at the front of the theater. Laura paid the driver, then stepped out into the heat, hurrying to the shade of the marquee. Joe, the theatre's security guard, opened the door for her.

"Afternoon, Mrs. Morgan."

"Hi, Joe. Good grief! It's suffocating in here!"

"Air conditioner troubles. It's been down all day but they're hopin' to get it fixed in time for tonight's show so's they don't hafta cancel."

Shaking her head, Laura made her way backstage to Taylor's dressing room. If anything, it was hotter backstage and she wasn't surprised to find Taylor shirtless, sitting in front of an inadequate fan.

"Hello, darling," she said as she came into the room. She leaned down to kiss him, gently running her fingers down his sweat-streaked chest before she pulled away. "How can you stand it in here? It must be a hundred degrees."

"Only ninety-five the last time we checked," Taylor said, smiling at her. "You should go on home where it's cool."

"And not see you again until the wee small hours?" she said as she sat on the couch. "I know this is your life, Taylor, but I can't say I'll miss it. It's going to be nice seeing you in daylight occasionally."

"You make me sound like a vampire!" Taylor laughed as he said it. "But I don't think I'll miss it either, at least not right away."

He poured a glass of iced water for her from a thermal pitcher on his dressing table. After she had gratefully downed it, she handed it back to him. "More please. Taylor, what do you think of Australia for our first trip?"

"Right now, skiing in the Alps sounds a lot more attractive."

She made a face at him. "It will be winter here by then, Taylor. You'll be glad of the summer weather. Look at this." She stood to hand him the brochures—and sank gracefully to the floor as she fainted. The next thing she knew, she was lying on the couch, looking up into Taylor's worried face as cast and crew crowded into the doorway.

"Laura?" Taylor's eyes were filled with concern as he took a damp cloth from the wardrobe mistress to put across Laura's forehead.

"What happened?" she asked, still slightly disoriented.

"You fainted, I think. It must be the heat. Joe's calling a cab. I'm going to take you home."

"Don't be silly, Taylor. You have to get ready for the show." She pushed him away and slowly eased herself up to a sitting position. "I'm fine. You're right, it must have been the heat." She glanced at the faces in the doorway and flushed in embarrassment. What a fuss Taylor must have made to bring them all crowding in here! "I'm fine, everyone. Honest!"

They slowly moved away and Laura tried standing, leaning on Taylor for support. She was a little unsteady at first, but that went away quickly. She brought her hand up to her husband's cheek. "See, Taylor. I am fine. But I think I will go on home."

He started to protest, but Joe appeared in the doorway to tell them the cab was here. Taylor pulled on a shirt then walked her to the stage door. Leaning in the door of the cab, he kissed her. "Sure you don't want me to come with you?"

"I'm sure, Taylor. Go on. Break a leg." He closed the door and watched as the cab drove away before heading back inside.

🍁 🍁 🍁

When Laura arrived at their building, she found Matteo waiting anxiously outside. "Taylor called you, didn't he?" she asked, shaking her head. Still, she was grateful for the support he gave her as they went into the building and rode the elevator up to the apartment where Rosina was waiting.

"Madonna! You shouldn't have been out in this heat, Laura! Taylor called and told me what happened. You need to go lie down for awhile—rest." Laura let Rosina fuss over her. Actually, everything she was recommending sounded good. Their bedroom was quiet and cool, dark as Rosina pulled the shades. Laura sank down on the bed, kicked off her shoes, and lay back against the pillow. She drank the water that Rosina handed to her then said, "I think I'll try to nap for awhile, Rosina. Wake me when the girls get home." She was asleep before Rosina pulled the door shut.

🍁 🍁 🍁

Taylor tried not to worry about Laura. It must have been the heat—but she'd been so pale! Laura was almost never sick. But Annie—Meg's mother and his first wife—had never been sick either. The brain tumor that had killed her made its presence known suddenly and had taken her in less than six months.

He shook his head as his makeup woman came in. Laura would be fine. She would…she had to be. He couldn't lose her, too.

Chapter 2

❀

Laura woke the next morning feeling remarkably well, much to Taylor's relief.

"You worry too much, Taylor," she said as she brushed her long red hair. "It was just the heat. It's so much worse here than at home." She looked out the window at the high-rise buildings that surrounded them. She loved Taylor and would follow him wherever he needed to be but she missed the clear blue skies and sweeping vistas of New Mexico. Sometimes she felt like she couldn't breathe in New York.

Taylor came up behind her and put his arms around her. "Homesick?" he whispered.

"A little. But it's nothing you can't fix," she said as she turned to him. She pulled his head to hers and kissed him. "I don't have anything on my schedule today. The girls are gone to school, Rosina's downstairs…"

"And me? What if I have something planned?" he said as he began to unbutton her shirt.

"Whatever you had planned, darling," her voice caught as he lowered his mouth to her throat, "will just have to wait."

Laughing, he picked her up and carried her to their bed. He only had one thing planned and he intended to give it his full attention for the rest of the morning.

🍁 🍁 🍁

The fainting episode was forgotten until Laura woke up a week later, nauseous, and barely made it to the bathroom before vomiting again and again.

By mid-morning she was feeling better and was able to convince Taylor to go on to the theatre. "It's only something I ate, Taylor. I'll stay home today and be fine by tomorrow."

It happened again the next morning and the day after that as well. Taylor was worried enough to override Laura's objection and made an appointment for her with their doctor. The time she was in with the doctor was an eternity to Taylor waiting for her in the outer office—too many memories of Annie's last months with doctors and hospitals and bad news…

Laura squeezed his shoulder as she and Doctor Bernard came into the room. She knew how hard it was for him to be there. If he'd just listened to her instead of panicking over a silly case of the flu, they wouldn't be here at all.

The doctor sat behind her desk and opened Laura's folder. "Well, Laura, I don't think this is anything you're going to throw off easily."

With her words, it was as if the past and the present had suddenly collided for Taylor. He was back in Annie's hospital room in Florida listening as the doctor told them she was dying.

Before the doctor could continue, Taylor, suddenly pale, demanded, "What are you talking about? What's wrong with Laura?"

Taken aback by the tone of his voice and his sudden intensity, she was quick to assure them both, "I'm sorry. There's nothing wrong. Laura, Taylor—you're pregnant."

Pregnant? Now? They had talked about children in the beginning and had even tried for awhile. When she hadn't gotten pregnant they decided that having two teenage daughters was more than enough and had gotten on with their lives.

But now? The girls were nearly grown. They were planning on traveling, concentrating on Laura's career for awhile. Taylor and Laura looked at each other in disbelief then burst out laughing while Renee Bernard looked on in amazement.

Chapter 3

❊

Taylor opened the door to the apartment and let Laura go in before him. Neither of them had said anything on the way home from the doctor's office. The reality was beginning to sink in—a baby. They were going to have a baby.

He watched as Laura opened the French doors that led to the balcony. She stood in the doorway making no move to go out.

"Laura? Darling?" He crossed the room and wrapped his arms around her, pulling her back against him where he could feel her trembling. "What are you thinking?"

"I don't know. It's all so sudden. A baby?" She turned to face him. "What do I know about having a baby? What do I know about being a mother?" She placed her fingers over his mouth before he could answer. "Don't, Taylor. The girls were thirteen when I came into their lives. I've been more of a big sister and friend than I have a mother. Babies are so tiny, so fragile. What if I do something wrong?"

Taylor saw the fear in her eyes. "What do I know about babies? Meg's eighteen. That was a long time ago. I'm almost forty, now. Too old to be a first-time father. No one ever believed that Meg was my daughter, I was too young. Now people will think I'm this one's grandfather." He smiled at her and brushed a strand of hair from her face. "I don't know nuthin' 'bout birthin' no babies, Miss Laura," he whispered and was rewarded with a small smile.

"Are you happy, Taylor? This means all of our plans will change and we'll be starting over."

"I was in shock in the doctor's office. I guess we should have been smart enough to figure out what was going on," he said with a rueful smile. "But now that it's sinking in…Yes, my darling Laura, I'm happy, I'm thrilled, I'm excited…and I'm scared to death, too. But this was meant to be. I know it. And we'll get through it together. We just have to start over again."

Laura leaned her head against his shoulder. He was right. They had each other. They'd get through it. Through the shock and the fear, she felt a glimmer of happiness. A baby! A part of her, a part of Taylor…suddenly it seemed very right. She raised her head and smiled at him. "I love you…Dad."

CHAPTER 4

❁

"What was with Taylor and Laura at dinner?" Meg turned from her desk to look at Betta. "They were off in some other world."

"Knowing them," Meg said, "they probably spent the afternoon in bed."

"Meg!"

"Oh, Betta, stop. You know it's true. They're still young enough to do it. Taylor's at the theatre 'til late, Laura's in bed early most nights. Afternoons are the only time they have!"

"Meg? Do you think you could ever love someone as much as they love each other?"

"First I'd have to find someone who could love me…and that's not going to be easy. Not with the schedule I'll have to keep to get into med school."

"I got a letter today. From Milan."

"Betta! Why didn't you say anything?"

"I haven't opened it yet. I'm afraid to. What if they hated my portfolio? What if I didn't get accepted? I'll die."

"They wouldn't dare turn you down," Meg said fiercely. "*Open* the letter!"

She watched as Betta slit open a creamy envelope covered with Italian stamps and drew a sheet of paper from inside. Betta read silently, the paper trembling as her hands shook.

"Well?"

Betta looked up with tears in her eyes. Uh-oh, Meg thought. They couldn't have rejected her!

"Betta! What did it say?"

"They accepted me. I'm going to go to design school in Milan."

Meg shrieked and threw her arms around her sobbing sister. "Why are you crying, you silly goose? This is wonderful! We have to go tell Laura and Rosina and Matteo. You should call Taylor at the theatre before the show starts!"

"Wait, Meg. Not yet. Let me get used to the idea. This is going to mean so many changes. I'll be half a world away. What will I do without you?"

Meg sobered instantly. They'd been talking about school for two years now. Meg was trying to get into the Stanford pre-med program but hadn't heard yet. Betta wanted to study fashion design in Milan and now she would. But neither of them was prepared for the reality—they'd been together since they were twelve and seen each other through all the changes in their lives. Now they would be alone.

CHAPTER 5

"Laura?" Taylor stood in the door of her study and watched his wife staring at a blank computer screen. She had made a name for herself in free-lance writing in the last few years and was finishing up a novel now. Words usually came easily for her but that obviously wasn't the case tonight.

He crossed the room and leaned down to put his arms around her. "I have to leave for the theatre. I'm sorry. I wish I could stay."

"It's alright. I'm fine. Just a little too scattered to write right now." She started the log-off sequence on her computer.

"Have you called your parents?"

"Not yet. Don't you want to be here when I do?"

"I want you to do what's best for you. I can get their congratulations later. I think you need to talk to your mother tonight."

"Maybe. Go on, Taylor. You'll be late."

She watched as he walked to the door and listened as his steps faded down the hallway, leaving her alone with too much to think about.

※ ※ ※

"Hi, Jason, it's Laura. Is Beth around?"

"She's feeding the monsters. I'll go relieve her so you two can talk. Everything ok?"

"We're fine, Jason."

"I'll get her then."

Laura could hear the sound of laughter in the background as she waited. Beth had married Jason four years ago. He was a fellow artist and the two of them had moved to Taos where they had opened a successful gallery. Beth had given birth to twins a year later and the boys were into their "terrible twos".

"Laura! Thanks for rescuing me. Tomás and Taylor were driving me crazy." She said it with a lilt in her voice that belied everything she said. Beth was a wonderful mother and adored her children.

"You love it and you know it, so don't try to fool me," Laura said.

"I do. They're wonderful, Jason's wonderful…I don't think I've ever been this happy. How are you and your gang?"

"The girls are fine. They're both waiting to hear from schools about next year. I can't believe they'll be going off on their own."

"But it will give you and Taylor a chance to have some time. That's good, isn't it?"

"It would be…"

"Laura? What's wrong? Has something happened to Taylor?"

"No, he's fine. He's still on schedule to leave the show in March. But we're going to have to change our plans a little." She took a deep breath then asked, "How do you feel about being a godmother in May?"

"A godmother? To whom? Ohmygod, Laura, you're pregnant! When did you find out?"

Laura's voice choked with tears, "Today, Beth…"

"You're not happy about it, are you?"

"No…yes…Beth, I don't know how I feel!"

Beth laughed softly, "Those hormones will get you every time, girl. Give yourself some time to get used to the idea."

"But I should be happy! Shouldn't I?"

"Laura, don't you remember when I found out I was having *twins*? I was devastated. I thought everything I'd planned and worked for was gone. But the day they arrived all that changed. I wouldn't give them up for anything."

"You're a wonderful mother, Beth. But I'm afraid I won't be!" Laura began to cry. "What if I do it all wrong?"

"You'll be great. You will. I promise." Half a continent away, tears streamed down Beth's cheeks as she tried to comfort her friend. "Have you called your Mom yet?"

"No. I needed to talk to you first."

"Call her now. Then I'll call you tomorrow night and we can talk."

"Thanks, Beth…what would I do without you?"

"I don't plan on letting you find out. I love you, Laura."

"Me, too…'nite."

Laura hung up the phone then washed her face. The woman in the mirror looked so lost…maybe talking to her mother would help.

🍁   🍁   🍁

Laura glanced at her watch as the phone began to ring in New Mexico. Taylor's curtain was going up right now and she sent a warm thought in that direction as her mother picked up the phone.

"*Buenas noches.*" Laura's mother, part of one of the Spanish land grant families, still found it natural to answer the phone in the musical language of her childhood.

"*Mamá*? It's Laura."

"Laura! How good to hear your voice. I've been thinking about you all day and was going to call you in awhile. How are you? The girls? Taylor?"

Laura laughed. "We're all fine, Mom. The girls send their love and said to tell you they'll call soon. Right now they're busy with homework."

"No word from schools yet?"

"No, but it's early. They still have several months of school to go."

"They'll both be accepted where they want to go. No one would dare turn those two down. Your father is still hoping one of them will decide on UNM."

Her parents were both professors at the University of New Mexico and Laura had graduated from there with her journalism degree. "I don't think it's going to happen, Mom. Meg is set on Stanford and Betta wants to go back to Italy."

"*Sí*. It will be hard for you and Taylor to have them both leave at the same time. But you have a lot to look forward to as well, *mi'ja*."

"A little more than we had planned, Mom."

"Laura? Is something wrong?"

"No…not really. Mom, I have some news for you. How do you feel about being a grandmother again?"

"You're taking in someone new? Now?"

"Not exactly. This one we're starting from scratch."

"Laura? I'm not sure…*ay, Dios mío*! You're going to have a baby!"

As her mother began to laugh and cry at the same time, so did Laura. In the background she heard the rumble of her father's questioning voice then he was on the phone.

"Laura? Your mother is hysterical. What's wrong? You're alright…all of you?"

"Nothing's wrong, Dad. She'll be ok. But you might want to start work on that cradle you always wanted to build."

"Cradle…Laura?"

"I'm pregnant, Dad. The baby's due in May."

"Well…well! I guess I had better get to work. Here's your mother, my girl."

"He's crying, isn't he, Mom?" Laura said with a smile, her own eyes filled with tears.

"He is. We're both so happy for you, Laura. Taylor's pleased?"

"He is. At least I get to stay home and get used to the idea. I hope he makes it through the show tonight."

"And you, *mi'ja*?" Her mother's voice was tender as she asked.

"Oh, Mom...I *think* I'm happy but I'm also really scared."

"I was, too, when I realized I was pregnant with Tomás. It's a scary thought. Suddenly everything's different, isn't it?"

"Taylor was right, Mom. He said I needed to talk to you."

"So, let's talk…"

Laura kicked off her shoes and sank down into the armchair by the bed and let her mother's love surround her.

❧ ❧ ❧

Laura had been asleep by the time Taylor had gotten home from the theatre and she'd been so tired she hadn't heard him come in. When she woke in the morning, their room was filled with light. She turned over to look at the clock and found a vase of yellow roses—six of them—sitting on the nightstand. She smiled as she reached out and touched one of the soft petals then picked up the envelope that leaned against the vase. Opening it, she read the small card inside:

Darling mother of my child—

Roses for you.
$^1/_2$ now, $^1/_2$ on delivery.

Love always—
Taylor

She was laughing as she looked up to find him standing in the doorway.

"Too cute?" he asked.

"Too something," she said as she held out her hand to him. "But, I love you," she continued as he sat on the bed beside her.

"Good talk with your Mom last night?

"With Mom and with Beth."

"I should have known," he said with a smile. "How is she?"

"Frazzled. If we have twins, Taylor, I'm never forgiving you."

"I don't have any say in it, Laura!"

"You should of thought of that when you got me pregnant," she retorted then gasped as her stomach flipped. "Oh no! Taylor, move!"

He listened helplessly as the morning sickness gripped her again. Maybe twins weren't the only things she'd never forgive him for!

CHAPTER 6

❈

Taylor's show was dark on Mondays and they all made an effort to be together for dinner on that night. It gave them a chance to catch up on everyone's news and lives. Dinner was usually a lively event and the centerpiece of their weeks.

Laura had requested Rosina make the lasagna that the girls and Taylor loved. Personally, she really didn't care if she ever ate again! Her morning sickness wasn't having the decency to confine itself to mornings. She felt nauseated a good deal of the time right now and was already counting the days until the first three months were over. The doctor said the morning sickness usually went away then.

She was calmer now about the pregnancy. It still seemed unreal but she was getting used to the idea. She and Taylor had already begun to look at converting his study to a nursery. He would move his computer to a corner of their bedroom for now.

She was sitting on the floor in her study going through a box when Taylor came to the door.

"More from the fan club?" he asked as he sat down beside her.

"I've just started sorting this box. Did you finish what I gave you last week?" Laura had been sorting his fan mail since before they were married, when she had served as his assistant for a brief time.

"It's done. Here's the disk with the answers."

"I'll print them out this afternoon and you can sign them this evening."

"You know, Laura, all of this could wait."

"No. If we get behind on it, you'll never catch up. There's some stuff in this box from Elodie that she wants you to sign for fund-raising. You *know* how she gets when you don't get stuff right back to her."

Elodie Nee was president of Taylor's fan club. She had been the "poor little rich girl" of their group when Taylor and Annie had met in New York. As struggling young actors, they would often come together to pool their resources for cheap, but plentiful, group meals where they could compare auditions, complain about directors, and celebrate the small breaks that happened now and then.

Elodie had been part of that but everyone knew she came from "old money". She didn't flaunt it but if someone were desperate, they knew she'd come through with the money to see them to that next paycheck.

When Taylor got his big break and became the toast of Broadway, Elodie placed an ad in *Variety*. A joke for Taylor's birthday, it announced the formation of the Taylor Morgan Fan Club. The joke quickly turned into reality as requests began to come in. Before either of them knew it, Taylor had a real fan club and Elodie was its president.

She'd kept it up even when she left the theatre to marry the nice stockbroker her parents had picked out for her. Five years later, the childless marriage ended but her presidency went on. Her steadfast support meant a lot to Taylor and their friendship remained the basis for the fan club and the charity fund-raising that was done in Taylor's name.

He would have liked it if Laura and Elodie had become friends but there had been something between them instantly, a mutual antipathy that never showed in public. They avoided each other more often than not. Laura accepted her friendship with Taylor but had made it clear she didn't want to be part of it.

"Anything interesting in this one?" Taylor changed the subject. He didn't feel like having the same argument again. He reached into the box and pulled out a handful of envelopes.

"The usual. I've found a few that need answers. Taylor, you do know the fans are going to go crazy when they find out about the baby?"

"I've thought of that. I think I'll ask Elodie to come up with a fund-raiser for Shelters and ask them to donate there instead of sending gifts to us." Taylor was president of Shelters for Children, a charity that provided a safe haven for abused children. He'd met Laura when he'd been in Albuquerque for a concert benefiting the homes.

"That will help but we're still going to be inundated. Even if I do have twins, we're not going to need a gazillion pair of baby bootees!"

Taylor reached out and brushed a strand of hair away from her face. The morning sickness was still hitting her every day and he could see she'd lost weight. "Let's not worry about them now, Laura. It can wait until later. Have you thought about how we're going to announce it to the family tonight?"

She looked at him with a wicked grin. "Actually, I have. I'm going to let *you* figure it out!"

Dinner that night was their usual noisy affair. Rosina insisted on using the good china, silver, and tablecloth every week. There were candles on the table and they had all gotten into the habit of "dressing" for dinner…at least something a little more festive than their usual casual clothes.

"Rosina, you've outdone yourself on this batch," Taylor said as he took a second helping of the lasagna as everyone murmured agreement. He saw that Laura had taken a small serving and was mostly pushing it around on her plate. No one else seemed to have noticed. "So, what's happening at school?"

"The fall dance is coming up," Betta said. "Meg's got a date to it already."

"Betta!"

"Well, you do!"

Taylor put on his best fatherly air and asked, "Do I know this young man?"

Meg rolled her eyes before she answered, "No, Taylor. But he already knows he has to pick me up here and at least meet Laura before we leave. His name is Jared Brown. He's first chair french horn in the orchestra."

"And only the cutest guy in the whole school," Betta volunteered.

"Looks aren't everything," Laura said as she looked at her husband, "but being cute doesn't hurt."

"I am *not* cute," Taylor said. "Handsome, debonair, and charming, but never cute."

Meg and Betta looked at Laura and the three of them chorused, "Cute!"

It was Taylor's turn to roll his eyes as the three of them broke into giggles. They really were more like sisters. Laura was only twelve years older than the girls.

Rosina stood to clear away the dishes. "I made chocolate cake for dessert, Laura, with your mother's mocha icing."

"Thanks, Rosina," she said as Rosina took her plate. She didn't miss the look that Rosina gave her untouched food. "Chocolate's always a good choice."

The girls helped clear the table while Matteo and Taylor talked about the new car they'd just bought. Taylor had put his Jaguar in storage along with Laura's Opel GT when they moved to New York. They kept a sedan now and Matteo was their driver.

Laura thought it was a good thing that the girls were going off to school or they might find themselves stuck with a mini-van.

When the cake had been served and everyone was settled in again, Taylor waited for a pause in the conversation. When it came, he cleared his throat and said, "Laura and I have some news for you."

"A new CD, Taylor?" Matteo asked.

"Not quite, Matteo. But it is a new venture. I guess there's no clever way to say it. You girls are going to have a little sister or brother come spring."

There was a stunned silence around the table. No one had expected this. Taylor looked at Laura and smiled as they waited for the storm to break.

"You're having a baby?" Meg whispered then loudly repeated, "A baby?"

Everyone turned to look at Laura who smiled and said, "A baby. In May."

Then everything happened at once. The girls were hugging Laura, Matteo was slapping Taylor on the back, and Rosina was crying.

"This is so cool," Betta said. "I hope it's a girl."

"No way," Taylor responded. "We have enough girls around this house. I want another guy on my side."

"Too bad, Taylor," Meg said as she sat back down, "it's a girl. I just know it. And, if you think Betta and I are spoiled, just watch out when we get our hands on her."

Betta sobered and said, without thinking, "But I'll be in Italy…"

"Betta? Did you hear?" Laura asked

She smiled shyly. "Last week. I was accepted."

The scene from moments before was repeated as the women surrounded Betta with hugs.

"Betta! That's wonderful." Taylor said. Betta had always had a special place in his heart. They were very much alike on the inside and, for a moment, his heart hurt at the thought of her going so far away.

"Why didn't you say anything?" Laura asked.

"I guess I needed to get used to the idea first. But, now, with the baby, maybe I should start here in New York so I can be around to help."

"And California's too far away, too," Meg said. "I'll start here, then transfer later."

"Wait a minute," Laura said. "You can't make those kinds of decisions without thinking about it. Betta, you can't turn down this opportunity. Meg, Stanford won't wait if you turn them down. I'll have Rosina and Matteo to help."

"But she's going to be our sister," Meg said.

"Or brother," Taylor said dryly.

"Sister," Meg said firmly. "And I want to be here."

"Me, too." Betta said.

"Hold it," Taylor said. "You don't have to decide now. Let's all get used to the idea. And right now, I think we need that bottle of champagne I've been chilling, Matteo. We need to toast Betta's news."

"And yours," Betta said as she reached over to hold Laura's hand. "We have a lot to celebrate."

❋   ❋   ❋

"I think it went well," Taylor said as he and Laura got ready for bed. "They certainly appear to be pleased. And Rosina's beside herself at the thought of a baby."

"We can't let the girls give up on their plans," Laura said as she came out of the bathroom wearing green satin pajamas that matched her eyes. "Especially Betta! Taylor, this is a once in a lifetime chance for her. Meg might be able to transfer later and can certainly get a good pre-med education here but Betta *has* to go to Milan."

Taylor took her into his arms and used one thumb to smooth out the frown between her eyes. "Give them time, darling. It will all work out the way it should."

"How did we ever get ourselves into this?" Laura asked.

"I think it started this way," he said with a smile before he kissed her, eclipsing the future with the promise of now.

CHAPTER 7

Taylor had gone straight to the theatre following an afternoon interview. There wasn't going to be enough time to go home for dinner with his girls. Girls? Young women, all of them, even his wife, he acknowledged. He'd have to stop thinking of them that way.

He'd asked Matteo to pick up some soup for him and he settled down in his dressing room to answer some of the fan mail Laura had given him a few days before.

When the door opened, he said without looking up, "Thanks, Matteo, just put it on the table."

"Do I *look* like a Matteo?"

Taylor raised his eyes to see a woman in the doorway. "Elodie! What a surprise!"

"Hi, Taylor. I had some business in the city and just wanted to say hello."

Taylor stood and walked over to her, leaning down to give her a kiss on the cheek; a kiss that landed near the corner of her mouth when she unexpectedly turned her head.

"It's nice to see you. I'm glad you caught me here. I came in a little early this evening. Usually, I'm not here for another half an hour or so."

"I just thought I'd take a chance."

Matteo loomed in the doorway behind her. "Taylor, here's your soup. Hello, Ms. Nee."

"Thanks, Matteo. You can go on home now, if you'd like. I'll see you after the show."

"Not much of a supper, Taylor," Elodie commented as she took a seat on the couch. "I thought you and Laura had that fabulous housekeeper and cook." There was a touch of disdain in her voice but Taylor pretended not to notice.

"I was busy with an interview this afternoon and didn't have time to go home." He held up his hand to stop her as she opened her mouth to speak. "I know, I know. I'll have Laura call you as soon as we have a publication date."

"Well, you know how the members are, Taylor. They just can't get enough of you."

"That's true enough, although I never have understood why," he said as he opened the soup container. "Would you like some of this?"

"God, no! I have dinner reservations for after the show. I was hoping you might join me?"

"Thanks, but not tonight. I'll be heading home right after the show. Laura…" He paused, then went on, "Actually, I do have some news for you. I don't want it to get out just yet, but I do want you to turn that brain of yours into making it a great fund-raiser."

"Sure, Taylor. What's the news?"

"Laura may kill me for telling you, but the truth will get out soon enough. We're going to have a baby in the spring."

For once, Elodie Nee was speechless. A baby? It was bad enough when he'd *married* Laura. So many of the fans had left the club then. She'd had to work her tail off to keep it going when he went into seclusion in Italy with his new bride. The man simply did not *think* about the consequences of his actions.

She managed to summon a smile and, in her best cheerleader voice, said, "A baby? Taylor, that's wonderful! You and Laura must be thrilled."

He smiled, a shy smile that quickly turned into a cat-that-ate-the canary grin. "We are. So are the girls."

"Are you still leaving the show?"

"In March, as planned. The baby's due in May so we'll have time to get the girls settled into school. Betta's been accepted to design school in Milan!" he added.

"What will you do then?"

"I really don't know. We'd planned on traveling but the baby changes some of that. I think we're just going to take it day by day, let nature take its course, so to speak."

This was going to take some damage control, she thought. *Major damage control.* Her mind was already tumbling with thoughts and ideas of how she would handle this and the reactions it was bound to bring.

Smiling, she got up from the couch. "I know you need some time to prepare, Taylor—for the show *and* the baby." She gave him a hug then went to the door. "Keep me posted on how things are going. And be sure and congratulate your darling wife for me." She blew him a kiss and was gone.

Taylor shook his head. Elodie disliked Laura as much as Laura disliked Elodie. He didn't understand it; never had, never would. At least they'd learned to work together and play nice in public.

Glancing at his watch, he picked up the phone. There was just time to call Laura before he began make-up for the night.

As the curtain rose, Elodie Nee leaned forward in her front row mezzanine seat. Taylor didn't know just how often she came into the city to see him in the show. She always sat in the mezzanine, far enough away to make sure he didn't see her, close enough to see him and listen to that beautiful voice. As he made his entrance, she gave herself over to the fantasy that he was singing for her alone.

He smiled, a shy smile that quickly turned into a cat-that-ate-the canary grin. "We are. So are the girls."

"Are you still leaving the show?"

"In March, as planned. The baby's due in May so we'll have time to get the girls settled into school. Betta's been accepted to design school in Milan!" he added.

"What will you do then?"

"I really don't know. We'd planned on traveling but the baby changes some of that. I think we're just going to take it day by day, let nature take its course, so to speak."

This was going to take some damage control, she thought. *Major damage control*. Her mind was already tumbling with thoughts and ideas of how she would handle this and the reactions it was bound to bring.

Smiling, she got up from the couch. "I know you need some time to prepare, Taylor—for the show *and* the baby." She gave him a hug then went to the door. "Keep me posted on how things are going. And be sure and congratulate your darling wife for me." She blew him a kiss and was gone.

Taylor shook his head. Elodie disliked Laura as much as Laura disliked Elodie. He didn't understand it; never had, never would. At least they'd learned to work together and play nice in public.

Glancing at his watch, he picked up the phone. There was just time to call Laura before he began make-up for the night.

As the curtain rose, Elodie Nee leaned forward in her front row mezzanine seat. Taylor didn't know just how often she came into the city to see him in the show. She always sat in the mezzanine, far enough away to make sure he didn't see her, close enough to see him and listen to that beautiful voice. As he made his entrance, she gave herself over to the fantasy that he was singing for her alone.

CHAPTER 8

❀

The Morgan's annual New Year's Eve party was an event that their friends always looked forward to. Taylor had given up some other perks to have it written into his contract that he did not perform Christmas Eve through New Year's Day. This year, Laura's parents would be with them. As a surprise, Taylor had arranged for Beth to come as well. Jason sent Beth out the day after Christmas and would join them with the twins on the thirtieth. Now near the end of her fourth month of pregnancy, Laura was finally past the morning sickness. Her energy levels had returned and she seemed to be the picture of the perfect pregnancy.

Taylor looked up from his book when he heard the apartment door open to the sounds of laughter. Had Betta and Meg not been in Florida visiting Meg's other grandparents, he might have thought it was them. With a smile, he went down the hallway and looked into the foyer. The two women were removing coats, hats, and gloves, with dozens of shopping bags at their feet. They had set out to shop for the nursery and, from the look of things, managed to find what they'd been looking for.

"You know," he said with a smile, "the room is only so big. You are going to leave room for the baby, aren't you?"

"Oh, Taylor! We had such a good time. Wait until you see all the things we found." Laura came over and kissed him before pulling him over to the packages. Diving into one of them, she came up with a multi-colored caterpillar. "Isn't this just the cutest thing? Since we're doing the nursery in bright colors, it will be just perfect."

"We bought a few practical things, too, " Beth said. "Just in case you're wondering."

"You two? Practical? That will be the day!" he said then laughed as they stuck their tongues out at him.

"We bought lots of pink," Beth said with a wicked grin. Everyone knew that Taylor was sure the baby would be a boy. He was the only one who thought so and the rest of them were having fun teasing him about all the girl things they were buying.

"My son isn't wearing pink," Taylor said with mock indignation.

"Then it's a good thing Laura's having a girl!"

"I hope you kept receipts," he said as he leaned down to pick up a number of shopping bags. "It will make returning all this useless pink stuff so much easier."

"A girl, Taylor," Beth said. "I'm sure of it. And I am going to be the most indulgent aunt you ever saw!"

The two of them laughed as Taylor shook his head and rolled his eyes before proceeding down the hall to the nursery-to-be.

Matteo had made numerous trips to the airport but, finally, everyone was home. Meg and Betta complained about the cold after their trip to Florida. Laura's parents had arrived laden with insulated containers of Mexican food. Rosina had matched their offerings with Italian specialties and the table now groaned with food. Jason had arrived with the twins who now sat between their mother and their Auntie Laurie, so it was a large and noisy group that sat down to dinner.

"I will make the *posole* in the morning, Laura," her mother said as they all began to eat. "It will insure good luck for you and your friends."

"I can hardly wait, Mom! And these *tamales* are heavenly. I miss the food at home so much!"

"I hope you brought *biscochitos*, Maria." Taylor had developed an addiction to the anise flavored sweet that was the official cookie of the state of New Mexico.

"Would I forget you, Taylor?" Maria laughed. "I knew I wouldn't be welcome without them," she teased.

"Just more welcome *with* them, Maria."

There were several conversations going at once and Taylor listened in as he continued his dinner. The women were talking about the nursery and baby clothes. Sean and Jason were discussing art with Matteo and Betta. There was a lot of laughter and he was glad to feel their home full of happiness.

"So how many people are coming to this party this year, Laura?" her father asked.

"I have no idea, Dad. The usual and all of Taylor's cast and crew once the performance is over."

"You'll not be letting yourself get too tired over this, will you?" Sean tended to allow his Irish roots to creep into his voice when he was concerned about something.

"Not a chance, Sean," Taylor answered.

Laura shook her head. "Taylor's right, Dad. None of them will let me do anything. You'd think I was the first woman to be pregnant the way my gang is acting."

"As it should be," Sean said, refilling his glass.

"See, Laura, even your father thinks I'm right," Taylor said.

"Well, I might not go *that* far, Taylor," Sean said as everyone laughed. They all knew he was teasing his son-in-law. Maria and Sean loved him as dearly as if he were their own.

Sean turned to the girls, "So, which one of you is going to give up these wild plans of yours and come to the University of New Mexico?"

Betta smiled at him. "Not me, *Abuelo*. Milan is waiting. I wanted to stay here and help with the baby but Laura and Taylor won't let me."

"Me, neither," Meg added. "I've applied to schools here in the northeast to be closer but if Stanford says yes, I'm going to have to take it."

"Fine, maybe my new grandson will come when it's his turn." Sean was the only one to share Taylor's conviction that the baby would be a boy. "He could play for the Lobos."

"Your new granddaughter," Maria said, "can be a Lady Lobo, you know."

"Not the same," Sean muttered.

"With Laura and Taylor for parents, she can pretty much count on doing something with words," Meg said. "How about she becomes the next Sarah Bernhardt?"

"Or Jan Burke. We can always use another writer," Laura said.

"Maybe you'll have twins," Jason threw in. "Then you can have one of each."

"Not twins!" Beth said as she cleaned Tomás' face. "I wouldn't wish that on my worst enemy, let alone my best friend!"

It was quiet Matteo who brought the discussion to a close, "Whatever the bambino is, may it be healthy and as good as the parents that brought it into the world."

Murmurs of agreement were heard as glasses were raised around the table. "To Taylor and Laura," Meg said, "the best parents anyone could have."

Taylor's eyes met Laura's and he raised his glass to her with a smile. Boy or girl, there was no doubt that this baby would be loved.

CHAPTER 9

❈

The party was well underway when Elodie Nee stepped out of the elevator wearing a slinky black dress and heeled sandals, her black hair, worn short now, perfectly coiffed. Her fur coat was draped casually over her shoulders and she carried a ribbon-bedecked bottle of champagne. She looked, and felt, as if she belonged in this rarified world of theatre and music—a world she felt was rightfully hers.

Taylor saw her come through the door and went to greet her. "Hello, Elodie. I'm glad you could make it."

"You know I wouldn't miss it. How's our little mother? And when are you going to let me announce the baby to the fans?"

"Laura's fine. And we want to keep it quiet a bit longer," he said as he took her coat. "You know most everyone. Get yourself a glass of champagne and join the party."

Spotting Laura across the room, she said, "Thanks, I see someone now." It was time to pay her "respects" to the mother-to-be. Snagging a champagne flute from the tray offered by a passing waiter, she made her way through the crowd.

Laura was wearing a green pantsuit that matched her eyes. The crystal pleats of the top allowed the round of her pregnancy to show. Her face was fuller, too. If she weren't careful, she'd look like a pig soon, Elodie thought. She certainly wasn't going to look like Taylor's perfect little wife for much longer.

"Laura!" Elodie called when she got close enough. "You look positively radiant!"

Laura's heart sank when she saw who was talking. She really didn't want to make nice with Elodie Nee tonight. But she put on her best hostess smile and said, "Elodie. So nice to see you. I wasn't sure you'd make it this year." Wasn't sure and had been hoping you wouldn't, Laura thought.

"I wouldn't have missed this. If it hadn't been for your red hair, I might not have recognized you…the new roundness, you know."

Oh, I know, thought Laura. It's your catty way of saying I'm getting fat! "It goes with the territory. But you've never had children, have you?"

Meg could see what was happening and stepped in before Laura and Elodie could progress to name-calling. "Laura, your mother was looking for you. I think she and Rosina are in the kitchen."

"Thanks, Meg. You'll excuse me, Elodie?"

"Meg, you look so grown-up!"

"I *am* grown-up." Meg had always found Elodie to be cloyingly sweet. And clueless about her and Betta. She'd given them dolls for their sixteenth birthdays—dolls, for heaven's sake!

"Of course you are, dear." Elodie looked past Meg. "Why there's dear Michael," she said. "I haven't seen him in ages." She walked away from Meg without so much as a goodbye, heading for Michael Crawford who was trapped with no way to get away from her.

"Thanks, Meg." Laura came up behind her and gave her a hug. "You saved me. Too bad Michael doesn't have you in his corner," she went on as they watched Elodie take over the conversation in the little group she had invaded.

❦ ❦ ❦

Taylor had watched the scene from across the room. Since Laura couldn't stand Elodie, he made an effort to keep them apart. This was one of those events he couldn't manage, since he couldn't *not* invite her to the party. Thank heavens Meg had been there to separate them. With any sort of luck, they'd avoid each other for the rest of the evening.

❦ ❦ ❦

The party began to wind down after the traditional countdown. Taylor had been with Laura as the New Year arrived and they greeted it with a kiss. Neither of them saw the look on Elodie's face as she watched the man she adored kissing another woman even if she was his wife.

Taylor tapped on the glass he was holding to get everyone's attention after the traditional singing of *Auld Lang Syne*. When the room had quieted, he said, "Thank you all for joining us once again as we bid farewell to an old year and its problems and welcome the new with its possibilities. It will be a year of changes for the Morgans. Betta and Meg will graduate this spring and go off to find their own lives." A spattering of applause greeted this announcement. "Laura and I will begin anew when I leave the show in March and we welcome our son in May."

A resounding chorus of "It's a girl!" came from the women in his life and the guests all joined in the laughter. "Whoever our child is, he—or she—will be surrounded with the love of our friends and we look forward to this new adventure. Happy New Year, everyone!" Applause and cries of "Happy New Year" filled the room as Taylor kissed Laura once again.

People began to leave. By one a.m. most were gone. Laura's mother and Rosina were picking up from the party. Beth and Jason had gone downstairs to Rosina's to relieve the babysitter. Meg and Betta headed for bed. Finally, Elodie was the only one left. Laura wished her a terse "Happy New Year" then escaped to her bedroom.

"Lovely party, as usual, Taylor."

"I'm glad you enjoyed it. And I'm glad you came."

"I was serious—I *wouldn't* have missed it for anything."

Taylor was aware that she was a little drunk and more than a little maudlin. "Let me call down to get you a cab," he said. He arranged for the doorman to call a taxi then walked her to the elevator.

"We have a lot of work to do this year, Taylor, with the baby and the fund-raiser. I really do need to announce it soon if we're to make it work."

"I know. Laura and I thought we'd announce it when I leave the show in March."

"I think it should be sooner," she said a bit belligerently. "You have no idea how long it took to get things calmed down when you married *her.*"

"It's none of their business, really. I don't have to tell them—or you—anything." He was not in the mood to run interference between his wife and the fan club president. "We'll announce it when *we're* ready."

She was saved by the bell as the elevator discreetly chimed then opened its doors. She heard Laura's voice calling Taylor's name from the apartment and decided to give her something to remember. Just as Laura stepped into the open door to the hallway, Elodie twined her arms around Taylor's neck and kissed him hard.

What Laura saw was her husband in the arms of a woman she already hated, his hands on hers, looking for all the world as if he were holding her hands in place instead of trying to pry her loose.

"Taylor!" Laura's voice was soft but he could hear the pain in it as he finally succeeded in pulling Elodie's arms from around his neck. He saw her eyes fill with tears as she turned and fled back into the apartment.

"Damn it, Elodie! What the hell were you doing?"

"I'm sorry," she said. "I didn't know she was there and I've had too much to drink or I would never…"

He took her arm and practically pushed her into the elevator. "Good night, Elodie," he said, his voice full of barely contained rage. As the doors closed and he turned away, she ran her fingers across her lips, which curved into a satisfied smile. "Good night, my love," she whispered. "It's going to be a *very* interesting year."

CHAPTER 10

Taylor found Laura in their room. She was huddled in the armchair beside the bed, crying hard.

"Laura..." Taylor came across the room and sat on the floor in front of the chair. He placed his hand on her arm and cringed when she moved away from his touch. "Laura, that wasn't what you're thinking."

Her emerald eyes were shiny with tears. "No? It looked pretty clear to me."

"*She* kissed *me*. And it happened just as you came through the door. I was trying to peel her off me."

"It didn't look like you were trying too hard," she said, sniffling.

Taylor reached to the nightstand and handed her the box of tissues. "Laura, I swear it wasn't anything. Elodie is an old friend and she'd had too much to drink. She was going home alone. There won't be anyone waiting for her."

"I swear, Taylor," she snapped, her tears drying, "sometimes you are so dense. She's in love with you. She has been for years. Probably has been from the beginning."

"I don't think so, Laura. We're friends."

"Maybe you're playing at friendship but she's playing for *keeps*. I can't do this anymore. I want her out of our lives."

"But Laura…"

"No buts, Taylor! You have to make a choice, her or me."

"You're being unreasonable. I'll make sure she's not a part of our life. You won't have to see her again. But she's the president of the fan club. I can't just replace her. You know the charity would suffer without her influence."

"You mean you *won't*. She can be replaced easily enough. She delegates everything anyway, then takes the credit. The truth is that Teri Hanson has been running the club for the past couple of years."

"Darling, you have to calm down and see this for what it was…"

"I saw, Taylor. I saw way more than I wanted to and more than you ever will. Me or her, Taylor." She went into their bathroom and stopped just short of slamming the door in deference, he was sure, to her parents who were just down the hall. There would be no reasoning with her tonight, that much he was sure of. A hell of a way to start the new year, he thought, as he left their room for the sanctuary of his study.

🍁   🍁   🍁

She wasn't surprised that he was gone. She was relieved, though. She didn't want to continue this tonight, not with her parents here. As much as they loved Taylor, she knew her father would cheerfully kill him for hurting her.

She'd said things tonight that she promised herself she would never say. She'd known from the beginning that Elodie was in love with Taylor. All anyone had to do was watch her, her heart in her eyes, her hands constantly touching him.

At first, Elodie had been cordial but distant, treating Laura, as Taylor's assistant, like a paid servant. When she'd seen that Taylor was in love with Laura, her cordiality had changed to bare civility.

For awhile she had tried to find a way to gain Elodie's respect but it never happened. When he'd come home from Italy and married her, even the civility was gone, at least in private. Taylor was too important a commodity for Elodie to risk doing something in public that would embarrass him. The few times the three of them had appeared in public together, no one had ever seemed to notice the antipathy between the two women.

But tonight was too much! Elodie had crossed a line Laura wasn't able to overlook. And in the deepest recesses of her mind, she wondered if it had been the first time…

CHAPTER 11

Taylor slept in his study that night. He wasn't sure which one of them he was angrier with, Elodie for her actions or Laura for her accusations. With a house full of family and friends, there was no way to discuss it. He was hoping she would calm down by morning.

He awoke earlier than he'd planned but he wanted to be out of the study before anyone discovered him there. Rosina and Maria were already up fixing brunch for the crowd and he joined them for coffee in the kitchen as they worked.

The others wandered in a few at a time, helping themselves to plates of *huevos rancheros* and Italian bread. Laura was the last to make an appearance and she carefully avoided Taylor's eyes. Beth noticed immediately. It wasn't like Laura—or Taylor either—to avoid the casual contact they both usually enjoyed. Laura looked tired and Beth could tell she'd been crying. There was something seriously wrong with this picture!

After brunch, Taylor and Jason left for their tennis match with Sean and Matteo going along to supervise. The girls went out to visit friends and Maria and Rosina went to Rosina's apartment to discuss plans for the new baby while they watched the napping twins.

That left Laura and Beth with some time alone. They retreated to the bedroom where Laura stretched out on the bed with Beth in the chair beside it. They discussed the party and the baby until Beth took matters into her own hands.

"Alright, Laura. We've discussed everything else possible. Out with it."

"Out with what?"

"Do you think I didn't notice that you'd been crying? That you and Taylor were avoiding each other this morning?"

"Just a domestic dispute. No big thing."

"You can't lie to me, Laura Collins Morgan. I've known you too long and something is bothering you."

Laura's eyes filled with tears, "Oh, Beth…"

As her voice trailed off into heartbroken sobbing, Beth moved to the bed and hugged her until she could speak.

"What is it? What's happened?"

"It's Taylor. Last night—last night after everyone else had gone, I went looking for him and found him out in the hall with that witch, Elodie Nee, wrapped around him, kissing him as if she had a right. And maybe she did…"

"What? What could possibly give her the right to kiss *your* husband?"

"I don't think it was just her doing the kissing. Taylor certainly looked as if he was returning it."

"You know that can't be true! Taylor adores you!"

"And Elodie's been after him for years! Maybe there's been something between them all along!"

Beth didn't answer. Laura had told her often enough over the last few years that Elodie Nee was in love with Taylor but Beth never thought she really meant it. Elodie wasn't any more in love with Taylor than the rest of his fans were—was she?

"They were just standing there in front of the elevator where anyone could have seen them. My father would have killed Taylor if *he'd* seen them. What about the girls? How would he have explained it to them?"

"But none of that happened. So, how did he explain it to *you*?"

"He said she had kissed him—as if that made any difference! He tried to make me feel sorry for her because she had no one to go home to. As if that was an excuse!"

"Do you really think that Taylor's been seeing her all along?"

Laura was silent for a long time, staring down at the emerald ring Taylor had placed on her finger when he'd asked her to marry him. Did she believe he'd been cheating on her with Elodie? Raising her eyes to meet Beth's, she said, "No, I don't think there's anything between them—not on Taylor's part, anyway. There *would* be if Elodie had her way! But, you're right. I know Taylor loves me. But he's so blind to how she feels about him and I can't make him see it. Taylor's loyal to a fault when it comes to his friends."

"I'm glad you realize that it probably did happen the way he said it did. Laura, he loves you. From the day he met you, there hasn't been anyone else for him."

"I said such awful things to him last night, Beth. We never fight. We don't always agree but we never actually fight. But we did last night. Taylor spent the night in his study."

"You're going to have to talk about it, you know. You have to hear him out and you have to try to make him see how you feel."

Laura's eyes grew dark. "I said one thing that I won't take back and that I won't apologize for. I can't handle Elodie Nee in our lives anymore. If Taylor insists on keeping her as the fan club president and pursuing this friendship, it's going to have to be outside of our home. I simply won't put up with her anymore."

"Then tell him that and stick to it. But if he decides to keep her in his life, you have to believe that it's only as a friend."

"I know. At least my head knows. My heart still believes differently. I'll talk to him tomorrow after everyone leaves." Laura looked at the woman who had been her best friend through so many years—since they were thirteen years old! "I'm so glad you were here."

"I'm never further away than a phone call. You know that."

"My phone bill certainly does!" Laura answered as the two of them laughed.

CHAPTER 12

There were too many people around for Taylor to broach the subject with Laura. She had seemed calmer when he and Jason had returned from their tennis game and he was sure that she and Beth had had a long talk. The fact that Beth hadn't met him at the door with her claws out gave him hope that their talk had made Laura see that what had happened with Elodie was really nothing.

There had been a message with his answering service from Elodie asking him to call. He hadn't. He still wasn't sure what he was going to say to her and didn't want to talk to her right now anyway.

Everyone would be leaving tomorrow and he would be going back to the theatre tomorrow night. He needed to talk to Laura tonight no matter what it took. He waited impatiently through the last minute conversations and the frantic packing until the apartment was finally quiet.

He was relieved to see that Laura was still awake. She was propped up in bed, a book resting on the mound of her abdomen. As he watched, the book moved as the baby inside pushed at the unwelcome weight. Laura shifted the book and ran a hand lightly over the spot the tiny hand or foot had pushed against.

"He's going to have a fear of books if you keep reading giant novels that way," Taylor commented from the doorway.

"*She's* going to be a great reader," Laura commented as she looked at him. He looked tired, she realized, tired and tense. Today hadn't been any easier for him than it had been for her.

"May I come in?"

"Of course. It's your room, too."

He closed the door behind him then crossed the room and sat facing her on the bed. "We need to talk, Laura." He took her hands in his and never let his gaze waver from her eyes.

"I love *you*, Laura. I have from the moment I met you. What happened last night was…hell, I don't know *what* it was! But I promise you I wasn't a willing participant. You have to believe me."

She removed one of her hands from his and caressed his cheek. "I know, Taylor. I'm sorry for doubting you."

Wordlessly he reached out and pulled her close, savoring the moment of having her safely within his arms again. After a few minutes of silence that did much to heal their hearts, Laura gently pushed him away.

"But we do have to talk," she said. "What are you going to do about Elodie?"

"There's nothing *to* do—she was drunk and probably doesn't even remember what happened."

She shook her head in exasperation. "She remembers. She did it deliberately. I think she heard me call you and set the whole thing up to hurt me—to hurt us."

"You're wrong, Laura. Elodie's just a friend—a long-time friend," he said with a note of warning in his voice. "I know you don't like her but she's not out to hurt us."

Laura sighed and closed her eyes for a moment. How could he be so blind? Opening her eyes, she told him, "It's you who's wrong. She's in love with you and resents me for being the one you chose. I know you don't believe that and I'm not even going to try to convince you." She held up her hand as he took a breath to interrupt. "No, Taylor, no more. No more excuses for her. I'll work with her in her capacity as your fan club president, but she'll never be welcome in our home again. If you can't live with that, then I won't be living with you."

Her green eyes were cold and he knew her well enough to know that she meant every word she was saying—there would be no changing her mind on this one. If that was what it would take, he was willing to take this as a compromise.

"Fine. If it's that important to you, she's no longer welcome here. But that doesn't mean I won't continue our friendship—I'll just make sure that you have as little contact with her as possible. But you have to trust me, darling, or it will never work."

"I trust you, Taylor. But I will never trust her."

"Then can we call this closed and go back to our lives?"

"After one more thing," Laura said as she reached out to pull his face to hers. "I'm going to wipe out any memory of her kiss right now," she whispered against his lips then proceeded to drive any thought of Elodie Nee from his mind.

CHAPTER 13

Taylor had escaped the chaos of the family departures by pleading that he needed to be at the theatre early. It wasn't entirely untrue—he did need to do his vocal exercises and get back into the mind of his character after the week off. Mostly he just needed a space to think.

Laura had made it clear last night that she believed him—making up almost made the argument worthwhile, he thought with a smile. But in the clear light of a new day, a new year, he had to face what he was going to say to Elodie.

A part of him wondered if Laura was right. Was Elodie in love with him? Did she deliberately try to undermine his marriage? No matter how hard he tried to convince himself, he couldn't believe that it was true. Not Elodie. She was his friend and that was it.

Still, friend or not, what she'd done was completely out of line. He had to make that clear and he had to tell her what the consequences would be. It wasn't going to get any easier if he waited; might as well get it over with now. He reached for the phone and began to dial the number he'd called so many times in the past.

❋   ❋   ❋

The apartment was blissfully quiet. All of the visitors were gone. She missed them already but still enjoyed the quiet that surrounded her—the quiet that had been missing for the last week.

Going to her desk, she booted up the computer and opened the file for her novel. It was almost ready to send out, just a few more changes to make. She felt sure it would sell—as soon as she was ready to let it go.

Rosina cleared her throat so as to not startle Laura. When she was working, Laura was in her own world, unaware of the real one that surrounded her.

"Laura, these came for you." She held out a crystal vase overflowing with bright flowers. Laura smiled as Rosina placed it on the corner of her desk.

"Thanks, Rosina. They're beautiful, aren't they?"

"Very beautiful," Rosina replied. "As long as I've interrupted you, is there anything special you'd like for dinner tonight?"

Laura opened the card as she answered, "We must have enough leftovers to feed an army. Why don't we make do with those?"

"I'll see what comes together," Rosina said as she turned to leave the room. A loud crash of shattering glass stopped her and she turned to find the flowers on the floor, the vase shattered, and Laura, white-faced, looking at the card in her hand.

"Laura! Are you alright?" Rosina pushed the mess away from Laura's feet as she urged her to sit down. "What is it? What's wrong?"

"Nothing—nothing's wrong. I just knocked over the vase." The tremor in her voice told Rosina she was lying. "Please, just get rid of them," she said as she knelt down and began throwing the flowers in the trashcan. Rosina helped her pick up the debris and soak up the water with towels from the bathroom. Other than a damp spot on the carpet—and the note that had come with the flowers—there was no trace that they'd been there when Rosina left the room with the trash and wet towels.

Laura sat at her desk and picked up the card once again and read the handwritten message it held.

Laura, Taylor,

A wonderful party as always! Thanks for sharing so much with me.

Love—
Elodie

Taking a deep breath, Laura tore the card to shreds before she turned back to her novel. She'd be damned if she would shed any more tears over Elodie Nee.

※   ※   ※

The phone rang in Elodie's Westside apartment. She had a feeling she knew who it would be and she answered with a smile he could hear in her voice. "Good morning! And Happy New Year!"

How could she sound so unconcerned, Taylor wondered. Didn't she know what kind of chaos she had caused in his life?

"It's Taylor, Elodie."

"Taylor! Wonderful party! I had *such* a good time. Just the perfect way to kick off the New Year."

"I'm glad you enjoyed it, Elodie—even if you enjoyed it a little too much."

"Taylor?"

"Oh, stop it, El. You're not fooling me. You know exactly what I'm talking about."

"Oh," she said contritely even as she grinned at herself in the mirror. Laura must have been really upset at what she saw. Served her right. "Oh…my little indiscretion at the elevator. I was hoping you'd forgotten."

"You wrapped yourself around me like a boa constrictor! What the hell were you thinking?"

"That's just it, Taylor. I *wasn't* thinking. I'd had too much champagne, it was all so romantic...I am so sorry. Was Laura terribly upset?"

"You might say that," he answered.

"I will have to apologize to the dear girl. What can I do to make it up to her?"

"Nothing, Elodie. In fact, other than fan club functions, you won't be seeing Laura—or me—socially again. The fallout from your little performance is that you're not welcome in our home anymore, not if I want to keep my wife."

She was stunned. She'd never considered that Taylor would ban her from his life! It was all the doing of that red-haired bitch!

"Did you hear me, Elodie?"

"Of course I heard you!" she snapped before she regained control. "I...I just don't know what to say," she continued with a quaver in her voice. "Isn't there something..."

"Nothing. Look, El, we've been friends for a long time. I don't want to lose that. But you pushed Laura too far this time. She's got a right to want you out of our life. I'm sorry, but that's the way it's going to be. I'll talk to you in a few days so we can get the last pieces in place to announce the baby. Take care."

She was left with a dial tone. Taylor had hung up on her. Slowly, she replaced the receiver. Laura would regret this—Elodie would make sure of it.

CHAPTER 14

Laura woke from a nap just before the girls were due home from school. Napping was becoming a part of her daily routine. The naps were wonderful but they were taking up her afternoons; there wasn't a lot of time left to do her work. She'd gotten a little writing time in before lunch but the afternoon was a total waste.

As she walked into her study, she saw the box of letters from the fan club. They still needed sorting through and now was as good a time as any. Pulling out a handful of envelopes she began to open them and skim the contents looking for the ones that Taylor needed to answer.

Most of the letters came on fancy stationery; some scented with perfume, some calligraphed, some with cute little designs on the envelopes. She always tried to find the ones that were from the children—Taylor particularly enjoyed answering those, she thought with a smile as she lightly ran her fingers over her stomach before a plain white envelope caught her eye. There was nothing impressive about it, which was why it was so noticeable. In the rainbow of colors in the box, it stood out like a wallflower at a dance.

The address was typewritten or computer-generated. The envelope had been sent through the fan club, marked personal, with the required member number on the back flap.

She slit the envelope open with the letter opener Taylor had bought for her in Venice on their honeymoon. Even though the handle was made of beautiful Venetian glass, it had been a sturdy tool for the last five years. She put the opener in her lap as she pulled out a sheet of cheap white paper. When she read what it said, she dropped it on her desk and stood up as if to move away from it. The opener fell from her lap and shattered on the edge of the wastebasket but she never noticed.

"Laura? Are you alright?" Meg had come to tell her dinner was ready and was surprised at how white Laura was.

"What? Oh, I'm fine. I just dropped my letter opener and I'm afraid it's shattered."

"I'll go get a broom. Be careful, those slippers aren't going to be much protection."

Laura sat down and picked up the letter again. It was every bit as awful as she'd first thought. It described in graphic detail a sexual encounter between the writer and Taylor after he got "rid of that red-haired demon you married." Taylor had had his share of odd fans, some blatantly pursued him sexually, sent him trinkets and pictures. But never something like this! This was downright pornographic. Quickly, she folded it back into the envelope and hid it at the back of a drawer until she decided what to do.

When Meg came back into the room, she had moved the chair away from the desk so that they could sweep up the glass from the shattered handle of her letter opener. Her unpredictable emotions threatened to make her cry over the loss—and the letter that had led to its destruction.

She was startled when the phone rang and nearly dropped it as she picked it up. "Hello?"

"Laura? You sound strange. Is something wrong?" Taylor's voice surrounded her with his love.

"Hello, darling," she said.

"Hello, Taylor," Meg called as she headed out the door with the broom and dustpan.

"She sounds pretty cheery," Taylor commented.

"Why wouldn't she? She's eighteen, pretty, and has a date to the Valentine's dance with the best looking boy in the school!"

"What about you?"

"I don't want to go to the Valentine's dance, but thanks for asking."

"You'd be the prettiest girl there," he said, smiling at her teasing.

"Don't you have a show to do, Mr. Morgan?"

"I do. But I thought I'd check in before everything started happening. What was wrong when you answered the phone?"

"Nothing important. I managed to knock my letter opener off the desk and it hit the wastebasket and shattered. Meg and I were cleaning up the mess."

She was entirely too calm about it, Taylor thought. Something else was bothering her—he knew her well enough to tell that. Maybe it was just some pregnancy thing.

"I'm sorry. I guess we'll just have to go back to Venice to buy you a new one."

"I'll hold you to that."

"Just say when."

"Maybe when the baby goes to college?" She laughed but he wasn't sure that she was kidding.

"I'm sure we can find a babysitter before then," he said.

"Go do your show, Taylor—I love you."

"I love you. See you in the morning."

"Maybe I'll surprise you and be awake," she said in a throaty whisper that never failed to have an effect on him.

"Laura…"

All he heard was her giggle before she hung up the phone.

"Hello, Taylor," Meg called as she headed out the door with the broom and dustpan.

"She sounds pretty cheery," Taylor commented.

"Why wouldn't she? She's eighteen, pretty, and has a date to the Valentine's dance with the best looking boy in the school!"

"What about you?"

"I don't want to go to the Valentine's dance, but thanks for asking."

"You'd be the prettiest girl there," he said, smiling at her teasing.

"Don't you have a show to do, Mr. Morgan?"

"I do. But I thought I'd check in before everything started happening. What was wrong when you answered the phone?"

"Nothing important. I managed to knock my letter opener off the desk and it hit the wastebasket and shattered. Meg and I were cleaning up the mess."

She was entirely too calm about it, Taylor thought. Something else was bothering her—he knew her well enough to tell that. Maybe it was just some pregnancy thing.

"I'm sorry. I guess we'll just have to go back to Venice to buy you a new one."

"I'll hold you to that."

"Just say when."

"Maybe when the baby goes to college?" She laughed but he wasn't sure that she was kidding.

"I'm sure we can find a babysitter before then," he said.

"Go do your show, Taylor—I love you."

"I love you. See you in the morning."

"Maybe I'll surprise you and be awake," she said in a throaty whisper that never failed to have an effect on him.

"Laura…"

All he heard was her giggle before she hung up the phone.

CHAPTER 15

After hanging up the phone, Laura sat in the desk chair and stared at the drawer that held the letter. Maybe it wasn't as bad as she had thought on first reading. Maybe she was overreacting. But she knew she wasn't.

She unlocked another desk drawer and took out an envelope and dumped the contents onto her desk. The plain white envelopes lay scattered across the surface. She didn't need to read them to know what they contained.

The first one had arrived when they returned to Italy after their honeymoon. Taylor had tried to hide it from her but she'd found it crumpled in the trash. Now she picked it up and read it again…

Darling Taylor,

I can't tell you how devastated I was to hear of your recent wedding. It was too soon, Taylor, you haven't had enough time to recover from Annie's tragic death, not enough time to explore the possibilities…not enough time to let me show you how I feel about you. But it's not too late, my love. We can still be together when you leave that redheaded Delilah who's seduced you in your grief.

I'll be waiting…

Your TRUE love

It had only been the beginning. The letters had continued coming, never regularly, but always through the fan mail. Always in a plain white envelope with a printed address, sometimes on a label, sometimes directly on the envelope. As required, a membership number was always on the back of the envelope, but the same number had never been used twice. Tracing the numbers would have required working with Elodie and she was not known for being particularly cooperative when Laura made a request, so Laura had never tried. Besides, it was obvious all the letters were the work of one person—the sender had never tried to disguise it.

But none of the letters had been as blatant as this latest. Reluctantly, she opened the drawer and took it out. Forcing herself to read it slowly, she realized that it was as bad as she had remembered.

She'd never discussed the letters with Taylor. But this new one scared her. The writer seemed to be dangerously close to the edge that separated fan from stalker. Looking at the letters fanned out across her desk, she made a decision.

Pierce Albright was a local F.B.I. agent. He'd helped Laura out on some background information for an article she had written and had acted as her advisor when she decided to write her novel. They'd become friends and, as much as she hated to impose on that friendship, she knew he was the one person in her life that could advise her on these letters.

After looking up his number, she dialed and waited for his answering machine to pick up. He always screened his calls, never answering until he was sure who was on the other end. He was fiercely protective of his privacy and that of his newly pregnant wife. She knew that he had reason to be and waited patiently through his message before she said, "Hi, Pierce, Annette. It's Laura Morgan. Pierce, could you give me a call when you get a chance, I have…"

"Hey, Laura. Happy New Year!"

"To you, too, Pierce. Did you all have a good holiday?"

"A good one. Telling our parents about the baby was the highlight, of course…but you know all about that," he said with a laugh.

"Excited were they?"

"That doesn't even come close. We were sorry to miss your New Year's party, though. Was it as good as usual?"

"Better. My mom and Rosina tried to outdo each other on the cooking. I must have gained ten pounds."

"Oh, man! What I wouldn't give for some of your mom's *carne adovada*!"

"You're in luck. There's some in the freezer. Any chance you're available for a late lunch in the next few days?"

Pierce heard the note of tension that crept into her voice. "Something wrong, Laura?"

"Maybe…I'm probably just over-reacting. But I would like the chance to pick your brain."

"How about tomorrow? I can be there about two."

"That would be perfect, Pierce. Thanks. I'll see you then."

After saying goodbye, she hung up the phone. Her eyes were once again drawn back to the letters. So much *passion*! An obsession like that couldn't be healthy! She gathered them back into the manila envelope and locked them into her drawer. If Pierce said there was something to worry about, then that would be soon enough to bring Taylor into the picture.

CHAPTER 16

Taylor looked up from reading the paper as Laura came into the dining room. He knew that she felt she looked terrible but there was a glow about her and softness from the pregnancy that suited her right now. He smiled at her as he folded the paper before standing to give her a good morning kiss.

"How are you this morning?"

"Barefoot and pregnant...stop smirking, Taylor."

"And beautiful."

She shook her head at him with a small smile. Taylor had always been a morning person, awake early, ready to face the day no matter how late the night had been. She had *never* been a morning person but he could still make her laugh.

"Keep telling me that and I'll keep pretending to believe you."

She disappeared into the kitchen returning a few minutes later with a bowl of fruit and some toast.

"How's our son going to grow up to be a football player if you feed him that sissy food?" Taylor asked.

"Your *daughter* doesn't need to enter the world looking like a blimp like her mother. Anything interesting in the paper?"

"The usual murder and mayhem. Speaking of mayhem, how are you this morning?"

"What?"

"When I called last night, you sounded upset."

"Just hormones and the loss of my letter opener. You worry too much."

"Probably. But I'm not going to stop."

"When will you be going in today?" Laura said, changing the subject.

"I need to be in around noon. We want to run a tech rehearsal on act two. There have been some problems this week. What about your plans?"

"Pierce Albright is coming over for lunch. I had to ask him a technical question last night and he was whining about missing Mom's *carne adovada* so I took pity on him. He can help me with my research while he eats." She hoped Taylor didn't notice the tremor in her voice; she wasn't in the habit of lying to him.

"Tell him hello for me. Annette's feeling alright?"

"He says she's fine and their parents are thrilled about the baby."

"Good. We'll have to have them over for dinner before you get too uncomfortable to entertain."

"Too late for that, Taylor."

"I'll leave you to the paper, my darling grump. I'm going to go shower. Want to join me?"

"Only if we're using the tank at *Sea World*…the shower's not big enough for all three of us."

Laughing, he kissed her on the top of the head and went down the hallway to their room.

※　　　　※　　　　※

"You know, I might divorce Annette and marry your mother if she'd cook this for me all the time," Pierce said as he mopped up the last of the red chile sauce with a tortilla.

"Fine prospective father you are! Mom left you the recipe this time. But she said that you're the one who has to learn to cook it. No pawning it off on Annette."

"I can live with that." Taking a last swallow of iced tea, Pierce continued, "So, what's the problem, Laura?"

A frown creased the space between her brows. "Maybe it's nothing but I'd like you to look at something."

He followed her down the hall to her study where she unlocked the desk and took out the envelope that held the letters. He sat beside her at her worktable as she took them out and spread them across the surface.

"These have been coming off and on ever since Taylor and I got married. The first one was waiting when we got back from our honeymoon. The last one arrived in this week's fan mail."

Albright picked up the first letter and skimmed over it then read the rest in progression. He saw a pattern that he didn't like…the letter writer had a real obsession with Taylor and an equally real grudge against Laura. From the first letter with its scolding tone to the lasciviousness of the newest one, the writer was showing signs of a seriously deteriorating mind.

"Five years, ten letters. That's a lot, Laura. Indications of stalking include more than ten letters to a celebrity, especially written over a space of time. And this feeling the writer seems to have that she and Taylor are fated to be together…another real trouble sign. She obviously has met him, has plans to meet him again and seems to be getting pretty specific with those plans. This could be nothing, Laura, but I'd be more inclined to take it seriously."

Laura sighed. "That's what I was afraid you would say. Looking at them again last night, I could see that she's becoming more unstable."

"What does Taylor have to say about these?"

"He doesn't know."

"Doesn't know?"

"I sort his mail. I've never passed these along to him. I didn't want to worry him and I kept hoping she'd just give it up if she never heard from him."

Pierce looked back at the letters, catching phrases and words that rang alarm bells for him…"destiny"…"mine"…"us"…"together" …and the epithets aimed at Laura.

"Did it occur to you that, rather than protecting Taylor, you might be putting him in serious danger?"

Laura's face went white and Pierce kicked himself for the stark pronouncement.

"Do you really think he's in danger?" she whispered.

"Maybe not yet but I don't like the sound of these. And he's not the only one who could be in danger. What about you? And the baby?"

Laura's hands instinctively caressed the baby. "I'd never thought of that. Oh, Pierce, I've been so stupid."

"Not stupid. You just want to believe people are intrinsically good. I'm trained to look at it the other way. Now, take a deep breath and tell me more about how these have arrived."

🍁 🍁 🍁

An hour later, Pierce picked up the envelope containing all of the letters. "I can't make any promises, Laura. It's good you kept the envelopes with the letters but they've been handled a lot, going through the mail then sorting by the fan club. I don't think we'll find fingerprints but we might get lucky. I'll have someone start on these right away. And I'll be here at ten tomorrow morning to talk to Taylor with you."

Silently she let him out of the apartment and watched until the elevator doors closed. Fear clutched at her heart as she closed and locked the door. Pierce had succeeded in confirming all of her unspoken thoughts. There was someone who wanted to hurt them. A shiver passed over her as she opened the door to the sunny nursery that was usually so full of dreams. Right now it was filled with shadows.

❦ ❦ ❦

Taylor was surprised to find Laura awake when he came home from the theatre. She was sitting in the living room, reading, as he came through the door.

"Laura! Is something wrong?"

"Just can't sleep." She smiled past the fear that still swirled in her brain. She took his hand and placed it on her abdomen. "Your daughter's been practicing parallel bars all evening."

Taylor smiled at the movements under his hand. The baby was certainly active tonight. "Anything I can do to calm you both down?"

"I wouldn't mind being held for awhile," she said softly.

"Give me a minute to change and I'll be right back."

True to his word, he came back quickly, wearing soft sweats, carrying her favorite candle. He lit it and turned off the lights, then sat on the couch beside her, pulling her into his arms where she lay nestled against his chest. Gently he placed one hand on the baby and began to rub softly. Quietly he sang a Stephen Foster lullaby.

> "Slumber my darling, thy mother is near
> guarding thy dreams from all terror and fear.
> Sunlight has passed and the twilight has come
> Slumber my darling the night's coming on.
> Sweet visions attend thy sleep
> Fondest, dearest to me.
> While others their revels keep,
> I will watch over thee.
> Slumber my darling, the birds are at rest,
> Wandering dews by the flowers are caressed
> Slumber my darling, I'll wrap thee up warm,
> And pray that the Angels
> will shield thee from harm."

He could feel the tension easing in her shoulders as he sang and, before he had finished, she was asleep in his arms. He had never thought it was possible to love someone as much as he loved Laura—and now their unborn child, too. Humming the lullaby softly, he was content to hold them as they slept.

that was usually so full of dreams. Right now it was filled with shadows.

❦   ❦   ❦

Taylor was surprised to find Laura awake when he came home from the theatre. She was sitting in the living room, reading, as he came through the door.

"Laura! Is something wrong?"

"Just can't sleep." She smiled past the fear that still swirled in her brain. She took his hand and placed it on her abdomen. "Your daughter's been practicing parallel bars all evening."

Taylor smiled at the movements under his hand. The baby was certainly active tonight. "Anything I can do to calm you both down?"

"I wouldn't mind being held for awhile," she said softly.

"Give me a minute to change and I'll be right back."

True to his word, he came back quickly, wearing soft sweats, carrying her favorite candle. He lit it and turned off the lights, then sat on the couch beside her, pulling her into his arms where she lay nestled against his chest. Gently he placed one hand on the baby and began to rub softly. Quietly he sang a Stephen Foster lullaby.

"Slumber my darling, thy mother is near
guarding thy dreams from all terror and fear.
Sunlight has passed and the twilight has come
Slumber my darling the night's coming on.
Sweet visions attend thy sleep
Fondest, dearest to me.
While others their revels keep,
I will watch over thee.
Slumber my darling, the birds are at rest,
Wandering dews by the flowers are caressed
Slumber my darling, I'll wrap thee up warm,
And pray that the Angels
will shield thee from harm."

He could feel the tension easing in her shoulders as he sang and, before he had finished, she was asleep in his arms. He had never thought it was possible to love someone as much as he loved Laura—and now their unborn child, too. Humming the lullaby softly, he was content to hold them as they slept.

CHAPTER 17

❀

She'd wakened early in the morning to find them still cuddled together on the couch. Gently she woke Taylor and they'd gone to bed where he'd wrapped her in his arms again and they fell back to sleep.

It was almost nine when Laura woke. Taylor was already up and she listened to the quiet sounds of him moving about in the kitchen. For a moment she was happy before all the worry came crashing in on her again.

She got up, quickly washed her face, put on makeup and brushed her hair. Pierce would be here soon and Taylor still had no idea he was coming. Nor did she have any idea how to tell him.

In the end, she didn't tell him. When the doorman buzzed at ten, they were still at the table, sharing the paper and enjoying a quiet companionship.

"Who could that be?" Taylor said as he walked over to the intercom. "Yes, Brian?"

"Mr. Pierce Albright here to see you, Mr. Morgan. Shall I send him up?"

"Go ahead," he answered. "Pierce again? Should I be worried?" he asked with a teasing smile.

Laura just shook her head and went to open the door.

"Good morning, Laura. Taylor, good to see you."

"Pierce. Nice to see you, too. What brings you by this morning?"

Pierce glanced at Laura and saw the panic in her eyes. She obviously hadn't told Taylor about the letters.

"I needed to talk to both of you. Can I talk you out of a cup of coffee?"

"Of course." Taylor led the way back into the dining room. Laura picked up their plates and took them to the kitchen and returned with a cup and the coffee pot. Her hands were shaking as she tried to pour the coffee and Taylor stopped her.

"What the hell is going on? You two are scaring me."

"Laura asked me to take a look at these yesterday, Taylor. She said you hadn't seen them…it's some of your fan mail."

Puzzled, Taylor took the envelope from him and looked at Laura. Her face was white and her hands were twisted together as she watched him open the envelope. As he began to read the top letter, he glanced up at her again then read the rest of them through.

"Laura?"

"I didn't think too much about the first ones. I didn't want to upset you and I thought she'd go away but she seems to be getting worse. I asked Pierce to look at them to see if I was imagining things…"

Taylor looked at Pierce. "Not imagination, Taylor. I think you may have a serious problem here. It looks to me like you're being stalked."

❦   ❦   ❦

Pierce explained all the signs to Taylor. "I think this woman is serious. She's definitely stepped up her letter writing both in frequency and in intensity. She may be getting ready to make a move of some sort."

"This is ridiculous. It's just one of the fans who's just a little too interested. Why would someone stalk me?"

"Why wouldn't they? You're a public figure; well liked, kind to your fans, accessible—the dream mate of any unhappy woman."

"But look at all the different member numbers. How do we know it's the same person?"

"*Read* the letters, Taylor!" Pierce was exasperated that the man refused to see the danger. "This woman uses the same phrases. She always refers to Laura's red hair. She talks about a life for her with you. She signed them all with 'your true love'. It's the same woman!"

"Pierce, I can't take this seriously. God, if you could have seen some of the letters over the years."

"Did any of them threaten your wife?"

"What? No! You think this person might hurt Laura?"

"Laura and the baby. Do you think she's going to be happy when she hears that you and Laura are having a child?"

Taylor was speechless. He could dismiss the attack on himself—he really couldn't believe that would happen—but if Laura was in danger it was another thing entirely.

"What do you suggest we do?"

"For now, hire a bodyguard. Watch for repeat people at the stage door. Open any gifts carefully. And alert your fan club management to watch out for signs of problems in the membership."

"A bodyguard. That's the best you can suggest?"

"These are copies of the letters, Taylor. The originals are in the crime lab being unofficially examined. I want to make this an official investigation but I need you to swear out a complaint before I can do that."

"What good will that do?"

"It will allow me to investigate it openly instead of under the table, risking my job."

"Can you keep it quiet? Away from the tabloids?"

"I think we can. If you notify the fan club what to be watching for. Can you trust your people?"

"No!" Laura said at the same time Taylor said, "Absolutely!"

Pierce looked from one to other. "Which is it?"

"You can't trust Elodie," Laura said. "She's capable of anything."

"Laura. Enough! Elodie would not hurt me for the world. You have to get over that."

"Look, you two, I don't know what's going on with this Elodie. But you're going to have to decide if you trust her."

Taylor looked at Laura then said to Pierce, "I trust her completely." Laura burst into tears and ran from the room.

The two men sat in silence for a moment, then Pierce said, "I gather Laura's not fond of Elodie?"

"An understatement. Elodie's president of the fan club. She has been since the beginning. She and Laura do not get along—never have. Then there was an incident at the New Year's party. Laura wanted me to take the fan club away from her but I refused. But I had to agree that Elodie would be part of our public lives only."

"Tough one, Taylor. You and Laura will have to work this out. I'd advise you to alert them. The next time a letter comes, and another *will* come, we need to catch it as quickly as possible. We might be able to get a fingerprint or some other piece of identifying evidence if we do."

"I'll take care of Laura. And the bodyguard for her and the girls."

"I think the girls are safe. This woman never refers to them but it wouldn't hurt to have someone watching them. But what about you, Taylor?"

"I don't need a bodyguard, Pierce. I think you and Laura are wrong but I won't risk her or the baby. But I'll take care of myself. Now, what do I need to do to get this investigation started?"

CHAPTER 18

❀

When Pierce left it was nearly noon. He was on his way back to headquarters to file the official complaint and get this investigation started.

Taylor closed the door behind him then walked to the terrace doors that overlooked the city. He was more shaken by the idea that someone would seriously consider hurting him, or someone he loved, than he had been willing to show to either Pierce or Laura.

The odd ones he attracted were the price of his celebrity. And some of them had been a little scary. Before he met Laura, one woman had kept showing up at the stage door with little gifts and progressively blatant invitations. One night he'd found her sitting on the doorstep of his apartment building wearing a fur coat and nothing else. He'd had her escorted away by the police and she'd honored the restraining order that had been sworn out against her. He hadn't thought of her for years but he should let Pierce know. Maybe she'd gone round the bend again. Taylor had no idea what had happened to her.

The letters seemed harmless enough to him. He knew a lot of his fans had their fantasies about him. He usually found it flattering and more than a little silly but ultimately harmless. This letter writer just seemed to have a richer fantasy life than most of them, but if there was any threat to Laura or the baby, he had to take them seriously. It was Pierce's job to know to know about these things. Taylor would have to trust his judgment.

"Taylor?"

He turned at the sound of Laura's voice. She stood in the doorway to the living room looking pale and tired. He wanted to be angry with her for holding back the information and for her unreasonable reactions to Elodie but he couldn't. All he wanted to do was gather her into his arms and make the fear leave her eyes.

"Is Pierce gone?"

"He left a few minutes ago. He was on his way to make all of this official."

"Are you angry at me, Taylor?"

He sighed and shook his head. "Not angry, Laura." As he took a seat on the couch he gestured that she should join him. When she had and he'd pulled her close, he went on, "I'm a little surprised that you kept the letters from me."

"I just didn't want to upset you. They seemed so harmless in the beginning."

"There were other letters before you took over my mail. Some just as bad. I survived those."

"I know. Part of it was that…" her voice trailed off.

"Part of it was what?"

She took a deep breath and moved away where she could look at him. "I was jealous. I didn't want to know that your fans felt that way about you and I didn't want to share that information with you," she said defiantly, a blush rising in her fair skin.

Taylor couldn't help but laugh. "Oh, Laura, you never fail to surprise me. Come here, woman, and let me show you that you have nothing to worry about."

Taylor made an appointment to meet Elodie at her apartment the next day. Pierce had promised to accompany him so they could enlist her help with the letters.

"Taylor! A stalker? One of *our* members? I just can't believe anyone would do that."

"You know them all personally, Ms. Nee?" Pierce asked quietly.

"Of course not but I do know most of them. And none of them would hurt Taylor or dear Laura for anything."

"I agree with you, El, but Pierce deals with this kind of stuff all the time. If he says I'm being stalked, we'd probably better take him seriously."

"What do you need me to do?"

"The letters," Pierce said, "are coming through the fan club mail. Always with a different member number. The postmark is always smudged, sometimes non-existent as if the letters are being slipped into the mail by hand. It sounds very much like someone from the inner circle of the club might be the one who has the best access."

"What? You can't be serious. I've known these women for years. Some of them have been with me and Taylor from the very beginning."

"Could someone have worked her way into your management group? Maybe she started the letters earlier then found a way to get on the inside, making it easier to send the letters and giving her better access to Taylor?"

Pierce watched Elodie as she thought about the idea. He had the feeling she was a little less surprised by this than he had expected. His gut instinct said that Laura was right; Elodie Nee wasn't just the good friend that Taylor believed her to be.

"Well, I really don't want to cause trouble for any of my ladies but we did add someone new about three years ago...at Laura's request.

And, she's in charge of picking up and forwarding the mail from the postbox, which would make it easy for her. But I can't believe…"

"Ms. Nee, I'll need the names of all your 'ladies'. I'll be as discreet as possible when I investigate but I will have to talk to all of them—including you, ma'am," Pierce said with an apologetic smile. "I would appreciate it if you'd give me the name of this individual who does the mail so I can start there."

"Taylor, must I?"

"I'm afraid so, Elodie. If it were just me, I really wouldn't care. But there are some things that make us think that Laura might be in danger. With the baby coming, I just can't risk it."

"Can I tell them?"

"Ms. Nee, if we didn't need the information from you, we wouldn't be telling *you*. The fewer people who know this gives us a better chance of tracing the stalker. And I'm sure you clearly understand the risk that this could get into the tabloids—not something Taylor needs."

"No, that would be just awful. I still…well, I guess it can't be helped. If you'll wait, I'll print out a list for you. The girl that does the mail is named Teri Hanson. Sweet thing and very eager to help."

🍁 🍁 🍁

With list in hand, Taylor and Pierce left Elodie's apartment. As they waited for the doorman to hail a cab, Pierce asked him again if he was sure about Elodie.

"Pierce, I've known her since I was twenty. She's always been an asset to my career. And a good friend. I trust her completely."

"I'll take your word then, Taylor. I'll get someone started on this list. The Hanson woman? Do you know her?"

"I've met her. Written a couple of thank you notes for special tasks she's done for the club. But that's it. All of Elodie's inner circle seem to be normal. I've never noticed any problems from any of them."

"Looks can be deceiving, Taylor. Don't let down your guard."

※ ※ ※

In her apartment, Elodie Nee looked through the list she'd given to Albright. What a blessing this had turned out to be! Laura had insisted that Teri be added to the team and, while she was a hard worker and did anything she was asked, Elodie didn't like her just *because* Laura had championed her. Elodie had always felt that sweet little Teri was Laura's personal spy. Maybe now, Elodie could pin this letter thing on her and get her out of the picture. She poured a glass of champagne and started contemplating exactly how it could be accomplished.

CHAPTER 19

All too quickly, it seemed, the last week of Taylor's run in *Lorna* had arrived. Laura was now seven months pregnant but, miraculously, the word had not leaked out. They were planning to announce their news at the fan club party the afternoon before his final performance.

Graduation was rapidly approaching for Megan and Betta. Megan had been accepted at Stanford and both girls were frantically caught up in finals and prom and farewell plans.

There had been no more letters. Pierce had persuaded his supervisor to add the Morgan file to his caseload but, thus far, it hadn't made much of an impact. Taylor's earlier stalker had settled down in the Midwest and was no longer following his career, so she wasn't a suspect. None of the previous letters had offered any clues and, until another letter arrived, they would just have to wait.

None of Elodie Nee's inner circle had offered any red flags during his investigation. Still, he agreed with Elodie that the Hanson woman would be best removed from mail duty. And Laura never told him that Elodie had removed Teri from all her other responsibilities as well.

On the afternoon of the final performance, a gala luncheon was held at the Ritz for Taylor's fans. The big attraction was Taylor's scheduled appearance on his way to the theatre and the announcement he had hinted at in an invitation sent to the fan club membership.

The room was buzzing with speculation when a flurry of activity at the door announced his arrival. Flanked by their daughters, with his arm protectively around Laura, he made his way into the room flashing the beautiful smile that had captured Laura's heart.

She and the girls dropped back as Taylor made his way to the stage. No one noticed. They might as well have been invisible for all the attention the crowd paid to them. Their bodyguard and Pierce Albright stood by the doorway scanning the crowd and a number of "new members" seemed more interested in their fellow fans than in the man on stage.

The noise was awesome and Taylor egged them on with his engaging grin and flirtatious attitude. It was a full ten minutes before the cheers and whistles and flashing cameras calmed down as he finally convinced them to be seated.

As it became quiet, he looked at them and said, "So, what are you all in town for?" The laughter rocked the room again.

Elodie efficiently took over running the show, bringing up winning fans to accept autographed prizes and have pictures taken with the man of the hour. A gift check of money raised in fund-raising, marking the end of this run in the show, was presented to Taylor and the local representative of his charity, *Shelters For Children*. He made a gracious speech thanking them for all their support.

"Now, I promised you an announcement. I hope you'll all find it as happy an announcement as I do."

"A tour?" "New show?" "Another CD!" excited guesses rang out across the room.

"None of those but something definitely new for me." He turned and stepped down from the stage, taking Laura's hand to lead her back up the steps to stand beside him.

"I'm taking up a new role," he said as he removed the voluminous cape that Laura was wearing. "Laura and I want you to be the first to know that in two months, we'll be parents again—starting from scratch this time!" His face glowed as he put his arm around his obviously pregnant wife. "We hope that you'll join us in celebrating our blessed event by giving gifts to the charity. We promise you that *our* child will want for nothing and hope you will honor him…or her…with gifts for children who have so little."

A brief silence filled the room. No one had guessed this news! Then the applause started and grew and someone began a chorus of *Happy Birthday* for Baby Morgan. Taylor laughed and leaned down to kiss Laura…an act that broke more than a few hearts and set at least one set of teeth grinding.

Someone called out above the noise, "Is it a boy or girl, Taylor?"

He smiled and answered, "Yes!" bringing another round of laughter. "Thanks to all of you for being here today. The news will be public tonight on *ET* so you can run off to your laptops and announce it. Just don't be late for the show!"

With another wave, he escorted Laura from the stage where they and the girls were whisked out a back door to the safety of the waiting car.

༺ ༺ ༺

"Well, I think that went well," Taylor said as he loosened the tie he had worn to the party. "You're alright, Laura?"

"Stop fussing, Taylor. I'm fine. And it did go well."

"I can never get used to all that…that…" Betta was at a loss for words.

"Pheromone deluge?" Meg asked dryly.

Pierce burst into helpless laughter. "That's it exactly! I'm surprised you can walk out of there at all, Taylor."

"It's a little difficult sometimes, Pierce. Guess you FBI types don't get that kind of adoration much."

"Ever!" he said, as the car pulled up to the rear entrance of the theatre.

"Then I think I've definitely got the better job," Taylor said with a grin as he kissed Laura. "You—go home and rest. You two," he said to his daughters, " you see that she does. I'll see you all tonight before the show."

Laura's eyes met his and he could see the faint shadow of worry there so he leaned over and whispered, "Nothing's going to happen, Laura. I love you."

"I love you, too. Go get some rest yourself before everything starts happening. We'll see you in a few hours."

CHAPTER 20

The ending of a show was always a time of mixed feelings for Taylor. He'd given a lot of his time and energy to "John Ridd", as he did with every character he brought to life. Each cast was like the formation of a new family for him and it was hard to move on.

Still, he was tired. Not as young as he used to be, he mused, as he walked the empty backstage corridors. It was time for some quieter time, for a new life and this new responsibility of a baby. Deep in his heart he was scared to death of the idea but he'd never backed down from a challenge in his life.

He passed his almost empty dressing room. Most of his personal things had been packed up and taken home already. All that remained on the dressing table were the picture of his parents that had traveled with him all these years, a photo of Laura in Venice on their honeymoon, and senior portraits of Meg and Betta. Those would go home with him tonight.

He went out on the empty stage. The silence was overwhelming but he could hear echoes in his mind of laughter and music and applause from this show and all the others that had come before. Despite the ghost light, the stage was crowded with the spirits of the generations of players who had come before him and the promises of those who would come after.

"Saying goodbye, Taylor?" The voice came from the stage right shadows but he knew who it was.

"It's always a little hard to let go, El. You know that."

Elodie Nee stepped from the shadows and waited as he walked over to her. "So what are you going to do now? I can't see you staying home playing Daddy all day."

"Really? The funny thing is that I *can* see me doing just that. I'm really looking forward to a 'normal' nine-to-five life for awhile."

"You'll be so bored, Taylor. This is what you were born to do," she said as she swept her arm across the empty auditorium. "Can you turn your back on it?"

"For awhile, anyway. I have time to think about what comes next." He put an arm around her shoulder, the gesture of an old friend. She felt the difference from the protective arm he'd wrapped around Laura at the party earlier and a surge of jealousy went through her. He should have been mine, she thought. I'd have never held him back this way.

Taylor started walking back to his dressing room. "Nice party this afternoon. You outdid yourself this time. The check was way more than I expected. It's going to help a lot of kids. Think the fans will fall in with the plan for the baby gift?"

"I think so. They were pretty excited after you'd left. I have the feeling that a lot of those donations are going to come wrapped around baby booties."

"We'll send them on to the charity, too," he said with a laugh as he stopped at the door of his dressing room. "Where will you be sitting tonight, El?"

"Second row center," behind your *wife* she thought bitterly. "I think the fans have most of the first ten rows. You'd better have a speech planned for the ovations."

"I do but it won't be easy to deliver. Thanks for stopping by but I think I just want to be alone for awhile. I'll see you at the party tonight."

"Break a leg, Taylor," she said as she kissed him on the cheek. Her hand lingered a moment on his shoulder before she turned away so that he couldn't see the tears in her eyes.

🍁　　🍁　　🍁

Backstage began to fill up as cast members arrived. Everyone had a word for him and he was running late with changing into his costume when the door opened. "Taylor?"

He peeked out from behind the screen and leered at his wife. "I'm getting dressed. Want to help?"

"Running late?"

"Yeah. Curtain may not make it up on time tonight. It will be the first time but everyone's been by to say something and will you look at these flowers?" He stepped from behind the screen to the mirror and checked his makeup.

"You know, I never thought my husband would wear more makeup and spend more time in front of the mirror than I would."

"Occupational hazard, Mrs. Morgan."

There was a knock on the door. "Five minutes, Taylor" the stage manager called before he made a general announcement. They could hear the flurry of activity outside the door as people ran for places and lost props were located.

"Are you sorry, Taylor? To be leaving?"

"Sure. But I'm excited about us. It's time we had a life like other people. I'm looking forward to actually going to bed *with* you instead of hoping you'll wake up when I get home in the middle of the night."

"Me, too. I'd best get out there. A kiss for luck?"

"A kiss because I love you—you're all the luck I ever need."

Another knock at the door and a call for places broke them apart. "Later, love," he said as he ran out the door. She hurried around to the auditorium entrance, taking her seat just as the curtain rose.

"Bravo! Bravo!" The auditorium was filled with cheers and whistles as Taylor made yet another curtain call. The ovation showed no sign of stopping. Once again he took his leading lady's hand and led her to the apron to take another bow. This time she held up her hands to try to quiet the crowd and they slowly took their seats waiting for the farewell speeches.

"Oh, my," she said, her voice choked with tears. "I promised myself I wouldn't cry but I evidently didn't listen. Taylor Morgan has been my partner now for years—graciously loaned to me, to *us*, by his wife, Laura, and his daughters, Megan and Betta. He has been everything I ever dreamed of when I came to New York and I thank him for sharing his expertise and company with me. Taylor, we will all miss you. Not just the cast but all of New York. And we'll be here waiting when you decide to come home again." With that, she couldn't hold the tears back any longer and the audience rose to its feet again when he hugged her.

Finally, they fell silent again as she stepped back to join the ensemble, leaving Taylor alone in the spotlight. The tears flowed freely on the faces of cast, crew, and audience and he could see the tearful smiles of his wife and daughters in the front row.

He never looked past them to notice that Elodie had already fled, her tears, her disappointment, and her anger too much to handle in this public arena.

"I guess this is good-bye then—at least for a little while. I'm going to be taking some personal time now for awhile. My daughters will be going off to college this fall and Laura and I have a new plan of our own. In case you haven't heard the news, we're adding to our family in about two months." Another wave of applause shook the theatre and he waved and smiled his appreciation.

"This will probably be the most difficult role I've ever had to fill. I may be begging to come back after my first few sleepless nights and diaper duty. But it's time for me to move on, at least for awhile. But there's too much greasepaint in my blood now for me to even think of saying good-bye forever. When the right role comes along, I'll be back."

When the applause quieted he went on, "My thanks to Llewellyn for the magnificent music he wrote for 'John Ridd'." A spotlight picked out the composer sitting in the front row next to Laura and the applause rose again. When it died down, Taylor continued, "My thanks and love to these folks up here with me. They are every bit as much my family as those down there in the front row. I thank them for taking me in and giving me a place to play." Turning to his cast mates, he threw them a kiss. "You'll be forever in my heart."

Turning back to the audience he said, "Goodnight, my friends. I wish you great dreams."

As the audience rose to their feet once again, Taylor took a step back into the ensemble, leading them in a final bow before the curtain descended and it was, finally, over.

diaper duty. But it's time for me to move on, at least for awhile. But there's too much greasepaint in my blood now for me to even think of saying good-bye forever. When the right role comes along, I'll be back."

When the applause quieted he went on, "My thanks to Llewellyn for the magnificent music he wrote for 'John Ridd.'" A spotlight picked out the composer sitting in the front row next to Laura and the applause rose again. When it died down, Taylor continued, "My thanks and love to these folks up here with me. They are every bit as much my family as those down there in the front row. I thank them for taking me in and giving me a place to play." Turning to his cast mates, he threw them a kiss. "You'll be forever in my heart."

Turning back to the audience he said, "Goodnight, my friends. I wish you great dreams."

As the audience rose to their feet once again, Taylor took a step back into the ensemble, leading them in a final bow before the curtain descended and it was, finally, over.

CHAPTER 21

❈

The reality didn't sink in for Taylor until he read the reviews of his replacement's opening night. There were the inevitable comparisons to his own performance but his successor had held up well. Taylor felt a sense of loss as he realized the character he created was no longer his.

He was at a loss for what to do with his time so he threw his energies into finishing the nursery. He and Laura took long walks and spent the evenings catching up on movies they hadn't seen.

He was there to see Betta and Meg off to their senior proms. He'd missed all the other dances. When they came in dressed for the dance, they took his breath away and he said goodnight to their dates with a fierceness he hadn't expected to feel.

When the door had closed behind them, Laura came up and put his arms around him. "A little fatherly jealousy, Taylor?"

"I guess I just hadn't ever realized—let myself realize—that they're really grown now. They're young women and I know exactly what those boys were thinking!"

"You're probably right. And you can't do anything about it."

"I know—but if this baby is a girl, I'm locking her up 'til she's thirty."

Laura laughed and shook her head at him. "Then I guess maybe I had better start hoping it's a boy." She yawned suddenly. "I'm sorry, I just can't keep my eyes open. I think I'll go on to bed. You're not going to wait up for the girls, are you?"

"Isn't that what I'm supposed to do?"

"Not when they're going to an all night party after the dance. They'll be home after breakfast tomorrow."

"Then I'll read for awhile." He put his arm around her and walked down the hall to their room. "Are you feeling alright? You've been exceptionally tired the last few days."

"I'm just ready for this pregnancy to be done."

"Are you sorry, Laura? Do you regret that our plans were all blown apart by this baby?"

"Sometimes. It's a big change. But this baby is a part of you and me. And she'll be the most important thing we've ever accomplished."

He wrapped his arms around her and held her close until he felt her yawn again. Chuckling, he said, "Into bed with you, Sleeping Beauty. I'll see you in the morning."

※ ※ ※

The apartment was quiet—too quiet. And Taylor was restless. This leisure stuff was hard to get used to. He had just settled in with a book when the phone rang and he reached to catch it before it could wake Laura.

"Taylor, it's Sean."

"Sean, good to hear from you. Is everything alright?"

"'Tis. Maybe more than alright. Is Laura around?"

"She's gone on to bed. Her energy level seems to be pretty low these days."

"Maria was the same. Slept for hours before Toms was born. But it's you I wanted to talk to, anyway. This needs to be between you and me for the moment."

"Sounds interesting, Sean. What's up?"

"What are you going to do with your time now, Taylor? Other than being a new dad?"

"I hadn't really thought that far. I'm going to need to find something. All this quiet is driving me nuts."

"I thought it might be," Sean said with a laugh. "You're not known in the family for being the shy, retiring type. So, I have some news for you that might solve your problem. There's an opening for a visiting instructor in the theatre department here at UNM. They want to hire someone to run a two-semester course on musical theatre and they were hoping to get someone with some experience—an actor—to come in to teach it. The department head's a friend of mine and she suggested your name. The committee loved the idea and asked me to talk to you about it."

"Me? Teaching? I've never taught before, Sean."

"No, but you've lived it. You know the ins and outs. Laura's mentioned some of the workshops you've helped with there for the performing arts school and the inner city groups you've given time to. I think it would be a good thing for you."

Taylor could feel a spark of excitement building. This could be exactly what he was searching for and would have the advantage of taking Laura back to her beloved New Mexico. With the baby, being near her mother would mean even more to her.

"I don't know what to say, Sean. The idea's certainly exciting."

"Any chance you could fly out for a couple of days? I know you don't want to leave Laura but since the baby's not due for another six weeks or so, it should be safe. And, Taylor, it's not really any of my business, but I hope you won't discuss it with her until you make up *your* mind if you want to consider it. I don't want to get Laura's or Maria's hopes up. I hope you understand."

"I do. It wouldn't be fair to either one of them and I know it must be hard on you."

"Well, I have to say I wouldn't mind being around my new grandchild on a daily basis."

"Set up a meeting for me, Sean. Let me know when. I can do an overnight trip and tell Laura I have a meeting with producers in California."

"Is the California thing a possibility? Movies?"

"There have been a couple of nibbles but I don't feel like it's really what I want to do. I'd really like to come out and talk with the University before I consider anything with them."

"I'll call Kris Straub right now. She should be home and I'll try to get back to you this evening. I'm glad you're considering it. I hope you know it's not just having my girl and baby home—I'd like to spend some more time with my son-in-law, too."

"I'd like that, too. Let me know as soon as you have some information for me."

CHAPTER 22

"Morning, Taylor," Laura came into the dining room the next morning not looking a lot more rested than she had the night before. He noticed her face looked a little puffy and she wasn't wearing her wedding ring. She'd had some swelling problems with her hands before and had had to leave her ring off when it happened.

"Morning, love. How are you feeling?"

"I don't know, " she said as she pushed her heavy hair away from her face. "I feel a little off this morning. I have an appointment with Dr. Bernard this afternoon and I'll talk to her then, so just stop before you even start to lecture me."

"Me? I wouldn't do that."

"Only if you got a chance."

"Sit down and I'll get you some breakfast. Fruit and toast, again?"

"I think so. Would you ask Rosina if there's any of the cantaloupe left?"

As Taylor left the room, Laura acknowledged that she really didn't feel well. She had a headache and her hands and feet were swollen. This baby couldn't come too soon to suit her, she thought.

"Here you go, Laura." He set a bowl of cantaloupe and raspberries in front of her. "Rosina sent the yogurt, too. Said you need your calcium."

"I hate yogurt, Taylor."

"I know that but I'm not going to tell Rosina that I won't bring it to you."

"Good idea."

As Laura began to eat, Taylor said, "I got a call last night from that Hollywood producer. They'd like me to fly out for a day or so to discuss some ideas."

"Really? Anything exciting?"

"They aren't being real specific but I was considering it might be worth checking out. Would you be alright with me gone for a couple of days? I told them I could probably leave tomorrow morning and be back the evening of the day after."

"If you're interested in it you should go. I'll be fine. I think I'm probably just going to be doing a lot of sleeping anyway."

"I don't want to leave if you think you need me here."

She smiled at him. "I always need you, Taylor. But go. See if you can get them to put you in something with Pierce Brosnan. Then I can meet him and run off with him."

"I'll make a note of that," he said with a mock frown. "No Pierce Brosnan movies!"

"Sean Connery?"

"The man's old enough to be your father!"

"That doesn't make him less interesting."

"Eat your breakfast, Laura Morgan. I'm not discussing this with you any more."

Laura laughed as he turned back to the paper. As if she'd ever be interested in someone other than Taylor! Guys could be so insecure.

🍁   🍁   🍁

"The baby looks fine, Laura. Your weight is up but still within line. I am a little worried about this swelling in your hands and feet. Are you having headaches?"

"Some, and I can't seem to stay awake at all."

"Your blood pressure is up a little, too. I'll know after I get the results from your urine test but I'm thinking you might be developing pre-eclampsia." Dr. Bernard saw Taylor's mouth open and stopped him. "Just wait a minute, Taylor. Let me finish. *Then* you can ask questions."

"Pre-eclampsia just means we need to take some precautions so that it doesn't become eclampsia, which could be serious. This is not at all unusual especially with first pregnancies. I think right now we can control this with medication and bed rest. OK, now you can ask questions."

"How serious is this? Is Laura in danger?"

"Only if it should get worse. But I'll be monitoring her every day to make sure there are no further signs." She turned back to Laura. "I'd like to send a visiting nurse over to take your blood pressure every day and to check the swelling. I need to know if you're urinating as often as you should be and if the headaches get any worse."

Taylor said, "I'm supposed to leave town tomorrow for a couple of days. I can cancel the trip."

"There's no need. Laura has Rosina and the girls there to wait on her hand and foot, right? She just needs to stay in bed, drink lots of water. The nurse can monitor her vital signs and I'll see her every other day."

"Dr. Bernard is right, Taylor. I'll be fine. You need to go on this trip."

"Are you sure? Both of you?"

"Yes!" they said in chorus.

Taylor was still worrying about leaving the next morning. "Rosina, you'll make sure she does what she's supposed to while I'm gone?"

"*Sí*, Taylor. You know I'll keep her safe. This baby is important to me, too."

"I'm more afraid of Rosina than I am you, Taylor. She doesn't give in to me."

"She's not going anywhere," Meg declared from the doorway. "With me and Betta and Rosina on guard, Laura's going to be allowed out of bed only after she's submitted a request in triplicate that's been personally approved by God!"

"Fine—I guess. I'll call when I get there and Matteo has the number of the hotel. Call me if there is the slightest change!"

"Go on, Taylor. You'll miss your plane if you don't go. Give Pierce my love," she said with a wicked grin then kissed him and clung to him a moment longer than was necessary. She'd never admit it but she was scared and having Taylor gone wasn't going to help.

"I love you," he whispered, " and I'll be home soon." Another kiss and he was out the door. They could hear him talking to Matteo in the hallway and the door closing behind them as they left. Rosina left to make some tea and Betta tried to make Laura more comfortable as she settled onto her left side as the doctor had ordered. The waiting had begun.

CHAPTER 23

Taylor couldn't concentrate on anything on the flight to Albuquerque. He spent most of the time worrying and kicking himself for leaving Laura. What if she did get worse? He must have been out of his mind to leave.

Sean was waiting for him at the Albuquerque International Sunport and noticed the strain in his son-in-laws eyes right away. "Something's wrong, Taylor. What is it?"

"That obvious?" Taylor asked as the two of them made their way out of the airport to the parking garage.

"You look like you've been hit by a truck. Is it Laura?"

"She's not doing completely well right now. The doctor says it's nothing serious but it could turn into something. Pre-eclampsia, she called it. High blood pressure and a bunch of other things."

"I've heard of it," Sean said, fighting to stay calm at the thought of his daughter in any kind of danger. "I guess it's fairly common."

"That's what the doctor said. She's put Laura on bed rest and is sending a visiting nurse over to monitor her every day. Rosina and the girls are with her."

"I'd put you on a flight back right away if I could but you know that tonight would be the earliest we could do that."

"I know. We might as well go through with this. Your Professor Straub will probably think I'm a total idiot. I don't know that I can be coherent about this."

"You have until noon to get it together. We're having lunch with her and the committee. I thought I'd take you to the hotel so you could catch your breath. Maria's at home so we won't risk running into her on campus."

"Think we'll be able to pull this off, Sean? Keeping it from my wife and yours?"

"I hope so, but I won't be surprised if they put it all together somehow."

"Do you suppose if this baby is a girl, she's going to be able to see right through us, too?"

Sean laughed, "Without a doubt! We'd better keep our fingers crossed for a boy."

❦ ❦ ❦

Laura spent most of the morning napping in between being wakened to drink more water or tea. Despite all the liquids she didn't seem to need to get up for the bathroom as often as she would have thought. Her headache was still there and she was starting to feel decidedly grumpy. And bored! Nothing she tried to read caught her attention and what was on television was dismal.

Lunch was a rich broth that Rosina had made, with fresh bread and no salt! She ate some of it before pushing it away. "I'm sorry, Rosina. I'm just not hungry." The light from the window seemed very bright and she asked her to pull the heavy drapes. "What time is the nurse supposed to be here?"

"Around four," Rosina answered. Laura did not look well. The puffiness seemed to be increasing. "Should I call the doctor?"

"No, the nurse will be here soon. She'll know. I'm just being a baby about it."

The phone rang and Rosina answered it before Laura could reach for it. "*Sí*, Taylor. She's here. She's in bed and doing as she's told. I will put her on the phone."

Rosina handed her the phone then indicated Laura should scoot back down in the bed to lay on her left side as instructed while she was talking.

"Hello, darling."

"Hi, how are you doing?"

"About the same. And I'm bored to tears."

"I'm sorry I'm not there to keep you amused."

"How's California?"

"Bright and sunny. Full of suntanned blondes. Pierce Brosnan says hello."

"Right, Taylor. Stay away from the blondes or you'll have a redhead to contend with when you get home. What time's your meeting?"

"Meetings. I'm going to be busy the rest of the day and evening it looks like. I've left an itinerary with the hotel so I can be reached if you need me."

"Just land the job, Taylor. Right now, lying around on a sun-kissed beach sounds pretty good."

"Not with the way *you* sunburn. I'd be married to a lobster."

"Go to your meeting. You can pick on me when you get home tomorrow!"

His voice softened, "I'm sorry I'm not there, Laura. I almost caused a scene and made them turn the plane back around right after takeoff. I shouldn't have come."

"Don't be silly. We're fine. I'll see you tomorrow night and I promise I'll whine enough so that you won't feel like you missed anything."

"A threat or a promise, Laura?"

"A promise. See you then. I love you."

"Love you, too. Be good."

"Any change, Taylor?"

"It didn't sound like it. She's not liking the bed rest much."

"I'm not surprised."

"Do I have time for a phone call before we go?"

"Sure. Shall I leave?"

"No, I'm just going to call Beth and have her call Laura. That will cheer her up."

"Should I call Maria and tell her you called me?"

"If you think Maria won't jump on the first plane."

"I'll use my cell phone while you call Beth. Fifteen minutes?"

"That should do it."

The phone rang in New York half an hour later. Meg was sitting with Laura and snatched it up. "Hello?"

"Hey, Meg! It's Beth."

"Beth, how are you?" At the sound of her best friend's name, Laura's eyes brightened. Beth was just what she needed right now.

"I'm fine but Taylor just called me about Laura. How is she?"

"She's right here being a horrible patient. You sure you want to talk to her?"

"I'll risk it," Beth laughed. "I've seen her horrible before."

"I heard that," Laura said since Meg had handed her the phone before Beth finished speaking.

"Well, it's true. I've seen you every way you can be seen, girl."

"Except almost eight months pregnant and looking like a blimp."

"I don't have to see that. I've been there and done it. Taylor called. He said you're on bed rest for pre-eclampsia."

Meg waved from the door and left them to talk. "Oh, Beth, I've never been so miserable in my life."

"What does the doctor say?"

Laura filled her in and, in Taos, Beth's eyes filled with worry as Laura talked about her symptoms. She glanced at the medical dictionary she had open on the computer screen. Swollen feet and hands. Headache. Sensitivity to light. None of this sounded very good.

"You said the nurse would be there soon?"

"She's supposed to be. Then we'll talk to the doctor."

"Call me back after you talk to them, please?"

"Sure, if my guards will let me use the phone again."

"At least you still have your sense of humor."

"Not really," Laura eyes and voice filled with tears. "Beth, I'm scared to death. What if something happens to the baby?"

What if something happens to you, Beth thought before answering. "They know how to handle this, Laura. You're getting the best of care. I know it's uncomfortable and nerve-wracking right now but it will be all right. You have to hold on to that."

"I wish you were here to hold my hand. I feel like such a baby and I just want it to be over with."

"I know, sweetheart, I know." Beth's own voice was filled with tears. "I wish I was there, too. But I'll be there as soon as the baby arrives so I can start spoiling her right away. Laura? Do you want me to call your Mom?"

"No, she'd just go crazy with worry."

"And later she'll just kill us for not letting her know."

"You're right but I'll call her after I talk to the doctor, if there's any change."

"Don't forget to call me, too. I'll be waiting by the phone."

"Thanks, Beth. I'll let you know what they say."

"I love you, Laura Collins Morgan. You do what they tell you to and I'll see you soon."

"Bye, Beth…love you, too."

Laura reached out and hung up the phone. She took a drink of water and the effort seemed to leave her breathless and nauseated. The phone rang again as Meg came back in the room.

"I'm going to unplug this thing if it rings one more time, Laura. You're supposed to be resting!—Hello?"

"Megan! It's *Abuelita*."

"*Abuelita!*"

Laura's eyes widened. She knew Beth hadn't had time to call her mother even if she'd decided to break her promise not to. That left Taylor. He shouldn't have worried her mother, Laura thought as she reached for the phone.

"Hello, *Mamá*," Laura said.

"*Mi'ja*! Your father just called. Taylor called him from California. What is he doing in California when you're ill!"

"Mom, I'm alright. It's just pre-eclampsia. The doctor's got me in bed and is monitoring me. I'll be fine."

"*Ay, Dios Mío*," Maria said. "You should have called me. Your mother should be with you."

"Mom, I have Rosina and the girls. They won't let me move. There's nothing you could do here. You need to finish up your classes so you can be here when this baby arrives."

"But I feel so helpless, *mi'ja*!"

"I wish you were here, too, Mom. But I am getting the best of care. In fact, I just heard the doorbell. That will be the nurse. I'll call you back when she's left and we've talked to the doctor. It may take awhile."

"I'll be here, Laura. I love you."

"I love you, too, Mom. I'll talk to you later."

Laura handed the phone back to Meg as Betta brought in the nurse. "I swear I'm going to kill Taylor when he gets home. He shouldn't have called your grandmother!"

"Getting upset's not going to help your blood pressure, Mrs. Morgan," the nurse said briskly. "I want to take you through a calming breathing exercise before I take your blood pressure. We'll get a better reading that way."

Laura nodded and tried to pay attention to what the nurse was saying. How did her life get so out of control, she wondered, as she closed her eyes and tried to relax.

🍁   🍁   🍁

The meetings at the University were going well. Taylor had managed to pull himself together by the time he and Sean met the Theatre Department committee for lunch at the *Monte Vista Fire Station*, one of Albuquerque's original fire stations. It had been converted to a restaurant and the building's territorial style was one of Central Avenue's landmarks.

Taylor and Kris Straub hit it off immediately. Their visions of what this directed study in musical theatre could offer to the University's program were very similar. Most of the committee sat back and listened as the two of them hammered out details and discussed possibilities. By the end of lunch, everyone was sure that Taylor was the right person to take the visiting position and design the program.

Sean handed him off to Kris and headed back to his university office. She would take Taylor to meet the provost and the president. They would discuss salary terms and all the fine details. By dinner tonight with other theatre and music faculty, they would probably have a tentative answer—tentative to Taylor's discussing it with Laura. Sean wasn't too worried about what his daughter's response would be. The southwest was in her blood and she'd be thrilled to come back home.

A frantic message was waiting on his voice mail from Maria so he called her back before his class was due to begin.

"Sean, I should be there with her!"

"Maria, she has the best of care and you only have two more days of classes to go. You can't go running off now."

"*Madre de Dios,* Sean Patrick! Do you think I care about my classes?"

"Yes, I do. Wait until Laura calls back after talking to the doctor. If she's worse, I'll put you on the first plane out and teach your classes myself."

"Oh, Sean. I know I'm overreacting. I just can't lose Laura like we did *Tomás*."

The loss of their son had hurt them deeply when he died in his twenties from cancer. There was not a day that went by when he was not in their hearts and thoughts. Sean understood Maria's panic but tried to stay calm for her sake. His voice softened, "We won't lose Laura, darling. She'll come through this fine, you'll see. She's strong like her mother."

"I don't feel very strong right now, Sean. When will you be home?"

"Not 'til late, sweetheart. I have that committee meeting tonight. I can't miss it. I'm sorry." The timing on all of this was not working well. For a moment he considered telling Maria what was going on but the thought of getting her hopes up that Laura might be coming home would be too cruel if it didn't work out."

"I'll call you when I hear from Laura, Sean. You have your cell phone?"

"I do. Call me when you hear."

"There. Do you feel a little calmer now, Mrs. Morgan?"

The breathing exercise had calmed her but Laura was beginning to feel terribly nauseated. "Yes, it helped. Could we just do this so I can go to sleep for awhile?"

"Sure thing." The nurse put the blood pressure cuff on and went through the procedure. Laura closed her eyes and waited but the others saw the alarm in the nurse's eyes when she took the reading. "Well, that didn't work right. I need to try one more time, Mrs. Morgan. You go ahead and keep your eyes closed and I'll be through in a few minutes."

Once again she pumped up the cuff and took the readings. The reading was evidently the same and she wrote it down carefully before she pulled the cuff off. "I'll need to call this in to the doctor. Is there a private phone I can use?"

Laura's eyes flew open. "Private? What's wrong?"

"Nothing. I have some other patient information to pass on as well and you know the confidentiality thing."

"Come, I will show you where you may call," Rosina said.

Meg and Betta plumped up Laura's pillows and got her to drink a little water. Neither of them was happy with the way she looked or with the reaction of the nurse.

Suddenly she moaned and leaned over the edge of the bed and vomited up the little water she had just taken. "I'm sorry," she whispered as she fell back against the pillows. Meg soothed her as Betta ran to tell the nurse.

🍁   🍁   🍁

When his phone rang toward the end of class, Sean expected it to be Maria but was surprised when it indicated an out of area call. "Excuse me for a moment, class" He answered the phone and Matteo said, "Sean, I must find Taylor immediately."

"Hold on," Sean said then quickly dismissed his class. "Now, what is it, Matteo?" What's happened?"

"It's Señora Laura. She's very ill. They are taking her to the hospital now and say that the baby may have to come tonight. Taylor needs to get back here right away!"

"Oh dear Lord," Sean whispered. "Give me the number I can reach you at, Matteo. I'll get plane reservations made and get back to you as soon as I can. Matteo, how bad—"

"I don't know, Sean. But they are taking her by ambulance now."

"I'll call you back soon. Call me if there's any change."

Sean hung up the phone and looked at his watch. Taylor's meeting with the faculty was just starting so he decided to call the airlines first. Fate was on their side. A flight was leaving in two hours with three empty first class seats. It would get them into New York about one a.m. There was no faster way. He called Maria immediately afterwards.

"Maria, it's me. Don't ask me lots of questions now, darling. I'll explain it all later. I just got a call from Matteo. They are taking Laura to the hospital right now. I don't know the details but they seem to think they may have to take the baby tonight. Taylor is here with me—no time to explain Maria, not now! Just pack some stuff and meet us at the airport by six-thirty at gate B-6. Just hand luggage, Maria. You can buy whatever we need when we get there. I'll see you in about an hour. Drive carefully—Laura needs you."

Quickly he made one more phone call to the provost's office to notify them that he and Maria would be gone. Their exams were with their secretaries and student teaching assistants could administer them. Then he took off running across campus to the theatre where the meeting was being held in Popejoy's green room.

Everyone looked up startled as a disheveled, breathless, Sean Collins burst into the room. Taylor immediately rose to his feet, "Sean? What is it? Is it Laura?"

Gulping in air, Sean said, "Matteo called. They're taking her to the hospital. They may have to take the baby tonight. We have a flight at seven."

Taylor's face went white and he turned back to the group. "I'm sorry. I have to go. My wife…our baby…"

Kris Straub took over. "Go, Taylor. This can all wait. We'll all keep you in our thoughts that everything will be alright. Please let us know, Sean, when you have news."

"Of course."

Without a look back both men exited the room running.

🍁　　　🍁　　　🍁

Dr. Bernard was waiting when her ambulance arrived at the hospital. "Laura, like I told you on the phone, your blood pressure is up. The vomiting, nausea, and light sensitivity are all further signs that you may be developing full eclampsia. Right now," she said as she helped move her from gurney to examining table, " I want to check you and the baby out, see how much this is influencing the baby. If the baby's not showing signs of undue stress, I'll put you on intravenous drugs to lower your blood pressure. But if there's any sign of fetal distress, I'm going to have to induce labor or, possibly, perform a caesarean."

Tears ran helplessly down Laura's face as she held her hands over her abdomen where her precious baby might be in trouble. "Whatever you have to do to save the baby, Doctor."

"Taylor's still gone?"

"He wasn't supposed to be home 'til tomorrow. I don't know if Matteo has reached him yet."

"Nurse Mondragon, would you go see if Mrs. Morgan's family has arrived? Find out if they reached Mr. Morgan for us. Meanwhile, Laura, you and I have some work to do here."

"Damn it! I knew I shouldn't have left her, Sean. I should have stayed there."

"Should haves don't change anything, Taylor. We'll get back to her as soon as we can. There's Maria waiting for us."

Taylor's tiny mother-in-law was pacing in front of the check-in counter but she opened her arms to her son-in-law as he came toward her.

"Oh, Maria. What am I going to do?"

"You're going to pray and keep good thoughts, Taylor Morgan. My Laura is strong. She and the baby will be alright," she said fiercely. "But now, you two tell me exactly why Taylor is *here* while Laura is *there*. And you had better have a good reason."

Maria was quietly furious with Sean and Taylor. She understood *why* they had kept her and Laura out of the discussion and she knew there was no way Taylor would have left Laura if he'd really thought there was any danger. Yet all she could think of was her little girl going through all of this without the support of her husband.

Her little girl—soon to be a mother, God and the Holy Mother willing. Her fingers never ceased to move as she said her rosary over and over in offering for her child.

The phone rang in Elodie Nee's apartment. She'd been very depressed and angry since Taylor had left the show. He'd been so busy with Laura that she hadn't seen him since then. Not wanting to be out of the picture, she'd bribed an admitting clerk to find someone on every shift who would let her know when Laura was admitted in labor.

But she wasn't expecting the call this soon. Laura must still be over a month away from her due date. The clerk read her the admitting notes and acknowledged that it meant that Mrs. Morgan was in some trouble. Elodie thanked her then hung up the phone.

She called a good friend who was a doctor and told him what she'd just heard about a "dear friend".

"I don't think you have to worry too much, Elodie. Your friend will probably be fine, unless they don't get the blood pressure under control. But before it gets that bad, they'll probably take the baby by caesarean."

She thanked him then hung up the phone and paced her apartment for awhile. Laura could die. Taylor would be devastated, of course, but he'd need all his friends to help pick up the pieces. And if the baby survived—well he couldn't raise a baby on his own now, could he?

She smiled at the possibilities even as Taylor fought to stay calm high over the Midwest.

❦   ❦   ❦

"Have you heard from Taylor?" Laura asked Meg as she took a turn sitting with her. Laura's blood pressure was still high but she begged the doctor to wait as long as possible for Taylor to get there. Her anxiety wasn't helping.

"He called from the plane. They'll be in around midnight. Matteo will be there to meet them."

"Them?"

"Don't ask me why or how, but your parents are with him."

"What? But he was in California. Did he stop in Albuquerque?"

Meg watched the numbers fluctuate on the blood pressure monitor. "Laura, calm down. I don't know anymore than they're on their way."

"What time is it now, Meg?"

"Eleven-thirty."

"And as long as we can wait, Laura." Renee Bernard spoke from the door. "Your blood pressure is still going up and the protein levels in your urine are dangerous now. I'm seeing some distress in the fetal heartbeat."

"Oh, no, please, no. Isn't there anything you can do?"

"I'm going to give you something to induce labor but I can't promise we won't have to go to a c-section. Laura? Are you listening?" After Laura nodded and fixed her eyes on the doctor, she continued, "There are real risks here, Laura, and I'm not willing to take them. If Taylor's not here when it's time for this baby to come—by natural means or surgery—I am not going to hesitate. Do you understand?"

"I do. And I trust you. I just want him to be here."

"I know you do. And I'm sorry, since his absence is partially my fault. I didn't expect this to happen. Try to rest now for awhile. Meg, you'll be with her?"

"We're taking turns. Betta will be in soon."

"Good, just try to keep her calm for now."

When the plane finally landed, the flight attendants asked everyone to keep their seats while some passengers with an emergency exited first. Taylor, Maria, and Sean ran up the walkway to the passenger pickup area where Matteo was waiting. Taylor was on the phone as soon as he was in the car.

"They took her to delivery fifteen minutes ago, Taylor," Meg reported. "She's still in labor but I think the doctor is moving toward a c-section fast."

"How is she? Is she in danger?"

"Taylor, I don't know. Just tell Matteo to hurry. I'll meet you at the emergency entrance and get you up here as fast as I can."

"Meg—thanks. You've been wonderful in all of this. You're going to make a hell of a doctor."

"Not this kind, Taylor. Too nerve-wracking. I'll stick with counseling. Hurry but be careful!"

The car pulled up to the emergency entrance closely followed by the police car that had been trying to pull them over for speeding the last ten blocks. Taylor and Maria jumped out of the car and ran inside while Matteo and Sean stayed to face the music.

True to her word, Meg was waiting and she ran with them to the stairwell. "This is faster than taking the elevator. We only have to go to the third floor." Maria kicked off her shoes and left them behind as they began the climb.

Rosina was holding Laura's hand—an emergency, last-minute choice for birth coach. Laura was beginning to tire and her doctor glanced at the clock. This had been a hard and fast labor with all the trauma preceding it. Laura's blood pressure was down to an acceptable level but the exhaustion was taking its toll. The doctor decided to wait ten more minutes. No baby by then and she was doing a caesarean.

"Come on, Laura, we're almost there. You can do this. Get ready to push."

The door burst open and a masked, gowned figure flew into the room. The turquoise eyes above the mask locked onto Laura's and she began to cry. "Oh, Taylor, you're here. You're here."

Rosina moved away from her place by Laura's head and left the delivery room to brief Maria. "She is strong, our Laura. She'll be fine. The doctor thinks it will be soon but it may still have to be by surgery."

Taylor held Laura's hand tightly. "I am *so* sorry, my love. I should never have left you."

"Taylor," the doctor snapped. "You can apologize later. We have a baby coming so do your job."

Taylor slid his arm under Laura and supported her as she got ready to push again. "Now, Laura, I can see the head. Give us a good push—more—more—more—great! Breathe now. We have a redhead here but I can't tell if it's a red-haired girl or boy. You're going to have to give us another push. Taylor, help her."

Taylor held his breath as he concentrated on transferring all his strength to Laura. She was so pale, her hair matted with sweat, her eyes with circles under them. Still, she had never been more beautiful to him as she gave a cry that was echoed by the baby.

"A girl! Laura, Taylor, you have a girl! And she has her father's lungs it seems," the doctor said as the baby cried loudly. "You're going to have some competition, Taylor," she continued as they lay the baby on Laura's heart. Tears flowed freely down both their faces as a turquoise-eyed, red-haired angel invaded their hearts.

Taylor emerged from the delivery room and pulled off the paper cap that covered his hair. Matteo and Sean had reached an agreement with the police officer who had issued a warning rather than a citation when he'd heard their story, so the whole family was waiting.

He smiled, an ear-to-ear grin. "We have a daughter. Annie Collins Morgan. She weighs 5 lbs., 14 ounces, is 16 inches long. She has her mother's red hair and my eyes and is the most beautiful baby ever born. Laura was a miracle. I'm so proud of her." He broke down in tears. "So proud."

As the delivery room doors opened, a nurse peeked out and held her fingers to her lips with a smile before she very slowly walked past them pushing a bassinet. Sisters, grandparents, father, and friends got a good look at the baby before the nurse moved her down the hall to the nursery.

Next was a bed with Laura. "*Mama!* Did you see her? Isn't she beautiful?"

"She's beautiful, *mi'ja* just like her *Mamá*," Maria answered with tears in her eyes. "*Muy bonita.*"

Taylor took her hand and followed along as they went down the hallway to Laura's room while the rest of the family hugged and cried and rejoiced in the safe arrival of the newest Morgan girl.

CHAPTER 24

❁

The nurse chased Taylor from the room while they helped Laura clean up from the birth. By the time he came back, her hair had been braided and she was wearing a clean gown. Her eyes were closed but there was a soft smile on her lips.

"Hi," Taylor said softly from the doorway.

"Hi, yourself," Laura said as she held out a hand to him.

Taylor pulled his arm from behind his back and handed her six yellow roses. "I promised you half on delivery," he said with a smile. "They should be diamonds or rubies or emeralds but these will have to do for now."

"It's four a.m., Taylor! How did you get yellow roses this time of night?"

"One of the phone calls from the plane. I told Matteo to find some somewhere so I could keep my promise. For all I know, they came from someone's garden."

He took the flowers from her and put them in the water pitcher before he sat beside her and took her hand. "How are you, my love?"

"Tired. But I've never been happier."

"Me, too. I can't believe how close I came to losing you."

"That's over, Taylor. We can forget about it now and concentrate on that angel down the hallway."

"I went and looked in the nursery when they threw me out of here. She's easily the prettiest baby in there."

"Did everyone else go home?"

"Reluctantly. Dr. Bernard wouldn't even let your mother come see you."

"And I'm throwing you out, too, Taylor," she said from the doorway. "Laura needs to rest and, from the look of you, a few hours sleep wouldn't hurt you either."

"I'm fine. I'd like to stay."

"Sorry, Taylor. You can come back in the morning."

"It *is* morning."

"Not until nine o'clock, it isn't. Your wife and daughter will be waiting," she said as she casually took Laura's wrist to check her pulse then glanced at the monitors before writing some notes on the chart she carried. "You're looking much better, Laura. Your blood pressure is almost normal but I'm going to want to keep you for a couple of days just to make sure we don't have any lingering complications. You did a good job in there. I'm proud of you."

"Thanks. And thanks for helping me wait for Taylor to get here. She's all right—our Annie?"

"Absolutely perfect with the requisite number of fingers and toes. The nurses are already raving about the color of her eyes. Since she wasn't born with the usual dark blue, I'm pretty sure they'll stay this color. You're going to be beating boys off with a stick, Taylor."

"I've had practice with Betta and Meg."

"Good thing. You're going to need it." She paused at a sound in the hallway. "I think that's for you—fifteen minutes then you're out of here, Taylor." She smiled as a nurse carrying a pink wrapped bundle pushed open the door. She stopped and looked at the baby as she was leaving. "Hello, Miss Annie. Your Mom and Dad are waiting to meet you."

She watched as the nurse handed Annie to Laura and the three of them began the process of forming a family. It had been a good night despite the drama—the kind of night that reminded her of why she did this in the first place. Closing the door behind her, she smiled as she went to sign out before heading home for a few hours sleep.

※　　　　　※　　　　　※

Taylor and Laura spoke in whispers as they admired their sleeping daughter. Despite the trauma she had been through, Annie Collins Morgan showed no signs of the stress. In her parent's eyes, she was perfection.

Gently Laura unwrapped the blanket to free the baby's hands. "Look, Taylor. Such tiny fingernails!"

Taylor gently touched the soft little hand. Annie opened her eyes and yawned at her father before wrapping her hand around his finger. Taylor's eyes filled with tears. "She's so beautiful, Laura. How could we have made anything so beautiful?"

"Love, Taylor. She's pure love."

Like all parents throughout time, they counted her tiny fingers and toes and marveled at the shell-like perfection of her ears. She never let go of Taylor's finger until, all too soon, the nurse came to take her back to the nursery.

"So soon?" Taylor said.

"Sorry, Mr. Morgan. Doctor's orders. Besides, your girls need their rest."

Another nurse came in. "She's right. And I'm here to give Mrs. Morgan something to help her sleep and to see that you leave, Mr. Morgan. They'll be here in the morning waiting for you."

"May I stay until Laura falls asleep?"

The nurses looked at each other. "If you promise me that you'll leave right after that, I'll pretend I don't see you. But don't push your luck, Mr. Morgan." She helped Laura sit up to take a pill then lowered the lights. "No fair trying to stay awake, Mrs. Morgan."

"I won't—I doubt if I could anyway."

"Sleep well."

Taylor held her hand. "Laura, I wish I could tell you how I feel but there aren't words."

"I can see it in your eyes, Taylor. I don't need words—at least not those kind of words. Taylor, how did my parents end up with you?"

He laughed. "It's a long story, darling, too long for now. I promise we'll explain in the morning."

Laura yawned and fought to keep her eyes open. "It had better be a good story, Taylor."

"Oh, it is—with a very happy ending."

"I like happy endings," Laura murmured as sleep overtook her.

Taylor watched her for a moment before he released her hand and left the room. He waved goodbye at the nurse and waited for the elevator.

Matteo was waiting in the lobby. "Matteo, you should be home asleep."

"Sleep can wait. I wanted to drive you home. How is Laura? And little Annie?"

"Both sleeping. Both beautiful."

"*Sí, bellisima.* Congratulations, Taylor."

"Thanks, Matteo. Let's go home."

CHAPTER 25

❁

Taylor woke at seven, forgetting for a moment why he felt so tired. Then, as the memory flooded his mind, he smiled. They had a little girl! A perfect, beautiful little girl! And in two hours he would see her and her mother and he couldn't remember ever being happier than he was in this moment.

The rest of the household could hear him singing in the shower. No one had gotten much sleep but they all wanted to be together at breakfast to discuss the miracle that had entered their lives. By the time Taylor came into the dining room, his mother-in-law was carrying in a plate of *huevos rancheros* for him with fresh tortillas and butter already waiting on the table.

"*Buenos Dias*, Taylor."

"Good morning, *Abuelita*. I hope your newest granddaughter inherited your cooking skills."

"Laura and the baby were well when you left?"

"They were wonderful, Maria. They let us have her for a little while and we counted all her fingers and toes."

Megan said from the doorway, "So I guess Betta and I have been replaced?" Her words were teasing. She knew Taylor loved them both and had more than enough love left over for the littlest Morgan sister.

"No, not replaced. Redefined, maybe. How much are you going to charge for babysitting?"

"How much are you going to pay us to get her back?" Betta chimed in. "Once we get our hands on her, you may never see her again. We have a lot to teach her."

"That's what I'm afraid of!" Taylor said as he sat down to eat. Matteo and Sean came in with their own plates as the girls went to get theirs. In a few minutes, the family was gathered at the table.

"OK, enough of the mystery," Meg demanded as she buttered a fresh tortilla. "How in the world did you manage to get *Abuelo* and *Abuelita* here *with* you? You were supposed to be in California!"

"I wasn't. I was in Albuquerque but I can't tell you why just yet. I need to talk to Laura first."

"No fair, Taylor!"

"It is fair. I promise, I'll tell you the whole story tonight after I've talked with her. I'm going to the hospital at nine. You all can start visiting at eleven. You'll probably have to take turns but you can go admire Annie in the nursery while you're waiting."

"Does she really have your eyes, Taylor?" Betta asked.

"She does. Even the doctor remarked on it."

"Wow! What a combination—Laura's red hair, your turquoise eyes. It's a good thing she's our younger sister, Meg. We'd never be able to compete."

"I need to make a couple of phone calls before I leave. Did someone remember to call Beth last night?"

"Call her? She was calling us every half-hour for updates. Her phone bill is going to be enormous."

"You can call her again later with details after you've seen Laura. Right now, I need to go authorize the press release to the fan club and to the media. I should be ready to leave in about twenty minutes, Matteo."

Taylor called his agent first and authorized him to send out the press release he and Laura had prepared. All that needed filling in was Annie's name. Taylor accepted the congratulations cheerfully then called the director of the show he'd just left. The whole cast had been aware of the pregnancy and had helped to keep it quiet. They deserved to hear before the general public did.

His final call was to Elodie Nee.

"Elodie, it's Taylor. Sorry to call so early."

"It is early, Taylor. What's so important it couldn't wait until a civilized hour?"

"I could wait but then the fans would hear it on the news first. I thought you might want to get the news out right away."

"News? The baby's here? Already?"

"Last night—actually early this morning. We have a little girl, Annie Collins Morgan."

"Taylor, how wonderful! But she's early, isn't she?"

"She was but she and Laura are both fine. I'm on my way to the hospital to see them in just a few minutes."

"Give me the details, Taylor and I'll put it out on the Internet right away."

He gave them to her then hung up. As he picked up a few things to take to Laura, he realized that Elodie had never congratulated him. Probably too early for her to even think about it, he thought, and promptly dismissed it as he left for the hospital.

Elodie hung up the phone. So the great and wonderful Laura Collins had survived all the drama. Too bad. And a girl? Everyone knew Taylor had been hoping for a boy. He must be so disappointed. She'd find a way to console him later but for now she'd better get the message out before someone heard it first on the media. Then she'd send flowers to the wretched woman because it was the thing to do. Too bad she couldn't include something poisonous.

🍁   🍁   🍁

Taylor paused in the doorway. Laura was sitting up in bed, their daughter against her raised knees. A beam of sunlight streamed through the window and highlighted their beautiful hair.

"How are my girls?"

Laura's smiled. "We're fine. Come see Annie. Look who's here, little one. It's your Daddy."

Taylor reached out and gingerly took the baby in his arms. She waved her hands in the air and screwed up her face as if to cry. "None of that, Miss Annie. It's my job to make you happy, not to make you cry." At the sound of his voice she opened her eyes wide and tried to focus on the face behind the voice. "That's better, my girl. I brought a present for you." Taylor reached into the shopping bag he had carried in and pulled out a purple dragon that was almost as big as she was.

"It's darling, Taylor. She'll love it."

"Only the first of many things I'll be spoiling you with, my little love," Taylor crooned to her. "Mommy may never find you in the crib, with the toys we've all bought for you. You're going to be one pampered princess."

He looked up and met Laura's eyes. "Mommy and Daddy. Sounds a little scary to me, Laura. Are we ready for this?"

"We're in deep trouble if we're not."

The nurse came in a few minutes later to take Annie back to the nursery. "You can have her back at ten-thirty before visiting hours start."

Taylor handed her over reluctantly and followed the nurse to the door watching until she rounded a corner that took her from his sight.

❧ ❧ ❧

"You are in so much trouble, Taylor. If she's got you this wrapped around her little finger now, what will it be like when she's a teenager?"

"Can I help it if I have a weakness for redheads?"

He leaned down and kissed her softly then more deeply. "I love you, Laura. How are you this morning, really?"

"I'm fine. I slept well and ate breakfast and even managed a shower before you got here. Annie and I had a little time together about seven and I told her all the secret ways to get around you."

"I have a present for you, too." He took a small box out of his pocket and handed it to her. "Just something to mark this momentous occasion, my love."

She opened it and caught her breath. "It's beautiful." Her hands were shaking so he reached in and took out the ring and placed it on her right hand. "It's a family ring, Laura. Look, it starts over here with a sapphire for you, then an emerald for Meg, a diamond for Annie, another emerald for Betta, and a garnet for me. We've always been a family, Laura, it just seemed like a good time to mark it."

"It's beautiful. You're beautiful. When did you have time?"

"Tiffany's has had it ready for a couple of months. All they needed was the final stone. I picked it up on the way this morning."

She reached out and he drew her into his arms. They held each other quietly for a long time, enjoying the small space of peace in their lives before the new responsibilities took over.

When they finally broke apart, Laura held her hand up so the light could catch the ring. "You did that the morning after we got engaged, remember?" Taylor said.

"Always," she said with a soft smile before she changed the look to a glare. "It's beautiful but I'm not distracted. I want to know where you were and how you and my parents hooked up."

"I figured you'd get back to that. Can I get away with blaming it on your father? It was his idea."

"*What* was his idea? Tell me now so I can decide if I'm going to blame him when he gets here."

"I was in Albuquerque, not California. Sean had called with something interesting the night before we saw the doctor." He spent the next half-hour filling her in on the job offer and the mad race across the country to get to her.

"Did they offer you the job finally?"

"I don't know. I need to call Kris Straub and find out. They may have hated me and this could have all been for nothing. But, now that you know, I'd like to know what you think before I call her. If this isn't what you want, I can still explore that Hollywood thing." He said it with a grin because he knew her answer already. "I hear Pierce Brosnan is looking for someone to be the next James Bond villain."

Laura shook her head at him. "Pierce Brosnan or going home to Albuquerque? It's a rough choice. But, if you don't mind, I'd like to go home, please."

He picked up her hand and kissed the palm. "Your wish is my command. Let me call, then we can tell everyone when they get here."

CHAPTER 26

UNM's answer had, of course, been yes. They were thrilled to have Taylor join the faculty. Maria and Sean were beside themselves with joy and Taylor had heard Beth's scream from across the room when Laura had phoned her with the news. Meg and Betta were pleased as well. It meant there would be no choosing who to spend holidays with and New Mexico was much closer to Meg's school in California than New York was. Rosina was going to be their Nanny and Matteo had decided that New Mexico would be a good place to retire. He was looking forward to a little garden and a lot of time with Annie.

In the chaos of the new baby and the pending move, the fan club mail had piled up. Knowing they didn't want to take it cross-country with them, Laura corralled Taylor, Meg, and Betta one afternoon during Annie's nap to help her sort through it all.

The girls were put to work opening all the baby gifts. Most would be donated to charity but every gift would be acknowledged so they made a list of gifts and givers as they worked. Taylor's job was to open anything that looked like a letter and decide if it needed answering while Laura opened the envelopes that were obviously cards. Many of them would contain checks for the charity so she kept a notepad by her side.

There had been no threatening letters for some time now. Once Elodie had dismissed Teri Hanson, they had stopped. Laura hated to admit it but it looked like Elodie had been right about her.

There were only so many ways to exclaim over a cute bib or blanket or stuffed animal. After the first few, the girls quit commenting and worked quietly.

Taylor skimmed the letters as he opened them. Most didn't need answering but he made a small stack of those that did. Any checks, he passed across to Laura who added them to her list. As he ran his hand through the pile of envelopes in front of him, he thought he might never get through them all. Maybe quiet obscurity at UNM would have some advantages! As he reached to pick up another envelope, one caught his eye and his hand stilled before he carefully picked it up by the corner. Plain white, cheap paper, the envelope stood out among all the others. A mostly illegible number was scribbled in the corner and a clear label, printed with his name and the fan club address, stood out starkly against the white.

He didn't want to alarm the girls so he broke the silence to ask, "Meg? Would you go ask Rosina for something to drink? I'm getting parched here. And Betta? Would you go get my letter opener off my desk? This one is dull already."

The girls were glad of a chance to stretch and left the room. "Laura?"

She looked up from the pile of envelopes in front of her and her face went white when she saw the envelope in his hand. "Oh, God. That can't be what we think it is!"

"I hope not. But we'd better call Pierce."

Laura dialed his office. "Pierce? It's Laura. I think we have another letter."

He asked them to drop it in another envelope and send it over to him by courier. Taylor decided to deliver it to him personally.

Together they took it to the lab where Pierce asked a friend to take a quick look at it. The gloved lab tech carefully slit the letter open then slid it into a plastic protector before handing the letter back to Pierce. He turned his attention to the envelope while Taylor and Pierce read the letter.

Darling Taylor—

So you have a little girl! How wonderful! How sweet! But you wanted a little boy, didn't you? You must be so disappointed. Laura really let you down, didn't she?

And to give you a child with her horrible hair! A constant reminder of how she failed you.

My poor, poor Taylor.

It's time to leave her, darling. She can't provide what you really need. No son. No bright lights of Broadway. Instead she's offering you a life in the middle of nowhere? She's destroying you, Taylor.

Give me a sign, my darling, by staying here in New York where you belong. Give me a sign and I'll be by your side in moments and we can live the life you were meant to have.

Your TRUE Love

As usual, the letter was machine printed and unsigned. But Taylor suddenly knew who had sent it. Hoping he was wrong, he asked the tech, "Is there a postmark on the letter?"

"Postmark? Let me see. No postmark. Sorry."

"Anything else we can work with?" Pierce asked.

"Give me some time, Albright! Go get some coffee. Come back in an hour."

Taylor was silent as they made their way to the coffee machine then to a small staff lounge.

"What is it, Taylor? What did you see in that letter?"

"Two things. The writer knew I wanted a son. I didn't. I adore Annie. It was just a family joke—a *family* joke, Pierce. That means the writer has to be someone close to me. Only our close friends knew about it. The regular fans wouldn't."

"OK, that's one thing. You said there were two. What else?"

"The move. The writer knew about the move. It hasn't been announced yet. The only fan club person who knows is the president. Elodie knows. And she knows about the joke. Pierce, I think Elodie wrote those letters. Laura's been right about her all along."

"Don't jump to conclusions, Taylor. The pieces add up but maybe not to what you think. Could that Hanson woman be the one?"

"No, she's left the club entirely. When Elodie removed her from her responsibilities, Laura said Teri was devastated. She resigned her membership. She'd have no way of knowing about the move or the family joke. Elodie is the *only* one in position to know both things and still get a letter in my mail."

"We need more than that to go on, Taylor. We can't accuse her without more evidence."

"How's this for evidence?" Both men looked up as the lab tech walked into the room. "The letter writer left us a nice clear fingerprint on the back of the address label. Evidently forgot that the adhesive on those things picks up everything. I'm running it now."

"Let's go," Pierce said. "Start another search. Narrow it to here in the city."

Taylor felt sick as he followed them back to the lab. Elodie? How could it be Elodie? She'd been his friend for years. He could hear Laura telling him that Elodie was in love with him. She'd been right. Laura had been right all along and he'd never believed her.

The three of them watched the computer screen flashing as it ran thousands of possibilities. Suddenly, it stopped and a set of fingerprints came up on the screen. The tech moved the image he'd lifted from the label and superimposed it until it matched the first finger of the left hand. Scrolling down, he brought up the identity belonging to the fingerprint—Elodie Nee. Fingerprinted ten years ago for bonding as the chief fundraiser of a special charity. Elodie Nee of the Taylor Morgan Fan Club.

※ ※ ※

Elodie's maid answered the door and let them in. "I will go get Ms. Nee, Mr. Morgan. May I bring you coffee?"

"Thank you but no, Elsa. Please tell Ms. Nee that it's urgent."

A few minutes later, Elodie came into the sitting room. She was startled to see Agent Albright standing at the window while Taylor paced the room.

"Taylor?"

Taylor stopped and looked at her without saying anything.

"Taylor? What is it? Has something happened?"

"Why, El? Why the letters?"

"Letters? Have you gotten another letter?"

"You know damn well I have, Elodie! What I want to know is why? Why would you do such a thing?'

"Taylor, I don't know..."

"Damn it, Elodie. I know. The last letter. You gave yourself away. You're the only one outside the family who would know that I had said I wanted a son *and* knew about the move to Albuquerque. You're the only one with those two bits of information who would also have access to the fan club mail. How could you do that to me?"

"Taylor, I don't know what to say. I don't understand..."

"Ms. Nee," Albright said, "stalking is a crime in New York State. Threatening letters qualify as stalking. If Mr. Morgan chooses, we can prosecute you and put you behind bars."

Suddenly, Elodie dropped the façade. "Alright, Taylor. Yes, I wrote the letters. I was hoping they'd scare Laura away. You want to know why? Because I'm in love with you, Taylor. I always have been—from the beginning. But you never gave me a second look no matter what I did for you. I understood when you married Annie Miller. You had to. I understood that. But you broke my heart when you married Laura. I couldn't stand that you chose her over me. I did everything for you, Taylor. Why was it not enough to make you love me?" She sank into a chair and covered her face with her hands as she began to cry.

Taylor looked helplessly at Pierce. Pierce shrugged as if to say it was Taylor's call. But he knew Taylor would never file charges; never send the woman to jail. Elodie Nee would get away with it.

"Elodie, I'm sorry. I never meant to hurt you. I never knew you felt this way. I thought we were just friends. Laura knew. She tried to tell me but I refused to believe her. I told my wife she was wrong—that you and I were just friends. We *fought* because of you and you came close to getting her out of my life."

Elodie looked up with hope in her eyes.

"No, El. It's over. *You're* out of my life. I want you to announce your resignation as President of the fan club. You can choose whatever reason you wish but you *will* resign and you'll do it today. I'll swear out a restraining order against you and you *will* honor it if you don't want me to file stalking charges against you. If you come near me or my family ever again, I won't hesitate to file the charges."

"Are you sure, Taylor?" Pierce asked. "We have more than enough proof. You left a fingerprint on the letter this time, Ms. Nee. A fingerprint *under* the label. Only the person who labeled the letter would have been able to place a fingerprint there."

"No, Pierce. This is enough. Elodie? El, look at me."

She looked at Taylor and knew she had lost. Taylor Morgan would never belong to her and she was out of his life—out of the limelight. She'd be nobody.

"Tonight, Elodie. Your resignation needs to be on the Internet by seven o'clock tonight. I'll be checking. If it's not there, Agent Albright will be back to take you into custody. Save us all the trouble. Save yourself the humiliation."

Taylor walked to the door and Albright followed along. Elodie turned in her chair and watched as he walked out of her life without even a goodbye.

※　　　　　※　　　　　※

Taylor let himself into the apartment. He'd been silent on the ride back asking only that Pierce drop him off at home. He still couldn't believe what had happened.

He found Laura in the nursery, rocking Annie as she held her bottle. They were both so beautiful—they were his life. He'd put them at risk because he'd refused to believe that Elodie could betray him in such a way.

Laura looked up and was startled by Taylor's appearance. He looked haggard and tired. She glanced down and saw that Annie had fallen asleep. Holding her over her shoulder, she burped her then put her down in her crib.

Then she went to Taylor who took her in his arms and held her almost too tightly. She could feel the shudders that racked his body as he whispered, "I'm sorry, Laura, I'm so sorry."

Frightened, she stepped back and looked into his eyes. Taking his hand, she led him next door to their room and closed the door behind them. He stood there looking lost.

"You're scaring me. Has something happened? To the girls? To my parents? Rosina? Matteo? For God's sake, Taylor, tell me what's wrong!"

"No. None of that. Nothing's wrong with anyone. Everyone's safe. You're safe."

"The letter? There was something in the letter?" Laura asked even as she breathed a sigh of relief that those she cared for were safe.

"It was Elodie."

"What was Elodie?" Laura's eyes widened as the truth dawned on her. "Elodie's been writing those letters?

"We saw her, Pierce and I. We went to talk to her and she admitted it. You were right all along. I should have believed you. Elodie was in love with me and hoped to scare you away. Can you ever forgive me for not believing you?"

Elodie Nee hated her that much? Laura's knees were weak as she thought about the hatred in those letters. Even though she had despised the woman, she had never hated her enough to cause her worry or harm. She looked at Taylor, his heart in his eyes as he met hers.

"Forgive you? There's nothing to forgive." She walked over and held him. He rested his cheek on her hair and held her as if he'd never let her go.

There was a knock on the door and Meg called out, "Hey, you two, break it up. Dinner's ready!"

Laura pulled away from Taylor and looked at him before she went to the door. "Go on without us, Meg. I think we'll will be skipping dinner tonight."

"Is everything ok?" Meg asked as she caught a glimpse of Taylor who had turned to stare out of the window.

"It will be. We'll talk to you in the morning." Laura gently shut the door then turned back to Taylor.

"Come sit down. Tell me what happened."

He held her hand as he told her. She wasn't surprised to find that he wasn't pressing charges. It was a relief just to know who it had been and that they'd found her out. They would be starting a new life soon with no threatening secret hanging over them. Even as she felt Taylor's pain at his betrayal by his long-time friend, a part of her rejoiced that Elodie Nee was out of their lives—forever.

CHAPTER 27

Elodie's letter had appeared on the Internet list that night. Pleading poor health, she resigned. The next day, Taylor and Laura found Teri Hanson and asked her to take over the presidency. She agreed and brushed Taylor's apologies aside. She wrote a warm letter to the membership wishing Elodie well and announcing Taylor's plans for the future. The transition was accomplished with little fuss. Pierce checked on Elodie's whereabouts the next day and discovered she'd flown to Europe and was cloistered at an expensive spa. As far as Pierce was concerned, the further away she was from the Morgans, the better.

A month later, Meg and Betta graduated from high school with honors. They flew to Florida to visit Meg's mother's parents and would fly to Albuquerque from there.

Sean and Maria had found the perfect house for the Morgans. It was near the university with another house just next door for Matteo and Rosina. Sean had already taken down part of the fence and put in a connecting gate.

Rosina and Matteo had left earlier to fly to Albuquerque with three-month-old Annie. Laura and Taylor were taking a few days to drive there, their first time alone since Annie's arrival. The apartment had been sublet to a fellow actor. What furniture they were taking had already been taken by the movers. There was nothing left to be done but leave.

"Ready, Taylor?" Laura said as she came into the living room.

"I think so. It feels kind of odd to be leaving here."

"It's been a great home, Taylor. And we'll be back. New York can't do without you forever."

"And I can't do without *you* at all. Will you teach me how to speak Spanish on the way?"

"*Sí, Señor* Morgan. *Vamanos.*"

They pulled the door shut behind them, leaving behind an old life as they began a new one bright with promise.

CHAPTER 28

❀

Taylor couldn't believe it! The first day of classes at UNM, his class starting in fifteen minutes, and he was still cruising for a parking place! Damn it! He *had* a parking permit. Laura had tried to warn him but he figured how hard could it be? Well, he was finding out. It wasn't just hard, it was nearly impossible.

Finally, at the far end of "A" lot, he found a space and pulled the yellow Opel GT into it. The car had belonged to Laura's brother and when he died he'd left it to her. It had been in storage during their time in New York and now it was his. With Annie's arrival Laura had insisted on buying something safer—a Saturn station wagon. Funny how kids change your life, he thought.

As he got out of the car he glanced at his watch. Ten minutes! It was at least three or four blocks to Popejoy Hall, the University's performing arts center where his classes would be held, and it was ninety degrees out here. Still, if he was going to make it, he'd better run.

He took off, oblivious to the admiring looks he was getting from the women he passed. The sun glinted off his reddish-brown hair and there was nothing wrong with the view as he passed them and kept going. By evening, there were a lot of students considering changing to a theatre major.

He threw open the doors of the theatre building, ran down the stairs, and skidded into the classroom assigned to him. Only five minutes late. Not bad, except that he couldn't catch his breath long enough to speak. As he tried, he suddenly realized his new briefcase, a gift from Meg and Betta, was still in the car with all of his notes and his class list.

A young man in the first row got up and handed him a bottle of water, which Taylor took gratefully. He swallowed half of it before he finally found his voice.

"You know, I didn't plan it this way. I was going to be waiting for you. Tweed jacket, pipe, a volume of Shakespeare clutched in my hand. I even bought glasses with plain lenses. I was going to be the perfect picture of genius with *savoir fair*."

"Instead, I'm sweaty, out-of-breath and ready to give an "A" for the course to—what's your name?" he asked the boy who had volunteered the water.

"Colin James," the boy said, somewhat flustered at being pointed out by Taylor.

"Colin. I'll remember you. You saved my life today. As I was saying, instead of the professor type, you get the real Taylor Morgan who's scared to death of this class—especially now that I just realized my briefcase is still in the car parked at the other end of the universe. Do you all drive here everyday?"

The snickers and giggles that had been muffled during his speech broke out into laughter when he asked about parking. They all had been there. UNM's parking problems were legendary.

"So, since we've started with the real Taylor Morgan, I propose we continue that way. Those of you who wanted the other guy are free to leave the room."

No one moved, of course. Competition to enter this directed study with *the* Taylor Morgan had been fierce. Those who had been accepted were still in awe despite Taylor's precipitous beginning.

"The briefcase had my class list, too, so I can't call roll to figure out who you are. Instead, why don't we all sit and you can tell me a little about yourselves?"

"Just call me Taylor. I'm not much on formality. I assume first names are okay with all of you?" By the end of the hour and a half class, the twenty-five students felt like he was an old friend. " I'll be better organized Thursday, I promise," Taylor said as he prepared to dismiss them. "I know I have an office here somewhere but the room number escapes me. I'll be in on Monday and Thursday afternoons if you want to drop by. Other than that, I'll see you on Thursday."

A few of the students stayed and chatted for a few minutes and he began to put faces to names. When they were all gone, he went down the hall to Kris Straub's office.

"Hi, Taylor. How'd it go?"

"Other than a less than stellar beginning, it went okay, I think. They seem like a good group, really interested."

"Competition was rough, Taylor. We had one hundred applicants for the twenty-five openings. They'd *better* be interested."

"I think I'll hike back to my car now," he said as he stood to go.

"Parking problems?"

"You might say that. Is it always this bad?"

"Quite often it's worse. You bought a house over near the law school, didn't you? If I were you, I'd walk over there and catch the shuttle. It will let you off right in front of Popejoy."

"I'll give it a try tomorrow. Talk to you later, Kris."

Taylor got back to the house and sat in the car for a few minutes. He was exhausted. The run, the class, the walk back to the car. It really *would* be easier to walk to the law school.

He let himself into the house quietly. Annie should be napping which meant Laura might be as well. He could smell the sauce that

Rosina was preparing for dinner. Meg was off in California and Betta was in Milan. The house still felt empty without them.

Laura was not in the bedroom so he checked the patio. It was the most attractive feature of the house. Made of stone slates and shaded by an arbor of wisteria, it was always cool.

She was out there. Soft music played. He recognized "Pachelbel's Canon in D Major", her favorite piece of music. She had several different versions and had chosen Llewellyn's for today. The baby monitor was next to her.

Right now she was practicing T'ai Chi Chih. She had taken up the meditative form shortly after they'd come back to New Mexico. Her mother had invited her to a class and she found that it was perfect for her hectic lifestyle as a new mother who was also a professional writer.

He watched as she slowly moved into "Daughter On The Mountaintop". She stood tall, her eyes closed, her hands moving gracefully as if through heavy air. She was about halfway through her work out. That would give him time for a quick shower.

As he walked back to their room he heard the small sounds that meant Annie was waking from her nap. She always woke in a cheerful mood. She'd been sleeping through the night by the age of two weeks and rarely had a fussy time.

He walked into her room and to the crib. She looked up at him and smiled, kicking and waving her little arms and legs. He reached down and scooped her up.

"Hello, Princess. It looks like you've had a wonderful day."

On the patio, Laura heard his voice and smiled. She was looking forward to hearing about his day. As she continued her T'ai Chi Chih practice with "Daughter In The Valley", she listened in to his one-sided conversation with Annie.

"Mommy's outside doing that T'ai Chi stuff so you're stuck with me. I bet you need a new diaper and maybe some juice? I know I could use some juice. I must have sweated off five pounds running to

class." Annie gurgled at him and grinned her toothless grin. "Oh, you think that's funny, do you? I guess it was pretty funny when I think about it. There, you're nice and dry. Let's go find that juice."

Fifteen minutes later, Laura came in to find them at the kitchen table. Annie was happily gumming on a cookie while her father could only be described as scarfing them down.

"Eating dessert first, Taylor?"

"Well, you know what they say, life is short so…"

"Uh-huh," Laura said as she poured herself a glass of water. "What's this about running across campus?"

"Uh-oh, Annie. Mom's spying on us. We better watch what we say." The baby pounded her cookie on the highchair tray, happy to agree to whatever her father had said.

"So, tell me about the day, Taylor," Laura continued as she dropped a kiss on his head then took a chair across the table. "Sounds like it wasn't exactly perfect."

For the next fifteen minutes, he told her the story of his day. They were both laughing hysterically with Annie smiling along when Rosina came in the kitchen.

"What is so funny?" she asked as she checked the pot she'd left simmering on the stove. She put a colander of fresh vegetables into the sink then began to get down the ingredients she needed to complete dinner. By the time she'd heard the shortened version, she was laughing, too.

"How much time before dinner, Rosina?" Taylor asked. "I really need to get a shower."

"At least half an hour. Plenty of time."

"Then I'm off. Annie, you make sure Rosina cooks it right. No sneaking in any healthy stuff."

He stopped by Laura's chair and took her hand and gave her a look of pure invitation. Then he was gone, leaving her to make up an excuse to Rosina.

"Can you watch Annie for a few minutes, Rosina? I need to go return a phone call."

"*Sí*, Laura. Take your time. The *bambina* and I will take care of dinner."

"Thanks!" Laura called over her shoulder as she headed down the hall.

"Those two, Annie. They think I don't know what's going on. I remember what it was like to be young and in love. They'll enjoy their shower."

Annie clapped her hands. Everything was okay with her.

CHAPTER 29

Taylor's inauspicious beginning to his class quickly turned into a blessing. His students were comfortable with him right away and he felt at ease with them as well. They soon formed a working partnership that involved mutual respect—and copious amounts of laughter. He found that he loved teaching.

Laura was having a harder time adjusting. There was no doubt that she loved being home in Albuquerque again. Annie was all she could have ever wished for in a baby. The problem was that there wasn't enough to fill her time.

One night when Taylor came home from the University, Laura was waiting for him.

"Taylor, we need to talk."

"Aren't husbands supposed to cringe in terror at that phrase?"

"There's a reason for that."

"So, tell me. I can take it!"

"It's not funny, Taylor!"

He sat beside her on the sofa. "I'm sorry, darling. What is it?"

"It's not enough—my life right now. I know I have time for my writing and for Annie but there's something missing. I wasn't cut out to be a stay-at-home-mom. I need to do something more."

"That's understandable. I'd wondered when you'd realize you needed more."

"You knew?"

"Not for sure, but you've been very restless lately."

"Henry's offered me my old job back at the *Herald*. Part time this time. I can pretty much set my own hours. Annie won't be neglected."

"There's not much chance of her being neglected while she has Rosina around. That's why Rosina stayed with us. She's Annie's caregiver. We always planned that."

"I know that, Taylor. I just feel so guilty…"

"There's no reason to. Between Rosina and your mother, your Dad, Matteo and even me, she's never going to be with strangers. She needs a mother who's happy—and taking this job will obviously make you happy."

"Then you think I should take it?"

"As long as it leaves time for an occasional trip to the zoo with your husband and daughter—and an occasional escape with your dashing husband," Taylor said with a leer, "I don't see any problem with it."

"I should have known you would understand. There's just one thing—when do I get to meet the guy who's going to be my dashing husband?"

Taylor shook his head at her. "Maybe I should show you instead of telling you?"

"I think I could live with that. But it will have to be later. I hear noises in the nursery. Your daughter is awake."

Taylor kissed her soundly then stood to go to Annie. "This child has a lot to learn about timing," he muttered. "As for you, wench, prepare to be taught a lesson about dashing husbands later tonight."

Laura laughed softly as he stalked out of the room. "Wonder if swashbuckling is part of the package," she murmured as she picked up the phone to call Henry and tell him she was accepting the job.

CHAPTER 30

"Now that the drop/add date for classes is past, we're going to get down to some serious business," Taylor said to his class. "We've had some time to get acquainted and I have an idea where all of you are in your theatre expertise. But all that expertise is going nowhere if we don't have a place to practice it. It's time to decide on a play."

Various suggestions were called out until Taylor raised one hand for silence. "Not that easy. I have the librettos for three shows. I'm going to hand them out randomly—no fair exchanging with someone else. What you get is what you're going to read. You have one week to read it and come up with the pros and cons of doing that show. What are the problems and plusses? Great costuming but difficult sets? Archaic language? Next Tuesday you'll form into groups and compare notes with the others who have read the same libretto. You'll elect a leader or leaders to present your case for or against. All three groups will have half-an-hour to present their case. Then you've got a couple of days to think about it. You can trade show librettos at that time. On Thursday we'll discuss it all again as a group and then we'll vote. Majority will rule. No arguments. If there is a tie, I get to break it, but I'd rather it be your decision entirely."

"After that the work begins. First item of business will be auditions. These are mandatory—*everyone* will audition even if your interest is in tech. You'll need to prepare a song and provide sheet music to me and to the accompanist. We'll also work on a brief dance routine which you'll learn as a class but will perform solo at auditions."

After the groans and grumbles had died down, Taylor continued, "You need to know all about theatre production, not just the stage glamour or the secret tech societies. A play is put together by a group. Even a one-man show needs a director and stage crew. You'll need to have an acquaintance with everyone's job. You could be needed somewhere unexpectedly."

"Start working on your audition resume now. We'll be polishing them over the next few weeks. This is a professional resume, people. That means headshots, too. Those don't have to be professional. Get a friend to take a roll of film then have the best ones enlarged. Normally, a director will want black and white as well as color but I will allow you to submit only color this time."

"List every acting and tech credit you have. If you were Vitamin C in your kindergarten nutrition class, list it. If you made the paper crowns for Sleeping Beauty, list it. Your resume is not the time to be shy. Nor is it a time to pad. The theatre world is pretty small and insular. Lie on your resume and you'll be caught out."

"I'm increasing my office hours starting today. I am available by appointment to work with your on your audition or your resume. Any weekday except Friday—that's my day with my family, at least until we start rehearsals. There are sign-up sheets on my door."

Taylor looked around the room. Some faces were stunned. Some were smiling. All were apprehensive. "It sounds harder than it really is, honest. If you go on to New York after this, you'll stand out in the crowd because you'll know what you're doing."

"Read those scripts. And be prepared to participate in the discussions. Part of your grade will depend on it. See you on Thursday."

As the class gathered up their stuff to leave, a few hung back waiting to talk to Taylor. He offered what reassurance he could. This was a senior level seminar and highly specialized. The work had to be completed to pass the program. Taylor had already received inquiries from New York theatre friends about new talent he might send their way.

Last in line was a slim blonde. Allison had probably the best soprano voice in the class and she could dance beautifully. What she seemed to lack, surprisingly, was self-confidence.

"Taylor? I don't know if I can do that audition thing. It frightens me. What if I blow it?"

"Better here than someday in New York, don't you think? This is a necessary part of the training."

"I know but…"

"You'd like my help?"

Her blue eyes opened wide. "Would you, Taylor? I'd be ever so grateful."

"Let's go look on that schedule and see if your fellow students have left any room. I'll wager that you're not the only one signed up."

Allison gathered her books and followed Taylor down the hall. She was betting there was another way to pass this course and get that recommendation for New York. And Taylor wouldn't be such a hardship, she thought, as she observed the rear view of him in tight jeans. No, not a hardship at all.

CHAPTER 31

❃

Annie was six months old in October. She still ran her parents' world but with a cheery smile and ready laugh. On the day of the class decision about what show they would do, he found himself suddenly responsible for Annie. There was no other choice but to take her to class with him.

As he wheeled her stroller into the mural-decorated classroom, several hearts—female *and* male—skipped a beat. This was a whole new Taylor they hadn't included in their fantasies.

"As you can see, we have a guest this morning. She will take Broadway by storm someday." He leaned down and picked her up then turned to face the class. "With this smile, how can she miss?" Right on cue, Annie gave her best smile to the class. "This, ladies and gentlemen, is Annie Collins Morgan—she's one of the women who runs my life."

Annie regarded them solemnly until she spotted a bright toy key chain attached to one of the backpacks. Then she smiled and the owner stepped forward, "Let me take her, Taylor."

"Would you mind?"

"Not at all! She's adorable."

"Thanks. She takes after her mother, obviously."

After answering a few more questions about the baby, Taylor turned to the discussion at hand.

He wandered the room, listening to the arguments, stepping in only when they began to become a little too heated. When Annie began to fuss, he picked her up, and continued his pacing as Annie snuggled into his shoulder and fell asleep.

"Class is almost over. Are we ready to vote?" There were a few minor grumbles but the voting began. In the end, Llewellyn's *Lorna* won out.

"I'm very pleased with your choice, since Llewellyn gave me special permission to use it. But if you think that you're going to get off any easier with one of my shows, you're mistaken. From here on out, the work is yours. I just supervise. So, that's it then. We won't have class next week but I'll add that time to my office hours to help with auditions. Tuesday after next, auditions will begin. It will probably take two class sessions and Kris Straub will be sitting in. Have a pleasant weekend."

Carefully, he placed the sleeping Annie in her stroller. Immediately after class he had a session with Allison. Having listened to her father's vocalizing all her life, Annie was never disturbed by music.

"So, Allison, what music have you settled on?"

"I haven't. I don't know what to choose. What would impress a New York director?"

"He doesn't care what you sing. He needs a feeling for your range and delivery. You could sing the ABC song but it has to work to sell you."

"I was hoping you'd choose for me," she said with her best pout.

"Allison, my job is to teach you to do—not to do for you. Either get serious about this or drop out of the class. Come prepared on Tuesday."

Taylor picked up his briefcase and guided the stroller out the door without a backwards glance. He had most of an hour left before his next appointment so he went to his office.

He couldn't understand how someone with talent like Allison wasn't willing to work for the payoff. He supposed she might have gotten along on her looks so far, but she had to have had decent grades to get into this seminar.

He realized that she reminded him of Elodie. El had just sailed along on her looks and when that wasn't enough, she dropped out. He had a suspicion that Allison was going the same way.

Allison fumed all the way back to her apartment. How dare Mr. High-and-Mighty-God's-Gift-to-the-Theatre shut her down that way. She needed that recommendation! It was her only hope of escaping her parents and starting a new life in someplace other than backwards Albuquerque. Fine! If playing the sweet helpless thing didn't work, she'd try for super student. But she was also determined to get him into bed before the year was over. Let him see what he'd be missing when she dropped him and moved on.

Laura came into the house quietly. It was Annie's naptime. Taylor had promised to bring her home in time and she'd promised to come take over for him. Poor Rosina had the flu and Laura's mother was teaching. No one had been available and Laura had an important interview that wasn't going to work if she had the baby along. It had been easier when Annie was still tiny but she was much too active and alert now.

Taylor was in his study, the baby monitor turned quiet on his desk.

"Hey, Prof, what does a girl have to do to get an A in this class?"

"Funny you should ask. I think I just had that same conversation with a student."

"Really?"

"I'm not sure. It was weird."

"Be careful, Taylor. It would be a good idea to not work with her without someone else there. It's so easy to charge 'sexual harassment' without any grounds. The burden of proof would be on you."

"I see living this close to the law school is rubbing off on you."

"No, just dealing with daily reality. Be careful, love."

"I will. It wouldn't work anyway. Why would I be interested in a young, pretty blonde when I can have you?"

"Uh-huh. Sure, Taylor. Just remember, if you succumb, you'd better hope the police lock you up before I get to you."

He reached out and caught her wrist, pulling her into his lap where he kissed her. "Never happen, Laura. I'm hooked on a redhead."

"See that you stay that way, Professor," she murmured as she settled into his arms.

CHAPTER 32

When Annie began to stir, her parents lay cuddled in bed.

"I'm so glad your appointment cancelled."

"Mmm—me too." Taylor ran his hand down Laura's side and rested it on her hip. "Want me to go get Annie?"

"I'll do it. But you should get up. Without Rosina, one of us is going to have to go get dinner."

"Beautiful but can't cook. So close to perfect."

"Well, you can't cook either so we're even. Decide what you want while I get the Princess."

I have everything I want, Taylor thought as Laura left the room. My life is as close to perfect as anyone's can get. He reached out and knocked on the wood of the bedside table. No sense in tempting fate.

As they ate pizza later, Taylor said, "Something else happened today—something good I think."

Laura wiped strained pears from Annie's face. "Something good? What?"

"The symphony would like me to do a Christmas concert with them. The soloist they had scheduled had to cancel so I'm second choice."

"Hardly! They must be thrilled to get you."

"They seemed pleased."

"Will you have time?"

"I should. The rehearsals for *Lorna* won't start 'til next semester. It's only October and the music the symphony's been rehearsing should be fine with just a couple of changes. I insisted they add "Ave Maria" for your mother."

"That's sweet, Taylor. She'll be pleased."

"It's mine if I want it."

"You haven't accepted?"

"It will take me away from you and Annie for more evenings. I've gotten used to this domestic bliss."

"It's your decision but I think you should do it. Annie and I will survive."

"I think I should, too. I'll call the symphony manager later to confirm."

"What about the fan club?"

"It's going to be on the fifteenth. That's a little close to the holidays isn't it?"

"True, but they'd leave their families on Christmas morning to come hear you sing."

"Which is exactly what I don't want."

"Ask the manager if he can set aside a block of tickets, maybe 150? I'll get in touch with Teri and have her see what kind of response we get. They'll be thrilled, Taylor."

"What about Teri? This will take a big bite out of her holiday time."

"I'll ask her. Don't forget, I can do a lot of the advance work here for her."

"Let me talk to the symphony first."

"Don't forget to stipulate I get front row seats."
"Always, my love."

"Don't forget to stipulate I get front row seats."
"Always, my love."

"Don't forget to stipulate I get front row seats."
"Always, my love."

CHAPTER 33

❀

The rest of the semester passed in a blur. As he had expected, the concert rehearsals had really cut into his home time. They were lucky if they managed the weekend together. If it wasn't his schedule, it was Laura's calling her out to cover some event.

Despite the butterflies and hesitations, all of his students did well on their auditions. Some were obviously destined for a backstage career but they all braved through the audition ordeal. He and Kris Straub had announced the cast at the end of November but, for now and until the end of the semester, the whole class was involved in pre-production details. Rehearsals, set building, and all the other myriad details would be covered in the second semester and culminate in a week of shows.

Betta would be home from Italy in time for the symphony concert and Megan would arrive a few days later. They'd have almost a month together before he and the girls had to return to their respective classrooms.

Laura and Teri had done a terrific job of arranging the fan tickets and a party after the concert. Taylor had promised to show up and talk with them for awhile. Besides the fan club, he'd arranged tickets for his students as well – nosebleed seats but the best he could do for a subscription event. They were invited to the party as well. Their class was being dismissed a week earlier than other UNM classes since there was no final to take. They'd still be around for the finals in their other classes and were looking forward to the concert.

Especially Allison. She still saw Taylor as her ticket out of Albuquerque. She'd been frustrated when he insisted on having an accompanist around when they worked on her audition number. If she showed up unscheduled in his office, he suddenly had another appointment. If she was meeting with him, it was strictly open-door policy.

She had overheard him talking with his wife on the phone one day about the plans for his fan club party. It was to be his last appearance before the semester break. He told his wife he would come back the morning after to close up his office then his time was "all hers."

Allison would be waiting in his office. What happened after that – well, time would tell.

She watched him hungrily. He was so beautiful…and that voice. Her blonde hair shimmered in the dim light as she lost herself in daydreams about what he would do when he saw her and, in her mind, there was no one else in the theatre but Taylor as he sang only to her.

The concert was a great success. Taylor had waived his fee in favor of this being a benefit concert for the theatre department and the symphony.

He'd forgotten the rush of coming out on stage to applause and cries of admiration. It was intoxicating and he quickly moved back into his rightful place on stage. The concert was perfect. And he'd won over the Albuquerque audience. Afterwards, the symphony conductor asked him to do the Christmas concert again the next year. Taylor laughed it off. Who knew where he would be next year?

The fan party was a great success. His students had never seen him in his "celebrity" persona. It was a whole different world and more than one of them imagined that they would be the ones walking into a room of adoring fans someday.

She was obscured in the shadows at the rear of the room, basking in the warmth of his smile. He was answering questions and talking about his teaching when Laura came into the room with baby Annie in her arms. Her heart twisted as she watched him kiss them both then turn to introduce his daughter to his fans. They certainly made the perfect picture of a happy family and she wasn't alone in imagining Laura gone from the picture and herself standing next to Taylor instead.

Taylor had stayed up late talking to Betta but he was still awake early. The house was quiet—his girls still asleep. Quietly he made coffee then headed over to campus. On this Sunday morning, just before winter break, the campus was mostly deserted. He found a parking space close by and walked to his office.

The building was deserted and his footsteps echoed in the basement hallway as he approached his office. His mind was still on the concert the night before. He'd missed the attention, he realized. Teaching was great for now but it wouldn't hold him long. He knew that New York was in his blood and he'd be going back.

When he opened the door to his office he was startled to see someone sleeping on the couch. Blonde hair peeked out from under the coat pulled around the sleeper as a blanket and he realized it was

Allison. How the hell had she gotten into his office? He turned to leave when she said, "Wait, Taylor, don't go!"

He turned back. She was still dressed in the skimpy black dress she'd worn to the concert last night. He'd noticed—it was hard not to, he was human and male, after all. He'd noticed the short skirt that showed off endless legs and the low neckline that was designed to enhance, not hide, her attributes.

"Allison, what are you doing here?" he said from the doorway.

"I wanted to see you before I left. Last night...oh, Taylor, you were incredible last night. I've never felt that way. You made me laugh and cry and soar with you."

"You could have written it all in a note, Allison. It's not appropriate for you to be here like this."

"Oh, but it is, Taylor. Think about how your lovely wife will feel when the rumor gets around that I was seen leaving your office in the early hours of the morning—obviously rumpled," she said as she raised her arms to run her hands through her hair, "heavy-eyed and smiling. Don't you think she'll find it interesting?"

"What kind of game are you playing, Allison?"

"An important one. You, Taylor Morgan, are my ticket out of Albuquerque. All it will take is a recommendation from you to some of your Broadway friends and I'll be on my way. Just a phone call or a letter and we can part friends. If not, I'll put all my talent into a scene back in my apartment, when I tell my boyfriend how the great Taylor Morgan took advantage of me. They take sexual harassment seriously at the university in case you didn't know."

"Allison, why are you doing this? You've got talent. Why can't you depend on that?"

"A thousand other girls have talent, Taylor. What they don't have is a recommendation from a Broadway legend. And since you think I'm so talented, I'm sure it won't be too much for you to contact your friends. I'll drop out of school and leave for New York right away and everyone will marvel at your perception and generosity."

"Not a chance, Allison."

They both turned in shock to find Kris Straub standing in the doorway. "I heard your threats, Allison. You *will* be leaving UNM but it won't be with a recommendation. Whether you do so quietly or Taylor chooses to press charges for stalking and harassment will be his choice."

Allison stood frozen. It was all over! She'd blown it. And to be kicked out of the University! Her parents would never let her forget it. "Taylor? I was desperate. I wouldn't have done any of what I said! I..."

Taylor shook his head. "Save it, Allison. Withdraw from UNM and I won't press charges. I won't even blackball you on Broadway because I still believe you have talent. But if you're going to make it, you're going to do it the same way the rest of us did. No shortcuts, no bodies to leave behind as your staircase."

Kris asked, "You're sure, Taylor?"

"I'm sure."

"Then, Allison, I think you had best leave. I will expect a letter withdrawing from UNM to be in the registrar's office by the first of the year, with a copy to me, of course. One hint that Taylor was in any way responsible and I will see that charges are brought. Do you understand?"

Allison nodded. She picked up her coat and tried to find something to say. There wasn't anything. Instead, she burst into tears and fled.

Taylor sat behind his desk, still shaken by the encounter with Allison. If Kris hadn't come along...he didn't want to think about all he would have lost. Kris? He looked at her and asked, "How come you were here, Kris?"

"Don't look a gift horse in the mouth, Taylor. I called your house and Laura said you'd left a note that you were coming on over here."

"That still doesn't explain why you were here."

"Seems pretty obvious to me. I wanted to talk to you."

"So, I'm fired after all?"

"Hardly. We had a meeting yesterday afternoon and we found funding to continue your program. We'd like you take on the seminar on a year-to-year basis. It's brought some great press and prestige to the University already. If we hadn't already taken a vote, that concert last night would have clinched it."

"What?" Taylor was still muddled from the earlier encounter.

"We're offering you a yearly contract, Taylor. It will be renewed at the end of each year for as long as we have funding and you want it. You won't have to decide until the spring of each year so if you get a better offer, you have an out."

"God, Kris, this is last thing I was expecting. You don't need an answer today, do you?"

"No, I just wanted to catch you before the holidays and let you know it was a possibility. Talk it over with Laura. We'll make you a formal offer in the spring. You can decide then." She stood to go. "Are you alright, Taylor?"

"It's a lot for this early in the morning."

"Go home. Enjoy the holidays. Your other daughters are coming?"

Taylor smiled. "Betta's home from Italy already. Meg should be home mid-week."

"Then you have a lot to be thankful for. Go enjoy your family."

"Kris? Thanks—for everything."

"Merry Christmas, Taylor. I'll see you in January."

Taylor sat at his desk for a long time after she'd left. What a morning! Thank God he didn't have to make a decision about the teaching right away. Right now, teaching was not high on his list of favorite things.

CHAPTER 34

❀

Taylor broke into a smile when he saw a red Jaguar convertible blocking his spot in the driveway. Meg was home—days before they expected her. He pulled up at the curb and was barely out of the car before she came running out of the house to greet him.

"Taylor!"

"Meg!" Even though she was nearly as tall as he was, he picked her up and whirled her around. "I am so glad to see you! How did you get here so early?" He set her back down and walked arm in arm with her to the house.

"I talked a couple of professors into letting me take the exams early. Not early enough to get me home in time for your concert, although I did try. I'm sorry I missed it."

"It was my best performance ever and you'll regret forever that you missed it."

"Right—don't you know that voices like yours are a dime a dozen in California?"

"Maybe, but you can't understand what they're singing."

"Who would want to?" she asked as they went inside.

Betta, Laura, and Rosina had Christmas ornaments spread all over the living room. Annie, safely in her playpen, watched it all with huge, fascinated eyes, until she saw Meg. She laughed and held out her hands to be picked up. Meg was happy to oblige.

"Hello, darling," Laura said as she looked up from the box she was sorting through. "We were just getting a head start on things. The tree's still on the patio waiting for you and Matteo to do your macho thing and wrestle it into the stand and bring it in."

"While you ladies do all the fun stuff, right?"

"Of course," Laura said, laughing at him. "We only keep you around for your brute strength."

"I will fetch Matteo," Rosina said as she dusted off her hands.

"No, Annie and I will go do it," Meg said. "You can do some limbering up exercises while we're gone, Taylor."

He flexed his arm muscle and frowned when they all laughed. "Some harem I've got. No respect for their absolute ruler."

"Not a bit," Meg said as she ducked into the kitchen and out the back door.

🍁   🍁   🍁

Laura's parents joined them for dinner. The tree had been decorated and stood in the corner of the living room waiting for a formal lighting ceremony. As Annie's first Christmas tree, it was an important moment. She had been napping by the time Taylor and Matteo had brought in the tree and had not seen it in its glory. Sean had come armed with his video camera, a gift from Taylor and Laura when Annie was born. He seemed determined to document every moment of her life.

The friendly rivalry that existed between Maria and Rosina had resulted in another enormous dinner. Maria had passed on her Mexican cooking to Rosina and now Meg groaned as she pushed her plate away.

"Wonderful dinner! You would not believe what passes for chile in California!"

"Ha!" Betta said. "At least you can get chile. I can't get it in Italy and I'd probably have died of deprivation by now if Laura and Rosina didn't send me regular care packages of that canned stuff."

"You get care packages? Hey!"

Laura laughed. "All you have to do is ask, Meg. We can put you on the mailing list."

"Like I have time or a place to cook. I'm thinking about moving off campus. I'd like to get an apartment with a roommate. The noise in the dorms drives me crazy."

"I don't know," Taylor said. "I feel safer with you living on campus."

"Have you ever actually been in a dorm, Taylor? Check one out here and you'll see what I mean. Besides, Betta lives on her own."

"That's different. She doesn't have a dorm option."

"Taylor!"

"We can discuss this all later," Laura said before it could escalate into an argument. They all knew Meg would win anyway. She had always known how to get around Taylor. "I think it's time for Annie to see her tree before she falls asleep. Mom, why don't you give us a minute then you can bring her in."

They all pushed back chairs and went into the living room. The plan was to leave it dark until Maria arrived with Annie. Then the tree's tiny white lights would be turned on. The angel on top was the only thing missing and Taylor would put it on with Annie's "help".

"Ready?" Maria called from the dining room.

"Come on in!" Laura called back and, in a moment, they could see her and the baby silhouetted in the doorway. Annie made a little questioning sound at the darkness then Taylor turned on the lights. Her question turned to amazement as she saw the beautiful tree with all its shiny ornaments and sparkling lights. Her eyes were wide as she tried to take it all in, then she broke into a delighted laugh and clapped her tiny hands. Her first Christmas tree had her approval.

Taylor stood with his arms wrapped around Laura as they watched the delight on their baby's face and he whispered, "I love you," into her ear before everyone began to laugh with Annie.

Laura turned to him with a smile, her eyes returning his whispered message. "It's time for the angel," she said as she handed him the angel that had graced her childhood trees. Maria had passed it on to her the first Christmas she and Taylor had been together. Someday it would pass on to Annie and Laura felt the family ties so strongly as she held it that tears filled her eyes.

"I'll need my assistant," he said as he took the fragile angel from her. "Come here, my princess." He took Annie in one arm and the angel in his other hand. For a moment he stood by the tree letting her gaze at it closely. "Here's your angel, Annie Morgan. Let's put it on the tree." He stepped up on the small stepstool carefully and reached up to settle the angel on her perch. Then he held Annie up where she could see it.

"Happy First Christmas, Annie."

Betta said, "There's one more ornament to be added."

"What did we miss?" Laura asked as she looked around the room.

"This one," Betta continued as she brought a small package out from behind her back. "It's for Annie from Meg and me."

Laura sat down with Annie in her arms as they opened the package together. Inside was a silver ornament, three girls holding hands, two of them larger, with a smaller figure between. Three names—Megan, Annie, Betta—were engraved on the skirts of the three figures. Laura looked at them with tears in her eyes as Annie reached for the silvery toy. "Oh, it's beautiful," she whispered.

"Read the back," Meg said quietly.

Laura turned it over and read aloud, "For our sister Annie with love on her first Christmas". The date was engraved as well. "It's perfect. She will always treasure this. Shall we hang it on the tree, Annie? Near the bottom where you can see it?" She stood and knelt down by the tree and hung it on a low branch. "Isn't it pretty? Your sisters love you very much." Annie cooed as she reached out and set the ornament twirling.

Taylor had gone to stand between Betta and Meg. He had an arm around each of them and he kissed their cheeks. "Thank you. Annie's a very lucky child. And we're very lucky to have three beautiful and loving daughters."

Annie made a grab at one of the lights and Laura pulled back to keep her from it, forgetting that there was a step behind her. As she tumbled backwards, Annie still in her arms, everyone gasped but Annie laughed thinking it was all a part of the festivities. Laura laughed with her as Taylor reached down to help her up. Christmas had come to the Morgan family—and it was bound to be merry.

CHAPTER 35

It wasn't until after the New Year, and their traditional party, that Taylor and Laura had a chance to talk about his job offer. He'd phoned his agent and discussed upcoming possibilities. There were several concert bookings that were pending but they could be worked in around his teaching schedule. The way seemed clear for him to continue teaching. Now that the shock of Allison was over, Taylor realized he still wanted to teach.

Their Christmas gift from Laura's parents was a week at the Amizette Inn in the Taos ski valley. Laura was determined that it was time Taylor learned to ski…and the Amizette, with only twelve rooms, offered privacy as well. Long afternoon naps came to mind.

Laura was thrilled with the gift but Taylor wasn't so sure. "You want me to go out and put sticks on my feet and hurtle down a mountain in the cold? What if I break my leg? Run into a tree? Think what a loss it would be for the world."

Betta laughed. "There are no trees on the bunny slope, Taylor. And it's hard to 'hurtle' when it's mostly flat. Come ski with me in the Alps. That's skiing."

"The bunny slope. I'm going to be skiing with five-year-olds?"

Meg answered, "Oh, no, Taylor. Some of them will only be two or three."

Laura was laughing at the look on his face. "If you're very good and a quick learner you'll move up to the beginner slopes quickly enough."

Taylor glanced at Sean and Maria. "This is all just a plot to get your hands on Annie for a week, isn't it?"

"Of course it is," Sean answered as he handed Annie another bow to play with. "Since Meg and Betta will be in Florida to see her other grandparents, it will give Rosina and Matteo a break as well."

Maria smiled. "It will be alright, Taylor. I'll make you an extra large batch of *biscochitos* to take with you. And I've already given Laura a little something to help keep you warm."

※   ※   ※

"*That's* what your mother gave you to keep us *warm?*" Taylor was already under the covers of the queen-size bed in room nine tucked up on the third floor of the inn – "the girl's tree house" Laura had called it.

Laura stood at the foot of the bed wearing an emerald-green teddy. Her red hair cascaded to her shoulders and her legs seemed to go on forever. She smiled as she climbed on the end of the bed and then up to sit astride him. "It's not working, Taylor?" she said with a mock-pout and a flutter of her lashes. "You look a little flushed. Are you sure you're not *too* hot?"

"My God, Laura, if that thing was red you could start a fire with it!" He said as he slid his hands down her bare arms to rest lightly on her thighs.

"Wrong color?"

"Perfect color," he said with some effort as his fingers moved to trace the skin at the edge of the cups holding her breasts.

"I'm so glad you like it," she whispered as she leaned down to kiss him lightly, her hair curtaining their faces.

"Like doesn't even begin to cover it…anymore than *that* begins to cover you. I'm nice and warm now. Want to join me?" He lifted the covers so she could come in.

"You'll be sorry," she warned.

"Not a chance." He twisted his body to slide her off of him and under the heavy quilts and blankets, which he pulled back over them as she cuddled close and ran one foot up his leg.

"You're freezing, woman. Get away from me!"

"I warned you you'd be sorry."

"Then I guess I have no choice but to warm you up. Just keep those cold hands to yourself until they warm up a little or you could cause a major crash."

Laura laughed and moved her hands up to tangle in his hair. "No crashes, darling! Are you sure you're up to warming me?"

His answer was a deep, slow kiss as they snuggled deeper into the covers. Maria's gift had definitely heated things up.

🍁 🍁 🍁

Over breakfast, the best french toast he'd ever had, Taylor told Laura about the offer to continue with the University.

"That's wonderful! At least I think it is. What about you, Taylor? Are you ready to go back to New York?"

"I could be, but New York isn't ready for me to come back; at least according to my agent, they're not. I've had a couple of offers I'm not interested in. There are some scattered concert dates and the summer off might allow a small tour. When the right thing comes along, I'll head back to Broadway. Right now, I'm pretty happy with where we are."

"You know what my answer is, Taylor. I couldn't be happier but I worry that you're not really finding what you need in teaching."

"Remember what you said to me after we went to that cast party back in Sacramento?"

"I know we had a great time and you were wonderful with the kids."

"You told me that I would have been a great teacher if New York hadn't worked out for me." He reached across the table and took her hand. "You were right. Maybe not the "great" part but I really am enjoying the teaching. And it seems to be the thing I'm meant to be doing right now."

Laura smiled at him, "Not quite, Taylor. What you're meant to be doing right now is learning to ski. Quit stalling!"

"Wouldn't you rather go back and snuggle under the covers?"

"After your lesson and a sauna when we get back, that's exactly where we'll be."

"You're really not going to let me out of this, are you?"

"Not a chance!"

❦   ❦   ❦

An hour later, she introduced him to his ski instructor. Heather looked barely old enough to be in high school let alone capable of teaching someone to ski. "You'll love it, Mr. Morgan. There's nothing to compare to it," she said perkily. "Why don't you come back in an hour, Mrs. Morgan?"

"I thought I might stay around and watch," Laura answered directing a wicked grin at Taylor.

"I'm sure that Heather knows what's best, Laura. Why don't you go ski on the big kid slopes while I try to figure this out?"

"Shouldn't I be here to kiss any boo-boos?"

Taylor pulled her close and whispered, "The boo-boo kissing comes later…and I expect to have a lot for you to kiss."

Laura laughed as she headed over to the chair lift. "Be a good boy, Taylor!"

Taylor shook his head and turned back to Heather. "So, where do we start? About the only thing I know is that these things are called skis and that stuff is snow. Somehow they're supposed to go together."

Heather laughed and began his first lesson.

CHAPTER 36

Laura stepped out the bathroom and started over to the bed. She felt wonderful after the exhilarating day on the slopes and the slow, lazy sauna they'd taken when they came back to the Amizette. Taylor had showered and told her he'd wait for her to come kiss the "boo-boos". He hadn't made it—the poor boy was sound asleep. Laura wasn't surprised. He'd tackled his ski lesson full-tilt, as he approached everything, and was actually ready for a run down the beginner's slope before they headed back to the inn.

Smiling softly, she drew the curtains then slid into bed beside him. He moved closer, pulling her against him as he mumbled something incoherent into her hair before sinking back into a deep sleep. Laura lay there enjoying the quiet sound of his breathing, the warmth of his body next to hers, the weight of his arm around her. He would be hurting when he woke up, she was sure, but the bottle of massage oil warming in the bathroom and the champagne she'd set to chill outside their door would take care of that. She closed her eyes and drifted off to sleep, secure in the joys of her life.

※　　　　　※　　　　　※

She woke to the sound of a groan and turned to see Taylor grimacing as he tried to stretch. "My God, woman, you didn't tell me that all of that was a prelude to torture."

"You'll get better. You need to get up and move around a bit. We'll eat and then I'll help work those kinks out of you."

"Kinks? Try knots the size of basketballs! It will be a long time before I have any kinky thoughts."

"Get up, Taylor. Go take a hot shower." She smothered her laugh as he moved gingerly to the bathroom. She was sore, too, but it was a pleasant soreness after a day of exertion. Poor Taylor was never going to believe that he would be a new man once he hit the slopes tomorrow.

※　　　　　※　　　　　※

All too soon, the semester started and the year began rushing by. The older girls were back in their respective schools, Laura and Taylor at work. But when April came, they all were together again to mark a milestone.

"…Happy birthday, dear Annie, happy birthday to you!" Annie clapped her hands and laughed at her grownups. But when Rosina set a tiny cake in front of her with one candle, her eyes grew round and she whispered, "Hot!"

Laura, beside her, took her hand. "You're right, Annie, the candle is hot. But wait until you see what happens. Can you pretend you're blowing up a balloon like we do at story hour?" Annie puffed her cheeks out. "Beautiful! Now what do you do?" Annie stopped holding her breath and blew out, right in the direction of the candle just hard enough to make it go out. Everyone clapped and Annie looked bewildered. "Gone, Mama?"

"The 'hot' is gone, Annie. Now you get to eat your pretty cake." Laura pulled the candle out and pushed the cake toward Annie. She looked at it and touched it tentatively. "No. Pretty!"

"It is pretty, Annie. Rosina made it just for you."

"*Si, Bambina*, the cake is for eating…for you."

Annie's lip quivered and her beautiful turquoise eyes filled with tears. "Pretty, Mama. Pretty."

Taylor stepped in. Annie's tears could get around him every time. "It is pretty, Annie. Let's save it for bedtime so you'll have pretty dreams." Annie flashed a beautiful smile at her father and nodded. "Besides, Miss Annie, you have presents to open and we're going to go someplace special. Cake can wait!"

Taylor handed her the first package. She'd been a little young at Christmas but had quickly gotten hold of the idea of opening packages. Now, a young lady of one year, she knew all about presents and launched herself into tearing into the wrapping paper. Laura shook her head. "The father in shining armor rescues the princess once again from her evil ogre of a mother."

"Somebody's got to do it, Ogress," he answered with a totally unrepentant smile. "I'll see to your punishment later."

It took two cars to get them all down to the Albuquerque Botanical Park. It would be Annie's first trip and there were so many cameras amongst them that not a moment would miss documentation. They took her stroller for later but Taylor perched her up on his shoulders. First stop was the Children's Fantasy Garden with its oversized plants and a golden dragon guarding the entrance. Annie fell in love with the dragon and wanted to take the concrete beast home.

"No, Annie, that dragon has to stay here. Custard is waiting for you at home and he might be afraid of such a large dragon." Taylor carried her away, reciting Ogden Nash's "*Tale of Custard the Dragon*" as they headed for the Butterfly Pavilion. On the way they stopped to watch the model trains. Annie was so delighted when the train came out of the tunnel that the operator backed the train up then brought it through the tunnel again just for the joy of watching her smile.

As they approached the Butterfly Pavilion, Annie pointed at the bright windsocks that flanked the entrance. "Burfly, Daddy, Burfly!" She began bouncing up and down on his shoulders. "Mommy! Mommy! Burfly!"

Laura laughed as she lifted Annie down from her father's shoulders. "Calm down, little one. We're going to see lots of butterflies." The others said they'd wait outside and take turns coming in. It was a small butterfly house and they didn't want to crowd it.

Taylor opened the first door and then closed it carefully behind them. Even though they knew Annie wasn't capable of understanding much of it, they made a point of explaining that the second doorway was to help keep the butterflies from flying away. As they entered the beautiful garden, Laura put her down and they each took a tiny hand.

Annie's eyes were enormous. To her, it must have appeared that they'd entered one of the stories that Mommy read to her each night. As they came to the fence that surrounded the center area and the garden below, a yellow swallowtail swooped across in front of them and settled on a branch where Annie could take a good look. She stood very still and quiet, mesmerized by the beautiful creature leisurely sunning its wings in front of her. Then suddenly, up it flew and skimmed across Annie's nose to land on Laura's bright hair. Annie began to laugh. "Silly burfly. Mommy not flower!" Laura stood very still while Annie laughed and Taylor lifted her to see the butterfly in her mother's hair. "I think it's a smart butterfly, Annie. Mommy is pretty enough to be a flower." Then, as quickly as it had come, it flew away. Annie's eyes clouded until Taylor pointed out Zebra striped butterflies, a whole flock of them, hanging in the tree in front of her. Annie's love affair with butterflies had begun.

CHAPTER 37

Taylor watched from the wings as the curtain rang down on the final performance of his final year of teaching. What had been planned as a one-year stint had stretched to four. In this group, as in the others, a couple of them would be heading off to New York to give it a try after graduation. Taylor thought they had a good chance.

But now it was over. The theatre department had lost funding for his class this year. Truth was, Taylor had been restless for the last few months, ready to move on to something else. He just wasn't sure what.

This had been a perfect job for him at this stage of his life. He'd been able to spend time with Laura and Annie. Unless it had been a performance night, Taylor had been home to tuck Annie in every night, often leaving rehearsal long enough to do it. He would rush home and sing her Stephen Foster's *Slumber My Darling*, the lullaby he'd sung to her before she was born and countless nights since. It was hard to believe she would be four years old this week! He'd promised her a trip to the Butterfly Pavilion. It had been their favorite father-daughter get-away since the first time he'd taken her there.

Laura's part-time job at the *Albuquerque Herald* had allowed her to be home with their daughter every night and she'd somehow found time to finish a second novel. There were times he was addressed as Mr. *Collins* at one of her book signings and they both found it funny that no one really knew who he was. One of the joys of these four years had been coming home to a wife who was still awake and the chance to go to bed together—time for loving and sharing they'd not had while he was in a show.

Meg would be graduating from Stanford in a few weeks. She'd be home for the summer then back to medical school in California. Betta was still in Italy and was beginning to make a name for herself as a fashion designer. She would be home for Meg's graduation then back here to Albuquerque with them for a couple of weeks.

Sean and Maria were a major part of Annie's life. She now spoke Spanish as easily as she spoke English and adored her "Abbo" and "Abby". It was mutual. Her grandparents spent a lot of time with her and Taylor was glad she'd had a chance to be part of their lives.

Matteo had his garden. Annie helped him plant it this year and delighted in eating the carrots and lettuce she had helped to grow. And Rosina was happy devoting her time to caring for the *bambina*.

The truth was, all of their lives revolved around Annie. Taylor still sometimes found it hard to believe that this bright and beautiful child was his. Surely she was a changeling from the wee folk. No human child could be so enchanting.

Suddenly, he was drawn back to the present as he became aware of the cast and audience chanting, "Taylor! Taylor! Taylor!" The leading lady drew him out onto the stage to tumultuous applause and yet another goodbye speech in a career filled with them. Kris Straub, head of the theatre department, presented him with specially commissioned comedy and tragedy masks made from Nambe silver.

Laura joined him backstage as he said goodbye to the life he'd led for the past four years. She knew him well enough to know that, while he was disappointed in the loss of funding for his program, he had been ready to move on for some time now. She was fairly sure they would be going back to New York soon. During their years in Albuquerque he'd turned down several offers to return to the stage but she knew he missed it. When the right offer came, he'd be back there again—and she'd be beside him. She knew now that although Albuquerque was her childhood home, her heart's home was wherever Taylor was.

CHAPTER 38

Good morning! (or Evening as the case may be!)

How are my girls? It seems much too long since either of you have been home to visit. Even though we have Annie to spoil, your grandmother and I miss you.

I have a conference in Belfast in mid-June, after your graduation, Meg. Since you'll already be here for the ceremony, Betta, I have a proposal for the both of you. I'd like you to come along to Ireland with me. My conference is only 4 days. I thought maybe we could take the rest of two weeks to explore my homeland before the chance is lost. A colleague of mine will be away for the month and has kindly offered us the use of his house while he's gone. Your grandmother can't go since she'll be running a retreat. So I thought I'd see if the two of you would like to come keep your old Granddad company.

Ireland's beautiful then…let me share it with you.

Your loving Abuelo

Megan logged into her e-mail briefly. She really had to study for her chemistry final tomorrow but she simply could not look at one more formula right now. Telling herself that it was almost over was a lie—it would all start over again in the fall when she began med school. But that was not until fall. Once tomorrow's exam was over there was only graduation then a blessedly carefree summer!

She smiled as she read her grandfather's message. He was so much fun to be with that she knew this trip would be great. It was only two weeks. That still left her time to visit her Florida grandparents and spend time with Laura and Taylor and Annie. Meg hadn't realized that it was possible to love someone as much as she loved her baby sister!

Before she answered Sean, she sent a quick note to Betta in Milan. They'd already made plans for Betta to take time off so they could be home at the same time. If they worked this out right, they could spend some time in Albuquerque with the family then Betta could fly back to Italy from Ireland. Maybe she'd go back with Betta for a few days, too. As she wrote the message, Meg could feel some of the pressure receding and a smile lit up her face as she typed.

Betta really didn't care if she ever saw another pin or swatch of cloth again. Fernando had been a total slave driver these last few weeks as they readied the fall collection for showing. This week had been beyond awful as he threw temper tantrums and fussed at every stitch and fold. Still, he'd chosen one of her designs to feature—a soft copper-colored silk dress and shawl that she'd designed with Laura in mind. It wasn't by accident that the sample was being made in Laura's size either.

Noting Meg's message that followed, she opened Sean's message first. Her grandparents had never made any difference between her and Meg. They loved both of the girls as if they were granddaughters who had been born to them. This family had been woven of heartstrings not blood ties.

Ireland! Just the three of them. What fun that would be. Fernando was closing the studio for June and she'd already planned on being home. She was pretty sure that Meg's message had it all figured out.

As she opened her sister's message, her exhaustion fell away and she smiled.

༺ ༺ ༺

Taylor held Annie as they watched her sisters and grandfather disappear from view. Annie's eyes filled with tears, not at being left behind but at the loss of the company of her sisters. She'd just gotten used to them being home again and now they were gone.

"Shall we go watch the plane take off, Annie?" Taylor asked as he gently wiped a tear from her cheek. "They'll be back soon, sweetheart, almost before you know it. And I'm sure they'll bring you presents—you'll like that, won't you?"

Annie nodded solemnly then laid her head against her father's shoulder. "Go home, Daddy?"

"Sure, little one. Let's go see what Mommy's been up to."

Once Annie was down for her nap, Taylor knew he'd have to talk to Laura about the offer that had come this morning—a new show that would mean a move back to New York. Taylor knew that Laura would support him in this but he hated the thought of taking her away from her home again. The truth was that even he wasn't sure he wanted to leave Albuquerque but his contract at the University was over and he was officially unemployed—again!

CHAPTER 39

Annie fell asleep on the ride home. Laura had heard the car and was holding the door open as he carried in their sleeping daughter. She watched as he tucked her into bed, making sure that she had Custard, her guardian dragon, tucked in beside her to keep her safe while she slept. Annie was convinced that Custard was the one that kept bad dreams away.

Taylor pulled the door almost closed then put his arm around Laura as they walked down the hallway.

"Get any work done this morning?"

"A little," Laura said, "but it was too quiet with everyone gone. I got so used to all the activity with the girls home."

"I know what you mean but, after the last few weeks, I'm ready for a little peaceful."

"We still have Annie to keep us busy. Did she enjoy the airport?" Laura said as she took glasses from the cupboard and poured lemonade for both of them.

"She did until Sean and the girls disappeared. Then she was ready to leave. I think the planes weren't fun anymore since they were taking her best friends away."

Taylor opened the door to the shaded patio that always seemed to stay cool despite the summer's heat.

"She adores Meg and Betta. They certainly have never given her a reason not to," Laura laughed as she thought of all the ways their two older daughters spoiled the baby. "Annie's resilient though. By tomorrow she'll be ready to go back to pre-school and Sarah will be her best friend again."

As they sat on the glider, Taylor put his arm around her and she leaned her head against his shoulder much as their daughter had done earlier. They sat in silence for awhile watching the hummingbirds flocking to the honeysuckle that surrounded the porch. Finally Laura broke the silence.

"Your agent called while you were gone. He wanted to know if you got the fax he sent."

Taylor sighed. "I suppose he told you what was in the fax."

"Something about a new show being offered to you," she said as she moved to one end of the glider so that she was facing him.

"I was just waiting until it was quieter to talk to you. There was so much going on this morning that it didn't seem like the right time."

"I know, Taylor. He was pretty excited about the offer."

"Remember the show that was my first break? They're doing a revival this year on Broadway and they want me to take the other male role—the older husband this time instead of the young lover," he said with a rueful smile.

Laura laughed at the chagrin in his eyes. "It's alright, Taylor. In real life you're still the young lover."

"I'm glad you still think so! Anyway, the husband has always been the more challenging role. He has to be the heavy without losing the sympathy of the audience."

"Do you want to take it?"

"I don't know, Laura. There's you and Annie to think about. This is the only home Annie's ever known. I hate the thought of uprooting her. Your parents will be heartbroken and you…"

Laura reached out and took his hand. "*I'll* be fine, Taylor, as long as I'm with you."

"It will mean moving back to New York."

"How much time will we have? We'll have to give the apartment tenants notice."

"They want an answer as soon as possible—by the end of next week at the latest. Then rehearsals will start in August with the opening set for mid-October."

"What do you want to do, Taylor? I can write anywhere as long as I have my computer."

Taylor was silent. They'd made a home here. These last few years had been a lot less hectic than the theatre life had been. Except for rehearsals, he'd been home most nights in time to tuck Annie into bed. His teaching schedule had left time for a normal life with Laura. Sean and Maria had been an active part of their lives, especially Annie's.

Still, a new show? As soon as he'd read the fax this morning he'd known that he wanted to take it. He had felt the excitement of new possibilities, a chance to return to the stage, a chance to be back where he belonged.

"We don't know that the show would be a success, Laura. We might be uprooting everyone for something that could close the first week."

"With Taylor Morgan starring in it? Not a chance!" She smiled as she reached out to push an errant curl from his brow. "You really want to do this, Taylor. I can see it in your eyes and hear it in your voice."

"I do, Laura."

"Then we move."

"As simple as that?"

"As simple as that, Taylor. Wherever you are is where Annie and I belong."

CHAPTER 40

Their flight arrived at Gatwick early in the morning. They made it through customs in good time and found a cab to deliver them to the house they would be using. A motherly little woman met them at the door.

"Welcome to Ireland, Dr. Collins. I'm Katyrose and I'll be keeping house for you while you're here. Let me help you with those bags and show you and the young ladies your rooms." Katyrose efficiently took charge and had them sorted out quickly. "You must be starving by now," she said as she turned to go downstairs. "There's a bit of breakfast in the dining room if you're feeling up to it. Come down whenever you're ready." Meg and Betta looked at each other then broke into muffled giggles as the housekeeper went down the stairs.

"She's just like Rosina!" Meg whispered.

"If she is, we're not going to get away with anything!" Betta whispered back. "I'll bet you anything that the 'bit of breakfast' is a huge meal."

"No bets! I'd lose. I'll meet you down there."

Sean was already in the dining room when the girls arrived. Warming trays on the buffet held a dozen different breakfast offerings and Sean was tucking into them with enthusiasm.

"Well, my dears, we're here. What shall we do today?"

"Sleep?" Meg ventured knowing that it was out of the question.

"Sleep! You girls are young enough a little jet lag shouldn't slow you down. We need to be out exploring!"

"Maybe time for a little nap this afternoon?" Meg pleaded.

"Okay, a nap later. Eat now and we'll head out. Professor Wolf has left a whole pile of brochures and maps for us to use. I want to check on the conference hotel as well so I can find my way there in the morning."

True to his word, Sean took them sightseeing until late afternoon, returning them to the house in time for tea and the nap he'd promised Meg. He had told Katyrose not to make anything for dinner, as he wanted to take the girls to the local pub that evening.

"So, what do you wear to a pub?" Meg looked at Betta, stunning as usual in simple tailored slacks worn with a blouse of her own design. Meg had quit growing at five foot six but Betta was tall and willowy at five foot ten.

"How should I know?" Betta answered. "I'm Italian!"

"Something simple I guess. It's not like a fancy restaurant."

"What about that new skirt you brought and your blue sweater? It's just the color of your eyes. You can charm all the local guys."

"Me? You're the one with the glamorous job in Milan. Betta Morgan, fashion designer to the stars!"

"A lot you know! It's more like Betta Morgan, slave-girl."

They were interrupted by the sound of Sean calling up the stairs. "Are you girls coming this evening or not?"

"We're coming!" Betta called as Meg quickly slipped into the sweater and skirt. After running a brush through her short dark hair, she put on some lip-gloss and called it done.

The pub was busy when they arrived. Not a lot of strangers visited the little neighborhood pub and there were a lot of whispers and quick glances at the newcomers. Sean found a table for them and the barmaid arrived quickly.

"What can I get for you this evening?" she inquired. Sean ordered three pints of Guinness and asked what the dinner menu was.

"Dinner tonight is soup and roast beef sandwiches," she replied. "The soup is good and hearty."

"Sounds fine to me," Sean said as he looked at Meg and Betta for their opinion. They nodded their agreement. "We'll take three."

"Three 'tis. I'll be back with your pints in a few."

Meg tried to look around without being too obvious. They were so out of place here. Everyone knew everyone else. Her eyes caught those of the bartender, a young man near her own age with dark red hair and deep green eyes. He stared at her for a moment before turning back to building the pints Sean had ordered.

Meg lowered her eyes, her heart pounding. Was it really possible to have that strong a reaction to someone you'd never met? It certainly had never happened to her before. She stole another look at him when their pints arrived only to find him looking at her. He smiled slowly and gave her a wink before Meg quickly dropped her eyes again, intent on her study of the grain of the old wooden table.

"You'll be the Americans that are staying at the Professor's place," the barmaid said as she delivered their pints. It was more statement than a question and Sean confirmed she was right.

"He told us to be watching for you and Katyrose was in earlier today to say you'd arrived. I'm Maureen Kelly. Welcome to O'Hearn's."

"Thank you, Maureen. We're glad to be here. I'm Sean Collins and these are my granddaughters, Megan and Betta."

Meg raised her eyes from the table to say "hello" only to find the bartender standing beside Maureen.

"I'll add my welcome, too, Mr. Collins. I'm Jamie O'Hearn." His words were for Sean but his eyes never left Meg. "We hope we'll see more of you on your visit."

"You will, Jaime. But please call me Sean. These are my granddaughters Betta and—"

"Megan" Jamie finished Sean's sentence. "I'm pleased to meet you."

Megan blushed as he made it clear that she was the one he was welcoming. Before she could catch her breath, he turned to her grandfather and said, "We're here most nights except Sunday. Friday is for music and we offer some of the best. You'll be joining us, I hope."

"I don't know that I can be here this week—I have a pesky conference to get out of the way. But I'm sure my girls will be glad to attend."

"And we'll be glad to have them," he said, his eyes returning to Meg's. "I'd best be getting back to work. Enjoy your meal." He turned away just as Maureen delivered their soup.

Betta leaned over to whisper to Meg, "Wow, Meg. On the first night you find the most gorgeous guy in the place. Nice work!"

Meg shook her head. "Don't be silly, Betta. He was just doing his job." At least she tried to believe that was true but her hands were trembling as she picked up her spoon to eat.

❦   ❦   ❦

At closing, Maureen polished up the clean glasses and placed them in their rows behind the bar. "Nice lot, the Yanks, eh, Jamie?"

"Nice enough," Jamie replied as he wiped down the bar.

"They don't look much like sisters. The one—Betta?—looked foreign. But the other—Megan, was it?—looks like the all-American girl." Maureen stopped what she was doing to look at Jamie when she said, "She certainly caught *your* eye."

Jamie continued to wipe down the bar, each swipe of the cloth taking him a little further from Maureen. "She was alright, I guess."

"Just alright?" Maureen said with a laugh. "She was a lot more than alright judging by the way you couldn't keep your eyes off her."

"What do you want me to say, Maureen? She was pretty? She *was*—very pretty. And a rich Yank tourist who will be gone in a fortnight." He threw the cloth into the pile on the floor then picked the lot up, heading for the laundry basket in the back.

"A lot can happen in a fortnight, Jamie O'Hearn!" she called after him as she shut off the lights.

"Let's go, Maureen. It's been a long day."

Maureen smiled as she followed her cousin out the door. The girl had gotten under Jamie's skin. This was going to be interesting to watch.

Jamie saw Maureen safely to her car then got his bicycle and headed home. Maureen saw way too much for her own good, he thought. He'd be teased about that girl, that Megan, for a good long while.

She *was* pretty—more than pretty, actually. A real beauty with that coal-black hair and eyes so blue you could practically swim in them. He'd heard her laugh with her grandda' and it was like listening to music.

He glanced up and realized he'd taken a different turn than usual, one that brought him past the professor's house. He stopped in the shadows across the street and looked up at the second floor windows. They were dark and he wondered which one was hers before he shook off the mood. Mooning after a tourist girl when he could have any of the local lasses with just the crook of his finger. She wasn't for him, Jamie thought as he pushed off again. But he couldn't help hoping she'd be in again tomorrow.

CHAPTER 41

❈

The girls spent the day sightseeing in Belfast. Mostly wandering with the help of a guidebook, they got lost more than once. But the people they spoke with were quick to help get them turned round again in the right direction. They managed to have lunch at the Crown Liquor Saloon, an 1880's Victorian wonder that was now owned by the National Trust. A tour bus took them past the busy harbor to see the site where the doomed *Titanic* had been built. They enjoyed poking into small shops and listening to the lilt of Irish voices all around.

By the time they made it home, they were footsore but happy. They ate the "wee bite" that Katyrose had left for them. After they ate and did up the dishes, Betta suggested another trip to *O'Hearn's*. "I'm sure Jamie will be hoping you'll stop by," Betta teased.

"Don't be silly, Betta. He was just being the good host."

Betta merely looked at her until Meg blushed. "Alright! So he was cute!"

"And interested in you!"

"Maybe. Fine, we'll go to the pub and I'll bet you ten that he ignores me."

"Good, I really would love to buy that woolen shawl I saw today. Ten dollars from you should make it just about reasonable for me."

The pub was more crowded than it had been the night before. They could hear the music that Jamie had mentioned as they made their way to the door. Slipping in, they stood back to watch and listen as a band played a lively melody that had a number of the crowd up on their feet dancing. The rhythm was infectious and it was impossible not to join the rest of the crowd who was clapping along.

Maureen spotted them by the door. "Fergus, you and Thomas move yourselves from these barstools. There's ladies standing by the door." As the two men got up, with good-natured grumbling, Maureen caught Betta's eye and waved them over.

"Welcome back," Maureen almost had to shout as the music came to an end and the bar erupted in cheers.

"Thanks," Betta said. "You weren't kidding about the music!"

"That one was a bit rowdy. It will get quieter now. Look, there's Jamie going to sing."

A plaintive fiddle began to play and the crowd quieted. Jamie, in a simple sweater and slacks, stepped forward with a tin whistle and played a tune that echoed and swooped around the fiddle's theme. After a moment, he began to sing. They didn't need to know the Irish to understand the song was about love and loss and longing. It was all there in Jamie's face and voice.

When the song ended, he took a quick bow and jumped lightly from the small stage and took his place again behind the bar, going immediately to Megan and Betta. "Sorry you had to hear my caterwauling right away. I thank you for not running away and staying to hear the good music to come."

"Nonsense, Jamie O'Hearn. You're fishing for compliments," Maureen chided him as he loaded her tray with drinks. "Quit your fishing and find out what these ladies need to drink—something strong enough to counteract having to listen to you!"

"She's right. I'm not doing my job. What will it be tonight, ladies? May I build you a couple of pints?"

"Sorry, Jamie, it's white wine for me," Betta said and Meg nodded her agreement, tongue tied at the looks Jamie was giving her.

"Wine it is. But we'll get you converted to Guinness before you leave."

Megan and Betta watched the other patrons of the bar and got lost in the music. Soon the tiny band—violin, accordion, and banjo—began another dance tune held together by the strong beat of the *bodrán*—the traditional handheld drum so important to Irish music.

Suddenly Jamie was out from behind the bar and in front of Megan. "Dance with me, Megan!" he said as he reached out and lifted her from the barstool. He carried her out onto the floor despite her protests.

"Jamie! I can't do this! I don't know how!"

"Then we'll teach you!" Maureen was suddenly on the other side of her, one of the young men from the bar beside her. Betta was drawn out to the floor by another man and the band began their song again, a little slower this time as the two American girls began to try the traditional patterns as the rest of the patrons made a circle 'round them to watch.

Meg's mother, Annie, had been a dancer, good enough for Broadway and a teacher for many years. Her training and genes belonged to Meg who picked up the dance steps quickly. Betta and her partner dropped out as the music increased tempo, then Maureen drew her partner off the floor so that all eyes were on Jamie and Megan.

She forgot her embarrassment and began to enjoy herself. As the music got faster and faster, she could hear the crowd clapping round them. Jamie never missed a step and neither did she as the music swept her away. As it came to a close in a swirl of sound, Jamie lifted her easily from the floor and put her on his shoulder just as the music ceased.

Meg was laughing and telling Jamie to put her down when her grandfather came into the pub. As Jamie finally lowered her, slowly, and returned her to the barstool he'd stolen her from earlier, Sean Collins saw the look in his granddaughter's eyes, a look echoed in the eyes of the young man who held her. He could see the bright color in her cheeks, not just from the dancing but also from the wordless promises held in those looks. His Megan had fallen in love.

CHAPTER 42

Meg was nervous as she dressed for dinner with Jamie's family. What was she doing? She'd only met him a few days ago...but it had been an eventful few days.

As she leaned into the mirror to apply lipstick, she found herself smiling as she remembered Jamie's kisses. He hadn't wasted much time, kissing her the day after they met—and as often as possible since then!

Still, it was too soon to be meeting his family. That meant something. A boy didn't bring home a girl to meet his family unless...unless what? Meg made a face at herself in the mirror. This was just a fling, she reminded herself. She'd be leaving in less than two weeks and Jamie would go on to the next pretty girl he met. But the thought of him kissing someone else made a lump rise in her throat and tears come to her eyes.

"You've fallen in love with Jamie, haven't you, Meg?" Betta had asked the question last night as they were getting ready to leave for an evening at O'Hearn's.

"Of course not, Betta. He's just a friend."

"That was no friendly kiss I saw you give him last night. And there's no friendship in the looks he gives you either. If you're not in love with him then you're going to be breaking his heart. Jamie O'Hearn's head over heels in love with you!"

Could Betta be right, Meg thought as she ran a brush through her hair. Was Jamie in love with her? Was she in love with Jamie? Love at first sight was a family tradition. Laura's parents had known the day they met. That was their story, anyway, and it was easy to believe it was true. Taylor and Laura, too, although it had taken them longer to admit it. So *was* she in love with Jamie O'Hearn? Deep inside she knew the answer was "yes"...but there was no point in knowing it. They were from two different worlds with too little time. Nothing would come of it.

As she heard the sound of the doorbell, her heart skipped a beat. Maybe nothing would come of her feelings for Jamie but today was today, and Scarlett O'Hara had the right idea. She picked up her jacket and ran down the stairs to meet him.

Jamie was chatting with her grandfather and looked up at the sound of Meg's feet on the stairway. She was wearing the blue sweater she'd worn the night they met, the one that matched her eyes—those deep blue eyes that seemed to see into his very soul. What was he thinking taking her home to the family dinner? She'd go back to America and the family would never let him hear the end of it. He'd be eighty-seven someday and they'd still be telling the story of the Yank girl that had stolen his heart.

"Jamie!" Meg's voice was filled with joy as she said his name. Sean took one look at her and realized that he was in deep trouble. He'd brought Meg to Ireland and she'd lost her heart to this young man. What would happen when it came time to leave? Surely Meg wouldn't throw away all of her hard work and skip med school to stay here?

"Megan," Jamie said as he held out his hand to her. "Are you ready to meet the whole clan?"

Laughing, she answered, "Ready? I don't think so but here I am anyway."

Jamie turned back to Sean. "You and Betta would be most welcome as well, Mr. Collins. My mother always cooks enough for an army and the table is large enough to make room for more."

"Thank you, Jamie. Betta and I have plans already so I hope you'll forgive us."

"When you come back to Belfast next time, we'll be expecting you."

"Next time it is. You two run along. Meg, don't forget the flowers you bought." Sean turned to the table and took up the bouquet that was waiting there.

"Thanks, *Abuelo*." She stood on tiptoe to kiss his cheek. "You and Betta have a good time."

Sean watched as the two young people went down the steps, hands held fast as they walked away.

"Did I miss Jamie?" Sean turned at the sound of Betta's voice and reluctantly closed the door behind him.

"He was here and they were gone almost right away." He looked at his other granddaughter and asked, "Did you know she's fallen in love with him?"

"I think she fell for him that first night. But Meg's not admitting it yet."

"Oh, Lord, your parents and Grandmother are never going to forgive me if I lose that girl to Ireland."

"Don't worry, *Abuelo*. Meg's not going to give up med school. If Jamie wants her, he'll have to come around to accepting her ambitions." Betta gave him a hug. "Enough about Meg. I have a date with the best-looking man in Ireland and I'll not have him mooning over some other girl—even if she is my sister! You promised me *Carrickfergus* today. I want to see if your Irish Castle can be more impressive than my lovely Italian palazzos."

CHAPTER 43

Jamie and Meg walked through the quiet Sunday streets of Belfast. They didn't need words but were content to merely be in the other's company. But Jamie's steps slowed the closer they got to his home.

"Jamie? Is something wrong?"

He stopped and turned to look at her. "Just some cold feet about taking you home."

"Why?" She might not have known him long but she knew enough about him to know that Jamie O'Hearn rarely had second thoughts about anything. He made up his mind and went after his goal without looking back. Her heart sank at the thought that he might be sorry he'd invited her.

Jamie saw the hurt in her eyes. "No, Megan, it's not you. Put that thought out of your head." He leaned down to kiss her gently. "It's not you—it's the family. There are such a lot of them. It's a lot to ask of you."

She laughed. "It can't be any worse than when my grandmother's family gathers. She has five sisters and three brothers and I have no idea how many grandchildren there are now. When they get together, it's so noisy with everyone talking and eating and the children playing. But it's a lot of fun, too. Big families are nothing new to me."

"You'd not told me about that part. Maybe you'll survive this after all." He kissed her again before leading the way to a house down at the end of the street where he opened the door and let them in.

Jamie's mother, Moira, welcomed her, blushing when she took the flowers Meg carried. "I can't remember the last time anyone gave me flowers, Megan. You'll not be minding if we use your given name?"

"Not at all," Meg replied. "Thank you for having me today."

"Any friend of young Jamie's is welcome. He knows that. Your grandfather and sister were welcome, too."

"Thank you. Jamie told them but they had plans to visit *Carrickfergus* today. My sister lives in Milan and has been teasing our grandfather that her *palazzos* are better than his Irish castles so he's off to prove her wrong. They sent their thanks for your kind invitation."

"Perhaps next time you're in Belfast, then. I'll go put these in some water. Jamie, introduce your Megan to the family."

Meg was quickly bewildered by the numerous cousins, uncles and aunts. It seemed that every second boy was named Jamie but no one seemed to have trouble figuring out which one was wanted when the name was called.

"Da, this is my friend Megan Morgan. Megan, Jamie O'Hearn, the patriarch of the clan."

"Welcome to our home, Miss Morgan."

"Thank you, sir. But please call me Megan."

"Megan it is, then. Jamie, where are your manners? Get your young lady a pint."

As her Jamie turned away, the door opened and a lovely woman came in. She had dark red hair, lightly streaked with gray, and the kindest face Meg had ever seen. She was dressed simply in a dark skirt and sweater with a white blouse. No makeup, but with skin as beautiful as hers, she didn't need it. Several of the children cried out, "Sha'leen!" and went running to shower her with hugs and kisses.

"That's my Aunt Sha'leen," Jamie said. "I'd forgotten this was her Sunday but I'm very glad you'll get to meet her." Jamie pulled her along with him as he made his way to his aunt and waited for the younger children to clear away.

"Jamie! You're looking well and happy. Could this lovely creature be the reason why?" she teased as she hugged him.

Jamie blushed. "Auntie Sha'leen, this my American friend, Megan Morgan. She's visiting here with her grandfather and sister."

Sha'leen saw the look in Jamie's eyes when he brought Meg forward to greet her. Jamie had fallen in love! She smiled as she greeted the object of his affection. "It's lovely to meet you, Megan." She cocked her head to one side as she looked at her. "Have we met before? You look very familiar."

"I don't think we have. We've only been here a few days but I'm sure I would have remembered you."

Sha'leen was swept away to greet other family members but her eyes strayed more than once to the American girl. She was quite beautiful—some would say striking, with her dramatic coloring. Sha'leen could not shake the feeling that she'd seen this girl before.

CHAPTER 44

Dinner was a noisy occasion. Everyone except the children was crowded around the huge dining table and there seemed to be a hundred different conversations going on. Meg was able to figure out some of the relationships and was surprised when someone asked Sha'leen about "the convent". The woman caught her surprised look and said, "No one warned you there was a nun in the family? There I'm known as Sister Eileen but I can't get anyone around here to use anything but my worldly nickname."

Jamie's mother continued. "Sha'leen is short for Shannon Eileen, her given names. She was the only girl and youngest child with all these very protective older brothers. I think she joined the convent just to have some female companionship!" The laughter that followed was a little forced and Jamie's mother seemed embarrassed by what she'd said.

"That would have been enough reason for any girl to join a convent." Sha'leen filled the awkward silence. "Three enormous brothers and two of them members of the *gardai*? Not only did they scare away any boy who got up the courage to come courting but I could see they'd be wanting me to take care of them until they found women desperate enough to marry them."

The laughter that followed smoothed over the awkward moment. Jamie gave her hand a squeeze under the table.

"Enough about the O'Hearn's," the elder Jamie said. "Tell us about your family, Megan."

"Oh! We're certainly not much like you." There was a brief silence then Meg laughed. "That didn't come out right at all! I meant we're not nearly as large a family and the relationships are much less defined."

She explained, "My sister, Betta, and I are both adopted. Our father is Taylor Morgan—the musical star?" Her questioning tone was answered by murmurs of recognition. "Our mother is Laura Collins Morgan. She's a writer and you may have seen some of her articles in magazines. I have one other sister, much younger, who *isn't* adopted. Annie is five and would fit right in here. She has beautiful red hair and turquoise eyes. So we're really kind of a mixed up group. Laura's father, my grandfather, is Irish, but our grandmother is an Armijo from one of the Spanish land grant families in New Mexico."

"An interesting mix to be sure," Sha'leen commented. "Were you adopted as an infant?"

"No, I was adopted when I was 12. My mother, also an Annie, was Taylor's best friend and he was my godfather. They'd been in the theatre together when they were very young, before I was born. When she and Taylor married, Taylor adopted me. My mother died shortly after that but I had Taylor to hang on to." Even now, her voice filled with sorrow as she thought about her mother and Jamie's mother dabbed a tear from her eye with the edge of her napkin.

Maureen chimed in, "Your sister? Betta? Hearing that you're both adopted explains why you don't look like each other. Where is she from?"

"Oh, yes! Betta, that's short for Elizabetta, is Italian. After my mother died, Taylor and I moved to Italy. Betta's aunt was our housekeeper. She lived with them because her parents had been killed in a car accident a year or so earlier. Betta began to come to work with Rosina and she and I became inseparable—the sister each of us wanted but had never had. When it came time for us to move back to New York for Taylor's career, I'm afraid I threw a fit at the thought of leaving Betta behind. Laura persuaded Rosina and her husband Matteo to move to New York with us and when Betta turned sixteen, Taylor and Laura asked to legally adopt her. She agreed and we were finally officially sisters."

"Family is family," the elder Jamie pronounced. "Sounds like yours is one to be proud of."

"I am proud of them…of us, really. I wish my *Abuelo*—my grandfather—could meet you. I think you'd get along splendidly."

CHAPTER 45

"They liked you, you know," Jamie said as they left the house to go to a concert in the park.

"I liked them, too. You weren't kidding about it being a crowd! How many Jamies are there in your family?"

"At least one a generation, sometimes more."

"Your Aunt—Sister Eileen? She's really very beautiful."

"She always has been. She was our favorite when were kids. Always full of laughter and fun…at least until just before she chose the convent. I never knew what happened but all the adults talked in whispers and Sha'leen cried all the time. But she seems happy enough now."

"Is there any way I could see her? I'd like to ask for her help. My father—my birth father, not Taylor—died here."

"Here? In Ireland?"

"Actually, here in Belfast. He was a television newsman and something happened here. I was thinking I might like to find his grave."

"Auntie Sha'leen would be able to help, I'm sure. I'll take you round to see her tomorrow if you'd like."

"Thanks, Jamie. I don't know why I care—he abandoned me before I was born. But it seems like the right thing to do." Meg turned to smile at him. "Enough of that, Jamie. You promised me music. Let's hurry!"

> * * *

Meg was late getting back to the house but the light was still on in her grandfather's room. She knocked softly then opened the door. "Abuelo, I just wanted to let you know I'm home."

"Come in and tell me about it, Meg."

She came in and sat on the end of the bed. "They're a nice family. A *big* family! Bigger even than *Abuelita's*. And they made me feel very welcome."

"Meg? I wasn't very good at this with Laura. Probably worse now but are you sure you and young Jamie aren't moving a little too fast? He's a nice boy and I don't want to see him left with a broken heart when we leave."

"I don't know, *Abuelo*. I'm not sure what's happening. Maybe it's just because we're here for such a short time, it makes it all seem more urgent. I like Jamie a lot—maybe more than is good for either one of us." Meg took Sean's hand. "But we're not children, *Abuelo*," she said gently.

"I know, Megan. It would be easier if you were."

She stood and leaned down to kiss top of his head. "Thanks for worrying about me. Goodnight."

"Goodnight, Meg." Sean watched as she closed the door. She was right. Meg and Betta were young women now, more than capable of making up their own minds. He just hoped that Meg was using her mind and not just following her heart this time.

> * * *

"I'm home, Betta."
"About time!"

"Meet me in the kitchen in ten minutes if you want to hear the details."

By the time Betta came downstairs in robe and slippers, Meg had made hot chocolate for the both of them. A plate of Katyrose's cookies was on the table.

"If we keep eating like this, Betta, we're both going to be huge by the time we go home."

"I know," Betta answered. "It would help if Katyrose wasn't such a good cook. So, how was dinner with Jamie's family?"

"Overwhelming and a lot of fun. He has zillions of cousins it seems. And half of them are named Jamie, too! But they were very kind to me. Jamie's father has let him take a few days off from the pub so we can spend some time together—if you and *Abuelo* don't mind him tagging along with us."

"It will be better that way. Remember, *Abuelo* wanted to spend some time with us."

"I didn't expect to meet Jamie!"

"It's okay, Meg. I understand. We just missed having you with us today. *Carrickfergus* was pretty impressive."

"After tomorrow, we'll be at your disposal."

"Why? What's happening tomorrow?"

"Jamie has an aunt who's a nun. Hard to believe because she's really very beautiful and, from what the family said, she could have had anyone she wanted. Jamie said something happened when he was a kid and it was like all the light went out of her and she joined the convent. He's taking me by to see her tomorrow."

"Planning on joining her?"

"No, silly." Meg toyed with the cookie she held. "My father died here, Betta. I found an article years ago about it. I thought I might try to find his grave."

"Meg! You never told me."

"It wasn't important, Betta. But, now that we're here, it seems like I should."

"And Jamie's aunt?"

"I thought she might help me find him—find where he was buried."

"Well, *Abuelo* is busy at the University in the morning. I think I'll just tag along."

Meg sighed then smiled at her sister. "I was hoping you would. Jamie will be by about ten-thirty to take us to see her."

"In that case, we'd better get some sleep. Think one of those cousins of his would like to tag along to keep *me* company?" The two girls giggled as they made their way upstairs to bed.

CHAPTER 46

Jamie arrived early and was fed by Katyrose while he waited for Megan and Betta to be ready. He was a little disappointed that Betta would be joining them but it couldn't be helped. He smiled at them both as they came into the kitchen.

"Lucky me, Katyrose. I'll have the two prettiest girls in Belfast to spend the day with."

"Not that you deserve them, Jamie O'Hearn. You take care where and how you go with them."

"Now, Katyrose. I'm taking them to the convent to see my Auntie Sha'leen. How could that get us in trouble?"

"You're an O'Hearn boy, Jamie. Trouble usually finds *you!*"

The three of them were laughing as they left the house.

"It's not too far to the convent. I rang there earlier and left a message for her that we'd be by this morning. She's a teacher at the school. Her lunch break is early so we'll be able to see her then."

She was waiting for them in the convent gardens. Meg was struck again by how lovely she was, while Sha'leen struggled to catch that elusive familiarity she saw in Megan.

"Megan, it's lovely to see you again. This must be your sister—Betta?"

"Hello, Sister Eileen. Thanks for seeing us this morning."

"Come and sit here under the tree. I've made some lemonade. You must be thirsty after your walk."

As the four of them sipped the cool drinks Sha'leen asked. "How can I help you, Megan?"

"I don't know if you can, Sister, but I thought I'd start with you. Maybe you can point me in the right direction. I'm trying to find my birth father's grave. He died here in Belfast several years ago."

"You didn't mention your birth father yesterday," Sha'leen said.

"I don't talk about him much. He abandoned my mother and me before I was even born. It wasn't until a few years ago that I found out he was dead. When I realized we would be coming to Belfast…" Meg sighed and said, "I don't really know. It just seems finding his grave is the right thing to do."

"I'll help if I can."

"Thank you. It was about ten years ago. He was a television reporter and his name was Cary Edwards."

With that simple sentence, Sha'leen's world came crashing in on her as she realized why Megan seemed so familiar. A face she'd carefully shut out of her memory suddenly loomed in her mind. Raven black hair…cobalt eyes…as handsome as Megan was beautiful. She was the image of her father—the man who'd changed the course of Sha'leen's life ten years before.

Moira O'Hearn, Jamie's mother, opened the door to find Sha'leen standing there. She was rarely able to leave the convent during the day so Moira was surprised to see her. "Do you have time for tea, Moira?" Sha'leen had been close to Moira before and their friendship had helped her through all that had happened; had supported her when she made her decision to enter the convent. It had been Moira who had broken the news to the family and helped her brother Jamie accept the decision.

"Of course, Sha'leen. Come in. You look as if you could use a friendly ear."

Sha'leen's eyes filled with tears. "More than you can imagine, Moira."

With Sha'leen seated at the table, Moira set two cups of tea on it then removed her apron to hang it by the door. She waited patiently for Sha'leen to begin but was surprised at what she finally said.

"It's that girl of Jamie's, Moira."

"Megan? He's certainly old enough to be looking at the girls, Sha'leen. And you'd think it would be his mother not his Auntie who would be having trouble with him bringing home a young woman he's so obviously interested in."

Sha'leen wrapped her hands around the hot cup. They'd been freezing ever since she had realized the truth about Megan. It wasn't until Moira reached across the table and took one of her hands that she looked up and the tears she'd held back all afternoon overflowed.

"Sha'leen! What is it? It must be more than Jamie and that girl!"

"It's her, Moira. She's…she's *his* daughter." At the confusion on Moira's face, Sha'leen whispered, "Megan is Cary Edward's daughter."

Moira crossed herself and whispered, "Holy Mother of God! How do you know?"

"When Jamie introduced her, she seemed familiar but I couldn't place where I might have seen her. This morning, Jamie brought her and her sister by to see me. Megan was looking for a grave—her father's grave. She said his name was Cary Edwards." Moira was speechless. It had all been so long ago—more than ten years now. Sha'leen had been a barmaid at the hotel, working with her oldest brother, Jamie. The American newsman had taken a liking to their Sha'leen and no one saw the harm in it—until the morning they'd found her in her room nearly dead from an overdose of sleeping pills, a note on her pillow telling them that Cary Edwards had raped her and she couldn't live with the shame.

Moira would never forget the rage that filled her Jamie's face as he and his brothers rushed off to the hotel to find the man. Had the others not been *gardai*—policemen—Jamie might have killed him then and there. Instead, they hauled him off to jail and a fancy lawyer had gotten him a sentence that had him deported, hardly a punishment for the taking of a young girl's innocence.

Never once in all these years had she asked her Jamie where he'd been that night the newsman had disappeared from his guarded hotel room—never asked what he knew about the battered body that had been found out in the woods on Cave Hill.

She'd stood beside her weeping husband as his adored baby sister had taken her vows and renounced the world. It had been the right answer for Sha'leen but Jamie had wanted so much more for her. He'd never forgiven himself for inviting the wolf into their fold.

"Sha'leen, what did you tell her? What could you say?"

"Certainly not the truth! There's no harm in the girl, Moira. She's not responsible for what her father did. I told her I'd see what I could find out and send word by way of Jamie."

"Are you going to tell her where to find him?"

"She has a right to know. I'll let you tell Jamie I rang up to tell him where. You know where he is as well as I do."

"And you, Sha'leen? Are you going to be alright?"

"I'll be fine, Moira. I shouldn't have to see her again and I don't mind admitting that's a comfort. But we can't let my brother know. Jamie wouldn't let it be. Moira, I'd best be getting back to the convent and explaining to Mother Superior why I had to go running out."

The two women stood and hugged one another. "Sha'leen? I'm here if you need me—you know that."

Sha'leen smiled into Moira's worried eyes. "I know that. No one could have asked for a better sister than you. Jamie chose well when he let you catch him."

CHAPTER 47

Jamie borrowed two scooters and his cousin Diarmid for the afternoon so they could take Meg and Betta to Cave Hill, the natural landmark that dominated Belfast. Home to Belfast Castle and the Belfast Zoo, it had miles of paths for exploring the woods; miles of paths for Meg and Jamie to get "lost" on for stolen kisses.

On one of these "lost" moments, Jamie had nervously presented her with a small box. "Just something to remember Ireland by," he said as he handed it to her. Something to remember *me* by, he thought as she opened it.

It was a *Claddagh* ring. Two hands holding a heart topped with a crown. "It's beautiful, Jamie. Thank you."

He took it from her and placed it on her right hand with the crown pointing outwards. "They say that if it's turned round the other way with the heart on the outside it means that love is at least being considered." Then he kissed her again.

"Jamie!" Diarmid's voice came from a distance. "Jamie! Lunch!"

With another quick kiss, Jamie took her hand and followed the path to the glen where they'd agreed to meet. He opened his backpack and brought out bottles of water and thick sandwiches that he'd gotten from the pub while Meg and Betta were getting ready and he was waiting for Diarmid.

The four of them were famished and chose food over conversation, at least for the moment. The sun was bright, the day was warm, and they all felt content with the world.

Diarmid was the one who broke the silence. "Do you remember when they found that body up here, Jamie? We must have been thirteen or fourteen then."

"A body!" Betta's eyes were huge. "We're picnicking where a body was found?"

"No, it wasn't found here but up over the crest near MacArt's Fort."

"That's still too close for me!"

"It's much too nice a day to be thinking of that, Diar," Jamie said.

"It was such a big thing, though…him being a famous American newsman and all."

Betta looked at Meg who sat up suddenly from where she'd been leaning against Jamie's chest admiring her new ring. "A newsman?"

"I think that was the story. He worked for the television and disappeared suddenly. They found his body up here a few days later."

"Had he wandered away and gotten lost?" Meg asked, knowing that it probably wasn't true.

"If he did, then *somebody* found him. They said he'd been beaten to death."

Meg's face went white and Betta moved over to her. "We'll be right back," she said as she took Meg away from the glen and into the shelter of the trees.

"You idjit!" Jamie chided his cousin. "That's not a subject to be bringing up with ladies around."

"I just thought they might be interested…him being American and all. It's not like he haunts the place!"

Suddenly, Jamie remembered what Megan had told Sister Eileen that morning. *"He was a television reporter…"* It couldn't be! Diarmid's story couldn't be about Megan's birth father—it was too much of a coincidence! He looked toward the wood where Meg and

Betta had vanished and he knew it was true. He'd brought the woman he loved to the very place her father had been murdered.

Betta made sure they were out of hearing range of their companions before she found a rocky outcropping to seat Meg on. By then her sister was shaking so hard she could barely walk. Betta knelt in front of her and took Meg's icy hands. "Megan, it doesn't have to be him. It could just be coincidence."

Meg could barely speak for the tremors that shook her. "No, Betta, it couldn't be. It was him. My father…my father was murdered! When I was growing up, I always thought he stayed away because he didn't want me. When I found out he died, it was easier thinking that he hadn't chosen to stay away; that he might have come back for me one day. But I always imagined he'd died peacefully somehow, not beaten to death on a lonely hillside!" Meg's voice dissolved into sobs that even the waiting men could hear in the distance.

Jamie had been silent when Betta led an obviously shaken Meg back into the glen. He moved to take her in his arms but Betta shook her head furiously. "No, Jamie, just take us home, please."

The four mile ride had seemed endless. Jamie could feel Meg's tears soaking the back of his shirt as she held on to him on the back of the scooter. What a difference from their ride up in the afternoon. Then she'd been laughing and teasing, holding on to him because she wanted to, not for dear life as she was now.

Betta sent them away once they had gotten them home. Jamie tried to speak to Meg but she'd waved him away, "Not now, Jamie. I can't…"

"I'll be at the pub if you need me, Meg." His eyes begged her to see how sorry he was at the turn things had taken but she only turned away to be led into the house by her sister.

❦ ❦ ❦

Jamie slammed into the back door of the pub, dumping off his knapsack and the helmets he and Meg had worn. Maureen was in the kitchen getting things ready for the evening rush and his father was in the front serving the early birds who'd stopped off for a pint on the way home.

"Trouble in paradise, Jamie?" Maureen asked.

"Not now, Maureen," Jamie said, his voice weary.

"Jamie? Are you alright? You didn't have an accident—you're not hurt, not Megan?"

"Everyone's fine, Maureen. Just let me be."

While it was obvious that everything was far from fine, Maureen did back off. She knew better than to keep at Jamie when he was angry. She'd just never seen him *this* angry before and she watched as Jamie moved with tight control to put on his apron and get ready for an evening of serving at the bar.

As Jamie came through the kitchen doors, his father looked up. "Jamie! Did you and the American lass have a good afternoon?"

"Good enough, Da," he said quietly. "You can go on home now. I'll take over."

The elder Jamie loved his son. He was the only child he and Moira had although they'd tried hard enough to give him a brother or sister. He could see the lad was hurting.

"Are you alright, Jamie?"

"I'm fine, Da! Just fine! I wish you'd all quit asking me!"

"I will then and go on home to your mother. But," his father rested his hand briefly on Jamie's shoulders. "I'll be there if you need me."

Jamie sighed. There was no point in lashing out at everyone. "Sorry, Da. Something happened today and I'm not sure what it's going to mean to Megan. She was pretty upset when I left her and Betta at the professor's. And I don't know what to do to make it right."

Girl trouble. That he understood. It was something he and his lass would have to work out between them.

"Call me if you need to leave tonight."

"Thanks, Da." Jamie managed a smile for his father. "I appreciate it.

❦ ❦ ❦

Their grandfather hadn't returned when they got home and Betta was relieved. Sean would be beside himself with worry if he saw Megan in the state she was in. Betta could hear Katyrose bustling about in the kitchen so she hurried Meg up the stairs and into the bathroom.

"I'm running you a bath, Meg. You need to get warmed up. I want you in it by the time I get back from the kitchen with some tea." She took Meg's face between her hands. "Meg? Did you hear me?"

"Yes…a bath. It won't help, Betta. I'll never be warm again."

"You will, Meg. You're just in shock right now. Be a good girl and get into the bath. I'll be back in a few."

Betta ran down the stairs and nearly ran into Katyrose who was gathering her purse and apron to take home.

"Oh! Child, you scared me to death. Slow down! Where's your sister? Your grandfather called to say he would be late and that the two of you should go on without him. I've left a bit of cold chicken and salad in the fridge for you if you've a mind to eat it and aren't heading straight down to the pub."

Betta was impatient at the rush of words from the housekeeper. "Thanks, Katyrose. Meg's not feeling well so we'll be staying in tonight."

"Is there something I can do? I can stay until your grandfather's home if you'd like."

"Thanks, but no. We'll be fine. You go on home and have a nice evening."

"If you're sure then. My favorite show is on soon and I'd like to be home in time for it."

"Good night, Katyrose. I'll see you in the morning."

Betta breathed a sigh of relief once the door closed behind her. Katyrose was a dear woman but she could be trying!

Quickly she brewed two cups of tea from the kettle that was always on the stove. She laced Meg's with lots of sugar and took a couple of cookies from the well-stocked jar before she went back up the stairs.

Meg was in the old-fashioned bathtub deep in bubbles that obscured everything but her face. She opened her eyes as Betta came back into the room. "Think you could have used a little more of the bubble bath?" she asked.

Her joke and the fact that color was coming back into Meg's face eased some of Betta's worries. "I didn't exactly take time to measure," she replied as she held out a cup of tea. "Take this and drink it."

Meg took a sip of the tea. "My God, Betta, how much sugar did you put into this!"

"Enough to try to counteract the shock you were going into."

"I don't remember them teaching us to use sugar when we were Girl Scouts."

"They didn't. *Abuelita* did. She said it's what her grandmother would do when she was upset."

Meg sighed and closed her eyes. "It's helping. I'm warmer now." She kept her eyes closed and Betta sat on the stepstool beside the tub. She watched as two tears squeezed out from under Meg's lashes.

"Betta? It has to be him, don't you think?"

"Has to be."

"Why should it matter so much to me? I was never anything to him."

"Do you remember what you said while we were out there? About how you'd been relieved he hadn't just abandoned you?"

"I was. It was silly. I knew it in my head but my heart wanted to believe that there was still a part of him that had cared for me and my mother."

"Letting go of dreams is never easy, Meg."

"Even the bad dreams?"

"Those are probably hardest of all."

☙ ☙ ☙

Sean came into the busy pub and looked around for his granddaughters. Jamie was behind the bar and beckoned him over.

"My girls not here yet, Jamie?"

Jamie set a pint in front of him. "No, sir. Meg wasn't feeling well and they decided to spend the evening in. Nothing serious!" he added at Sean's look of alarm. "I guess I haven't been letting her get much rest the last few days."

Sean laughed. "That's putting it mildly, Jamie. You two have been together almost constantly. I brought her along so I could spend some time with her. I never figured that I'd lose her to a local lad."

"I'm sorry. If you'd like, I'll…"

"Wait, Jamie! I was only kidding you. You're making Meg's trip truly memorable. She said that you'd arranged some time off and that you'd like to come with us on some of our excursions. I think it's a fine idea. What did you all do today?"

"We took a trip out to Cave Hill and explored the ruins. My cousin Diarmid went along to keep Betta company."

"I thought we'd take a trip out to the Giant's Causeway tomorrow or the day after. Would you be free to join us?"

"The day after would be better for me. I promised Meg I'd take her somewhere tomorrow—if you'd not be minding?"

"Either day is fine with me." Sean stood and reached into his pocket but Jamie interrupted.

"No, this one's on me."

"Then I thank you. Anything I should tell my Meg for you?"

A shadow crept into Jamie's eyes. "Just tell her I'll see her tomorrow." At least I hope I will, he thought as he waved goodbye to Sean and turned to building another pint.

※　　　　※　　　　※

Sean came into the house to find Betta in the sitting room reading.

"Hello, Betta," he said as he dropped a kiss on her head before he took the chair opposite her. "I stopped in at the pub expecting to find you there. Jamie said Meg wasn't feeling well."

"She's okay, *Abuelo*. Just a little too much going on at once. She's sleeping now and will probably be fine tomorrow."

"That's good. We've only got a few more days here and I would hate to see her sick."

Betta longed to throw herself into her grandfather's arms and tell him all that had happened. But it was Meg's story to tell and Betta wouldn't betray her. Still, it would have been nice to have talked it out with someone.

"I asked Jamie about going with us to the Giant's Causeway. It will take the whole day and he said the day after tomorrow would be better for him. He said he and Meg had plans for tomorrow. Are you going with them?"

"I was planning to. It seems like we're leaving you alone a lot and this trip was supposed to be so we could spend some time together."

"I can't compete with the local lads—and don't want to try. I wanted to make a trip to Linden Hall Library. They've got some manuscripts I'd like to take a look at. I didn't think you girls would be interested so I'll do that tomorrow and we'll have our outing on the day after."

Betta came and stood behind his chair. Leaning down, she hugged him, pressing her cheek against his still red hair. "We're pretty lucky to have you, *Abuelo*. Don't think we don't know that."

Sean patted the arms around his neck. "I'm the lucky one, Betta. Go on and get some sleep for your big adventures tomorrow."

CHAPTER 48

Jamie came home late, still half out of his mind with worry about Meg. He'd been hoping Betta would ring the pub and let him know she was alright but there'd been no word.

He was surprised to find his mother waiting up for him. "Ma? Is everything alright?"

"That's what I was wondering, Jamie. Your father said you were upset when you came to the pub tonight. I wanted to see if I could help."

"Thanks but there's nothing to help with."

"Sha'leen called. She told me that you'd brought Megan to see her this morning…and why. Shall I fix a cup of tea and we can talk?"

Jamie gave a sigh of relief. If his mother knew that much already, it would be okay to talk to her about what had happened on Cave Hill. He leaned down and gave her a hug. "Tea and talk are just what I need, Ma."

She was always there, his Ma. He couldn't remember a time he hadn't depended on her; even now when he was a grown man he still needed his mother. Not an easy thing to admit when you're over six foot tall and shaving.

His mother set the mugs of tea on the table along with a plate of cookies. No matter how upset he was, she knew her boy never turned down food.

"What did Auntie Sha'leen say?"

"She said that Megan was looking for her father's grave. That he'd died here in Belfast a few years ago."

"That's right. She said he abandoned her mother right after she got pregnant with Megan. She never saw him. He never inquired after her or sent money to help with her raising. He wasn't anyone to her, really. This Taylor, her adopted father, was always there for her and more of a father than her own ever was."

"And she still cares enough to see his grave?"

"I think it's all so unfinished for her, Ma. I think she's looking for a way to put him finally behind her but what happened today may make it worse."

"Tell me."

"I asked Diarmid along to keep Betta company and provide the second scooter to get us all up to Cave Hill. We had a wonderful time until we stopped for tea. That idjit Diarmid brought up that body that was found up there when we were kids. He went on about it until he mentioned the guy had been a television reporter and that he'd been beaten. That's when Megan lost it. Betta took her off into the woods but I knew what was going on. She'd told Auntie Sha'leen he was a reporter. It had to be the same guy. How many American reporters turned up dead in Belfast ten years ago?"

"The poor girl! She must have been devastated."

"I've never seen anyone so white, Ma. She was moving like a sleepwalker when Betta brought her back to the glen. I dropped them off at the Professor's house and went on to the pub. No one called me so I guess she's alright."

"She's a strong one, Jamie. I could see that in her. Give her some time to get used to the idea and take her to the grave to say goodbye. She'll get through it."

"Auntie Sha'leen found him then?"

"He's in the Protestant cemetery down the road from the convent. Sha'leen says his grave is in the northeast corner under that crooked old tree."

"If she's still wanting to go, I'll take her there tomorrow."

"Jamie? Have you lost more of your heart to this girl than you should?"

"If you're asking if I'm in love with her, Ma, I am. From the moment I saw her across the pub, I knew she was the woman I'd been waiting for…the one I'll probably always wait for since she'll go back to America soon. She's going to be a doctor, Ma, and will start her studies this fall in California. She's not going to give that up to have anything to do with an Irish barkeep. I'm in love with her but I'm wise enough to know that nothing's going to come of it."

"She might surprise you."

"She might—if I gave her a chance. But I won't, Ma. I'll wave goodbye and we'll write a few letters but then she'll be gone. Hopefully it will be a pleasant memory for the both of us someday." Jamie stood up from the table. "Thanks for listening, Ma."

"Goodnight, Jamie. Sweet dreams." She'd said the same thing to him every night for all of his life but there wasn't a chance it would happen tonight, Jamie thought. He'd be lucky if he slept at all.

Meg slept late the next morning. Her grandfather was gone by the time she came down and Katyrose was off to the market. Betta was sitting in the garden sketching out new designs. It was a soothing activity for her; a place she could be where all the troubles seemed to be less important.

"It's beautiful, Betta," Meg said as she came to sit beside her.

"Just something I'm playing with," Betta replied as she closed the sketchbook and set it on the table beside her. "How are you this morning?"

"I don't know yet. I feel a little numb."

"It was a lot to find out in one day. Are you still going to want to go to find his grave? Jamie called a little while ago. Sister Eileen found the information for you."

"I think I have to, Betta. Maybe then I can put this all aside…at least 'til we go back home. I know that Taylor knew my father and I'm going to ask him to fill in some of the blank spaces."

"Are you sure, Meg? Sure that you really want to know anymore?"

"I guess I need to know where I came from before I go on with who I'm going to be."

"Jamie said he'd be by about noon. Do you want some breakfast?"

"I'm sure I can find something to nibble on." Meg stood, stretched, then turned to go in the house. But she stopped at the doorway, "Betta?" She waited until she had Betta's attention then blew her a kiss. "Thanks for being there for me."

"It's what sisters do," Betta said with a smile.

CHAPTER 49

Jamie clattered down the stairs and into the kitchen where his father was having a cup of tea before heading off to the pub. "Good Lord, Jamie, how do you manage to make so much noise?"

"Noise? What noise?" Jamie replied with a cheeky grin.

"You seem to be feeling better this morning. Had a talk with your Ma, did you?"

"I do and I did. She knows the answer to everything. I can see why you married her."

"It wasn't for her brains alone, boy!"

"Da! That's my mother you're talking about!"

The elder Jamie laughed, glad to see his son back in fine spirits. "So where are you and your American off to today?"

Jamie's smile faded. "Not for anything fun today, Da. I promised to take her to visit her father's grave."

"Here? Her father's buried here?"

"Auntie Sha'leen found it for us. Megan's father was a newsman here about ten years ago. Do you remember when they found his body up on Cave Mountain?"

He heard a gasp and looked up to see his mother in the kitchen doorway, her face white with shock, his father's almost as pale.

"What?" he said, looking from one to the other.

The elder Jamie's voice was tight as he rumbled, "Tell me again what you just said."

"Meg's father—her birth father—was a television reporter here. I remember the fuss when he disappeared from his hotel. He was already in some sort of trouble—we kids picked that much up. They found his body up on Cave Hill a few days later. Meg didn't know any of this, except that he died here, until yesterday."

"And you made your Auntie find his grave for you?"

"Da, what's wrong? Meg thought Sha'leen might be able to help and she did. She told Ma where the grave was so I could take Megan there today." Jamie looked at his mother in confusion. "I don't understand…"

"You're damned right about that, Jamie O'Hearn! You *don't* understand! And you shouldn't be poking around in things that don't concern you."

"Jamie!" His mother reached out to her husband. "He doesn't know, doesn't *need* to know!"

"Doesn't need to know *what*?" the younger Jamie asked.

"He's old enough to know now, Moira. He's old enough to know that the father of the girl he's seeing ruined our Sha'leen's life."

His son stood very still. "What are you talking about, Da?"

"Your sweet Megan's *bastard* of a father raped your Aunt Sha'leen ten years ago. *That's* why she went into the convent. She couldn't face trying to build a normal life after that. And you dragged her into it again!"

"Da! I didn't know! How could I know? And it's not Megan's…"

"Not Megan's fault? Is that what you were going to say? No, it's not her fault but she's of his blood. I already ruined one life by bringing that man into my family. I'll not be letting you do the same. You'll not be seeing her again, Jamie O'Hearn! I forbid it."

"You can't forbid me to see her. I'm twenty-six years old and I'll see who I please."

"Not while you live under this roof you won't!" his father roared.

"Then I guess I'll not be living here any longer," Jamie shouted back with his eyes blazing. "I'm in love with Megan and I'll not let what her father did come between us!" He rushed out the door, slamming it so hard behind him that it bounced back from the latch and the window shattered.

Moira watched helplessly as her husband stormed out behind him.

Meg finished getting dressed. It would be a solemn afternoon but it would be easier with Betta and Jamie beside her. She ran her fingers over the *Claddagh* ring Jamie had given her yesterday before everything had come crashing in on them. With a smile, she turned it round so that the crown turned inwards. She'd see how long it took Jamie to notice.

Glancing at the clock, she realized it was already past noon. It wasn't like Jamie to be late. Something must have come up at home or at the pub. He'd be along soon, she was sure and she started down the stairs to wait with Betta.

The elder Jamie stomped into the pub. No one was there yet and that was just as well, he thought. He pulled down a bottle and a glass and poured himself two fingers of the finest Irish whiskey and drank it down neat. He rarely drank at all and never in the morning. But there had to be something that would remove the ache from his heart.

Ten years. Ten years ago he'd lost his baby sister. Sha'leen had been the light of all their lives. She was a late baby, her brothers all nearly grown before she came along. They'd each sworn to keep her safe, but he was the one who had failed.

Cary Edwards. Sly, smooth bastard—he'd duped them all into thinking that he was someone they could trust with their Sha'leen. Every boy in the neighborhood had been after her as well as half the news contingent at the hotel where Jamie had been keeping bar. But none of them wanted to cross the O'Hearn brothers so they watched from a distance and with respect. But Edwards had outdone them all and he'd convinced Jamie to leave her alone with him.

No one had ever blamed Jamie but himself. And the guilt only got deeper when their mother had died a year later and their father soon after—of hearts too badly bruised to go on he'd always thought. And Sha'leen—she'd never said a word of blame against him, still claiming to love him as she always had. But how could she when he'd failed her so miserably?

By the time Maureen arrived to help with the opening, the elder Jamie was cross as a bear and more the worse for drink than she'd ever seen him. Treading gently around him, she opened the door for business.

One o'clock came and went with still no sign of Jamie. Megan began to fear that he'd somehow decided that he didn't want to be mixed up with the daughter of a murdered man—although what difference that could make she was at a loss to explain.

By two o'clock she decided to ring his house but there was no answer. At two-thirty, she told Betta she was running down to the pub to see if Jamie was there. She was out the door before Betta could stop her and at the pub before Betta could catch up.

All young Jamie could think of was that he had to get away; had to find out if it were true; had to figure out what it would mean to love Megan if her father had truly been the one to so hurt Sha'leen. Finding himself in front of the library, it struck him that they would have newspapers, newspapers old enough to recount the story. There was no reason for his father to have made it up, but he had to see it in black and white before he could finally believe.

Forgetting his promise to pick up Megan, he settled in at a microfilm machine and began his search for Cary Edwards and the truth.

🍁   🍁   🍁

Megan opened the door to the pub that was emptying now that the lunch rush was over. Only a few of the regulars with nothing better to do lingered over an extra pint. Maureen called out a greeting to her, which caused the elder Jamie to turn with a ferocious glare.

"What will *you* be wanting, miss?"

Megan was startled by his tone. This was far from the genial man who'd been their host in the pub and the loving patriarch who had welcomed her into his home.

"I was looking for Jamie, Mr. O'Hearn. He was going to..." her sentence was cut off when he interrupted her.

"Go on back to America, girl, and leave my boy alone. Your family's already done enough damage to this one."

Betta stepped through the door in time to hear his statement. What was the man talking about? They'd done nothing to the O'Hearns. She exchanged a puzzled look with Maureen who was just as confused about what was going on as they were.

"I'm sorry?" Meg's voice was puzzled. "I don't know what you mean. If I've done something to offend you..."

"Offend? Offend? Is that what you Yanks call it? First your bastard of a father comes and destroys Sha'leen. Now, ten years later, you aim to do the same to my son? It won't be happening this time! I'll not let it happen again. Go on! Get out! You're not welcome here and you'll not be seeing my Jamie again if I've a say in it."

Meg turned to Maureen then to Betta. "What's he talking about? What have I done?"

"Jamie? You've had too much of the creature. Apologize to Megan right now!" Maureen stood with her hands on her hips and glared at him, angry as she'd ever been.

"Apologize? Not in this lifetime! Her father *raped* your Aunt Sha'leen—and you want me to take the viper's daughter in?"

"No! Oh, no…" Meg's eyes filled with tears. "It can't be true."

"True enough—you can look it up in the papers. And you needn't wonder any longer why he died."

With a strangled cry, Meg turned and ran out the door.

"You horrible man!" Betta turned on him. "Meg had nothing to do with who her father was or what he did! She loves your Jamie and wouldn't hurt him for the world. And now you've gone and destroyed the both of them. I hope you live a very long time with the memory!"

She turned on her heel and ran out after her sister, praying that Meg would head for the house and not run headlong away somewhere. The shocked silence she left behind in the pub was broken only by the sobs from the man behind the bar.

※ ※ ※

Moira O'Hearn stood waiting in the Mother Superior's office for a novitiate to fetch Sister Eileen. The scene in her kitchen played over and over again in her head. The long kept secret was out at last—and it may have destroyed the two she loved most in the world.

"Moira! What is it? What's wrong?" Sha'leen knew her sister-in-law would never intrude at the convent if it weren't an emergency.

"Oh, Sha'leen! Jamie knows!"

"Jamie? Which one?"

"*Both* of them. My son told his father he was taking young Megan to see her father's grave and your brother lost any of the good sense he'd ever had and spit the truth out at young Jamie. It ended with both of them rushing out and I don't know what's to come." With that, she dissolved into tears and Sha'leen could only hold her helplessly as she cried.

After the library, Jamie walked mindlessly, pointlessly until, at dusk, he found himself at the Protestant cemetery standing in front of a simple stone that held only a name and the date of death.

What kind of man was it that would abandon a young wife, pregnant with their child? How could he have turned his back on that child, his innocent daughter? Why would he have had his way with another innocent girl, only a few years older than his own daughter?

As he stood and stared down at the grave, he knew he'd never know the answers because he couldn't think in the same warped way as the man that lay buried there. He'd never understand because he, Jamie, was everything that Cary Edwards had never been.

With a heavy heart, he knew there was one more person he would have to talk to before he could turn to finding Megan. He left the cemetery and headed for the convent. He could hear sweet voices raised in praise to God as Vesper hymns were sung. He leaned against the wall to wait, wondering how Sha'leen could still find the faith to pray to a God who had betrayed her.

Megan had gone back to the house. Betta found her there crying hysterically in their grandfather's arms. He stood there hopelessly confused as he held her, his eyes asking questions of the breathless Betta who ran in the door.

"Meg? Meg!" Betta shook her head at her grandfather, wordlessly asking him to wait to have his questions answered. She drew her sister to the couch then sat beside her and held her as she cried. Sean could only sit helplessly by, waiting for an answer.

"Meg, he was drunk—crazy! He was just lashing out at you."

Sean's eyes widened at her words and he silently mouthed "Jamie?" Meg shook her head. "His father" she mouthed back to him.

"No, Betta. How could he make something like that up—*why* would he? Sha'leen is his sister. He'd never say such horrible things if they weren't true."

"Alright, Meg, but even if they were true, it has nothing to do with you. You're not responsible for what your father did."

"Jamie's father thinks I am! And so must Jamie. That's why he didn't come today. Now that he knows the truth, he wants nothing to do with me."

"You don't *know* that, Meg." Betta took her by the shoulders and made her sit up and look in her eyes. "All you know is what that spiteful old man said. Maybe Jamie just needed time to think."

"No. If he still cared he would have been here by now. It's over. And I loved him, Betta. I loved him."

※ ※ ※

There was no reasoning with Megan after that. Betta filled Sean in on the whole story while Meg huddled in a chair, tears still pouring down her face.

"It was awful, *Abuelo*, he was so horrible to Meg."

"I think I'll head down to the pub and have a word with Mr. O'Hearn myself," Sean said as he stood.

"No, *Abuelo*!" Meg's cry stopped him. "Just take me away from here, please."

"Where to, Meg?"

"I don't know! I don't care! I just can't be here. I can't face Jamie. Betta, take me back to Italy with you. I can't go home to face Laura and Taylor, yet. I need to have some time…"

Betta met her grandfather's eyes and nodded. "Maybe that would be best. I'll go pack our things. Would you go call the airport, *Abuelo*—see how soon we can leave?"

Sean came over and knelt down in front of Meg. "Are you sure this is what you want, Meg? Don't you want to give the boy a chance to have his say?"

"I can't, *Abuelo*. Please, just take me away from here."

"I'll call, then, sweetheart."

It was just before dusk when their rented car left for Belfast International. The girls would catch a flight to Heathrow in London then make connections to Milan. Their plane took off at about the same time Sha'leen came once again to Mother Superior's office—this time to meet young Jamie.

※　　　　　※　　　　　※

"Jamie, I'm so sorry." Sha'leen came to where her nephew was sitting and took his hands in hers. "You should never have had to find out and certainly not the way that you did. How's Megan?"

"I don't know. I haven't seen her today."

"Haven't seen…Jamie, you're not blaming her for what her father did?"

"No…at least I don't think I am. I feel like my whole world's been turned upside down and I can't go to her until I get it all back together."

"Jamie, look at me."

He raised his eyes to hers and saw only love there.

"Your father has blamed himself for years for what happened to me. It wasn't his fault any more than it's Megan's. There was only one person responsible that night and that was Cary Edwards. He's the only one to blame—but I quit placing blame the day I came here. It happened. It was horrible. I still sometimes have nightmares but some good came out of it, Jamie. I found where I was supposed to be—here in the convent with my sisters and God."

"But how can you still have faith after something so terrible happened?"

"Sometimes it makes it easier; makes you focus on what's important and what isn't. I'm happy here, Jamie. Happier than I could have been out in the world with a husband and family of my own."

"What do I say to her?"

"Tell her what's in your heart. That's what she needs to hear and what you need to say. Go, Jamie. Find your Megan and tell her you love her."

Sha'leen walked him to the door then gave him a quick hug. "She's a lucky girl, young Jamie. I hope she knows that."

❧ ❧ ❧

Sean pulled he car into the narrow driveway of the borrowed house. It looked so empty. They'd left in such a hurry that no one had thought to turn on lights to welcome him back.

Wearily, he got out of the car and started for the door. He was startled when a shadow moved from the porch and formed itself into a young man—Jamie O'Hearn. Not now, Sean thought, not now. I'm not ready to deal with him yet.

"Mr. Collins, there's no one at home. Is Megan with you?"

"No, Jamie. She's gone."

"Gone? She'll be back won't she?"

Sean shook his head. "Come into the house if we're going to talk, lad. I have a real need for a solid drink right now."

Jamie followed him into the house and was surprised at Sean's appearance as he turned on the lights. He seemed to have aged years in the few short hours since last night.

"Can I fix you something, Jamie?"

"I'd not turn down a whiskey if you've got it."

Sean busied himself pouring the two drinks then turned back to Jamie. "Sit down, boy," he snapped.

For a moment the two of them concentrated on the drink and the warmth of it spreading through their hearts. Jamie broke the silence with a tentative question.

"Megan? You said she was gone. She and Betta are just off sightseeing?"

"No, Jamie. Meg's gone. So is Betta. I was just coming back from the airport. They've gone to Italy."

"But why?"

"After what your father told her and you not showing up, she was devastated."

"My father? Dear God! What did he tell her?"

"You've not seen him then?" When Jamie shook his head, Sean continued. "She went to the pub to look for you when you were late coming to pick her up. She thought you might be there. She needed to reassure herself that you were not rejecting her because of who her father was. Your father was cruel enough to tell her the rest of the truth about her father. Not only had he abandoned her mother and their unborn child but he'd also raped another young girl. According to your father, his blood runs in her veins and that makes her no better than he was."

"No! He was wrong. Meg's wrong. I *love* her, Mr. Collins. Today was the first I'd heard of the whole story. I needed time to think, to take it all in. I didn't mean to hurt her by not coming round…"

"But, meaning to or not, Jamie, you did hurt her. She had only your father's words telling her that you wouldn't see her again. I tried to talk her into waiting to see if you would come but all she could think of was getting away. She doesn't even want to go home with me. She's chosen to hide until she can face the world again."

"Tell me how I can find her," Jamie stood as if to run out the door as soon as he had the information.

"I can't. I made her a promise that if you came round, I'd not give her away."

"But I have to see her! I have to explain!"

"I can't, Jamie. The best advice I can give you is to forget we were ever here and go back to your life. I'll be leaving tomorrow myself and Belfast will have no reason to remember Sean Collins or his granddaughters."

"That's your last word, then? There's nothing I can do to change your mind?"

"I promised Megan and I'll not break my word to her."

Jamie took a deep breath and closed his eyes for a moment. When he opened them, Sean could see them shimmering with tears.

"Would you tell her someday that she was wrong—that I loved her more than life itself? I was just too slow to tell her."

Sean nodded. "If there's a time that it can be said, I'll tell her. I'm sorry, Jamie, for the turmoil we brought into your life. It's amazing how one man—one *worthless* man—can still cause so much havoc from his well-earned grave."

Sean stood and walked Jamie to the door. As he opened it, they were both startled to find the elder Jamie standing there.

"Da! What are you doing here?"

"Jamie, Mr. Collins, I've done something awful and, while I know all the apologizing in the world won't fix things, I've come to do my best to make it up to young Megan."

Jamie laughed bitterly. "You're too late, Da. Megan's gone. Between us, we succeeded in breaking her heart and driving her away."

"Mr. Collins? Is this true? The lass is gone?"

"It's true, O'Hearn. And it's just as well because *nothing* you could say to her would make any difference. It was bad enough that she learned her father was murdered but to learn the why of the murder was more than she could bear." Sean stopped and took a deep breath. "I'll thank you to leave now—both of you—before I say or do anything that could shame me as much as you've shamed yourselves."

Silently, young Jamie stepped through the door and headed down the steps. His father opened his mouth as if to speak then closed it and turned to follow his son. Sean closed the door behind them and poured himself another glass. He missed Maria desperately. If only she wasn't on that damned retreat...

🍁 🍁 🍁

Jamie was several steps in front of his father, already turning into their garden gate, when his father finally asked him to slow down. "Jamie, please, we need to talk before we see your mother."

"Why'd you have to tell her what he'd done? Is your heart that full of hate?"

"You can't understand what it was like. To see someone I loved so hurt and me being powerless to help." He heard the sound of his own words and saw the look on his son's face. "I'm sorry. You do understand. I'll never finish regretting what I said to the lass. I've no excuse, Jamie, but my love for Sha'leen—and my love for you."

Jamie looked at him long and steady. For the first time, the elder Jamie really realized his son was no longer a boy but a man—a man who'd lost the woman he loved through no fault of his own.

"Answer me one thing, Da."

"If I can, I will."

"Were you one of them who was responsible for her father's murder?"

Of all the questions possible, the elder Jamie had never expected this one.

Jamie read the answer in his father's eyes. "'Tis what I thought. Megan's gone—thinking that I don't love her because of what her father did. And I can't go after her because what would she think if she found out the man who murdered *her* father was mine."

He turned and walked into the house leaving his father—and his youth—behind.

CHAPTER 50

Sean Collins looked around the lovely house that was supposed to have been the setting for one last trip with his granddaughters before they grew too far away from him—a trip to give them memories to share for years to come. There would be memories alright but none they'd be taking out to polish and share.

It had been a long night. He'd never really been to sleep. He'd repeatedly thought of calling Maria or Taylor but finally decided this was news best shared face to face. So he'd packed his things then straightened up the place. Finally, just as the sun was coming up, he sat down at the desk and wrote a note to Katyrose explaining that they'd been called back home suddenly. He left a tidy bonus for her in the envelope and thanked her for her kind care of all of them during their stay. He added a note asking her to deliver an envelope he would be leaving with hers.

Then he took another sheet of paper and wrote a short note. Sealing it in an envelope, he wrote a name across it and left them both on the kitchen table where Katyrose would be sure to see them when she arrived.

He left for the airport shortly after that. It was time to leave this place behind and go home. He didn't care if he ever set foot in Ireland again.

※ ※ ※

The pub was not yet open when Katyrose came to the kitchen door. Calling out a greeting to Maureen, she let herself in.

"Good morning, Katyrose. You're out and about early today."

"The strangest thing, Maureen, when I got to the Professor's house this morning, I found a note from Mr. Collins. He and his girls are gone! Called back home suddenly but he didn't say why. Left me a tidy bonus, he did," she said as she patted the drawstring purse she wore at her waist. "And he left an envelope for me to deliver to young Jamie. Is he about?"

Maureen was rocked by the news but didn't want to let it show to Katyrose. How hurt Megan must have been by old Jamie's drunken accusations yesterday! It was no wonder they'd gone.

"He's not in yet, Katyrose. I'll be glad to take it for you and give it to him when he comes in."

Disappointment filled Katyrose's eyes. She'd been hoping to find out what was in the letter. She didn't think it was from young Megan since the name on the envelope was in her grandfather's writing but she was nearly consumed by curiosity at what it could say. Still, she needed to get back to the Professor's house and wash the linens and put the house back to rights, so she reluctantly handed it over to Maureen.

"See that he gets it soon as he comes in, Maureen. I think it might be important."

"The minute he arrives, Katyrose." Maureen held the door open so the older woman could leave then tucked the letter into her apron pocket. Jamie should be along soon.

※ ※ ※

Jamie was late, arriving at the pub just before the doors were to open. He'd been out looking for a place of his own since he could no longer live under the same roof with his father. His decision had devastated his mother but she understood it was time. For awhile he'd thought about pulling up stakes altogether and heading to Dublin or even London. But the only place that Meg would know to find him—if she ever wanted to—was at O'Hearn's. If he left here…it was a tenuous connection at best but it was all he had.

He came in and grabbed an apron, tying it around his waist as he went into the public room. Maureen was just finishing wiping down the tables and Jamie began to do the same to the bar. She hadn't heard him come in and was startled to turn and find him there. The boy looked like hell. She'd have been willing to bet that he had not slept at all.

"Jamie?"

"Yes, Maureen?" He kept his back turned to her as he checked the stock behind the bar.

"Katyrose was by earlier. She said that Professor Collins and his girls have left."

"That they have, Maureen." He was glad to busy himself with straightening bottles and glasses so he'd not have to look at her face.

"She brought something for you—a letter."

He turned quickly, hope alive in his eyes as Maureen handed the envelope to him. She watched as he tore it open and read the short message, the light dying in his eyes.

"Jamie? 'Tisn't bad news, is it?"

"Neither good nor bad, Maureen. Thanks for taking it for me. I need to get some whiskey out of the back; we're a bit low. I'll be right back."

He went through the kitchen door and down the stairs into the basement storage room where he opened the single sheet of paper again. It was from her grandfather and read,

> Jamie, I'm sorrier than I can say at the way things turned out for you and my Megan. I hope that somehow the two of you will find a way to work it out.

I can't break my promise to her and tell you where she's gone. But I can give you my address if you choose to try to reach her. I'll forward it on for you if I think she's strong enough to handle it.

Sean Collins

Jamie folded the note and put it in his back pocket. He'd keep it but he knew he'd never use it. What had happened between their fathers would forever be a barrier between them. He'd always love her—but he'd never be part of her life again.

CHAPTER 51

Taylor and Laura waited at the airport for Sean's plane to arrive. He'd called last night to say that he was coming home early and the girls had gone on to Milan for a few days. He'd assured them that nothing was wrong but both Taylor and Laura heard something in his voice and Laura had insisted on coming along to pick him up.

Maria had called to let them know she would be home early as well. She'd left her car at the airport and would go on out to the house leaving Taylor and Laura to pick up Sean and bring him home.

"They couldn't have had a fight? Not Dad and the girls? Could they, Taylor?" Laura was worrying herself sick over the sudden change of events.

"I doubt it." Taylor took her hand and brought it to his lips. "Your Dad will be here soon. He'll tell us what happened when we get him home."

Laura sighed. "I know. I'm just so worried."

"Me, too. But we know that it's nothing life threatening or we'd be going there instead of him coming here."

"That's not a lot of comfort, Taylor!"

"It's all I can offer." He glanced at his watch. "His plane should be touching down any minute now. We'll know soon."

This was all too much at once, Laura thought. First the offer from New York and all the details that were going into getting them ready to make the move. They had chosen to wait until the travelers all returned before breaking the news to them. Her parents were going to be heartbroken. They adored their youngest granddaughter and spent as much time with her as they could. If some rift had happened with her Dad and the girls in Ireland, that would only make it that much harder on him to lose Annie. She sighed impatiently and tried to find a comfortable spot in the chair. The airport's territorial décor was striking but these had to be the worst chairs in the world!

"They just announced his plane, Laura." The two of them stood to move to the arrival gate where they waited, hands entwined, for the latest blow to rock their world.

※ ※ ※

"There he is!" Laura spotted Sean first and waved to him. Returning her greeting, Sean's heart lightened at the sight of his daughter and the man who stood so protectively beside her.

"Let me take that for you, Sean," Taylor said as he reached out to take the shoulder bag that the older man carried. Their eyes met and Sean shook his head slightly at the question he saw in Taylor's eyes.

Laura missed the look as she threw her arms around her father and hugged him fiercely. He looked so fragile and tired!

"Let's go see if we're lucky enough that they'll send your bag through right away," Taylor said. "Then we can head out to your house, Sean. Maria's waiting."

"Maria? But she's still at her retreat."

"Not anymore, Dad. She came home this morning and said she'd be waiting for us there."

While Taylor waited by the luggage carrel, Laura asked, "Dad? What happened?"

Sean put his arm around her and squeezed her shoulders. "When we get home, Laura. I don't want to have to tell the story more than once."

Patience was not one of Laura's strong points and the curiosity and distress were nearly killing her but she smiled and hugged him back.

Sean breathed a sigh of relief as Taylor pulled into the curving driveway that hid his home from the street. Finally! Home! Knowing that Maria was there waiting for him made all the difference in the world.

"I'll get the bags," Taylor said. "Laura, would you help me?" She looked at him in surprise and he nodded his head toward her father. "We'll be there in a minute, Sean."

As her father went through the door, Laura looked to Taylor for an explanation. "He'll need a minute with your mother."

"Of course he will. Thanks for thinking of it. I'm just so frazzled by all of this."

"C'm'ere," Taylor said as he drew her into his arms. "Whatever this is, we'll get through it." She tilted her head back to look up at him in the moonlight and accepted the gentle kiss he gave her.

"Sean!"

His eyes filled with tears as his wife hurried up the sloping entryway to hold him in her arms. She was the love of his life and the other half of his heart. Only now did he feel complete and ready to face what was ahead. They held each other for a long moment until they heard the door open to admit their daughter and son-in-law.

"Come in. I've made chocolate and biscochitos. There's green chile stew on the stove if you're hungry." Laura kissed her mother and went into the kitchen. Taylor dropped a kiss on his mother-in-law's head. She was so small that he never quite believed that Laura had come from her.

Once they were all settled around the table, Sean began his story.

"First of all, no one was physically hurt and the girls are both fine."

"And you, *mi amore*?" Maria asked as she covered his hand with hers.

"I'm alright, too, Maria. It all began the day we got there. I took the girls to a local pub called *O'Hearn's* where Megan met a young man named Jamie O'Hearn…"

🍁   🍁   🍁

The chocolate had grown cold by the time Sean finished his story and both women were weeping. Taylor sat in stunned silence at the twist of fate that had brought Cary Edwards back into their lives. He'd always known that someday Meg would want to know about her father and had been prepared to deal with it when the time came. But he'd never imagined that she would find out in such a way—find out details that even he hadn't known.

"Meg begged me to get her away from there. It wasn't just young Jamie's betrayal that had done her in. She was feeling such tremendous guilt at what Edwards had done to Jamie's aunt. All she could think of was getting away. Milan seemed like the best choice at the time."

"Betta e-mailed us that they had arrived safely. She said she was going to go back into the studio in a day or so and Meg was just going to do some exploring on her own." Laura's voice was choked with tears. Meg should never have found out what her father had been—must never find out, even now, what he'd done to Laura. Her eyes met Taylor's and he took her hand, knowing what she was thinking. There wouldn't be much sleeping in these two homes tonight.

"You've not heard from them since?" Sean asked, his voice filled with worry.

"It's only been a day, Sean," Taylor said gently. "I'll call Betta in the morning to see what's happened. Right now, you need some rest so we'll go on home and talk to you after I've called Betta tomorrow."

Taylor took Laura's hand and started to the door. When he got there, he turned to look at his parents-in-law, the people who had taken him and Megan into their hearts without hesitation. "Sean, she couldn't have had anyone better there with her. And you've got to quit blaming yourself for what happened. You had no way of knowing."

"My head knows that, Taylor. It may take a little longer to convince my heart."

CHAPTER 52

Betta opened the door to her apartment. "Meg? I'm home!" she called as she carried her portfolio over to the drawing table.

"Hi," Meg said as she looked up from the book she had grabbed for camouflage when she heard Betta's key in the door. She hadn't done anything today—or the past two days for that matter. Nothing held her interest and she found herself going over and over that last horrible day in Belfast.

"Feel like going out to dinner tonight?" Betta asked, knowing the answer before Meg said it. She hadn't left Betta's apartment since they'd arrived here three days ago.

"I don't think so, Betta. If it's friends who are asking you, go on without me."

"It's not friends. It's just me. You've been locked up in here too long. It's not an invitation, Meg. Get up and get ready. We *are* going out to dinner."

"And if I don't?" Meg's eyes turned stormy.

"If you don't, I'm kicking you out of my apartment and abandoning you!"

"You'd never do that!"

"Try me," Betta challenged as she locked stares with Meg.

Meg knew when she'd lost. "Fine. Just no place festive or dressy, please."

"Getting dressed up would be good for you, but we're only going to the place on the corner. It's a beautiful evening and we can sit outside and people watch for awhile. You have half-an-hour to get ready." Betta turned her attention to the letters she had picked up from her mailbox downstairs. She heard Meg pad softly into the bedroom and breathed a sigh of relief. At least she'd get her out of this apartment—out where Meg could see that the world was still going on.

🍁   🍁   🍁

It *was* a beautiful evening. Meg realized that she was glad to be out of the apartment. There was no one here who knew what had happened and she began to relax as they shared a bottle of wine while they watched the world go by.

Betta ordered dinner for them both and, for the first time since Belfast, Meg realized she was hungry. She cleaned the last of the sauce from her plate with a piece of bread then leaned back in her chair.

"Okay, you were right, Betta. I did need to get out."

"Am I ever wrong?"

The two of them smiled at each other and Meg raised her glass in a silent toast.

"What now, Meg?" Betta's voice turned serious as the evening shadows crept across the street.

Meg shook here head and sighed. "I don't know, Betta. I still feel so confused and don't know what to make of all of it. I've been thinking of going to the villa tomorrow."

Meg and Taylor had stayed at the Mediterranean villa after her mother had died. That was where Betta had come into their lives and Meg always thought of it as a retreat and a place for healing. Taylor had bought it shortly after he married Laura. The main house was rented out most of the time but the guesthouse was always kept ready for any of the family who cared to use it.

"Will you be all right there alone?" Betta asked.

"Alone is what I need right now, I think. I've always loved it there. I'll rent a car and drive down tomorrow."

"If you want to wait for the weekend, I'll go with you."

"Thanks, Betta. But I think I'm really ready to go now."

"Just promise to check in with me every day so I don't worry."

"I will—and if I'm really leaving tomorrow, we'd probably better go back so I can make arrangements for the car and get packed."

CHAPTER 53

Taylor had spoken with Betta every day to check on Meg. When he heard that she had left that morning for the villa, he was worried.

"Should she be alone, Betta?"

"I think she needs to be for awhile, Taylor. She's got a lot to work out in her mind."

"I'm just not sure she should be alone while she does it."

"You know Meg. There was no way I could get her to stay once her mind was made up."

"I know. Betta, I'm glad you were with her. You've been wonderful through all of this."

"She's my sister. I had to be there for her. I made her promise to check in with me everyday so I'll keep you posted."

"Thanks, Betta. I hope you know how much I love you?"

"I know, Taylor. Give Annie and Laura a kiss from me."

Too much at once. Everything was changing too fast. Both Laura and Taylor were feeling the tension.

Once they'd made sure that Meg and Betta were safe in Milan, Taylor and Laura had turned to the difficult task of telling her parents that they would be moving to New York in August.

Her parents had been supportive, of course, but it was breaking their hearts to lose Annie. None of them even wanted to think what the separation would do to Annie when the time came. For now, her grandparents were spending as much time as possible with her, saving up memories for the days to come.

It had been nearly a week since Sean had come back from Ireland. Taylor had been wrapped up in worry about Meg and guilt about their upcoming move. He wasn't sleeping well and Laura often went to bed without him only to wake and find him gone in the mornings.

On one of those sleepless nights, he'd rummaged around in the top of a closet looking for a box they'd stored there when they'd moved to New Mexico. He had found it when he took Meg back to close up and sell the Florida house she'd grown up in. When he'd realized what it contained, he'd called Laura and they had agreed that Meg was not ready yet for the contents. Someday she would want them—would want to know about her father—and, when that time came, Taylor would give it to her.

He carried it out to the patio and sat in the dark, his hands caressing the smooth wood of the box, and remembered that time that seemed so long ago.

It had only been a little over six months since Annie had died. With Betta's help, Meg was healing. The pain was still there below the surface but she was learning to go on. She'd been very enthusiastic about his marriage to Laura and welcomed her. Meg and Betta had stayed with Laura's parents while Taylor and Laura were on their Venetian honey-

mooned. When they came back to get the girls, Laura and Betta remained in Albuquerque to close up Laura's apartment, while Taylor and Meg went to Florida to close up and sell Annie's house and his condo. Then they were all going back to Italy to begin the work of forming a new family.

The house had been closed for more than six months by then. Sheets covered the furniture. The plants Annie had so lovingly attended were gone, the windows tightly shuttered. He and Meg had stood in the doorway, unsure what to do, where to begin. Finally, Taylor began to open the shutters and asked Meg to uncover the furniture. For the time they were there, he'd make it as much like home as possible.

It had been particularly hard for Meg. This was the only home she had ever known and she was packing away her memories. Remembering how he had felt when he had finally gone back to his own childhood home, Taylor gave her time alone there, time to remember—time to grieve.

He made sure that Meg had a chance to see and say good-bye to her friends. He arranged a luncheon for them at a nearby restaurant and sent a limo to pick up the girls. He deliberately did not attend, letting Meg act as hostess.

The night before they were to leave for Europe, Taylor and Meg hosted a dinner for the people who had been a part of their lives. Jane, Annie's assistant, had taken over the dance school and retained the Miller Dance Studio name. Susan, Meg's former babysitter, had gone to work for her. Jude MacMurray had stopped by to assure herself they were doing well. Her law firm would be handling the paperwork when the house and condo sold. David, best man at Taylor's wedding to Annie, was there, understanding now why Taylor had left Laura to marry Annie.

When it came time to leave the house for the last time, Taylor told Meg he'd wait for her outside. She'd wandered through the empty house and felt both the presence and absence of her mother in every room. Her face was tearstained as she came out of the house and pulled the door *shut behind her, shutting her childhood inside. She never looked back as they drove away, but she held on to Taylor's hand as tightly as she could.*

※ ※ ※

When she woke to find him gone again, Laura decided it was time for them to talk. She found him outside sitting on the patio in the pre-dawn coolness and shadow. Quietly she came out and sat beside him and wrapped her arms around him. She could feel his tension and understood why. Meg had been his since she was born, first as his goddaughter then his daughter when he married her mother.

He turned to pull her into his arms where he could rest his chin on her head. They sat in silence for a long while, drawing strength from their closeness until Laura said, "She's strong, Taylor, like her mother."

"Annie wasn't that strong, Laura. She just never let anyone see if something bothered her. I always knew that someday Meg want to know about him. I've saved this box of her mother's for her thinking that when the time came, I'd have it for her and I'd be there for her. She just wasn't supposed to find out this way…"

"But she knows now, so it's probably time to take her that box. You'll go to her?"

"How can I leave now with all that's happening with us?"

"I can handle things here. Megan needs *you* there."

He held her in silence then said, "What about you, Laura? What about what this must have brought up for you?"

"Cary ceased having the power to hurt me the day I bluffed him into signing away his rights to Meg. But I don't want her to know what he did to *me*. If she's so devastated over what he did to that boy's aunt, how will she feel if she finds out her father raped me, too? We can't add that to her burden."

"Secrets have a way of coming out, Laura. Look at how this one did. Can we risk not telling her the whole truth?"

Laura turned to face him. "No one will ever tell her. You and I, Beth and my lawyer, are the only ones who know. This secret will stay safe. But I think it's time for you to go to her and give her the rest of it. Then maybe she can get on with her life."

He nodded silently then pulled her close once again. They stayed wrapped in each other's arms as the sun climbed over the Sandia Mountains and the morning brought a new beginning.

CHAPTER 54

Meg woke with a feeling of peace. The villa always had that effect on her. There was a serenity about the old stones that seemed to seep into her soul whenever she came. Today, for the first time since that horrible day in Belfast, she felt like she might survive all of it. A few days here to get herself centered and she'd head home to New Mexico.

The first thing she was going to do was go for a swim. The tenants of the main house knew she was here and she had asked permission to use the pool. She'd always loved the water and swimming was the only form of exercise she could tolerate.

She swam for half-an-hour. By the time she was finished, the sun was up and the heat of the day was moving in. And she was starving. There were fresh eggs and fruit in the refrigerator and she hurried back to the guesthouse.

As she came around the curve of the path that separated the guesthouse from the main house, she was surprised to see someone sitting on her doorstep. The figure was in shadow and she cautiously slowed down as it began to move.

"Morning, Munchkin," Taylor said as he stepped into the light.

"Taylor!" Meg ran the few steps between them and threw herself in his arms. "Where did you come from? How? I can't believe you're here!"

Taylor laughed. "And I can't believe I'm standing here holding you while you're soaking wet."

She took a step back but he still held her hands. "How are you, Meg?"

"Let's not talk about it right now, Taylor. In a little while, I promise. Right now I just want to hear all the news from home."

She went to shower as Taylor cut up fruit and made omelets for them both. By the time she came back into the kitchen, breakfast was ready.

While they ate, Taylor filled her in on the news.

"Of course, home will be New York again," he said. "I've given the apartment tenants notice and they'll be out the first of August. I need to be there for rehearsals by the end of the month."

"And I'll be back in California by then. Maybe it's not too late to go to Med School in New York."

"Why, Meg? There are planes between New York and California all the time."

"I...I don't know, Taylor. A part of me really doesn't want to be that far away from family right now."

"Because of what happened in Belfast?"

"I don't know, Taylor. I'm still really confused by all that happened there."

"There's more, Meg. Your mother left a box for you. She wanted you to have it when the time came that you'd want to know more about him. I brought it with me."

Meg was silent. "I guess I should get all the bad news at once and get it out of the way. Maybe then I can get on with things." As Taylor started to stand she held out her hand to stop him. "This evening, Taylor. Right now, I just want to spend some time with you. Let's walk down to the village and see what's changed."

"You can't put this off forever, Meg."
"I know and I promise I'll look at it later. Please…"
"Let me change my shoes then we'll go."

❦   ❦   ❦

They had a wonderful morning together and renewed some old friendships with people they had known before. Mother Caterina was particularly glad to see them when they stopped by the Convent school that Meg and Betta had attended. She had to be caught up on all the news and was reluctant to let them go. "You were always one of the special ones, Megan, you and Betta. It was as if Heaven realized a mistake had been made in sending you to different families and gave you a new one where you could be sisters in more than your hearts."

The village was shutting down for the afternoon siesta by the time they started back to the villa. Taylor was beginning to feel a little jet-lagged and told her he was going to settle in for a nap when they got back.

The cool and quiet of the old stones welcomed them home. As Taylor started for his room, Meg said, "The box, Taylor. I might as well look at it now."

He didn't argue with her but went to his room and came back holding a cherry wood box. Meg remembered it being on her mother's dressing table. It had held her jewelry and Meg had always been allowed to play with the contents whenever she'd had to stay home sick. She smiled at the memory but her hands were shaking as she reached out to take it from Taylor. "Meg? Would you like me to stay with you?"

"No, Taylor. This is something I think I have to do on my own. I'll probably have questions later…will you answer them for me?"

"If I can." He walked to the door then turned back. "Meg…please remember your mother loved you with all her heart. And so do I."

He left her behind with the ghosts she would find, wishing that he could protect her from the past.

🍁 🍁 🍁

Meg sat back in the chair, her hands stroking the wood. Now that she had it, she wasn't sure she really wanted to open it. So many secrets. So many memories. So much she might not want to know. With trembling fingers she opened the box.

A ghostly scent she recognized was there for a moment, then gone—her mother's cologne—bringing Annie back to her. Meg felt the pain all over again of losing her mother long before either of them was ready for her to go.

On top of the contents in the box was a letter addressed to Meg in the handwriting she'd known so well. Beneath it she could see the edges of photographs and a glint of gold, but she set it all aside and opened the letter.

> My darling Megan—
>
> I knew the day would come that you would want answers about your father. Everything I know about him is in this box. It's not very much, I realize, but Cary was like that. I came to realize later that he was a chameleon, taking on the colors he wanted or needed at the time, but he never let me, or anyone else see anything real.
>
> We married in haste, Meg. I was hopelessly in love with him and thought he was perfect. He was gorgeous—his eyes that same fathomless blue as yours; his hair just as black as yours is. When he looked at me, I thought I'd died and gone to heaven. That Cary Edwards would look at me! He could have had his pick of girls. And there were a lot to choose from in our little world of the theatre, but he chose me. I was mesmerized by his style, his charm, and his good looks. I never saw that beyond the veneer he was hollow.

Oh, my Meg, I know this isn't what you wanted to hear! You wanted to hear he was wonderful and special and the prince you've always hoped he would be.

But he wasn't, Meg. I have to trust that you're old enough now to hear the truth. I found out later that he'd married me because I was available and presentable. His boss believed in family and marrying me was Cary's way of proving his worth. It didn't take me long to figure that out. It didn't take long for him to throw it at me in a rage—a rage that also allowed him to hit me. And it happened again and again. I was too proud to admit I'd made a terrible mistake, even to Taylor who knew what was happening and begged me to leave.

Then there was you. My wonderful miracle. I was so happy when I found out I was pregnant. I wanted you with all my heart. And I knew that Cary would have to come around; would have to be as happy as I was. But he wasn't.

His boss had fired him that day. When he came home, he'd managed to work it around that it was my fault. When I told him I was pregnant, he laughed, said he wasn't falling for that old trick. Once I'd convinced him it was true, he told me he didn't want me, didn't want a baby, and accused me of getting pregnant on purpose to trap him.

He beat me that night; tried to make me lose the sweet life I was carrying inside. I think he would have killed me but I managed to get away...and I ended up at Taylor's. I knew he'd take us in.

Taylor is the one who took me to the hospital; who stayed with me while they assured me you were safe. He took me home with him and made it *our* home while I waited for your arrival.

Cary came after me a few days later. He was drunk and more abusive than ever, but Taylor stood by us. He broke Cary's perfect nose and threw him out. Then helped me file for divorce and attended childbirth classes with me.

He was there when you were born, Meg, and he loved you from that first breath. He wanted me to stay and marry him but I didn't love him—not in the way he deserved, not enough to risk another marriage. I've often wondered if that decision was a mistake. Maybe I should have married him for all our sakes.

I never saw Cary again, Meg. He never tried to find us—not that I knew of, anyway. It was just another part he'd played and he moved on to the next.

When I got sick, Meg, we had to find him to get him to give up his rights to you so that Taylor could adopt you. He made a show of wanting to meet you; wanting to be a father—but it was all show, darling. He never cared. When it came to a choice between you and his career, the career won and he moved on again. The last I heard of him, he was a rising star on TNC reporting out of Ireland.

Meg, my sweet girl, I wish you were not reading this alone. I wish you'd never felt a need to know. But I knew you would, someday, and you had a right to know. So here's what little marked my marriage to Cary Edwards.

Meg, if you have some romantic fantasy about him, please believe me and what I've told you here. Don't try to find him. He'll only hurt you.

And, remember, I loved you. You were worth it all.

Mom

Meg silently folded the letter and slipped it back in the envelope. She closed her eyes and leaned against the back of the chair. Her mother had been so small, fine-boned and fragile. There was a picture in the box, a wedding picture of her parents. Her mother, young and beautiful, so obviously happy and in love, her gaze directed at her groom not the camera. Her father, young, handsome, tall and strong, staring at the camera with barely disguised disgust—far from the happy bridegroom. To imagine him striking her mother! Tears crept from beneath her lashes as she thought of the mother she'd only had for twelve years, her mother so full of laughter and fun and *love*. What kind of monster was he that he was able to hurt someone so fine?

In her heart, Meg had always cherished the illusion that her father had just been confused and young and afraid of the responsibility of a wife and a child. She'd always thought that someday she'd meet him and he'd see what he'd given up.

Meg leafed through the handful of pictures that remained in the box, pictures that told so little about who they had been, this dark man and his sunny bride. Their wedding license was there. Cary Edwards, no middle name. Anne Elizabeth Miller. Shadows of her past.

The final item in the box was a gold band. It had to have been her mother's wedding ring. Meg, marveling at the small size of it, slipped it on one finger after another until it finally fit the little finger of her left hand. She closed her eyes and let memories of her mother wash over her.

A soft knock at the doorway and the sound of Taylor's voice woke her. The shadows had lengthened into early evening while she had slept.

"Meg? May I come in?"

Closing the box, she said, "Of course, Taylor." Her eyes filled with tears as she saw the concern in his.

"Are you alright, Meg?" he said as her crossed the room. Kneeling in front of her, he took her icy hands in his. "Meg, I'm here. Tell me what I can do to help."

Taylor's love for her shone in his eyes and she threw her arms around him and broke into heartbroken sobs.

CHAPTER 55

When she had quieted, Taylor rose and handed her a box of tissue then brought her a glass of water.

"I'm sorry," she sniffled, her voice thick with tears.

"You've nothing to be sorry for."

"I know this is hard for you, too. You loved her…"

"I did love her, Meg, and wanted her to marry me. But she was wiser than I was and saw that it would never have worked out. She needed a security I couldn't give her."

"She thought *he* could?"

"I don't think she *thought* at all, Meg. She was in love with him and love has a tendency to obscure the truth sometimes."

"Was he…" She took a deep breath before she continued. "Was she right? Was he as awful as she said. Did he truly hurt her?"

"I'm sorry, Meg, it's true. Whatever his reasons were, he chose to use your mother as his target. She was too proud to admit it, to me or to anyone. That pride nearly cost her your life. But that was the price she refused to pay to him. She loved you from the moment she knew you were coming and she wasn't going to stand by and let anyone hurt you."

"Is there anything else? Where did he come from? Do I have another set of grandparents somewhere? Do I have cousins? Aunts? Uncles? Maybe I have siblings."

"I don't know. He never talked about where he was from. He told Laura once that his parents were dead and he had been an only child."

"Laura knew him?"

"Before we were married. He was a reporter in Albuquerque. She knew him then."

Taylor watched as she tried to process it all. "Meg, give yourself time to take this much in. Don't try to deal with it all at once."

Meg nodded slowly then replaced the pictures and the letter in the box, the ring still firmly on her finger. She closed it then stood and handed it to him. "Will you keep this for me, Taylor?" She leaned down and dropped a kiss on the top of his head. "Thanks…for everything."

❦   ❦   ❦

Meg and Taylor talked until late that night. He answered her questions—when he had the answers. They remembered Annie with laughter and with tears. Finally, the subject came around to Ireland and all that had happened there.

"I love him, Taylor. Jamie's everything I never even knew that I wanted."

"Betta and your grandfather seem to think he felt the same about you."

"I think he did, at least until the truth came out about my father."

"You never gave him a chance to tell you what he thought, Meg. You ran away."

"I couldn't bear to hear what he thought. I don't want to remember hateful words. I want to remember what we had for the fairy tale it was."

"Maybe his words would have been the ones you wanted to hear. You can't run away in case something will hurt. That's not giving yourself a chance."

"They're a close family. Jamie's father still carries a lot of hate and anger for what Cary did to his sister. If Jamie and I had gone on, where would I have fit in? How could I ever face Sister Sha'leen again? How could I force Jamie into the position of choosing between them and me? It was better this way. Fast and clean. He'll find someone else and I'll go back to school."

"And never give yourself a chance to love again?"

"Not a great track record in my family for love—except for you and Laura. I think I might have had a chance at that with Jamie…"

Her voice trailed off and Taylor pretended not to see the tears in her eyes even as his heart was breaking for her pain. Gruffly he cleared his throat and changed the subject. "I need to get back to Albuquerque soon, Meg. The move is coming up and I can't let Laura deal with all of it on her own. Are you going to stay on here for awhile?"

"No, I'd like to go home with you and help. Can we stop in Milan to spend a day with Betta first?"

"Great idea, Meg. Shall we call her in the morning and drive up tomorrow?"

"If we are, we'd better get some sleep. It's already after two."

"I'll wake you bright and early then."

Meg stood and glared at him. "Do not even think about it, Taylor! We can leave at ten."

Laughing, he stood up and gathered her into his arms. "How I ever came to be stuck with such a group of sleepyheads, I'll never know. Ten it is, then, Megan. But not a moment later!"

"Goodnight, Taylor." She hugged him hard then kissed his cheek. "I hope you know that in all the ways that matter, you have always been my father and I love you."

His eyes answered her, filling with tears as he said, "Goodnight, Munchkin. Sleep well."

She blew him a kiss as she left the room. He picked up the box she'd entrusted back to his care. He ran his hand lightly over the top then stepped outside to look into the night sky.

"Goodnight, Annie," he whispered to the stars. "I'll always love you."

A gentle breeze came up and caressed his cheek and he could have sworn he smelled the scent of her cologne. He was smiling as he went back in the house to a well-earned sleep.

CHAPTER 56

Meg surprised Taylor by being awake early the next morning. Together they went through and closed up the guesthouse. They had to caravan, both with their own rental cars, until they came to the first place they could turn one in. After that, they traveled together, arriving in Milan in the early afternoon. Betta had been thrilled that they were coming and had taken another afternoon off from the studio despite the fit that Fernando threw. She was waiting at her apartment when they arrived and leaned out the window to call down to them, "*Ciao!* Come on up!"

Even though it had been only a few weeks since Taylor and Betta had seen each other, she greeted him with an exuberant hug. "I'm so glad you're here!"

"So am I, Betta. The apartment looks wonderful…so do you!"

She poured them all a glass of wine and they sat down to talk.

Meg could see the questions in Betta's eyes and answered before she could even ask. "I'm alright, Betta. Taylor brought me some things my mother left for me. Cary Edwards was a loser from the first. I had a much better life without him."

"And Jamie?" Betta asked quietly.

"And Jamie will have a better life without me. That's over. I'm going home to help with the move back to New York…"

"Move?" Meg looked at Taylor. "You're moving back to New York?"

"Oops," Meg said, "I forgot you didn't know. Taylor only told me last night."

"All of this came up after you'd left for Ireland. We didn't want to spoil your trip so we saved the news for when you came home. What with all that's been happening, I never had a chance to tell you. I've been offered a role back on Broadway, Betta. I get to play the old guy instead of the young lover this time in the musical that gave me my start. We'll be going back the first part of August."

"That's big news, Taylor. How does Laura feel about it?"

"She says she's happy for me and ready to move but I think deep down it's breaking her heart. Your grandparents are trying to be upbeat about it but I know that it's horrible for them."

"And you're feeling guilty because you're excited about it," Meg said.

Taylor laughed. "I am. Excited *and* feeling guilty. It's the right thing for me to do now. And Annie will have so many more opportunities in New York. It will put Laura back in the center of the publishing world, too."

"You don't have to justify it to us, Taylor," Betta said.

"I'm not…yeah, I guess I am. I think the guilt's winning right now."

"Well cut it out," Meg said. "Betta, you'd better get to work on designing our dresses for the night he wins the Tony."

"Green for Laura, of course," Betta began to tick off on her fingers. "Blue for you again, Meg? I think I'll try burgundy this time."

"No, I think I'm ready to give up schoolgirl blue for a sexy black number," Meg said with a wicked grin. "Maybe one of those low cut things you have to glue on to keep from showing everything."

"Over my dead body," Taylor said with a raised eyebrow. "How about something with sashes and maryjanes and ribbons in your hair? The three of you sisters could dress alike." He put the wine glass down just in time to protect himself from the barrage of pillows they threw at him.

❦ ❦ ❦

Taylor called Laura while the girls got ready for dinner. It was morning in Albuquerque and he caught her as she was coming in from taking Annie to pre-school.

"Taylor! I'm so glad you called. I've been worrying."

"I'm sorry, darling, there was no time yesterday. Meg and I sat up most of the night talking."

"How is she?"

"Hurt and confused but ready to get on with her life. She's coming home with me."

"I'm glad. When?"

"I've made reservations for tomorrow evening. We're in Milan now. We drove up here today. This way we'll have another day with Betta before we leave."

"How is Betta?"

"I'm not sure. She was happy to see us. A little too happy maybe. I think there's something on her mind. I'll try to get her alone to talk sometime this evening."

"Then you'll be home on Wednesday."

"Late. Our flight's not due in 'til 11. We have a fairly long layover in New York. The producers are going to meet me there for a meeting since I'll have to hang around so long. Don't forget, I left the car at the airport so I'll drive us home. Don't wait up."

"Right, Taylor," Laura said with a decidedly unladylike snort. "Like I'm going to sleep with you due home."

"Hmm…then I guess I'll have to think of some way to make it worth your while."

"I'm counting on it, Taylor. I miss you."

"I love you, Laura. See you soon."

❦   ❦   ❦

Meg was the first to emerge from Betta's bedroom. "We're almost ready, Taylor."

"There's no hurry, Meg. But I did want to talk to you for a minute," he said quietly. "Is Betta alright? She acts like there's something on her mind."

"I think she is…and you're right. She asked me if I could give you two some time together later so I thought I'd come back here early after dinner and leave you two to talk. All very casual, of course," she said with a smile.

"Thanks, Meg. You don't mind?"

"How could I mind, Taylor? You came riding to my rescue and you might as well do two for one."

"Two for one what?" Betta asked as she came into the living room.

"Two beautiful girls and one old man." Taylor said.

"Uh-huh. Right. I don't know what makes those producers of yours think that you're going to convince anyone you're old, Taylor."

"Betta! Have you no faith in my acting ability?"

"Sure I do. That's why no young guy, no matter how handsome and charming, is going to be able to hold a candle to you and this show will be yours the same way it was the first time around. Now let's go to dinner. I'm starving!!"

CHAPTER 57

More than one person took a moment to smile at the three of them as they sat at the sidewalk café. With no time schedule, they were enjoying the evening, the food, the wine, and especially the company. A few of Betta's friends happened by and she introduced them but the evening was for father and daughters. Something they hadn't had in a long time.

After dessert and coffee, Meg pleaded exhaustion and said she'd go back to the apartment. "Taylor made me get up at the crack of dawn this morning. I need to catch up. You two had better be quiet when you come in if you know what's good for you."

They watched as she headed down the street to the apartment only half a block away. Taylor signaled the waiter. "More coffee, please. Betta?"

"Maybe another glass of wine, Antonio." She waited until he was out of earshot then told Taylor, "Antonio thinks he's an actor. He's not." She quickly suppressed a giggle as he returned with their drinks then finally got up enough courage to ask Taylor for an autograph.

When Antonio was gone, after profusely thanking and praising him, Taylor grinned at Betta. "There but for the grace of God…"

"What?"

"I could have been a poor waiter somewhere. It's mostly a matter of luck."

"Luck and talent, Taylor. You've had both but without the talent, all the luck in the world wouldn't help."

"What about you, Betta?"

"I'm fine, Taylor. I know I've got the talent and I've decided it's time for a little try at luck. I asked Meg to go on home early so we could talk," she confessed.

"So did I."

"Why?"

"I know my daughters. I could see there was something on your mind. Good or bad?"

"Good, I hope." She paused to take a sip of her wine and followed it with a deep breath. "I think I'm ready to leave Milan, Taylor. I want to go back to New York."

"But things have been going well for you here in your apprenticeship."

"Too well, Taylor. I'm past needing a mentor. I'm ready to try striking out on my own. I've been thinking about it a lot and I want to go back to New York and open a boutique. Knowing that my family will be there is just the icing on the cake," she said as she reached out to squeeze his hand before she rushed on. "It doesn't have to be a big place. I'd like to have my designs of course and those of a few others, almost a gallery for clothes as art, if that makes any sense."

Taylor nodded but didn't interrupt her. He was enjoying seeing his usually quiet Betta stirred up about something.

"And I want to make a specialty of wedding gowns, Taylor. I've designed some and people have raved over them. I want people to think of one of my gowns on the same level as one by Vera Wang."

"How can we help, Betta?"

"I have the money that Rosina and Matteo put in trust for me when my parents died. That's about half of what I would need for start-up capital."

"You still have a pretty good chunk left in your college fund, too," he reminded her.

"I was hoping you'd say that. With those two, I'd have the capital I'd need for everything except a place to open. I was hoping you'd co-sign a loan to help me pay the first year's rent on a place in Soho."

"Why not your own building, Betta? It makes more sense than paying rent."

"I'd never be able to afford that...not at first, Taylor."

"Then what about a partner? A silent partner? Laura and I could buy the building as our buy-in to the company."

Her eyes widened. "You would do that for me, Taylor?"

"Betta, you're our daughter and we'll do anything to help make your dreams come through. We'll expect a return once the profits start coming in, of course. And I think it's going to be as good as and probably a cheaper investment than Meg's medical school tuition."

Betta stood up and came around the table to put her arms around him. "I don't know what I did to deserve a second family as wonderful as my first. But I'm so grateful for all you've done for me. I love you, Taylor."

"I love you, too, Betta. I have from that first morning I came downstairs to find you and Megan giggling over something. I knew then that you were a part of me."

Wiping tears away, Betta returned to her chair as Taylor asked, "Tell me more about what you have in mind."

"First, Taylor, I want to call the store *Morganna's* and my line of clothing, *Elizabetta*." She went on to tell him all of her plans and they talked until the sidewalk café closed and they were gently reminded it was time to leave. They walked back to her apartment arm in arm still lost in the plans they were discussing, enthusiastically building castles in the air.

※ ※ ※

Meg heard their voices as they came in and Betta's gentle laugh before she called a quiet good night to Taylor. She sat up as Betta came into the room.

"So, I gather the talk went well? When do I get to hear what's going on?"

"Oh, Meg, I am so happy! I'll be home in New York shortly after the family moves back. I'm going to open my own place, with Taylor and Laura's help."

"Betta! That's wonderful. Tell me about it."

※ ※ ※

Taylor tried to make himself comfortable on the sofa in the living room. He could have stayed in a hotel but didn't want to miss a minute of time with his girls. He could hear them talking in the bedroom even after the light went off.

Betta would be coming back to New York. Maybe…just maybe, Meg's idea of med school in New York was not such a bad idea after all.

Smiling, he found a semi-comfortable place and fell asleep to the murmur of their excited voices.

CHAPTER 58

The lights were on as Taylor pulled the car into the driveway. It had been a long trip. First the day with Betta, then the flight to New York. Taylor had met with his producers while Meg had napped on a couch in the VIP lounge. Then the flight home…wherever Laura was, that was his true home. He knew that.

He had so much to tell her. His heart lifted as he saw her silhouetted in the doorway. "Go on, Meg. I'll get the luggage."

She didn't have to be told twice and was out of the car in an instant, running up the steps and into Laura's outstretched arms.

By the time he made it to the door with the luggage, they were gone. He could hear their voices down the hall in the guest room and he left Meg's bags outside the door. A second trip brought in his own luggage and he deposited it in their bedroom.

He was standing in Annie's doorway watching her sleep when Laura came up beside him. He draped his arm around her and pulled her close as they stood silently watching their third daughter safely asleep before they turned to go down the hall to their bedroom.

He closed the door behind them then kissed her, a gentle kiss quickly turned ardent. He broke away and leaned his head against her hair. "God, I've missed you, Laura."

"I've missed you, too, Taylor. Come to bed and let me show you just how much. The news will wait until morning." He followed willingly...home again.

CHAPTER 59

Taylor stood on the balcony of their New York apartment. After almost five years in New Mexico, the city he looked at was crowded and noisy. The sweeping view lifted his spirit, as always, even with the emptiness where the towers had once dominated. He felt his heart and head responding to the ever-present beat of the city and knew that he'd come home at last.

Taylor felt Laura put her arms around him and lean her head against his shoulder. "What are you thinking, Taylor?"

He turned to take her in his arms. "Just resting a minute before I go tackle more boxes."

"Liar. You're out here because you're enjoying being home."

"How can I tell you that when I've just ripped you from your home? I know what a sacrifice this move was for you."

Laura shook her head, kissed him, then said, "Taylor, don't you know by now that my home is wherever *you* are? It's true that 'home is where the heart is'. My heart is always with you."

"How did I ever get so lucky to marry you?"

"Obviously, you did something very bad in a previous life."

"No, it was something good."

The sounds of giggling and delighted shrieks reached them before Annie tore out of the doorway and hid behind her father. "Help me, Daddy!" she cried as Meg came out the door after her.

He scooped her up and said, "Why Princess Annie, what is this creature chasing you?"

"It's Megan! Megan the…the…" Annie thought hard to find something horrible enough to name her sister. "Megan the Monster! She's after me, Daddy! Save me!" she shrieked in his ear as she wrapped her arms tightly around his neck.

"A monster am I, Annie?"

"Must be," Taylor answered. "The Princess says you are, so you must be."

"Too bad. I was going to take Her Highness for ice cream but she wouldn't want to go with a monster like me. I guess I'll have to go by myself."

"Wait! You're not a monster." Annie wiggled out of her father's arms and ran to hug her sister. "I'm sorry, Meg. You're not a monster. I love you!" she said as she held her arms out to be picked up.

"Sure, I'm not a monster now that I mentioned ice cream." Meg said as she kissed Annie's cheek.

"I don't know, Annie. Maybe it's a trick. I'd better come along to protect you."

"Right, Taylor," Meg said. "The ice cream's no attraction to you at all, is it?"

"Me? Never touch the stuff unless I'm alone or with somebody. Want to come along, Laura?"

Laura laughed at them. "No, I think I'll stay here and enjoy a little peaceful. But you can bring me back a scoop if you'd like."

"Annie, what flavor shall we bring Mommy?" Meg asked.

"Chocolate!" Annie shouted. "Mommy loves chocolate!"

"Almost as much as I love you, little one. Have fun."

Laura watched as they went out the door then went back down the hall to their bedroom. So much unpacking still to do but at least this room was done. The whole apartment was freshly painted, arranged by phone ahead of their move with the building manager. Meg had volunteered to fly back from New Mexico early to make sure Annie's room was ready. It had been so hard for Annie to adjust to the idea of the move. All she'd ever known was New Mexico and the ready presence of her beloved grandparents. Having her room ready and waiting had been a help in the transition and now, almost two weeks later, she seemed to have settled in.

Copper and Penny raced into the room as fast as their little legs could carry them. The miniature dachshund siblings had been a gift for Annie's fourth birthday. Taylor's idea, but they had all grown to love the mischievous pair. "Hello, guys," Laura said as she leaned down to rub their ears. "At least you seem to have adjusted."

Meg was another matter. Ever since she'd returned from Ireland, she'd been more subdued than usual and had spent a lot of time on her own. What had happened there was weighing heavily on her and no one could help. She'd have to make her own peace about Jamie.

Looking out the window at the city below, Laura was overwhelmed with a wave of homesickness. It didn't matter that she was a grown woman with children of her own, she missed her mother and father desperately. Tears came to her eyes and, rather than holding them back, she picked up a box of tissue and allowed herself to cry the hurt out.

Taylor was pleased to be out in the bustle of New York. He still had a talent for being invisible in public and still loved the vibrant sidewalk parade. Unless people were expecting to see "Taylor Morgan", all they saw was a father out with his daughters.

Annie seemed to find the city as stimulating as he did. She chattered about the cars and had developed a love of taxis. She waved at every one that passed and, usually, got a wave in return. Even the most curmudgeonly taxi driver found it hard to resist the happy little girl with the halo of red curls.

As they went into the ice cream store and began the decision making process, they didn't notice the blonde woman who came in behind them. Since Annie was weighing her choices, the clerk helped the woman first. She took a seat in the corner where she could still see Taylor and his daughters. Her ice cream melted as she concentrated on the man who never left her thoughts.

🍁 🍁 🍁

The phone rang and Laura took a few deep breaths to clear her head before she answered.

"Hello."

"Hi, Laura. It's me."

"Hi, Beth."

"What's wrong? You've been crying. I can hear it in your voice."

"Sometimes it's a real pain to have a friend who knows you so well."

"So give. What's the matter?"

"Nothing. Everything. Taylor and the girls are gone for a little bit so I was indulging myself in a good cry. I'm homesick."

"I miss you, too, Laura. I got used to having you just a couple of hours away."

"I know. Me, too. It was great being able to see you every couple of weeks. How's Jason? And the boys?"

"Jason's wonderful as usual. He's working on a new series of sculptures using the boys as models. You'll love them. The boys are their usual terrible selves. I can't believe they'll be starting full-day school this fall! But I think the kindergarten teacher is relieved to have them moving on," she said with an indulgent laugh. Her twins, *Tomás* and Taylor, were high-spirited boys, full of mischief but impossible not to love instantly. "They miss Annie and want to know when we can come and see you. They don't seem to get the concept that New York is much further away than Albuquerque."

"Annie, too. She wants to know when they'll be coming for a visit. Soon, I hope?"

"We'll try, Laura. It will be harder now. We have to be here in the summer for the tourists. And with the boys starting school in the fall, there's not a lot of open time there."

"I know, Beth. Just wishful thinking on my part. I'll try to come out before Annie starts school but it will depend on how things are going here."

"How's Meg?"

"Still not her usual self but I think she'll be ok. I have the feeling that she's going to want to have a talk with us soon but I don't know for sure what she's thinking. This boy in Ireland meant a lot to her. I'm certainly not in a position to tell her that love at first sight isn't real. Besides me and Taylor, there's Mom and Dad."

"Whatever she's thinking, it will be right for her. Meg has always been practical."

Laura heard the door open and the sound of her laughing daughter coming down the hall, as she was welcomed with hysterical barking from the dogs. "They're back, Beth. Want to say hi to Annie?"

"Sure. And I'll talk to you soon. Love you."

"Thanks. Love you, too." She held out the phone to Annie. "Want to talk to Auntie Beth?"

Annie plopped down on the floor and took the phone. As she began an earnest conversation, Taylor came through the door carrying a container of ice cream. "Chocolate fudge this time, Laura." He stopped as she came over to take it from him, "Tears?" he asked as he ran his hand gently over her cheek.

"Just a little homesick. I'm fine. Beth called and I talked it all out with her."

He drew her into an embrace and whispered in her ear, "I'm sorry, my love." Stepping back he said, "Let's go out for a grown-up dinner tonight. By the time we get home, maybe there will be an opportunity to make you feel more at home." He smiled at her and she fell in love all over again. "Eat your ice-cream before it melts. I'll go let Rosina know that we'll be out this evening."

CHAPTER 60

The next night, after Annie had been safely tucked into bed, Meg knocked at their open bedroom door. Taylor looked up from the script he was studying as he lay propped up against the headboard of the bed. "Hi, Meg. Come in."

Laura turned away from her computer to smile at her daughter. "At last. Human companionship. Taylor seems to think that script is more important than talking to me!"

Meg hesitated. "If you're busy, Taylor, I can…"

"Never too busy for you, Meg. You know that. Come sit here and tell us what's been bothering you."

"That obvious?" she said as she sat on the bed where she could see both of them. "I thought I'd been hiding it pretty well."

"You have, except from your nosy parents," Laura said.

"Then I guess it's time to talk," she said. "Please hear me out before you say anything. I've decided to put off medical school." She raised her hand as Taylor opened his mouth to protest. "No, Taylor, wait. Let me explain."

"What happened in Ireland has hit me harder than anything since my mother died. It's brought up a lot of feelings of grief and loss and I'm not doing well dealing with it. I've found a counselor here and am going to be seeing her once a week. It's not something that I can solve in a few weeks and I can't handle med school on top of it."

"I talked to Stanford and I've received a year's deferment for entering. I'll be part of next year's class if I still want to go. And I've talked to Betta. She'll be home in a few weeks to start building *Morganna's*. She's hired me to be her assistant. I'll deal with the contractors and remodeling while she works on the merchandise end of things."

"Please believe I've given this a lot of thought. Maybe too much," she said as her eyes brimmed with tears. "I just need to get myself together before I can even think of going back to school."

"Oh, Meg," Laura said as she came over and hugged the now sobbing girl. Taylor sat up and held them both until Meg quit crying. He released her and lifted her chin to look into her eyes.

"Meg, whatever you chose to do is fine with us. You have to do what's best for you no matter what other people expect. We're here to support you in whatever way we can."

"I knew that. I don't know why I was so worried that you would be upset with me."

"Meg, we could never be upset with you over such an important decision," Laura said. "Now that you've made it, we need to know what we can do to help."

"I need to stay here for awhile longer. At least 'til Betta gets back and we find someplace to live. Poor Betta's never going to get rid of me as a roommate."

"This is your home, Meg, for as long as you need it. Even if you leave to go live with your sister, this is still your home, yours and Betta's. The door is always open to you and you never have to ask permission to be here." Taylor held her hands. His eyes could see the woman she'd become but his heart was remembering the little girl he'd had to tell that her mother would never be getting better. "You're our daughter, Meg, and we love you."

"Thanks, Taylor. Your love and support—and yours, Laura—have been the only thing holding me together."

"Then I guess you're 'stuck' with us," Taylor said grinning at his pun as they both groaned. Beneath the smile, his heart was breaking because he knew this was a journey she'd be making on her own. All he could do was stand by to help if she needed him. It wasn't enough but it would have to do for now.

CHAPTER 61

The directors had narrowed it down to two actresses, both unknowns, to play the part of the young wife in the new production. They wanted Taylor to read with her before they decided. Both had worked well with the actor playing the part of the young lover so Taylor was to be a tiebreaker.

He hadn't met either actress beforehand. It was to be a cold reading strictly to see how they would fit with Taylor. The first callback was a dark-haired young woman who looked the part and read well with Taylor. There was enough chemistry between them to work with.

With that reading over, Taylor thanked her for coming and said they'd be in touch soon. Rehearsals would be starting next week.

There was a half-hour between readings. Taylor spent the time studying his script, trying to get a feel for his character. When they called him for the second reading, he went out on stage to see the second candidate.

"Hello, Taylor," she said in a silky voice. "Long time, no see."

"Allison."

"You said I had talent and I guess the producers and director agree."

"I won't work with you, Allison, so this reading is over."

"Don't do it, Taylor. You're a professional. We can work together. A little ice between the husband and wife will be useful."

"Not the way I see it. I have casting approval. And I will not work with you after your performance in Albuquerque."

"I'll go to the Union. And to the tabloids."

"Go ahead, Allison. You'll only be hurting yourself. I have a witness, remember?"

With that he turned and walked to the front of the stage. "I won't work with this woman," he announced to the stunned director who had been watching. "Let's go with the other one." He left the stage and returned to his dressing room, slamming the door behind him.

Allison stood frozen on the stage until the director said, "That's it for now. We'll let you know in the next few days. Thanks for coming."

She left the stage without a word. Taylor *would* pay for this. He hadn't seen the last of her yet.

CHAPTER 62

❁

"So what do you think, Betta?" Taylor had taken on the task of finding space for Betta's dream—the designer clothing store to be called *Morganna's*. He'd only had a couple of weeks before rehearsals started but Meg had helped scout out possible sites. Then Taylor would look at them in the mornings before he left for the theatre. It had been hectic but they'd been successful. At least he hoped it was successful. Today was Betta's first look at the building.

Betta turned slowly in a circle looking at the first floor. Located in Soho, it was an older building with three stories, just as she'd hoped. The first floor had polished wooden floors and huge windows to let in the light. It would be perfect for the trendy, designer clothes she'd feature.

"So far, so good, Taylor. What about the second floor?"

"One of the things I liked about this place was that it actually has an elevator. The building was a garment factory so it had to be big enough for clothing racks…which will allow a wheelchair and ADA approval." He pulled back the decorative metal grating that covered the door to reveal the industrial gray elevator. Betta immediately made a note that it would have to be wood-paneled and carpeted. The transition from everyday to the magic she had planned for the second floor would start here.

As they stepped off the elevator onto the second floor, Betta gasped. Floor to ceiling windows covered the front of the room and flooded it with light. She could see how the crisp white wedding dresses she had designed would capture and reflect the light. The hardwood floor would have to be covered with deep carpet but that couldn't be helped. The mood upstairs was to be elegant not modest, a place where dreams came true.

"It's perfect, Taylor!" Betta turned around and smiled at him. "It's everything I dreamed of."

Taylor felt a wave of relief. He had been fairly sure she'd like it but there was always a chance…the building, and he, had passed the test. "You still have to see the third floor. After all, you'll be living in it."

"It could be a dump and I wouldn't care. This room is…Taylor, I might as well have designed it."

"Still, you should look at the living area. If that meets with your approval, too, we can close on the purchase of the building by the end of the month."

Betta took one more look around what would become her Bridal Salon. Perfect. Absolutely perfect.

"Betta?" She turned to find Taylor holding open the door to the elevator.

"I'm coming, Taylor. But there's nothing up there that could possibly talk me out of this building."

The third floor had only the rudimentary necessities of living. A small bathroom was sectioned off in one corner. A kitchen in another. Other than that it was open space. She could instantly see how she could add walls for bedrooms but preserve the majority of the space for casual living. "Did Meg like it?"

"She said you'd know exactly what to do with it."

"She's right. I do. How did you know this was the right place?"

"Well, Meg found it first but I knew right away it was what you were looking for. The location's good. The building is sound—I had an inspector check it out. All it needs is the Betta touch and it will be *the* place to see and be seen."

"Thank you, Taylor. How can I ever thank you enough?"

"I have all the thanks I need in that glow on your face. I have to run to rehearsal now. Here's the key. It's yours, so you can stay as long as you like." He put his hands on her shoulders and kissed her cheek. "I'm so proud of you. Enjoy your dreaming, Betta, but try to come home in time for dinner, okay?"

"*Sí*, Taylor." He could see she had already drifted off to the visions that claimed her attention right now.

"Have fun," he said as he entered the elevator. She never heard him but he didn't mind. He stepped out onto the sidewalk and locked the door behind him. Looking back at the building he imagined what it would look like with color in the windows. Then he turned and hailed a passing taxi. Time to pursue his own dreams.

She watched from the doorway across the street, a scarf covering her blonde hair and dark glasses hiding her face. She had no idea what Taylor had to do with this building but she didn't really care. The key to Taylor's heart was Annie. That's where she had to start.

Chapter 63

Betta made it home for dinner but only because Meg came to find her. She'd been lost in doing sketches of how the rooms would appear when the door buzzer startled her out of her planning. It took a few minutes to find the intercom before she answered.

"Yes?"

"What took you so long?"

"Meg! Come on in." She pushed the button to release the door then ran down the stairs to meet Megan.

"Taylor suggested I might want to check on you and remind you that it's getting dark and the electricity is not on yet."

"I had lost track of time but I've been having so much fun. Look at these sketches."

The two young women looked at the drawings while Betta clarified where each would actually be. Megan was caught up in the dreaming and it wasn't until they both realized they could barely see anymore that they noticed how much time had passed.

"Yipes! Laura will be frantic if we don't check in soon."

"You call her on your cell," Betta said. "I'll use mine to call for a taxi."

* * *

As they waited inside the door for the taxi to arrive, Betta turned for one last look. Even in shadow, the room was perfect and she could see how it would gleam. Track lighting down here…could she dare to dream of a chandelier for the salon?

"Hello?" Betta turned to find Meg smiling at her. "Where were you?"

"I was thinking about the lighting. Oh, Meg, I just love this place. I feel like I've come home."

"You have. I'm looking forward to being part of this."

"I'm so glad you're staying. I mean…I don't want you to give up on medical school but I'm still glad you're here."

"I'm not giving up. Just postponing."

"How are things, Meg? Is the counselor helping?"

"I think so, but there's a long way to go. She asks questions that I find hard to answer sometimes."

They were interrupted when the taxi honked outside. Meg showed Betta how to set the alarm system then they left for home. Betta couldn't resist turning and looking back as long as she could see the building. It was hers. Soon *Morganna's* would be real.

Taylor didn't have rehearsals in the evenings so he was home for dinner and anxious to hear what Betta had been doing all day.

"After dinner, Taylor," Betta said. "We can talk during dinner then I'll show you the sketches afterwards. Right now, I'm starving! I never even thought to eat lunch."

"Betta!" Annie exclaimed. "Tomorrow I'll ask Rosina to make you a peanut butter and jelly sandwich. She uses grape jelly and it's really good!"

"Thank you, *bambina*. It sounds delicious and I appreciate you taking care of me."

Annie fisted up her hands and placed them on her hips. "Well, *someone* has to," she said sternly, sounding just like her mother. She didn't understand why everyone laughed but she laughed with them anyway. She was always happiest when she made people laugh.

"Let's go eat, Annie." Meg said, still giggling.

"Eat Annie? What a wonderful idea!" Taylor growled as he scooped his youngest daughter up and carried her to the dining room. "What kind of sauce shall we use?"

It was good to be home, Betta thought as she looked around the table. Her Aunt Rosina and Uncle Matteo had been wonderful to her after her parents' deaths and they'd understood when she decided that she wanted to be adopted by Taylor and Laura. It wasn't that she loved them any less but she had been a member of the Morgan family from the beginning and it was nice to take the name.

"Betta has the most wonderful ideas for *Morganna's*," Meg was saying. "We were looking at some of the sketches and they're great."

"Tell us some of the details, Betta," Laura said as she helped Annie wipe her hands.

"Laura, it's a wonderful building. Exactly what I wanted. Taylor and Meg must have read my mind. I want to use the natural lighting as much as possible, all those wonderful windows! But I thought track lighting for the first floor, keeping the hardwood floors. I want it to be inviting, vibrant, friendly…maybe a small coffee area in one corner for customers."

"That sounds perfect. What about the salon? I'm really curious about what you plan there."

"The hardwood has to be covered with carpeting. Plush, extra thick. Pale gray like a dove, I think. If I can find one I can afford, I'd love to have a crystal chandelier. It would reflect the sun during the day and fill the room with rainbows. I won't have music on the first floor, or if I do, it will be very quiet, but in the salon, it will be strictly classical and instrumental. A lot of Yo-Yo Ma and Llewellyn. The wedding dresses will be displayed on dressmaker's dummies; the walls will be light, maybe a pale, pale yellow to reflect the sunshine. It will be a place that inspires dreams."

"Wonderful, Betta. I can almost see it. Would you let me do a photo essay about the building of your dream? I'm sure I could sell it to one of the magazines, maybe even the *New York Times*. It would be wonderful publicity for you."

"Really, Laura? I'd be thrilled to have you do an article about *Morganna's*. Will you do the photography?"

"No, I think I'll ask my friend Christopher to do it. He's a wonder with light. I could have him drop by every day in between other jobs so he'd get a variety of pictures."

"*Grazi*, Laura. I'm overwhelmed."

"We'll work on the details. Right now, there's a certain young miss who needs her bath before bed."

"Betta! Come give me my bath, please?"

"If you promise not to splash and to let me play with the rubber ducky."

"Sure. Come on!"

She ran out the door with Betta following her. "I have some lovely soap from Italy, Annie. Let me get it and you will smell like a garden!"

Meg excused herself to go help, leaving the older generation at the table.

"She is so happy, Taylor," Rosina said. "You've done a wonderful thing."

"Not me. All I did was find a building. The rest is up to her."

"*Morganna's* will be a great success. She's going to be a famous designer," Matteo said with pride. No one disagreed.

CHAPTER 64

Betta's hands trembled as she signed the last set of papers. With that signature she was in debt for probably the rest of her life but the building was hers! *Morganna's* was going to be real. Crystal, the closer for the mortgage company, shook Betta's hand. "It sounds like such a wonderful project, Ms. Morgan. I hope you'll send me an invitation to the opening. I can't wait to see it."

"I will. Right now, we're aiming for the beginning of November so we're open in time for Christmas. I'm not sure we'll make it."

Taylor heard the edge of panic in her voice. "You'll make it, Betta. Everyone's ready to help." She smiled at him. Without Taylor's help, this wouldn't be happening. He'd put up a large amount of investment money for the store – a silent partner but she wanted to make sure he got back every penny he put in.

"Shall we go see if it's still there, now that you own it, Ms. Morgan?" Taylor asked with a teasing smile. They said their goodbyes and hurried out of the building.

As their cab pulled up in front of the building, Betta was overwhelmed by a sense of panic. She sat frozen in place, her hand on the handle of the car door, staring at the building. "*Dios Mio*," she whispered. "Taylor, what have I done? What if it doesn't work?"

Taylor got out of the cab and came around and opened the door and helped her out. "I remember feeling the same way when the plane was about to land in New York when I first came here. Maybe my parents had been right. Maybe I should have gone to school. I was never more scared in my life. But I knew in my heart it was the right thing to do. I think you know the same thing in your heart, Betta." He gave her a hug then said, "Let's go see your new home."

Taylor stood back and let Betta open the door. As she stepped through she was greeted with cries of "Surprise" and "Congratulations". They were all there. All of her family and friends. Even her beloved grandparents from New Mexico were there. And Aunt Beth, too! The tears she'd been holding back finally overwhelmed her when she saw the banner they were holding. "*Morganna's* – When You Want To Be Noticed!"

Meg was beside her with her arm around Betta's shoulders as Betta tried to speak. "*Grazi, grazi*! I don't know what to say. It's been an incredible day and I've been feeling a little overwhelmed and lonely—so much resting on my shoulders. But finding you all here, I realize I'm not alone at all. *Morganna's* will be fine as long as I have such wonderful friends and family."

A cheer was raised and someone put a glass of champagne in her hand. Raising his own glass, Taylor said, "To Elizabetta Morgan and *Morganna's*. New York isn't going to know what hit it!"

"To Betta!"

Two of the young men from the crew that had been doing some of the preliminary work on the building disappeared up the stairs. A few minutes later they called down, "Ready!" and everyone ushered Betta out the door.

"Close your eyes, Betta, no peeking!" Annie ordered as she took Betta's hand to guide her. She could hear whispers around her and someone turned her around so that she was facing the building. "Okay," Annie said, "You can look now."

She hadn't noticed the white sheeting that had hung from the second floor windows when they had arrived. It was gone now and in its place, raised, gold, calligraphic lettering flowed just under the second floor windows—*Morganna's*. It was her sign, the sign she'd designed. She smiled with delight. It was exactly as she'd seen it in her mind and translated to paper. Exactly—only better!

She turned to find Taylor and Laura standing behind her. "Oh, how…"

"We stole your design and had it made," Laura said with a smile. "A housewarming present. I hope it's right."

"It's perfect! Thank you!"

Betta became aware of a photographer recording the moment. When he put his camera down, Laura beckoned him over. "This is Christopher, Betta. He'll be keeping the photo log of your progress for my article."

"It's nice to meet you, Christopher," Betta said as she shook his hand. She registered that he was almost as tall as Taylor and quite good-looking – dark hair, eyes the color of amber. He actually distracted her from the excitement of the moment as she felt a reaction she'd never felt for *anyone* before.

"Nice to be part of this, Ms. Morgan. Looks like it's going to be pretty posh."

"Betta—please call me Betta. It's so much easier than Ms. Morgan."

"Betta it is, then. And only your mother calls me Christopher. Make it Chris, please."

"Come back inside, Betta," Meg said. "You, too, Chris. We have food and more champagne."

As the two young women turned away, Meg whispered to Betta. "He is gorgeous, Betta. I'll give you first dibs but if you don't make a move quick enough, I may snatch him up!"

"Megan! He's a friend of Laura's. She sent him to take pictures not to romance one of her daughters."

Meg stopped and looked at her, "Are you sure, Betta?" she asked with a wicked grin.

"She wouldn't!" Betta exclaimed, her eyes widening at the idea.

"You've been away from home way too long! C'mon. We've got some celebrating to do."

CHAPTER 65

"Morning, Laura."

Laura looked up from the paper. "You're up early, Meg."

"I know. And it's not fair since I have today off."

"Isn't that the way it always goes?"

Meg poured a glass of juice then sat down at the table.

"So what are you going to do with the day?" Laura asked.

"I have a couple of errands to run this morning, then I thought I might take Annie to the zoo."

"She'd love that, Meg. But you must have more exciting things to do than baby-sit your little sister."

"Not one. Babysitting Annie is about as exciting as it gets."

"That's not good, Meg. You need to start getting out again."

"That's what my counselor says, too. But I'm not really interested, Laura."

"It's none of my business but did you ever try to contact Jamie?"

Meg stared silently into her glass for a moment then lifted her head to look at Laura. "I did—once. The letter came back unopened."

"I'm sorry, Meg."

"Me, too. But life goes on. And today I choose to spend it with my little sister. Has she got anything to get in the way?"

"She has dance class at ten but then she's free the rest of the day."

"I'll pick her up from there if that's ok."

"It would be great. Matteo can drive you."

"I thought we'd take a cab. You know how crazy she is about them."

"I know and I'm hoping she outgrows it before she has to choose a career. I never imagined any of my daughters being cabbies."

"Not to worry. Annie is destined for the stage."

"Taylor been brainwashing you?"

"No. You just have to watch her. She's going to light up a theatre someday."

"Am I being replaced?" Taylor asked as he walked in the door. He gave Laura a lingering kiss then dropped a quick one on Meg's head before he took a glass of juice and joined them.

Meg grinned, "Honestly! You two. Don't you know you're too old to be behaving that way?"

"What way?" Taylor asked, playing innocent.

"As if you can't wait for me to get out of the room so you can be all over each other."

"Hmm, not a bad idea. So, when *are* you leaving, Meg?"

"Never. I'm going to be around and in your way forever."

"We'll manage somehow. Now, who's this new gift to the theatre?"

"Meg thinks Annie is destined for a theatre career. I think she's going to be a cabbie."

"Meg's thoughts make a lot of sense," Taylor said, "but I've got to agree with you, Laura. I've already repainted her room yellow. The next thing will probably be a checkerboard floor!"

"You laugh," Meg countered, "but you'll see."

The person in question came into the room and ran and threw her arms around her father. "Daddy!"

Taylor scooped her up and kissed her. "Pretty fancy this morning, Miss Annie."

"I have dance class, Daddy. These are just my leotards. We don't get to wear the tutus until recital."

"Okay, I understand now. What's up after dance class?"

"I wondered if Annie would like to go to the zoo with me?"

Annie's eyes lit up. "The zoo? Will we see the butterflies?"

"We will."

"Oh, Mommy, can I? Can I go to the zoo with Meg?"

"I think that would be alright. As long as you promise to stay right with her and not wander off."

"I promise!"

"Then I'll pick you up at class, Annie. After breakfast, we'll find some zoo clothes for you to change into."

"Hooray! Butterflies!" Annie shouted as she jumped down from her father's lap and ran to her own chair. "Butterflies, butterflies, butterflies!"

CHAPTER 66

Laura glanced at her watch as she waited for the elevator to their apartment. She'd cut her last appointment short hoping to get home in time to spend a little quality time with Taylor before he went to the theatre. Since Meg had promised to pick up Annie after her dance lesson and take her to the zoo, Laura didn't have to feel guilty about engineering this time without child or work. Annie would have a wonderful time with Meg—while her parents, with any sort of luck, would have a wonderful time *without* her.

As soon as she stepped off the elevator she could hear the "dog-bells" start up—Copper and Penny made it their job to announce every visitor. So much for a surprise arrival, she thought, as she used her key to open the door. "Hush, you two! No barking." Copper stood there hoping for a biscuit while Penny rolled over hoping for a tummy rub. They were both disappointed. As Laura dropped her purse and briefcase onto the chair inside the door and she headed for the bedroom. Without the dogs barking, the apartment was quiet and, for a moment, she felt a keen disappointment of a lost opportunity. Then she realized that she could hear the water running in the master bath and she smiled in anticipation.

In their room, Laura quickly undressed then let herself into the bathroom. She paused to admire the silhouette of her husband's body then opened the shower door and stepped in.

Taylor turned in surprise then smiled at her, the slow, lazy, "cat that ate the canary" smile that never failed to turn her knees to jelly. Pulling her under the warm cascade, he said, "You're home early."

"Early enough?" she replied as she ran her hands down the length of his back.

"Early enough." He leaned down to kiss her and that was enough for awhile. Then he lifted her, bracing her against the wall as he joined their bodies. Wordlessly, he looked into her eyes, the green eyes that had so bewitched him from the beginning, and was rewarded with the pure pleasure he saw reflected there.

Sliding his hands from behind her, he brought them to her breasts, caressing the nipples, slippery now with water and laughed as she caught her breath, then catching his own as he felt her tighten around him. She wrapped her arms around him, one hand behind his head, pulling his mouth to hers greedily. As he slid deeper into her, she felt the wave begin that, much too soon for both of them, crested, leaving them breathless, hearts pounding, as the water wrapped them both in warmth.

※ ※ ※

Meg watched with the waiting parents as Annie's class finished their ballet lesson. They tried so hard. At only five years old, they'd begun to master the intricacies, some demonstrating remarkable grace. Meg was pretty sure it wasn't just her imagination that Annie was one of the ones who seemed to have the gift. She remembered the hours she had spent in her mother's studio at the same age.

When the class was released, Annie ran across the room and launched herself into Meg's arms. " Meg! Are we still going?"

"Of course we are, silly girl! I promised. And I don't break my promises, you know that. Get your things, go change, and we'll go."

Hand in hand the two of them left the studio, Annie chattering all the way down the stairs, barely pausing for breath as Meg hailed a taxi. Taylor had tried to get her to let Matteo drive them but Meg had protested that a cab would be fine. She was too busy laughing at Annie to notice the blonde woman who watched them intently from the shadows; the woman who heard Meg tell the driver, "To the zoo, please."

Taylor came out of the bathroom, already dressed and ready to leave for the theatre. Laura sat on their bed, wrapped in a green silk robe he'd given her because it matched her eyes. Her long hair was still wet and she was drying it with a towel as she sat there. Not for the first time, he regretted that his career took him away from her at night. These stolen times were hard to come by with a lively five-year-old in their life. He was contemplating just *how* late he could be when the phone rang and Laura reached across the bed to pick it up.

It happened so quickly. Meg was watching Annie as she ran after the butterflies and lectured everyone who would listen. She could name most of the butterflies now but some still had nonsense names she'd made up. She was chattering at the zoo docent when a school class came in with two teachers and several mothers. There was plenty of room but Meg thought she ought to be where she could keep a closer eye on Annie. When she stood, she scanned the crowd for her sister's red hair and finally saw it bobbing off in the distance. Beside Annie was a blonde woman who had come in with the school group and they seemed to be hurrying away.

"Annie!" The panic in Meg's voice alerted the adults in the crowd that something was wrong. "Annie!" Meg broke into a run and ran toward the rapidly disappearing woman and child. Weaving through the children, she tried desperately to keep the woman in sight as they headed for the exit.

"Annie!" The woman turned at the sound of Meg's voice, then scooped up Annie and began to run. Meg ran behind them but was suddenly caught up in another school class exiting the monkey house. By the time she pushed her way through the crowd and made it to the Southern Boulevard gate, the woman and Annie had vanished.

❧   ❧   ❧

"Hello?" Laura watched her husband as he braced one foot on a chair to tie his shoe. She'd always liked this view and was not really paying attention as she answered the phone.

"Laura…it's me, Meg. I can't find her. Someone took her." Meg's voice was choked with tears and hysteria. Laura's heart seemed to quit beating. Taylor turned and saw the blood drain from her face, her hand holding the receiver in a death grip.

"Megan! Slow down. Take a deep breath and start over." Laura didn't feel nearly as in control as she sounded. Her eyes met Taylor's and he saw the panic there. He turned and ran down the hallway, picking up the portable phone just in time to hear Meg continue.

"She was right there. I was watching her. She was chasing butterflies and then she was gone. There was a woman…" Meg's voice was lost in helpless sobbing.

"Meg! Megan!" Taylor nearly shouted into the phone trying to get her attention. "Where are you? " He made his way back to the bedroom, his own face nearly as white as that of his wife. "Where are you, Meg?"

"The zoo. Oh, God, Taylor…please come…"

"We're on our way, Meg. Try to stay calm. Have you been to the security office yet?" He took the receiver out of Laura's hand and pointed to the closet, telling her to get dressed.

"That's where I am now. They're looking for her but she's not here. That woman took her, Taylor. She took Annie!"

With those words, Taylor felt their world shatter around him.

CHAPTER 67

Laura was too calm, too controlled. She'd been that way ever since Meg's call. After hanging up the phone, Taylor had turned to find her dressed, in black jeans and a black shirt, an unconscious reflection of her state of mind.

"I'll call Matteo. He's expecting me to leave for the theatre so he'll be ready to go. I'll ask Rosina to wait here. Laura? Laura, did you hear me?" She nodded mutely and he could see she'd withdrawn deeply into herself. Dropping the phone on the bed, he came to her and held her in his arms. There were no words he could say, no comfort he could offer, and no response from her. It was like holding a wooden doll. He released her and headed for the intercom in the kitchen that connected their apartment with the one on the floor below.

"Matteo?"

"Sí, Taylor? You are ready?"

"There's a problem. Please send Rosina up here and go get the car. We have to leave right away." Out of the corner of his eye he saw Laura come into the hallway, turning into the living room. He heard Rosina's footsteps on the hidden staircase between the two apartments before she opened the door. Quickly, he told her the little they knew, his brief narrations punctuated by soft exclamations from Rosina.

"We're going to the zoo now. We need you to stay here. Call me if you hear anything at all. I'll have the cell phone with me." He hurried into the living room followed closely by Rosina. "We'll call you as soon as we know something," he said as he took Laura's hand and headed out the door.

The ride to the zoo was silent. Laura was still very calm and composed. Her hand in his was icy cold and there was no response when he squeezed it. Matteo paid no attention to the driving regulations as he took shortcuts and chances to get them to the zoo quickly. Taylor hardly had enough time to call the theatre to notify the director and his understudy.

"Robert, please, don't give out any information. Just announce that I'm ill. I'll tell you all of it when I have a chance."

Meg was hysterical by the time they got there. The security office had called the paramedics who were trying to calm her down. As Taylor came through the door, she pushed them aside and ran into his arms. He held her tightly and murmured reassurances until she calmed a little. Laura couldn't touch her, could only watch. She had to conserve her energy for the effort of holding *herself* together awhile longer. Taylor loosened his grip on Meg to shake the hand of a man who had obviously been waiting for their arrival. "Mr. Morgan, Mrs. Morgan, please sit down."

Laura sank onto the couch, Taylor beside her, his arm still around Meg.

"I'm Vincent Hobbs, Detective, NYPD. The zoo security staff called as soon as your daughter came to them."

"What happened? Meg wasn't making much sense when she called." Taylor softened his words with a gentle squeeze to her shoulders.

The detective recapped what he had been able to get out of Meg. "The woman who took Annie…"

Laura drew a shuddering breath at the sound of the name. Taylor took her hand and held it hard, as if by holding her he could reclaim their child.

"…the woman didn't seem to intend the child any harm from what Ms. Morgan was able to tell us. Annie didn't appear to be scared."

Laura spoke softly, her first words since Meg's call, "Annie wouldn't go with a stranger, not willingly. She knew about strangers…we *taught* her about strangers. She wouldn't go!" Her voice rose, high and tight with strain.

"I'm sure you did, Mrs. Morgan." Hobbs's voice was gentle. "It's possible that she called your daughter by name, having heard Ms. Morgan call her by name in the park. Children don't always recognize someone who knows their name as a stranger."

Laura caught back a sob and Taylor ached for her, knowing the pain she was feeling, knowing it as his own.

"Mr. Morgan, you're a high profile person. This is probably about money." Hobbs hoped it was about money…didn't believe it, but hoped. The kidnapper sounded more like one of those desperate women who wanted a child. It was harder to find one of those sometimes. "Is there someone at your apartment who could let in some of my team so we can set up call monitoring equipment?"

"Our housekeeper. I'll call her and let her know they're coming."

"Good. That will give us a head start. Go ahead and call her and I'll get my team rounded up. We'll meet them there shortly."

CHAPTER 68

They arrived home to a scene of controlled chaos. Technicians were setting up and testing various machines, wires snaked across the polished hardwood floors. Laura took one look, gave a strangled cry, and retreated to the relative quiet of their room. Taylor had phoned their doctor from the car and he handed Meg off to Rosina who would stay with her until the doctor arrived. Then he followed Laura hoping to, *needing to,* break through the barrier she had built around herself.

When he came to Annie's room, he stopped, compelled to look in. He almost needed the assurance that Annie actually existed. She seemed so completely gone from their lives. His eyes filled with tears as he saw her favorite toy, her guardian dragon, Custard, propped against her pillow. Annie couldn't sleep without Custard! What would she do tonight? *Where* would she sleep tonight? He turned away, unable to face the questions that had no answers.

He opened the door to their room and saw Laura sitting in the window seat, staring out at the city, where dusk was creating shadows. He could see the matching shadows that had formed under her eyes and the tension that had pushed him away. He crossed the room and sat facing her.

"Laura?" Her eyes turned from the street and met his. "Laura…" his voice trailed off. There was nothing he could say that would chase that look from her eyes. He knew only Annie could do that.

"It's my fault, Taylor." Taylor was stunned by her statement and could think of nothing to say before she went on. "It's my fault. If I hadn't been so selfish, it would have been me who picked her up. I'd have brought her home. She wouldn't have been there for someone to take." Her voice broke, the strain—finally too much to bear—racked her slender body with sobs. Taylor moved closer, pulled her into his arms and let his own tears mingle with hers as the evening shadows filled the room; just as shadows had suddenly filled their lives.

After awhile she quieted. Taylor loosened his hold on her and moved back to where he could see her face. Gently, he wiped the tears from her cheeks. "Laura…you're wrong, darling. This wasn't your fault. You could just as easily blame me for not insisting that they take Matteo and the car. Or blame me for being known, tempting someone to do this. But, not you, Laura. It's not your fault. There's no one to blame but the woman who took her." He took a deep breath and then went on. "I need you, Laura. Don't shut me out again, please. I'll never get through this if I don't have you to lean on."

For the first time since the phone call had disrupted their lives, he could see in her eyes that Laura had come back to him, that they would face the rest of this nightmare together. Gratefully, he pulled her back into his arms, resting his cheek on her hair.

A knock at the door broke their small respite. Standing, his hand still on Laura's shoulder, he called, "Come in."

"Taylor, I've just come from Meg." Joseph Barry, their family doctor and friend, stood in the doorway. He quickly took in the scene. Laura was obviously at the end of her rope. Taylor wasn't much better. "Rosina's with her. I've given her something to help her sleep. Right now she's so torn up with guilt…"

"Meg?" Laura said in surprise. "But it's not her fault!"

"She thinks it is, Laura. She feels responsible."

Before either of the men could say anything, Laura was on her feet and out the door. They heard a door open and Rosina's voice before it closed again.

"And you, Taylor? How are you holding up?"

"I don't know, Joseph. I feel like it's all some kind of nightmare and I'll wake up soon. What will we do if—if Annie doesn't come home?" The doctor knew there was no answer he could give. He put a hand on Taylor's shoulder and the two men stood in silence.

Finally, Taylor spoke. "I'd better go check on Meg and Laura."

"I'll leave some pills here for Laura. It wouldn't hurt you to take them as well. You both will need to get some rest. Call me if you need me. It doesn't matter what time."

❦   ❦   ❦

"Meg? Dr. Barry said you think this is your fault." Laura knelt beside the bed and smoothed the dark hair away from Meg's face. "It's not your fault. You mustn't think that."

Sleepily, Meg replied, "But it was, Laura. If I'd only watched her closer…if I'd just kept hold of her hand. I'm the one who let her go."

"Meg, you and I both know that holding onto Annie is like trying to hold on to fog. You didn't do anything wrong." Laura's eyes filled with tears again. "Right now, Meg, you need to sleep. We'll wake you if anything changes, I promise."

Taylor stood in the doorway watching his wife and their eldest daughter. Laura had been a good mother to Meg. And to Betta. She'd given them her whole heart and had never made a difference between them and Annie. They were all equally her daughters even if only one had been born to her.

He crossed over to the bed and sat beside Meg. "Laura's right, Meg. It wasn't anyone's fault. It's happened and we have to get through it. We're going to need all our strength to survive this *together.*" He leaned down and kissed Meg's forehead as her eyes fluttered closed and her breathing became regular. Taylor and Laura sat beside her for awhile longer until Rosina interrupted them.

"Taylor? The policeman wants to see you."

They rose and followed her into the hall.

"Rosina? You'll stay with her?" Laura asked.

"*Sí.* I'll be here if she wakes. I've called Betta. She was not home but I left a message to call our apartment. Matteo will be waiting."

"Thanks, Rosina." Taylor replied.

"We have to call my parents, Taylor," Laura said. "They have to know, too."

"Matteo has already called," Rosina said. "They will be here the first flight they can get. Matteo will pick them up." Taylor hugged the small woman who had been so much a part of their lives. "Rosina, I don't know what we'd do without you and Matteo."

"Go! The policeman is waiting." Rosina gave Laura's hand a squeeze and watched them walk down the hall. So beautiful they were and so troubled. She took her rosary from her pocket, sat down beside Meg's bed and began her prayers.

CHAPTER 69

❦

Pierce Albright was waiting in the hallway. "I have a friend at NYPD. He knows we're friends. Don't tell the Detective about my job. The locals get a little testy when the FBI steps in. And I can't step in officially—not yet."

Detective Hobbs was waiting for them in the dining room. After being introduced to Albright, he asked them all to be seated. "It's a little quieter in here. I need to ask you some questions. Maybe we can figure out who this person is, why she took your daughter."

They sat at the table, Taylor holding Laura's hand as the detective took out a notepad. He looked curiously at Pierce.

"I'm an old friend of the Morgans." Hobbs noted it carefully on his pad before he began.

"Mr. Morgan, Mrs. Morgan..."

Laura interrupted him. "That's going to be very time consuming. My name is Laura, just use it, please." Taylor nodded to indicate he agreed and Hobbs started again.

"Taylor, Laura, we're hoping to hear from the kidnapper with a ransom demand soon. The longer they wait—well, the less chance it is that it's a money thing."

"What else could it be?" Taylor asked then went white as he thought of the answer. "Are you telling us that some—some pervert might have Annie?"

"It's a possibility. I can't rule it out. But I'm thinking it might be another answer yet. I'm not sure that this is a ransom driven kidnapping. I think it could be something else—given your celebrity. There are a lot of strange people out there; fans who think that someone famous owes them something. In this case, I'm wondering if the woman thinks you owe her your little girl?"

"That's insane!" Taylor said angrily. "Why would someone think I owe them my child?"

"These types aren't sane, Taylor. They get involved in some fantasy of their own and build up a whole scenario. There was that actress who got killed several years back by someone who admired her. And that other one who kept breaking into that talk-show guy's house. Something goes wrong in their minds and that fantasy becomes a reality to them."

"But why Annie?"

"To hurt you—hurt your wife. Maybe even take your wife's place."

"Elodie." Laura's voice was so low that none of them was sure she had spoken.

"Ma'am?"

"Elodie. It's Elodie, Taylor. It must be."

Hobbs looked at the two of them. This wasn't making any sense. "Who's Elodie?" he demanded.

"Detective?" Albright stepped in. "We haven't been completely honest about my identity. I *am* a close friend of the Morgans but I'm also FBI. I'm here in the friend capacity. Now, about Elodie Nee. She's the former president of Taylor's fan club. She'd become obsessed with him a few years ago and began stalking him. When we found evidence it was her, Taylor and I confronted her. She resigned, left the country, and joined the European set. A few months ago she stopped attending parties and became a recluse. The rumor is that she's gravely ill."

"And you're sure she's still in Europe?"

"I was until right now. I'll see if I can e-mail someone over there to check her out."

"Elodie might have been obsessed with me but she doesn't have it in her to hurt a child."

"Taylor, that may or may not be the case," Albright said gently.

"And it may not be Elodie. All we have to go on is that she's a blonde woman. Elodie's dark."

"She could have dyed her hair but you've got someone else in mind." Hobbs said.

"A former student. Allison something…I can find out her last name. She was thrown out of UNM when she tried to blackmail me into giving her a letter of recommendation. Then she showed up as one of the finalists for the female lead in this show. I refused to work with her. She'd have enough reason to pull something like this."

"I'll check her out," Albright said. "I'll call the theatre to get her name. And I think you can be sure that Annie's safe for now. Whoever this woman is, Annie's her ticket to you."

The door to the living room opened and one of the police force stuck his head in. "Trouble, Hobbs. You'd better come see."

They all followed the officer into the living room where a special report banner was emblazoned across the television set. It dissolved into the concerned face of a local news anchor who announced:

> *"Real Time News has learned that the daughter of Broadway star, Taylor Morgan, was snatched at the zoo today. Annie Morgan, seen here with her father at a recent social event, was at the zoo with her sister, Megan, this afternoon when an as yet unidentified woman took her. Reporter Nick Redfern and cameraman Ed Schultz were at the zoo on another assignment when Morgan and his wife, author Laura Collins, arrived at the zoo and they were able to take this footage of the dis-*

traught parents entering the zoo's security office. No further details are available at this time but we have learned that Morgan called in 'sick' for tonight's performance and no one has been reached yet for comment. We'll keep you posted on this breaking story as new details become available."

The newsman's face was replaced with a close-up of Annie as the special report banner once again took over the screen.

One of the technicians turned down the sound, leaving a stunned silence among the watchers. It was finally broken when Detective Hobbs whispered a heartfelt and succinct, "Shit!"

CHAPTER 70

Annie yawned as she picked at the food the lady had placed in front of her earlier. Macaroni and cheese with green beans. The macaroni was from a box. Annie *hated* green beans. And she was tired. She just wanted to go home and go to bed.

"Will my daddy be here soon?"

The woman at the stove turned to face Annie. "He'll be here, sweetheart. I'm just not sure when."

"But I'm ready to go home now, please." Annie was trying very hard to be polite and to not cry like a baby would. "I'm sure Mommy or Meg would come get me if I called them. I know my phone number," she added hopefully.

"Why, Annie, haven't we had a nice time this afternoon? I can't believe you want to rush off so soon."

"I have been having fun," Annie said, not entirely truthfully. It had stopped being fun a long time ago. "But I'm really tired now and I'd like to go home." Right now, Annie really wanted her Mommy and she could feel the tears pushing against her eyes

"Of course you're tired, baby." Annie hated it when people called her "baby". "Why don't you come have a nice bath and then lie down on the couch? I'll wake you when Daddy gets here."

Too tired to argue, Annie climbed down from the chair and followed the woman to the bathroom. "I can take my own bath. I don't need any help," she said.

"But, baby, you're so tired! What if you fall asleep in the bath and drown? We can't have that, can we?" she said with a laugh as she turned on the faucet to fill the tub. She helped Annie undress and get into the tub then sat on the floor beside her talking and talking. Annie wasn't listening. The warm water made her even sleepier and she didn't argue when the woman helped her out of the bath and into a flowered nightgown.

As the woman covered her with a pretty quilt on the couch, Annie said, "You'll wake me when Daddy comes? Promise?" But she was asleep before the woman could answer.

Sitting on the floor beside the sleeping child, the woman smiled as she brushed back the damp copper colored curls from Annie's face. She reached to the end table for a pair of scissors and cut off a strand of that hair, tucking it into her pocket. "I'll wake you when Daddy comes, Annie darling…and he *will* come as long as I have you." She began to softly sing, "Slumber my darling, thy mother is near, guarding thy sleep from all terror and fear…" In her sleep, Annie frowned at the sound—Daddy's song but not Daddy singing. The thumb she had given up long ago crept back into her mouth as her free hand searched for Custard to keep her safe.

Still singing, the woman got up from the floor and went back into the kitchen. The child hadn't eaten anything! Too much excitement. She'd settle down when Taylor got here. And he'd be along—right according to plan.

CHAPTER 71

She'd moved in here and began to watch Taylor's daily schedule. At least once a week, she'd gone to the theatre, usually on the Wednesday matinee, to see Taylor on stage. She followed him to the park when he took Annie rollerblading with him. He was *such* a good father! He really loved that little girl and would do *anything* for her. Watching them together had made her realize that the way to Taylor was through little Annie. And she'd begun to watch for a chance.

It had come today. She'd been waiting near Annie's dance school to catch a glimpse of Taylor. He often picked Annie up and took her to the theatre with him for awhile before sending her home with that driver of his. But today, instead of Taylor, it had been Meg who came. Without Taylor. Without the driver. Without any clue that she had been listening when Meg had told the cabbie where they were going.

It had been simple from there. She had blended into the crowds while she kept the girls in sight. When Annie got caught up in that school class in the butterfly zone, she had known it had to be then. She'd slipped in beside Annie, taking her hand as if they belonged together. Annie never looked to see whose hand she had; she had just assumed it was Meg. It wasn't until they were on their way out of the habitat, that Annie had looked up and been startled to see a stranger.

"Who are you?" Annie had demanded. "Let me go!"

"Hush, Annie! Don't you remember me? You met me at the theatre where Daddy works. I help with the costumes."

Annie had been puzzled. She didn't remember this woman but she had met so many people with Daddy. She could never remember them all.

The woman continued, "Daddy sent me to take you to him. He missed picking you up this afternoon and wanted to see you. He couldn't come, so I said I would come *for* him. He trusts me with a lot of important things."

When Annie looked around for Meg, she had hurried her along. "Meg had to go. I already spoke to her. We need to hurry, baby. The car is waiting."

She'd taken Annie's hand and gently pulled her down the path. Annie followed along, still looking for Meg. They'd been almost out of the zoo when Annie had turned for another look and seen Meg behind them, waving her hand in the air. "Wait! There's Meg!"

The woman had turned then, scooped Annie up into her arms and began to run. "It's okay. She's just waving goodbye. We have to hurry now."

CHAPTER 72

All hell broke loose after the news bulletin. The phone began to ring almost immediately. Hobbs looked out to see a news truck on the street below. He knew it wouldn't be long before there were more of them.

"No, Robert. Thanks for calling. Please, let the others know we have to keep this line free. I'll let you know as soon as we know anything. " Taylor hung up the phone which instantly began ringing again.

Laura answered this time, "No, the Morgan's have no statement at this time, " she said firmly before hanging up. Again, it began to ring. She picked it up and went through the same routine but her voice had an edge of hysteria to it. When it rang again, Hobbs reached over and took it as Taylor pulled Laura into his arms.

"Cody! Answer this phone! Taylor, in the dining room, now!" Hobbs took charge, almost herding Taylor and Laura into the dining room with Albright trailing along.

"This is exactly what we didn't need," he said as soon as the door closed. "Those barracudas won't let up until they have some kind of statement. You're going to have to release something."

"Release what?" Taylor demanded. "They know every bit as much as *we* do!"

"Shh, Taylor." Laura seemed to pull herself together with great effort. "He's right. They won't go away until we give them something." She went on to explain to Hobbs, "I know. I was one of them."

"Neither of you has to make the statement. One of us can do it for you."

Hobbs was surprised when Laura shook her head. "It won't be enough. Besides, if it's us, that woman might see—might realize what she's done…" Her green eyes filled with tears again and she angrily wiped them away. "I'll call Heidi. She's a television reporter and our friend. We'll give her the exclusive video then release the same statement to the press."

"Laura, are you sure you want to do that?" Pierce was concerned.

"I'm sure I *don't* want to. But I'm also sure we have to." She turned and left the room.

"Taylor?"

Running his fingers through his hair, Taylor said, "She's right. We'd best get it done with, while there's still time to make the late news."

🍁 🍁 🍁

"This is Heidi Nesbitt and I'm with Taylor and Laura Morgan. As Ed just told you, their five-year-old daughter, Annie, was kidnapped from the zoo today. So far there has been no communication from the kidnapper but the Morgans do have a message for her. Taylor?" The camera came in tight on Taylor and Laura.

"Thank you, Heidi. We are appealing to the kidnapper to reach us as soon as possible. At least let us know that Annie is all right, please! Whatever you're asking, we'll do our best to get it for you so that you can return our daughter to us quickly."

The camera panned down to where Taylor's fingers were entwined with Laura's then dissolved into a shot of the interviewer holding a picture of Annie. "This is Annie Morgan. She's five years old and, as you can see, has her mother's beautiful red hair. If you were at the zoo today and remember seeing Annie, please get in touch with the police as soon as possible. You may hold the key that will return Annie Morgan safely home. The kidnapper is believed to be a blonde woman with a tall slender build. She and Annie disappeared mid-afternoon. If you saw them after three this afternoon, or have any other information that might help to return Annie Morgan safely to her parents, please call the NYPD and ask for the Morgan taskforce or call the station and we'll relay your information. Live from the Morgan home, this is Heidi Nesbitt."

The lights went off and silence filled the room. "Wrap it up, Jim, and we'll head back to the station." Heidi stood and handed her mike to the cameraman. "Give me a minute and I'll be ready to go."

"Laura, I'm so sorry. Call me if there's anything more I can do." She hugged Laura then Taylor before leaving with her cameraman. A police department spokesman followed them out, ready to read a statement to the print press and hand out the press release.

Across town, she watched the brief report. It hurt her to see Taylor so upset but that red-haired witch deserved all the pain she had seen in her eyes. "I'll be in touch, darling, soon, I promise." She kissed the tips of her fingers then placed them against the screen where Taylor's face had just been.

It was late. Hobbs had left an hour ago. Pierce had left after Taylor urged him to go get some rest. A police technician was camped in the living room with the recording equipment.

The calls had stopped shortly after their appearance on the news. Meg was still sleeping, Rosina steadfast beside her. Matteo was on his way from the airport with Laura's parents and Taylor and Laura had retreated to their bedroom to wait.

"Laura, you should consider taking one of these after your parents get here." Taylor held out the bottle of pills that Joseph Barry had left.

She shook her head. "No, Taylor. I don't want to be drugged out when Annie comes home."

"Laura…" His voice trailed off.

Hobbs had told them before he left that it would be unusual for a ransom call to come this late. "If someone is waiting to demand ransom, they're going to want to see you sweat first," he'd said. "We probably won't hear anything until morning. You should both try to get some rest."

"Laura, you'll just make yourself sick. Annie's going to need you when she comes home."

"It won't work, Taylor. Give it up, please." Laura's voice was weary. "All the arguments in the world are not going to change my mind."

"Not even from your mother, *jita*?" They turned to find Laura's parents standing in the doorway. The small, beautiful woman came across the room pausing only to touch Taylor's arm as she went by. Sitting beside her daughter, Maria Collins put her arms around her. They heard Laura whisper, "Oh, Mom…" before she began to cry.

Sean Collins knew that Laura would be fine with Maria. His job was to reach the man who was married to his daughter. "Taylor." Sean moved his head back in a gesture that they should leave. With another look at mother and daughter, Taylor followed his father-in-law out into the hall.

"Where shall we go, son?"

Taylor led the way to the dining room. "Thanks for coming, Sean," he said as he went to the antique sideboard and poured a glass of Sean's favorite Irish whiskey. Handing it to him, Taylor continued, "She needs you here, right now."

"I hope you understand that, Taylor." When Taylor looked at him in confusion he went on, "Understand that she needs her mother. It doesn't reflect on her love for you. When Tomás was diagnosed, it was her aunts and cousins Maria turned to. The loss of a child, no matter how temporary, brings up that instinct. Maria told me later that it was because with them she didn't have to be strong, didn't have to even *share* the burden—they carried it for her for that little while."

"She's needed someone. I can see now what you're talking about. With me, she feels she has to be stronger somehow. I'm glad that Maria is here, for Laura and for Meg."

"How is Meg?"

"She's devastated. Blaming herself, even though we've told her she's wrong."

"There's been no word?"

"None." Taylor sat down at the table across from Sean and began to fill him in.

※ ※ ※

It was more than an hour before Maria joined the two men in the dining room. Taylor got to his feet, ready to go to Laura, when Maria stopped him. "She's sleeping, Taylor. I convinced her to take some of the medication the doctor left. The pill and the fact that she's totally worn out will keep her asleep for awhile." She looked up at her tall son-in-law. "And you, Taylor? How are you?"

"Holding on, Maria. But just barely. Did Laura tell you that the lead detective, Hobbs, thinks it could be an obsessed fan?"

"*Sí*, she told me."

"So, if it's true, it's ultimately my fault that Annie is gone."

"Nonsense, Taylor!" Maria took his hands in hers, pulling him to sit beside her at the table. "You have no responsibility for what this woman has done. She's the only one responsible."

"Maria, my head knows that. It's my heart that refuses to accept it. If we lose Annie…" Taylor's voice broke and he leaned on the table as tears too long held back began fall.

Maria didn't try to comfort him with words, only stood beside him, her arms around his shoulders, her eyes meeting those of her husband as they helplessly stood by.

CHAPTER 73

It was morning. The light coming through the window played across Annie's sleeping face, teasing open her eyes. She stretched and yawned before she realized that the bed felt different. Opening her eyes, she saw that she was still in that woman's apartment. Daddy hadn't come!

She listened for a moment for voices but the apartment was quiet. She got up and padded silently to the bathroom. There was no sign of her anywhere. Maybe, Annie thought, maybe she could find a phone and call Mommy. Mommy must be wondering where she was. Annie had never been away from home this long.

But, when she came out of the bathroom, the woman was there. She picked Annie up in a tight hug. "Good morning, Annie! Did you sleep well?"

Annie squirmed until the woman put her down. "Where's Daddy? You said he was coming! I want to go home, now!"

"Daddy called late last night. He didn't want me to wake you. He said he'd be here later today. Now, baby, what would you like for breakfast?"

"Nothing!" Annie shouted as she ran to the door. "Nothing from you! I want to be home. I want Mommy and Meg and Daddy and Betta and Rosina and Matteo." No matter how hard she struggled, the door handle wouldn't budge. "I want to go home," she whispered as she sank to the floor, leaning against the door that wouldn't set her free.

❦ ❦ ❦

Taylor was up early. He hadn't really slept. Despite promising Maria he'd take one of the sleeping pills, he hadn't. He'd held Laura and stared into the darkness wondering where Annie was, aching with the fear that whoever had her wouldn't take care of her.

As the first light had begun to creep in around the drawn shades, Taylor had gotten up. Still in the same clothes from the day before, he'd splashed cold water on his face, looking at the man in the mirror who seemed boundlessly older than he had yesterday morning. After checking once more on Laura, he'd gone down the hall to check on Meg. She was still sleeping, the tangled sheets a sign of how restless she'd been. Rosina was gone, probably in the kitchen, he realized as the smell of coffee penetrated his mental fog.

Pushing open the kitchen door, he found Rosina and Maria preparing a breakfast. Most unusual for the two of them, great friends for years now, they were working in silence.

Normally, they would have been discussing everything. Maria looked up and saw him.

"Buenas dias, Taylor." She came over and gave him a hug as Rosina brought him a cup of coffee.

"Did you get *any* sleep, Taylor?" Maria's eyes were filled with concern.

"Not really. Has Hobbs come in yet?"

"I think I heard him awhile ago, Taylor," Rosina answered. "Take this to him," she said as she handed him another cup of coffee.

Taylor nodded and left the kitchen in search of the detective. He found him in the living room giving instructions to the man who was taking over the monitoring equipment.

"Hobbs?"

"You look like hell, Taylor. Didn't you sleep at all?"

"Thanks. And no. If it was your daughter, would you have slept?"

"I wouldn't have," Pierce Albright said as he joined them. In fact, he hadn't slept. His twin girls were just a few months younger than Annie. Hannah and Sarah had been sleeping by the time he'd gotten home last night and he'd spent a long time sitting in their room watching them sleep, grateful that they were safe.

"Sorry. I wasn't thinking," the detective said. "Is one of those for me?" he asked hopefully, pointing to the cups Taylor carried.

"What?" Taylor looked at his hands, surprised to find the cups there. "Here. Rosina sent it in."

Taking the cup, Hobbs led the way into the dining room. Sitting at the table, he opened the folder of Elodie's letters that Albright had had messengered over last night. "It was pretty interesting reading. She had a hard case for you. She was also very unstable. If that progressed, she could be dangerous."

"Dangerous?" Taylor carefully set his cup on the table. "Dangerous to Annie?"

"I don't think she considers Annie one of the obstacles between you and her. Laura, your career, the distance between your lives; those have to be removed. But I think she's including Annie in her planned life with you."

Pierce followed with, "And your Allison isn't a suspect. She's hates you, Taylor, but she didn't take Annie. She had a solid alibi and was quite upset that you'd think she'd do something like this. All she wants is you out of her life and career."

Taylor looked up as he heard the front door close. A moment later, Betta came into the dining room. "Taylor! I was out late. I never checked my answering machine 'til this morning. Has there been any news?"

"None. We're still waiting." Realizing that Hobbs was watching the reunion with interest, Taylor turned to him. "Detective Vincent Hobbs, our third daughter, Betta."

Hobbs rose and held out his hand. "It's nice to meet you, Ms. Morgan. I'm sorry it's not under better circumstances."

Betta nodded then turned back to Taylor. "Where is everyone? How is Meg? And Laura?"

"One question at a time, Betta! Laura and Meg are both still asleep. Rosina and your grandmother are in the kitchen." She didn't hesitate but headed for the hallway and the room she'd grown up in. Abruptly, she turned around and came back and threw her arms around him then held on tightly. "Shh, Betta. It will be alright. Say hello to your grandmother on your way to Meg. Take her some food, although you're the best thing she could find when she wakes."

"Thanks, Taylor." She kissed him then left through the kitchen door. The three men could hear the cries of delight as the two women saw her.

"If you don't mind my asking? You and Laura aren't old enough to have two daughters of that age."

"Meg is my first wife's daughter. I adopted her just before her mother died. Betta came to us shortly after that when we were living in Italy. Annie…" Saying her name was so painful that he had to wait a moment before he could go on. "Annie is our birth daughter but she was as much a surprise as the other two."

"A houseful of women, eh?" Hobbs shook his head with a smile. "I have one of those, too."

They were interrupted by the sound of the buzzer from the lobby of the building. The doorman had been briefed on what was happening and had promised not to buzz them unless it was important. Hobbs was at the intercom before Taylor could move.

"What is it?" he growled into the speaker.

"A letter for Mr. Morgan. It was just delivered."

They were all out the door before he could say anything else.

CHAPTER 74

Annie cried until she felt sick. Her head ached and her stomach hurt. The woman fussed over her, putting her back to bed on the couch and bringing her warm lemon-lime soda to drink. She refused to drink it, turning her back and stubbornly staring at the yellow and brown lines of the plaid upholstery.

Finally, the woman gave up trying to cajole her. "Annie, Daddy will be here soon and I don't think he'll be happy that you've been treating me this way. You wouldn't treat your mo..." She stopped herself just in time. The last thing she wanted to do was to remind Annie she had a mother. After all, by the end of today, they'd be a family. "You just lie here and rest. I'm going to go take a shower and I want to find you right here when I get out."

Annie listened as she walked away then heard the door close and the sound of the water running. Waiting just a few minutes to make sure the woman didn't come back out, Annie got up and went into the bedroom where she slept. Maybe that was where she kept the phone. Annie would call home herself and Matteo would come get her.

She tiptoed around the room. The phone wasn't on the nightstand or the dresser and Annie nearly cried. Maybe she really didn't have a phone. She almost gave up when she saw a tiny piece of thin cord peeking out from under the bedspread. Lying on her stomach, Annie saw the phone tucked back under the bed so she pulled on the cord until it came sliding out.

Carefully, she dialed the numbers that Mommy and Rosina had helped her learn. She listened to the phone ringing on the other end, waiting for Mommy or Daddy or Rosina to pick it up. She was very surprised when a strange man answered.

"Hello?"

"Uh…hello? This is Annie. I need to talk to my mommy, please."

The man's voice got very excited, "Annie? Just stay on the phone. I'll get someone. *Don't* hang up, promise? Keep talking to me!"

"I promise." Annie could hear him shouting at someone to "get one of the Morgans in here, now." She tried to imagine what was happening and forgot to listen for the sound of the water.

Suddenly, the phone was snatched out of her hand. "Annie! What are you doing?" The woman slammed the phone down and began to shout at Annie. "What have you done?"

Annie, who'd never been shouted at by a grownup in her whole life, began to cry again.

※　　　　　※　　　　　※

Laura woke when the phone rang. Automatically, she reached for it before the memory of what was happening flooded in. It was probably just another reporter—the police would get rid of them. Suddenly, she was aware of running feet and a voice shouting, "Mrs. Morgan!"

Throwing the covers back she ran to the door and pulled it open just as a policeman raised his hand to knock. "Quick," he shouted, pulling on her arm, "the phone. It may be Annie."

Laura turned and threw herself across the bed and snatched up the phone…in time to hear it being hung up. "Annie? Annie!" her voice rose into a scream as she realized there was only a dial tone.

"So you have no idea who gave you the letter to deliver." Hobbs was grilling the messenger who was obviously anxious to leave.

"Look, man, I just go where the boss tells me. I don't know who brings in the stuff, I just deliver it."

"Alright. Make sure the officer there has your name. We'll be checking with your boss to see if you're legit."

"Whatever! Can I go now? I'm already 20 minutes behind!"

Hobbs waved him away and turned back to Taylor who was staring at the envelope on the doorman's table. Plain white. Cheap paper. Typewritten address. Nothing to distinguish it from thousands of other letters. Everything to remind him of some. Hobbs picked it up just as a voice came crashing out of the doorman's intercom. "Hobbs? You there? Get up here right now. The kid's on the phone!"

Taylor beat Hobbs and Albright to the elevator. All of them silently urged it faster as it seemed to crawl up to the top of the building. When the door finally opened and they ran down the hall, the sound of Laura's scream was the first thing they heard.

Chaos greeted them in the apartment. The technicians were trying desperately to get a lock on the phone number. Laura was sobbing in her father's arms. Maria and Rosina stood frozen in the doorway as Meg and Betta arrived from the hall.

Taylor went to Sean and took Laura in his arms, trying to soothe her, trying to make sense of what she was sobbing. "Annie…Annie called. Oh, God, Taylor, Annie…I didn't get the phone… I heard it ring…reporter…but it was Annie." She would have crumpled to the floor if Taylor had not been holding her.

Hobbs turned away from the table where he'd been consulting with the techs. His face was grim. "Not enough time, damn it! Not enough time to get a lock on the number."

Sean asked him, "Are you sure it was Annie? Aren't there a lot of cranks out there? Maybe it was one of them."

Hobbs looked at the technician who shook his head. "It sounded like a little girl. She was so polite…" the frustration showed on his face as he realized he couldn't offer more.

"The tape? You got it on tape, right?" Pierce snapped at him.

"Sure. It's right here." He rewound the tape and the room fell silent as each of them strained to hear the words. "…this is Annie. I need to talk to my mommy, please."

Hobbs looked at Taylor who nodded. There was no doubt about it. The voice on the tape was Annie's.

CHAPTER 75

It was Maria Collins who spoke first. "Come. You all need to get some food into you. Today you are going to need all of your energy. Laura, you and Meg go get dressed. Pierce? Detective Hobbs, you and your officer will join us?" As they nodded assent, the various people in the room began to move. Maria, Rosina, and Sean went to the kitchen. Taylor took Laura back to their room while Betta went along with Meg.

Laura walked wearily to the bed and sat down next to the phone. She reached out and ran her fingers over it. "I should have answered it, Taylor. She needed me and I wasn't there."

"Laura, you had no way of knowing it was her." Taylor knelt down on the floor in front of her, taking her icy hands in his.

"I'm her mother. I should have known somehow."

Taylor just shook his head and brushed his hand across her cheek. "Go get dressed, darling," he said as he stood then pulled her to her feet.

Laura, like an obedient doll, went to the closet and pulled out a shirt and jeans. She put them on quickly, then twisted her long red hair and pinned it up. She didn't bother with makeup, which only emphasized her pallor. Then, without a word, she went out into the hall, Taylor following her.

"Betta, I'm so glad you're here." Meg embraced her sister.

"*Cara mia*, I'm so sorry I wasn't here sooner. How are you, Meg?"

"Me? I'm holding on. Did they tell you the whole story?"

"Rosina only told me that someone had snatched Annie at the zoo."

"She didn't tell you that it was *me* that let the woman take her?" Meg's back was to Betta and her voice was bitter with self-loathing.

"Meg?" Betta walked to the dresser where Meg was standing. Taking her by the shoulders she turned Meg to face her. "Megan Elizabeth, you love Annie almost more than anyone else does. We all know that. If there'd been a way to stop it, you would have found it! You didn't *let* anyone do anything! What was done was done *to* you and to Annie."

"But she was with me. I was supposed to be watching her, keeping her safe."

Betta took her by the hand and led her to the bed. "Meg, sit here and tell me what happened. All of it. Maybe if you go through it you'll see that you didn't do anything wrong." Betta got on the bed beside her and, leaning against the headboard, prepared to listen as she had so many other times.

"Hobbs? Mr. Albright?" Cody, the sound technician spoke quietly so as to not be overheard. "I didn't play all the tape. But there's a little more that I didn't want her parents to hear. It's not much but maybe you'll pick up something."

The tape began to turn and they heard again the child's voice, the voice that reminded Pierce of his own girls. "Uh…Hello. This is Annie. I need to talk to my mommy, please." Then the sound of Cody's voice urging her to stay on the line, Annie's voice again, then, in the background, the sound of a woman's angry voice, "Annie! What are you doing?" Only Annie's little gasp as the phone was evidently wrenched from her and slammed down was heard before her mother's frantic words took over.

Shaking his head, Hobbs said, "That doesn't sound good. She's losing control. Go ahead and make a copy of this. I'm going to have to get the parents to listen to it in case they recognize the voice." Cody nodded then turned to his task while Hobbs stared out the window, wrestling with the feeling that there was something he had missed.

Maria came into the living room. "Breakfast, Detective." He turned and smiled at her then told Cody to go ahead and get a plate. He'd stay with the equipment until Cody came back. He could hear the sounds of chairs scraping across the floor, utensils on plates, and the occasional murmur of voices. He was pretty sure that the family gatherings in this home were rarely this quiet. It was certainly a unique family structure with the multi-cultural background and three girls related only by love.

Cody came back out with a plate of food and took his seat back with the equipment. "Hobbs, you never did say what was in that letter for Morgan."

The letter! That's what they'd missed. Things had gone to hell so quickly, he and Albright had actually forgotten about it. Without answering Cody, he barged into the dining room. "The letter, Taylor! What did we do with the letter?"

Taylor's eyes widened in alarm. He couldn't remember picking it up—it must still be downstairs on the doorman's table. He pushed back his chair and followed Hobbs from the room, leaving Maria to explain to Laura.

CHAPTER 76

It was there, just as they'd left it. "I didn't touch it or anything," the doorman assured Hobbs. "I didn't want to go messin' up any fingerprints." Hobbs didn't have the heart to tell him that there probably weren't any to mess up.

Taylor opened it in the elevator. It was a single sheet of cheap printer paper. The message had been computer generated and printed.

"Taylor, darling,

By now you'll have figured out it's me who has Annie. Surprise! I've been watching you for the past few months—you and Annie, until I had her schedule memorized and I had only to wait for the opportunity.

Of course, that's how I knew about Annie's dance lesson. I've watched you take her and pick her up so many times. She's a beautiful child, Taylor. The three of us will be so happy.

Enough of that. I've left a letter for you at the theatre with instructions on how to find Annie and me. Don't bring anyone else, Taylor, especially not *her*! She has no place in *our* life.

I'll see you soon, my love, and all will be forgiven.

Elodie"

Taylor handed it over to Hobbs as the elevator came to a stop. Without a word, he went into the apartment and picked up the phone that was already set on speaker mode.

"Joe? It's Taylor Morgan. No, no news yet but we're hoping there will be soon. Yes, I'll tell Laura." Hobbs listened as Taylor tried to break in on the stream of concern being expressed by the man at the other end of the line. "Joe...Joe!" Taylor snapped at the affable theatre doorman. "Joe, I need to know if a letter's been delivered there for me."

The doorman chuckled. "A letter, Mr. Morgan? I'd say closer to two, maybe three, hundred. They've been arriving all morning along with flowers and lots of dolls and stuffed animals for Annie. She's going to have a ball when she gets home."

Hobbs met Taylor's eyes. Three hundred letters and only *one* of them held the key. It seemed an impossible task. Taylor thanked the doorman and asked him to have all the letters put in his dressing room. "Joe, send the flowers to the hospital. They can use them. Find someplace for the toys. We'll donate them somewhere later. Thanks."

Taylor turned to find Laura standing in the doorway. "What letter, Taylor?"

Hobbs handed her the one they'd just opened. She read it and, putting it together with what she'd heard, realized the task that faced them.

"I'll get my shoes, Taylor, then we can go."

Hobbs stopped her. "Laura, it's probably better if you stay here. One of you should be here if this woman calls. Or if Annie should get another chance. We can find the letter."

"You'll need help, Taylor." Meg and Betta stood in the hall. "We'll come with you."

"Me, too," Pierce said.

Laura looked at Taylor. "I *can't* stay here doing *nothing*, Taylor."

He crossed the room and took her in his arms. "Laura, you have to. Hobbs is right. What if Annie calls again?" He looked into her eyes then kissed her gently. "Please…"

Laura nodded her assent and watched as they all got ready to go. As Taylor opened the door she said softly, "You'll call me, Taylor?" and he nodded before closing the door behind them.

CHAPTER 77

Annie cowered by the bed as Elodie stalked around the room yelling at her. "Annie! Now he may not come. Daddy may *never* come and it will all be your fault." She jerked the cord from the wall and put the phone up high on the top shelf of a closet. She stood for a moment staring at herself in the mirror. With a conscious effort, she pulled herself together and came back around the bed and sat on the floor beside Annie.

"Annie, Annie, Annie. I'm so sorry. I shouldn't have yelled at you. But I trusted you to stay on the couch like I'd told you, trusted you not to sneak around behind my back. It scared me to find you on the phone. Who did you call, baby?"

Annie only stared at her, thumb in mouth, eyes wide and tear-filled.

"Oh, Annie, sweetheart. Did you try to call your Daddy? I told you he'd be here today. He *will*! I promise. Then the three of us will go away together and be a family. Won't that be nice?" Elodie got to her feet and began to brush her hair, chattering away about the new life they would have, how Daddy would love being with both "his girls", how Annie would like living in someplace called "the continent". Annie wrapped her free arm around her middle and let the words wash over her in a never-ending stream.

🍁 🍁 🍁

Matteo dropped Taylor and the others at the stage door. The theatre was still mostly deserted at midmorning, most of the cast and crew not coming in until the afternoon. Taylor led the way to his dressing room and opened the door.

There were letters everywhere! The makeup table was covered. So was the small table by the chair he kept in there. The chair and the loveseat were also covered. Letters had spilled off of surfaces and formed drifts across the floor.

Hobbs commented, "Well, it would have helped if you weren't quite so popular. Let's get started. I'm willing to bet that the letter we're looking for will look the same as the one I showed you in the car," he said to Meg and Betta. "For now, let's skip all the pretty ones and concentrate on the plain janes."

Each of them staked out an area in the dressing room and began to sort. Everything went unread as they searched for that plain envelope. They'd open envelopes and take a look at the contents later if it was necessary. Taylor's director appeared in the doorway. "Any news, Taylor? Anything I can do to help here?" He was quickly filled in on the task at hand and found a space on the floor and began to sort.

It was almost noon when they found it. She must have had it delivered late yesterday or early this morning. It had fallen off the makeup table and was half hidden under it on the floor. Taylor was the one who found it and he knew that it was the one they'd been looking for. With shaking hands he opened the envelope and pulled out the single sheet of paper. As he unfolded it, a bright red curl of hair spiraled down into his lap and his cry brought the others' attention. Meg reached out and picked it up. Annie's hair. Bright, vibrant, beautiful as she was. Taylor read the letter aloud.

"Taylor, darling,

It's time. I've been waiting ever so long for you to see that you'd married the wrong woman. But once you see me again and with your darling Annie, you'll know how perfect it will be.

So, come to me, my love. Today. As soon as you get this. We'll be waiting. You'll know where I'm hiding.

Elodie"

Pierce was the first to speak. "Where? Where would she be hiding, Taylor?"

"I don't know. It must be someplace from the early days. How am I supposed to tell how her wretched mind is working? Her Central Park apartment?"

"Not there," Pierce said. "Sorry, Detective, I pulled rank and checked out all the logical places last night. No sign of her at any of her regular places here *or* in Europe."

"Then where?" A brooding silence fell over the room. Only Taylor had the answer and he couldn't find it. "Damn it, Elodie. What game are you playing? Why would I know where to find you? You never…" Taylor's voice trailed off. No one dared to break the silence. Finally, Taylor spoke. "Her Aunt. Elodie had an aunt who lived here in the city. When she got tired of being around us or just wanted a little pampering, she'd head over to her Aunt Deborah's. It was a house in an artist's colony in the Village, just off Tompkins Square I think. I don't remember the address but I think I might recognize the building. Can we cruise the area?"

"It's all we've got. We'll have to run with it."

"You girls go on home. Matteo will take you. Laura needs you nearby."

Each of them solemnly kissed him and gave him a hug. "Bring her home, Dad. We all need her."

"I'll do my best."

Pierce rode with them in the unmarked car. As they neared the neighborhood, Taylor stared out the window as the car passed the parade of identical brownstones. One of them had to be Elodie's hiding place. Deborah had been a well-known glass artist and the house had featured a beautiful stained glass fanlight over the door. He had to hope the window was still there. Without it, it would be just another brownstone.

"Stop! That's it! Number 603!"

"You sure, Taylor?" Hobbs asked as he eased the car to the curb. "Let me go see whose name is on the mailbox."

As Hobbs started across the street, Pierce asked, "What are you going to do if it's the right place? Hobbs will want to play it by the book."

"Not a chance. His way may get Annie hurt. We're going to follow Elodie's instructions, at least until we get Annie out of there."

The car door opened. "The mailbox says D.Nee. D for Deborah. I think we have her." As Hobbs reached for the radio to call it in, Taylor stopped him. "No! We play it her way for now."

"You can't be thinking of going in there!"

"If I don't, Annie could get hurt. *You* told me to watch my back, how unstable she was. What's going to happen if she finds herself surrounded by cops? She could take it out on Annie. So, I'm going! And I'm going to get my daughter and take her home. Then you can have this woman, Hobbs. You can lock her up forever as far as I'm concerned. But not until I have Annie back."

"We can't go in there without some plan, Taylor. At least let us think this through for a few minutes so we can figure out the best way to get Annie out of there safely."

"Ten minutes, Hobbs. Then we go." Taylor's face was a grim mask that his fans would have been hard pressed to recognize.

CHAPTER 78

It was closer to an hour before the plan was in place. Pierce had helped convince Taylor to take the time; to make sure everything would work; to bring Laura into whatever plan they had. So they'd returned to the apartment, where the three of them and Laura had gone over every possible outcome. But, no matter the brainstorming, Taylor's plan to meet Elodie on her terms was the only one that he would accept. After a few final tweaks, they were ready to go.

Taylor pulled up in front of the house. It was an older neighborhood, a little seedy, like an impoverished dowager. Across the street was a non-descript car with tinted windows. Although he couldn't see them, he knew Laura and Hobbs were inside with Pierce in the driver's seat. They'd tried to talk Laura out of coming but there was no moving her. "She's my daughter, too, Taylor!" she'd declared in the tone of voice that Taylor had learned years ago wasn't worth arguing with. They wouldn't win.

He knew a swat team was out there somewhere. Other police, too. None of them would be any help if he couldn't accomplish his part. Taking a deep breath and sending a prayer to Genesius, the patron saint of actors, he knocked on the door, prepared to give the performance of his life.

※ ※ ※

Where was he? He should have been here long ago. Elodie paced past the window that faced a small back garden. She glanced over at Annie, huddled in a chair, her thumb still in her mouth, her eyes looking someplace far away. She'd had a devil of a time dressing her in the new dress she'd bought for her. "Annie, you want to look nice for Daddy, don't you?" Annie had just shaken her head—she hadn't spoken a word since this morning when Elodie had yelled at her. Elodie stopped in front of the chair and squatted down in front of her. "He'll be here soon, Annie. He will!" She was saying it as much to reassure herself as to comfort the child.

When the knock came at the door, Elodie smiled brightly at Annie. "He's here, baby! Now run into the bedroom like we talked about so we can surprise him with how pretty you are." She lifted Annie to her feet and nudged her into the bedroom, pulling the door closed as she whispered, "Quiet now, Annie. Wait until it's time."

The knock came at the door again, louder, more aggressive this time. She heard his voice, "Elodie? Are you in there?"

He was lifting his hand to hammer the door again when it opened. "Taylor!" She sounded like Elodie but she looked so different! She'd bleached her black hair to a gleaming blonde and cut it short. She'd been fitted for contacts that turned her eyes green. "Come in. We've been waiting for you."

Taylor registered that there were two suitcases to one side of the door as he came in. He looked around for Annie but saw only the living room with its run-down furniture, closed doors on the wall opposite the entrance. Where was she?

"I'm so glad you *finally* got here, Taylor. I was beginning to worry."

Taylor gave himself a mental shake then slid into the role he had to play. "I was delayed because a lot of letters about Annie had been delivered to the theatre. I came as soon as I found yours."

"Oh! I didn't think of that."

"Elodie, where's Annie?"

She fluttered around the room, touching the sofa, straightening a curtain, unable to stand still. "She's such a darling child. I've so enjoyed having this time with her."

He caught her arm, forcing himself to remain gentle, as she flitted past him again.

"Elodie, *where* is Annie?"

She laughed as she looked up at him. "Taylor, she's fine. I thought we could visit for a little while first."

"Elodie. Please. You have to realize I can't concentrate on *us* until I know she's alright."

"Taylor! I wouldn't hurt her. Not for anything. She's your daughter—*our* daughter now. But go on. She's in the bedroom. I'll give you a few minutes to check on her then we really must sit down and make plans. I already have tickets for us to leave for Europe tonight."

He walked past her and pushed open the door. At first, he didn't see her. He walked to the other side of the bed and saw Annie, dressed in some horrible lace and ruffled thing, huddling on the floor. He dropped down beside her and took her in his lap, his arms tight around her. "Annie...oh, my Annie..." he murmured as he stroked the bright curls.

She opened her eyes that had been scrunched up tight. "Daddy?"

"It's me, Annie. I've come to take you home."

She threw her arms around his neck and buried her face in his shoulder. "Daddy..." she said through the sobs that shook her body. "She said...she said you'd come but you didn't and I was so scared..."

"Shh, Annie, it's alright now. I'm here. You're safe."

Elodie spoke from the doorway. "You're such a good father, Taylor. I'll try to be as good a mother."

Annie's body tensed in his arms at the sound of Elodie's voice. He moved around to where he could see the doorway. "You've done okay so far, Elodie. She'll be fine. Just give us a few more minutes. Maybe you could bring Annie a glass of water?"

Elodie smiled and moved out toward the kitchen. He could hear her chattering away about how wonderful things were going to be. Shaking his head, he pulled Annie's arms loose from their chokehold on his throat. "Annie? Annie, I need you to listen to me carefully. Can you do that, darling? Just a little more then we'll get you out of here."

Annie nodded her head, her thumb once again in her mouth, her eyes never leaving his.

"Annie, I have to pretend to be happy to see this woman. I have to pretend that I'm going to do everything she wants. So some things may happen that you don't think are right but you need to remember I'm just pretending, like one of my plays." Annie nodded solemnly, responding to the serious tone of her father's voice.

"Good, sweetheart. I'm going to tell her you just want to lie down while she and I talk. But I want you to watch through a crack in the door, watch for a time she's not paying attention. Take off your shoes now so she won't hear you. When she's not paying attention, I want you to slip out the door as quiet as you can be. There's a car across the street with dark windows. Mommy's in there waiting for you. Do you understand all that, Annie?"

She nodded then moved to where she could unbuckle the shiny maryjanes that the woman had made her wear. When Elodie came to the door with the glass of water, Taylor was covering Annie with a quilt.

"She's worn out, poor baby," Elodie whispered as Taylor turned to her, one finger across his lips. "She missed you terribly. You can tell she's Daddy's girl."

Taylor put his arm around her shoulders and walked her from the room, pulling the door not quite shut behind them.

"That's a beautiful dress you got for her. You must have been planning this for a long time."

"It seems like forever, Taylor. When Meg's mother died, I knew that was a sign we should be together. But then you married *that woman*...what a mistake! But I knew that deep down you loved me, that you always had."

"I couldn't tell you, Elodie. I wasn't a free man. It wouldn't have been fair."

"Oh, I knew that, Taylor, and I would have waited forever, but I could see how Annie was growing and I didn't think *she* could raise her as well as you and I could. I needed to do something to make it happen...and now it has!"

Taylor sat on the couch and pulled her down beside him. Turning her to face him, he smiled at her, even as he fought the urge to retch. "How wise you are, Elodie. Wise and beautiful—what more could a man ask for?" He pulled her into his arms and kissed her. As he'd expected, she closed her eyes, leaning into his kiss. He kept his open and saw the door to the bedroom open wider, Annie looking at him in surprise. Please God, let her remember it was all pretend! He waved one hand behind Elodie's back toward the door and was rewarded with a conspiratorial grin from his daughter as she slid soundlessly across the floor and out the door that he'd left ajar when he'd come in.

🍁　　　🍁　　　🍁

"He's been in there so long." Laura nervously twisted her wedding ring.

"Not that long, Laura. This is going to take a little time. He can't just waltz in and pick up Annie, as much as we'd like that to be the case," Hobbs said from his place next to Laura in the back seat.

"I know. It's just—my whole life is in that house."

Pierce glanced at her in the mirror then turned his eyes back to the building. All was quiet. He knew that there were black and white units stationed around the corners in the next blocks. They'd be here within seconds as soon as the child was safe.

With nothing that could be said, they sat in silence as each minute ticked slowly by. While Pierce wouldn't admit it to Laura, he was beginning to get nervous, too. Taylor *had* been in there a long time. He'd refused to wear a wire, afraid that the woman would notice, so they had no way of knowing what was going on. He knew from seeing it time and again that jealousy could turn ugly very quickly.

Just as he was beginning to second-guess the wisdom of this plan, the door to the building began to push open.

Laura felt Hobbs tense beside her as they both kept their eyes on the door that was, ever so slowly, inching open. Laura caught her breath at the first sight of a face topped with red hair. "Annie!" she breathed the name and fumbled for the door handle. Hobbs stopped her. "No, Laura. Wait for her to come to us."

Laura wrenched her hand from his grasp with a wordless cry of frustration and watched as Annie slipped out the door, down the steps, and looked across the street to the car. She ran lightly to the curb and Laura laughed through her tears as Annie stopped and looked both ways before darting out into the street.

Hobbs pushed open the car door and Annie halted in the middle of the street at the sight of the strange man. He got out and moved aside so Annie could see her mother. "Mommy!" she cried as she ran to the car and launched herself inside, into her mother's waiting arms.

Hobbs quickly slammed the door and slapped the roof to tell Pierce to move out. Before the car was even out of sight, he was on his hand-held radio, calling in the waiting backup.

Pierce looked in the rear view mirror at his passengers in the back seat. He could see Laura holding Annie tightly in her arms, their faces curtained by the fall of her long red hair. This was why he went into law enforcement—the moments like this, few and far between, when everything went right. Smiling, he turned his eyes back to the road.

Laura held onto Annie until they both stopped shaking. Annie smelled differently to her, a combination of someone else's shampoo and the fear that Annie had been living with for the past…Laura was startled to realize that it had been only a little over 24 hours. Time had crawled along as if it were marking off years instead of mere minutes.

But the waiting wasn't over. Even as she rejoiced at the feel of her child back where she belonged, a part of her was back at that building with Taylor. The world would not be completely right until he was home with them and she sent another silent prayer for his safety, praying she'd be granted just one more miracle.

Where the *hell* were the police? Taylor wasn't sure he could keep himself together for much longer, listening to Elodie prattle on about "their future". It astounded him to realize she truly believed that he would turn his back on Laura, on his life, to go with her to Europe.

He heard a noise outside in the courtyard. Elodie heard it, too, even over the sound of her own voice. "Was that Annie, Taylor?"

No! She couldn't check on Annie now! Taylor reached out and caught her hand as she stood to go check on the supposedly sleeping child. "I think it was outside, probably a stray cat. Come tell me more about Paris, Elodie."

"In a minute, Taylor. I'll feel better if I just check on Annie first." She pulled her hand from his and was around the couch to the bedroom door before he could stop her.

"Taylor! She's gone. Annie is gone!" Elodie appeared genuinely upset by the discovery. And a part of Taylor that he didn't even know existed was very glad to see her anguish at the disappearance of "her" child.

"I know, Elodie. When I kissed you, she slipped out just like I'd told her to."

"But, Taylor, aren't we taking her with us?"

Annie safe, the secret out, Taylor finally lost it, "There *is* no *us*, Elodie. There never has been and there's not a snowball's chance there ever will be. I love my *wife* and I'd never leave her. You've been living in some kind of fantasy world for years now but it's not *my* world."

Her eyes filled with rage as she watched the plans she'd so carefully constructed for all these years fall into dust at her feet. Taylor didn't love her. He actually loved that red-haired witch. He would go back to her and continue with his perfect life. Not if she could help it! She'd be arrested, would go to prison…but first she'd see to it that Laura would never have him either.

🍁 🍁 🍁

Hobbs wasn't taking any chances. He sent men around to the back to cover the windows and the exits. There would be no chance for this woman to escape.

Once he'd heard that everyone was in place, he drew his gun and nudged open the unlatched door. He could hear Taylor's voice raised in anger before a scream rang out.

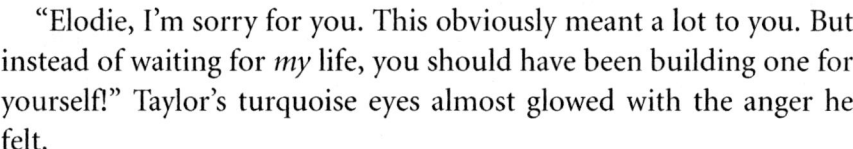

"Elodie, I'm sorry for you. This obviously meant a lot to you. But instead of waiting for *my* life, you should have been building one for yourself!" Taylor's turquoise eyes almost glowed with the anger he felt.

Elodie stood there watching him, seeing the anger in his eyes, and she knew it was all over. She'd given up her life for him for nothing. As Taylor turned to the door, she grabbed the scissors she'd used to cut the strand of Annie's hair and, with a blood curdling scream, plunged them into Taylor's back.

At the sound of the scream, Hobbs kicked open the door and rushed in. In the split second after he saw Elodie with the scissors raised, he chose not to shoot and, instead, dived across the room. He hit her with the full bulk of his weight, knocking her to the floor, landing on top of her. But he realized he hadn't been fast enough when he saw the blood pouring from the wound in Taylor's back.

Everything happened quickly then. The room filled with uniformed officers. Two of them rushed to Taylor to give first aid while another called for the waiting paramedics to come in. Two more pulled the now sobbing Elodie off the floor and cuffed her as Hobbs read her rights before they led her away.

Annie was welcomed home by her jubilant family. Meg kept crying and hugging her and it was Annie who patted her back and told her it was alright. She was surprised to find *Abuelo* and *Abuelita* there. Matteo was beaming as he watched and Rosina was crying. Laura looked over their heads and met her father's eyes. She could see the question in them and shook her head to indicate she didn't know what was happening back there, didn't know how Taylor was.

Pierce stayed in the car after dropping them off to see if he could find out what the situation was. Tuning in to the right band, he heard the call for an ambulance then the paramedics radioing the hospital that they were bringing in "a white male, approximately 40 years of age, stab wound with blood loss." He was patched through to Hobbs who told him to bring Laura to meet them at City Hospital right away.

When he arrived at the open door of the apartment he knew he was an unwelcome guest, as he pulled Laura to one side to tell her what had happened. She went to Annie and told her she had to go to be with Daddy.

"I'll be back as soon as I can, sweetheart."

Annie looked at Laura, her eyes the same shade of turquoise as her father's, and asked, "With Daddy?"

Laura didn't answer, only hugged her hard then kissed her. *Abuelo* came and picked her up saying, "Rosina made your favorite cookies, little one. Come see if she did it right." When he, having been quickly briefed by Pierce, had taken Annie from the room, Pierce filled the others in on the rest of what was happening. "I don't know how bad it is. Hobbs just wanted Laura there right away."

"We'll come with you, Laura," Meg said as Betta nodded agreement.

"No, darlings, thank you. Annie needs you here right now. I'll call you as soon as I know anything."

She left the now silent apartment that had only moments ago been filled with the sounds of rejoicing. Was Taylor to be the price they had to pay for having Annie home safely? Laura couldn't think about that. Wouldn't think about that. Taylor would be fine. Taylor would be fine, Taylor would be fine—the mantra ran through her brain during the ride to the hospital.

❦   ❦   ❦

Hobbs was waiting for them in the lobby. Quickly, before anyone could recognize Laura, he took her down the hallway into the emergency room and a cubicle at the back. He opened the curtain and stepped back to let Laura go in.

Taylor was sitting up, his shoulder heavily bandaged. He was pale from loss of blood but he was alive!

"Annie? She's safe?"

"At home being spoiled outrageously," Laura said through her tears as she crossed the room to him. "And you, my love?"

He held his one good arm out to her and pulled her close, resting his chin on her head. "I'll be fine. Just take me home, Laura. Take me home."

CHAPTER 79

Taylor was welcomed home with as much fanfare and fuss as Annie had received. She'd been changed out of the horrible dress Elodie had forced her to wear and was comfortable in her purple butterfly sweats, Custard tucked tightly under her arm. When Laura brought Taylor in, she hung back, looking at the sling on his arm. Finally she'd crept over and whispered, "Did she hurt you, Daddy?"

"She did, little one. But it will mend."

She thought for a minute then held out her beloved dragon. "Take Custard, Daddy, he'll make you feel better."

"Then what about you?"

She pondered the question and finally answered, "If I climbed into your lap, we could both hold him."

"I think that's the perfect idea. Ask Mommy to help you climb up here."

Laura lifted her up so she settled in on the opposite side from where he was injured. Even then, she knew it must be painful but the look of peace that came over his face as he held his daughter made her realize that Annie was the only medicine he needed. The two of them settled in and whispered for a few minutes before they both dropped off to sleep.

Laura shooed everyone from the apartment, telling them to come back tomorrow, she would call if there was anything to report. Finally, it was quiet. She stood in the doorway watching her sleeping husband and child, watching them safe, watching them home. And only then did she allow herself to cry.

🍁   🍁   🍁

When Annie woke hungry for supper, Laura warmed the chicken soup that Rosina had left and some of the tortillas her mother had made. Taylor insisted he was strong enough to move to the table so the three of them dined together. Even Custard was given a strawberry (his favorite) that he naturally shared with Annie.

After supper, Laura bathed Annie while Taylor watched. There were bruises on her little arm and Laura nearly cried when she saw them. Finally, with her own bubbles and her own pajamas, her hair dried, Annie smelled like herself again. The bruises would fade, so would the memories. Together they tucked her into bed where she quickly dropped off to sleep.

Taylor put his good arm around Laura and walked with her to their bedroom. The door safely closed behind them, he sat in the armchair near the bed. "Can you ever forgive me, Laura?"

She moved to sit at his feet. "Forgive you? For what?"

"Elodie. For all those years I never believed you."

"She wasn't the woman you knew, Taylor. Something had gone terribly wrong in her mind. But you weren't responsible, my love. You and Annie were her victims."

"You're right. She wasn't Elodie anymore. She was a lost soul with no place to be. I'm glad she's gone but I'll miss forever who she once was."

"Oh, Taylor, I've never been so frightened as I was when Pierce came to tell me you'd been taken to the hospital. I didn't know how badly you were hurt. I didn't know if you were dead or alive." Her eyes filled with tears and he gently brushed them from her cheek with his one good hand.

"I'm alive, Laura, and Annie is safe and I love you more than life itself." He winced as he leaned forward to kiss her.

"What am I thinking, Taylor? You need to take a pill and go to bed."

"Only if you come with me."

"I think that could be arranged."

CHAPTER 80

Jamie walked to work just as he had every day since he'd come to New York a little more than a year ago. He no longer consciously looked for Megan but she was always there at the back of his thoughts. She was the reason he'd finally pulled up his roots and emigrated soon after his father died. He'd never recovered from how he'd treated Megan and from losing his friendship with his son. He quietly slipped away in his sleep three months after she left.

Although he and the elder Jamie had made a peace of sorts, Jamie had never quite forgiven his father for his part in driving Meg away, for tearing him apart from the woman he loved. Still, he was man enough to take his share of the blame for taking so long to come searching for her.

Not that he'd found her yet. Instead, he'd found a bartending job here in Soho. A good job with a decent wage. He'd put down new roots and was doing well.

This morning, as he passed the big white building on the corner he noticed something new. A large gold sign proclaimed it *Morganna's*. Stopping to look in the window, he saw workmen painting the walls and hanging light fixtures. No clue what was going in there but it would add an interesting break in his walk. As he walked on, he missed the sight of Betta coming down the stairs and out the door, where she turned the other way to meet Meg for lunch.

❦ ❦ ❦

Soon the morning peek at *Morganna's* became the highlight of his walk. Since he didn't go into work until just before the lunch rush, there was always something going on, something new to see. The wooden floors had been stripped and polished to a high gloss. Fixtures and shelves that proclaimed it a fashion shop—a *boutique* he reminded himself—were being arranged.

One morning he watched in amazement as highly decorated wooden benches, tables, chairs, and stools were carried in. He'd never seen the like of them! As the parade continued, he'd been drawn to the door where he could hear a woman's voice directing where things were to be placed. A photographer was documenting the whole thing.

When the photographer put his camera down to change film, he noticed Jamie in the doorway. "Come on in and take a look," he invited. "I've seen you peering in lots of times in the last few weeks. By now you've earned a closer look.

"Thanks," Jamie said as he walked in. "It's quite a place. And I've never seen furniture like that."

"Those are Sarah Weatherington's pieces. She's a bright young artist/designer that the owner's decided to foster. She'll be introducing others as she goes along, especially up and coming fashion designers, including herself."

"Beautiful place. I work around the corner at *Barnum's*. Drop by and I'll buy you a pint."

"Chris? Can you come up here?" The woman's voice floated down the stairwell. For a moment, Jamie found it familiar but couldn't grasp from where.

"Gotta go. The boss lady calls. Name's Chris. I'll be by for that pint."

"Name's Jamie. Come by anytime," he answered as he headed out the door.

"Chris, were you talking to someone?" Betta asked as he came into the salon. "This could have waited."

"No one important. Nice guy who comes by here everyday—works around the corner at that bar. I think he found Sarah's work a little startling."

"Doesn't everyone?" she laughed. "But they always come back to buy it."

🍁   🍁   🍁

"Hey, Jamie, is that promise of a pint still good?"

"Sure and certain! And it's a good time for it, too. The place is quiet and I can join you for a bit."

The two men settled at a small table where Jamie could keep an eye on the door and the bar. It was always quiet this time of day with the lunch rush over and the happy hour crowd yet to arrive. "I haven't seen you come by lately, Jamie. New hours?" Chris asked.

"I think it's just a matter of our schedules meshing. How's the work coming?"

"It's really moving right along. Betta thinks we'll be able to open by the end of the month."

"Betta?"

"Boss lady," Chris said with a grin. "I'm actually working with her mother on an article about the startup of a new designer. Her name's Laura Collins Morgan. She's married to Taylor Morgan, the Broadway star, but she's a well-known writer on her own."

"And your boss lady—Betta?—is their daughter."

"She is. Betta and her sister Megan are opening the boutique."

Megan. After all this time, there she was just around the corner. He could stop in casual-like...

"Earth calling Jamie. Where were you, man?"

"Lost in the past. Chris, can you get me in to see Betta when her sister's not there?"

Chris backed off a little at the intensity of Jamie's gaze. The man looked as if his life depended on the answer. "Probably—but I'd want to know why before I did it. Their Dad just got rid of one stalker…"

"I'm not a stalker, I promise you, Chris. Let me tell you the story. If you decide not to help me after hearing it, please just promise you'll keep it to yourself."

Chris nodded and Jamie began, "It's been more than a year since I broke Megan's heart…"

Later that evening, Chris came to *Morganna's*. Betta had moved into the barely livable loft so she could fuss around the store as she wanted. Meg had opted for the comforts of home until the loft was actually furnished.

He rang the bell, even though he had his own key. It was late and he didn't want to startle Betta into thinking he was a burglar. Her voice, and the sounds of a vicious dog barking, came through the speaker, "Yes? Who is it?"

"It's Chris, Betta. You can turn off the dog-in-a-box." The barking abruptly ceased and he heard the buzzer that unlocked the door.

He went in, pulling the door securely shut behind him, then ran up the stairs. Betta, wearing pajamas and a robe, met him at the top. Chris registered that she looked sexy as hell, even in flannel pajamas. "Chris, what is it? Is something wrong, someone hurt?" The recent near-loss of Annie had affected all of them.

"No, nothing wrong. But there's something I need to talk to you about."

"This late?"

It was ten-thirty and Chris knew the bar would close at midnight. "I'm sorry, this couldn't wait until morning."

"Then let me pour some wine and we'll talk."

Chris sat on the futon sofa that also acted as her bed. As he watched her get out the wine from the miniscule kitchen, he wondered if she'd ever notice him. Not likely—at least not before *Morganna's* opened. He was patient. He could wait because Betta was worth waiting for.

She placed the wine on a small table then sat on a floor pillow facing him. "OK, what exactly was so important you had to keep me from going to bed?"

"That guy I told you about? From the bar around the corner?" She nodded and he continued. "Well, I had that pint with him today and he had quite a story to tell. It involves you and Meg. To start with, his name is Jamie O'Hearn."

Betta was speechless. Jamie? Meg's Jamie? It had been more than a year and here he was out of nowhere. She couldn't believe it.

"Betta? You alright?"

Taking a deep breath, she answered, "I'm just really shocked. I never expected to see him again.

"He told me what happened between them in Ireland. He's still in love with Meg—the real thing, Betta."

"Meg's been through so much pain because of him. So much confusion. She should have started med school but she put it off because she was so traumatized by all of it. Meg's always been vulnerable under that coat of confidence. He was the only man she ever fell in love with. The only one she risked getting close to. I don't know if she could manage having her life torn up again. First Jamie, then Annie's kidnapping, now Jamie again?" Betta shook her head.

"He wants to see you, Betta. I think he's hoping you'll act as an intermediary."

Betta stood up and refilled the wine glasses then sat back down wrapping her arms around her knees. She was silent for a long time but Chris knew her well enough to wait.

"Chris, do you trust him? He's not here bent on some kind of revenge?"

"I do trust him. I believe him. Just meet with him and see what you think."

"I guess I have to. Otherwise, I'll never know if I spoiled Meg's chance to be happy. When?"

"Tonight?"

"Tonight! You're crazy, Chris!"

"He gets off in half-an-hour. He doesn't want to be here when Megan might stop in. I think he's trying to protect her."

"So am I. But how do I protect myself? I've spent a year being angry at him," Betta almost shouted the words at him.

"I'll be here. Let me do the protecting. If you want him out, all you have to do is say so. I'll personally kick his butt down the stairs."

Betta laughed. "I don't think it will be that bad, Chris. Just be here as mediator…and my friend?"

"Does that mean you'll see him tonight?"

"Yes."

"I'll go meet him at the pub and bring him back here. Half an hour or so. It will give you time to get ready."

"Ready? I'll never be ready for this."

For the first time, Chris reached out to her as a person, not his boss. Hugging her lightly, he said, "It will be alright. You'll see."

Then he turned and left. She heard him clattering down the stairs until he hit the carpeting then heard the door slam behind him. For a moment she stood frozen in place. It had felt so right when Chris put his arms around her. As if she'd come home.

She'd been thinking about him a lot lately. She waited for the sound of his voice when he dropped in everyday. Not to mention some of the fantasies she found going through her mind when she should have been working or when she was trying to get to sleep. What was happening to her?

※ ※ ※

Jamie looked up, hope blazing in his eyes, as Chris walked through the door of the pub. When Chris nodded, he felt his knees turn weak. Seeing Betta was what he needed but her reaction could mean it was all over. There would be an end to hoping.

He managed to complete the close-up and locked the door behind him before either one of them spoke.

"What did she say?"

"She was shocked. Seems what happened between you and Meg caused a lot more damage than you'd thought. And Betta's still pissed at you."

"I expected that. She's my only way to Meg so I'll have to get her past that."

"You'd face anything for Meg, wouldn't you?"

"Aye, I have and I will. She's the only one for me."

"Here we are. Let's go talk to the dragon lady."

※ ※ ※

She heard them coming up the stairs. She'd taken the time to get dressed, consciously choosing a black sweater and leggings and twisting her hair into a neat bun in an effort to appear severe. It worked on Jamie but Chris only saw the beauty she was trying to hide.

"Hello, Betta. You're looking well."

"Jamie. Chris said you needed to see me urgently?"

"Mind if we sit down before we begin?" Chris asked as he sat on the futon and gestured for Jamie to join him. "Shall I pour some wine?"

"None for me, thank you," Jamie said. His stomach wasn't going to tolerate anything until this was over.

"Or for me, Chris. Help yourself."

Betta sat on the floor cushion as Chris poured his wine. Jamie looked older, even though it hadn't been that long. And she saw the same shadows in his eyes that floated in Megan's when she thought no one was watching.

"So, Jamie, what is it that made it so urgent to see me?"

"Megan, of course. I still love her and I want to marry her if she'll have me."

"What about your family, your father?"

"My father died three months after you left. He never recovered from what he had done. It drove a wedge between us that never really could be removed. We made a peace of sorts, so he had a quiet soul when he died."

"I'm sorry for your loss. It must have been devastating for you."

"'Twas, but that's the past now. I came to New York with the blessings of my family, of my mother and Sha'leen. They hold no grudge against Megan. It was her father, not herself, who did the terrible things."

"Why didn't you come to her that last day, Jamie?"

"I was confused. It was a lot to take in. I started there several times but found myself in other places where I'd no idea I'd been heading…including her father's grave, where I tried to understand what kind of man could have been the monster he was. By the time I made it to the house, you were gone. Even my father came by to try to make amends but it was all too little, too late. My life changed after that. I stayed at O'Hearn's for another six months in case she tried to reach me but I'd left my father's house and gotten a place of my own."

"It was my mother who talked me into coming here, into trying. She could see the good in Megan, just as Sha'leen did. It was only my own stubbornness and stupidity that kept me there. So, I came and found a pub job here. And I began to look for her but I didn't even know she was here until your little sister was kidnapped. I actually tried to come to her but the gardai made it clear that one madman on their hands was more than enough."

"I swear I didn't know Morganna's was yours. It was just an interesting place to watch on my morning walk to work. Thanks to the Good Saint who led Chris into the bar for the pint I'd promised, he ended up hearing my whole story and agreeing to act as intermediary for me and I thank him for that."

"So what now, Jamie?"

"I need to know. Does she speak of me at all? Is there any hope at all? Would I do more harm than good in coming back into her life? If it's harm I'll be doing, I'll walk away before it can even begin. I love her too much to see her in more of a hurt than she already is."

"Oh, Jamie. I can see you still love her. She doesn't speak of you but I see the same lost look in her eyes as I see in yours. So, I'll do all I can to help."

"Bless you, Betta," Jamie said with tears in his eyes. "What do you suggest we do next?"

"Next, you leave me be for a couple of days. I'll sound her out and if there's any hope at all, I'll invite you to the grand opening of Morganna's and I'll see that you meet again there. I won't tell her—you'll be on your own to win her back."

"Whatever you wish, Betta. It will be a hard wait but no harder than the last year has been." He rose to leave. "We've disturbed your sleep long enough now. We'll leave and I'll go light a candle in the church that the angels watch over your dreaming."

"Light another while you're there. This one for hope." She hugged him hard then kissed his cheek. "Goodnight, Jamie O'Hearn."

Jamie headed for the door as Chris slowly got up. Coming closer to her he said quietly, "See, it wasn't so bad. Do I get a hug, too, for bringing him along?"

Tentatively, she reached up and slid her arms around his neck. As his came around her, she leaned her head against his chest and heard the beating of his heart. "Betta?" he whispered. As she tilted her head to look at him, he kissed her, a gentle kiss full of promise. Then he let her go and joined Jamie at the door. "Goodnight, Betta. See you tomorrow."

As they closed the door behind them and started down the stairs, Betta hugged herself, remembering those few moments in his arms and the kiss…"I think I'm falling in love," she whispered to the empty loft. "How did that happen?"

❦   ❦   ❦

When Meg came in the next morning, she and Betta began to do the displays for the two designers who would be featured for the grand opening in two weeks. "Two weeks!" Betta exclaimed softly.

"You're talking to yourself again," Meg commented as she tugged a sweater by Liana over the model form and adjusted the cuff so that Liana's signature monkey showed.

"I am not," Betta responded while she arranged a rainbow of Samantha Darcy shirts across the wall. "You're here listening, aren't you?"

"Not when you start a conversation in the middle."

"OK, you win. I was talking to myself."

"Better get over that before the opening. Jennifer is going to think she's working for a nutcase."

"She will be! I have the worst case of cold feet."

"I imagine Chris would be glad to warm them for you," Meg said with a sly smile.

"What are you talking about?"

"Chris. That guy with the camera who's always hanging around? I've seen some of the proof sheets that Laura is going over. A lot of those pictures seem to be studies of you."

"Don't be silly. He's doing a wonderful job."

"Ask Laura. She'll show you the pictures. Or you could just go and take a look in the mirror there—that blush should tell you something."

"Don't push it. I still have to finish your dress for the Grand Opening. I got some totally yucky green silk in the other day. I was going to send it back but…"

"Okay, you win this time." She folded the last sweater and placed it in the rack. "I think it's time for a break."

"Good. Want to try the new espresso maker?"

"No way! That thing's terrifying. I'll settle for juice."

"Go ahead. I'll be right there."

She took a look around at what they'd done. Things were really beginning to come alive. The colors, Sarah's interesting furniture and mannequins—it really was all coming together just as she'd seen it in her head.

"Hey, stop daydreaming and get over here," Meg called from the area where the coffee shop would be.

As Betta joined her, Meg said, "I brought you a surprise. Raspberry almond chocolate croissants."

"You must have been at the bakery at the crack of dawn!"

"No, I was smart enough to order and pay for them yesterday so they saved them for me."

"This isn't going to help either one of us fit into our dresses for the opening."

"We'll work it off. Now, tell me what's been on your mind that has you talking to yourself. And don't try to tell me it's just the opening, something else is up."

"You almost had it figured out with Chris. I think there's something happening between us. It's been slow but suddenly took a new turn last night when he kissed me."

"Good kiss?"

"Very good kiss," Betta's eyes grew soft at the memory.

"I'm happy for you. Things really are coming together for you. Morganna's. Chris. All very good."

"But how do I know about Chris? I've never felt this way before."

"You just know. I did with Jamie. Sometimes it's instantaneous. Sometimes it sneaks up on you slowly until you just suddenly realize you're in love."

"Have you thought about Jamie?"

"Too much. That's what most of my therapy sessions are about. Despite everything, I'm still in love with him. I'm just too afraid to do anything about it."

"Has it occurred to you that Jamie might still feel the same, too?"

"Maybe. But I'm too frightened to do anything about it. Instead, I'm here helping you open *Morganna's* and that certainly wouldn't have happened if Ireland didn't happen. I'd be off in some stuffy chemistry lab somewhere trying not to gag."

Betta laughed, "Such a lovely image. I'm glad you're here, too. You've been so much help and it's been fun having you here. I won't let you give up on med school, but I promise not to push too hard."

"I love you, too. Now shouldn't we get back to work?

※ ※ ※

Chris came by late in the afternoon after Megan had left. As he came through the door, he saw Betta up on a ladder stretching out way too far for it to be safe. He dropped everything and ran to the ladder. His precipitous arrival caused Betta to lose her balance and fall neatly into his arms.

"You idiot! What would have happened if you'd fallen and I hadn't been here to catch you?"

"Maybe if you hadn't startled me, I wouldn't have fallen!"

"Betta Morgan, you drive me crazy." And he kissed her, not gently this time. He took possession of her mouth in a way that left no doubt how he felt.

"Wow!" Betta whispered when he finally lifted his mouth from hers and let her slide down his body to her own feet.

"We need to talk, Betta. Come upstairs with me," he said as he tugged her toward the elevator. Once inside he kissed her again, lifting her in his arms and bracing her against the elevator wall. When they arrived at the loft, he said, "You are so beautiful, Betta. Let me love you."

"Chris I've never…"

"Then we take it slow and if you want me to stop, tell me and I will." He walked to her and kissed her again. "I'd never hurt you, Betta."

She nodded shyly then slowly lifted her hands to his shirt and unbuttoned it, running her fingers across his lightly furred chest. He reached down and gripped her slender hips and pulled her against him so she could feel his arousal. Then he unbuttoned the shirt she wore and pushed it gently from her shoulders. The sight of the red lace bra against her faintly olive skin made him catch his breath and he tumbled her on the couch and patiently made her his own.

When they were finally sated, they cuddled together and talked about Meg and Jamie, about themselves. "I love you, Betta. I have from that first day. I thought I'd wait until after the opening to make a move but…well, I didn't."

"And I'm so glad you didn't. I was too busy to realize the changes until last night when you held me. It was if the world had opened up to me and I realized I loved you."

"This isn't just a casual thing for me. I love you. And, when we know each other better and are sure, I want to marry you."

"Is it possible to know each other better than we do now, right at this moment?"

He laughed and pulled her up until the length of her body stretched against his. "Let me show you. But, Betta, if we're going to continue there's one thing that's got to change."

Her eyes filled with concern as she traced his face. "What?"

"We have to get rid of this futon and buy a real bed!"

❦ ❦ ❦

When Chris left, he headed to Barnum's to hand deliver an invitation to the Grand Opening of *Morganna's* and a message from Betta that she would help him see Megan. What happened after that was up to them.

"You couldn't have brought me better news! I'll pay you now with a pint, but for the rest of my life with my friendship."

"Sounds like a deal to me," Chris answered.

"If it works out with my Megan, will you stand up with me?"

"I'd be honored, especially since I'm pretty sure who the bridesmaid will be."

"That's the way it is then? You and Betta have come to an understanding?"

"Only the beginning of one."

"Beginnings are good." And they raised their glasses in a toast to all that was good in their lives.

❦ ❦ ❦

The night of the gala arrived. Betta was beside herself with details and the anticipation of Megan's meeting with Jamie. The dresses she'd designed were ready when Meg, Laura, Annie, and Rosina arrived. Maria had received her gown earlier, since she needed something special for a formal dinner. She was already dressed in the striking scarlet silk that Megan had chosen for her. The dress had a slightly asymmetrical hem with just a hit of ruffle to suggest a flamenco dancer.

She'd asked the rest of them to trust her, so they had not seen the finished gowns yet. And she was wearing a long white lab-type coat over hers so they couldn't see it either.

"You first, 'Zia Rosina."

"All this fuss, Betta. I have clothes."

"Hush! Tonight you will be wearing *Elizabetta*!"

The others waited while soft outbursts of Italian came from the dressing room. Finally, Betta came out. "Ladies, our Rosina." She swept back the curtain to show a beaming Rosina wearing a soft rose pink dress with a high neckline and long sleeves decorated by tiny embroidered crystal roses. It swept to the floor to allow just a peek at the delicate rose-colored shoes she wore.

"Splendidamante!" Meg cried.

"Brava, Betta," Laura said. "Rosina, you are beautiful!"

After a little more fussing, it was Laura's turn. Rosina sat carefully in a chair, her hands touching the soft silk of the dress in wonder.

There was not as much chatting from the dressing room this time and Betta emerged quickly. "Signora Laura Collins."

Laura made her entrance in a floor length dress of what looked to be molten copper. It fell in one piece to the floor, sleeveless, undecorated, and incredibly elegant. "I love it, Betta," she said giving her a kiss. "Brava, once again, darling."

"Now, my Annie, it's your turn." As with the others, Betta helped Annie into her dress then made the grand introduction. "Mademoiselle Annie."

Annie stepped out wearing a pale blue velvet dress in a regency style. It was embroidered all over with metallic butterflies and a matching headband held back her riot of curls. It was her first "grown-up" dress and she moved very carefully to her mother's arms. "You are so pretty, Annie! Wait until Daddy sees you." Annie just smiled and sat carefully on a low stool, lightly touching the butterflies on her dress one at a time.

"My turn?" Meg said. "I love the others but I want to see mine!"

"OK, your turn."

They heard Megan exclaim, "Oh my God, Betta. Taylor's going to kill you!"

Mother, Aunt, and Grandmother turned to look at each other. This must be one very interesting outfit.

Betta stepped out with a wide grin. "Megan." As she swept back the curtain, Megan was posing for them. She was wearing a very short black dress with spaghetti straps. It clung to her figure like it...well, it had been made for her. The only decoration was a black scarf wrapped once around her neck then hanging down her back to show the two white antique lace medallions set into the ends. Stiletto sandals completed the outfit.

There was a stunned silence until Megan said, "This is the outfit I've wanted for years. Taylor's just going to have to live with it."

"You look stunning, Meg. Simply stunning," Laura said. "Maybe I'd better go down and warn Taylor."

"No!" both girls exclaimed at once.

"No," Betta said. "We are making our entrance together. No argument. Meg, keep an eye on them while I get ready. Don't let any of them sneak off." She went into the dressing room and emerged a few minutes later. Her dress was a forest green in a style that suggested the Renaissance. A long satin cape with open sleeves in a slightly darker shade of green was embroidered with tiny white unicorns around the hem.

"I am Elizabetta! Welcome to *Morganna's*."

"Perfection, Betta! You are perfection!"

"Then let's go make a grand entrance before the other guests get here and Taylor and I have to come hide before I make another grand entrance!" Betta exclaimed.

As they came out of the upstairs salon, Betta threw a switch that dimmed the lighting in the lower floor showroom except for a blazing light that encompassed the staircase. Soft music began to play and the room below fell silent as the Morgan women made their entrance.

Handsome in their tuxes, their men stared at them entranced. For a moment, Meg felt close to tears that there was no one waiting for her. She didn't see Jamie standing in the shadows, his heart in his eyes as he saw the woman he'd been searching for.

Matteo stepped forward as Rosina came to the bottom step and took her hand in his, raising her fingers to his lips. Then he swept her into his arms and they danced to the quiet music while the others watched with love. Taylor took Annie's hands and let her step on his shiny shoes as he waltzed her around the room. Chris, his heart in his eyes, led Betta into the impromptu dance and Sean literally swept Maria off her feet then on to the dance floor.

Laura put her arm around Meg and pulled her close. "He just hasn't noticed yet, darling. When he does, I tell you there are going to be fireworks." Their laughter was interrupted by a quiet voice with an Irish lilt. "Begging your pardon, Mrs. Morgan, but may I borrow Megan for this dance?"

Meg turned, her face white with shock. "Jamie? Is it really you?"

"'Tis…if you'll have me." He held out his hand to Megan who took it and stepped out on the floor with him, dancing with and inside a dream. The rest of them stopped to watch and Taylor, too surprised to notice the outfit, knew he'd lost this daughter to another man. Turning, he looked at Betta who leaned comfortably back into Chris's arms. Two in one night? That was more than a father should have to bear. He felt Laura's hand slip into his and turned to see her soft smile and the tears shining in her eyes. He still had Annie he reminded himself. And a true love of his own. As long as he had Laura, he had all he'd ever need.

A month later, Taylor won another Tony award and credited the women in his life. The Tony was nice…well, better than nice, but the more important event was taking place the next day as Megan married Jamie.

He hadn't been allowed to see Megan since the party last night. It wasn't until just before the wedding that he was allowed some time with her. The other women waited in the foyer while he entered the bride's dressing room.

She was standing next to the window. In her white dress, she looked like an angel come down to earth. "You're so beautiful, Megan," he said, his voice filled with awe.

"Thank you, Taylor." Far from being the nervous bride, she was calm and composed as she walked across the room to him. "You look wonderful yourself."

"I suppose I should have some fatherly advice ready but I don't. I've watched you and Jamie these last few weeks and there's no doubt in my mind that the two of you were meant to be together. I've had a chat or two with him about what he intends and I can trust him to take care of you."

"Did he tell you I'm going back to school? I'm going to get that counseling degree. Jamie will support me while I go to school and I'll support him when I'm finished, so he can get his business degree."

"You both have good heads as well as good hearts, darling. Whatever you set your mind to, you'll do it."

There was a knock at the door. "It's time," Laura said. She crossed to her daughter and kissed her lightly. "I wish you every happiness, Meg. I wish you and Jamie a love like I share with Taylor." Then she was gone and they heard the music start.

"You're sure about this, Meg?" Taylor asked, even though he already knew the answer.

"I'm sure."

"Just checking," he said with a grin as he pressed a tiny seashell into her hand. "You once told me love was 'stupid' and that you were 'never going to fall in love with anyone.'"

She smiled at the memory. "I guess you and Laura taught me well then."

˟   ˟   ˟

Betta followed Annie as she seriously dropped each petal from her flower girl basket. Then the music rose as Taylor escorted Megan down the aisle to be joined with Jamie as his bride.

Betta had designed Meg's dress when she first met Jamie. A simple column of white silk, it was bordered with embroidered crystal Claddaghs. Meg's bouquet was white lilies of the valley with shamrocks peeking through.

Her wedding ring was a Claddagh as well. As Jamie placed it on her finger, he did so with the crown facing inwards as he recited the traditional vow, "For better or for worse, for richer, for poorer, in sickness and in health, as long as we both shall live."

From their respective places as best man and maid of honor, Chris and Betta shared a look full of promise as the priest pronounced Megan and Jamie "husband and wife".

CHAPTER 81

After tucking an exhausted Annie into bed after the wedding, Taylor and Laura retired to their own room. It had been a memorable day. Jamie and Megan off to a good start and it looked as if Betta had found her love in Chris.

"At least we'll have Annie for a little longer," Taylor said.

"She's only five. I think it will be more than a 'little longer'—at least I hope so!"

"What about you, Laura? Are you ready to be a grandmother?"

"God, no! I'm still getting used to this mother thing."

"Well, you'll be the sexiest grandmother I've ever seen."

"You sound as if it hasn't occurred to you that you will be a grandfather if I'm a grandmother."

"Nonsense. I'm working towards the dirty old man role."

Laura giggled. "Want to practice?"

"I thought you'd never ask."

Laura woke later to find Taylor gone. She found him in Annie's room, singing her their lullaby. He held his arm out to her and pulled her close as he continued singing softly to their sleeping daughter.

> "Slumber my darling till morn's blushing ray
> Brings to the world the glad tidings of day.
> Fill the dark void with they dreamy delight—
> Slumber, thy mother will guard thee tonight.
> Thy pillow shall sacred be
> From all outward alarms,
> Thou, thou art the world to me
> In thine innocent charms.
> Slumber my darling, the birds are at rest,
> Wandering dews by the flowers are caressed,
> Slumber my darling, I'll wrap thee up warm,
> And pray that the angels will shield thee
>   from harm."

Afterword

Allow me to give you a more complete introduction to the music and poetry used in

When That Time Comes

Llewellyn and *Lorna* are real. I "met" Llewellyn on the internet when I wrote him a fan letter for his *Ghosts* cd and ended up ordering *Lorna*. The music enchanted me instantly and I knew I wanted to introduce that music and its composer to my readers. Llewellyn was agreeable and we formed a partnership that allows my readers to order the *Lorna* cd from his website or mine. And *Lorna*'s by far not his only recording. The *Pachelbel's Canon* that Laura uses to practice her T'ai Chi Chih can be found on his Pure Peace cd on the New World Music Label. Visit his website at **http://www.llewellynandjuliana.com** to meet this highly versatile and gifted artist.

Slumber My Darling, Taylor's lullaby for Annie, is an old Stephen Foster song. I first heard it performed by Alison Krause on Sony's *Appalachian Journey* cd that features the trio of Yo-Yo Ma, Edgar Meyer, and Mark O'Connor. While the album would be worth the cost alone just to hear her sing it, the music of these three musical geniuses is an added bonus. You can hear a brief excerpt at this address:

http://www.sonyclassical.com/music/66782/tracks.html

The Tale of Custard the Dragon was written by Ogden Nash. I first met Custard when I was about five years old and learning to read. He's been a good friend ever since. Recently, my own *Custard* was conjured up for me by my Aunt Marjorie and I'm now in the process of building, with the help of many friends, a "nice safe cage" for him. We'll be adding a website with our project to my Timing Is Everything website at

http://SabraS.homestead.com Please stop by and meet my Custard.

I want to recommend the practice of *T'ai Chi Chih*, the meditative form of this art. It's remarkably calming, centering, and clarifying. Check with your local community college, gym, or maybe a T'ai Chi Chih center. Just make sure you're asking for the *Chih* form developed by Justin Stone. The *Chuan* is the martial arts form.

While it's not music or poetry, the Amizette Inn in Taos Valley, NM could inspire you to write some. Room 9 does exist and Jim Walsh really does make the best French Toast on earth! Please check out their website at

http://www.amizette.com

I hope you'll check these out and allow them to add to your pleasure in reading the book.

Sabra

About the Author

Sabra Brown Steinsiek has not let her sudden fame as an author go to her head. She still is a native-born New Mexican who lives in Albuquerque with her husband, Will, and son, Jared, and their two cats, Vincent Vanilla and Hobbes America. She still pays the bills with her job of more than ten years as a library specialist at the University of New Mexico School of Law Library. And she still considers her "real life" to be that of calligrapher, storyteller, author, and e-mailer. You may contact her at **wordesmythe@hotmail.com** or through her prize-winning website **http://SabraS.homestead.com** where you can get a glimpse of some of the real places in the Taylor Morgan Trilogy. She is at work on the final book of the trilogy, *'Til The End of Time* which she hopes to see published in 2003.

0-595-22223-4

Printed in the United States
49456LVS00005B/28-45